DEFENSES DOWN

"I need your help to get Eclipse back on-line," General Patterson said. "When that little task is accomplished, we can all go back home, and I can celebrate the New Year with my family in Boston."

"I'm glad you have so much confidence in me, General," Julie said. "I wish I shared your optimism. Frankly, I don't give us high marks for success in just a couple of days. There must be tens of millions of lines of code controlling a system like Eclipse. And I'll be starting from scratch."

"I always have confidence in my people," he said. "Otherwise, I'd have to do all the work myself." His manner grew stiff, his eyes cold. "Besides, I don't want to think about the consequences if we fail."

"What's the worst that can happen?" Julie asked. "We postpone fighting wars until it's fixed?"

"If only it was that simple." The general looked at her, and she could see that his features were stone serious. Julie's grin vanished.

"If we fail," he said, "you and I will have a ringside seat to a thermonuclear war."

Other *Leisure* books by Joseph Massucci:
CODE: ALPHA

THE MILLENNIUM PROJECT

JOSEPH MASSUCCI

LEISURE BOOKS   L   NEW YORK CITY

To My Family, Patricia and Jennifer

A LEISURE BOOK®

December 1998

Published by

Dorchester Publishing Co., Inc.
276 Fifth Avenue
New York, NY 10001

ISBN 0-8439-4460-9

ACKNOWLEDGMENTS

I could not have written a credible sequel to *Code: Alpha* without the assistance of a few very talented people. First, my sincere thanks to Charles Barthel for sharing his extensive military and commercial flight experience for technical accuracy. Charles also brought to my attention the RAH-66 Comanche helicopter, and for that I am truly grateful.

Thanks to Bill Kelly and Joe Kramer for their support and counsel on Year 2000 issues, and for an appreciation of the daunting remediation challenges. To Dr. Leonard Adleman of the University of Southern California in Los Angeles for his paper "On Constructing a Molecular Computer." To William Burns, Jr., Marilyn Savage, Erin O'Rear, John Breckow, and Marlene Weigel for their suggestions and encouragement.

And to my wife, Patricia, for her support, enthusiasm, counsel—and help with transcribing!

PREFACE

THE MILLENNIUM BUG

As strange as this premise may sound, I assure you it's not fiction. The Millennium Bug is a computer glitch created decades ago by programmers who, to save money, expressed years in two digits instead of four. Simply stated, many software programs lack the first two digits to distinguish years in the 1900s from years in the 2000s.

The problem has been written into the computer software that runs everything from elevators to nuclear reactors and carries over to date-aware embedded microprocessors that keep time in devices such as thermostats, VCRs, ATMs, traffic lights, telephone systems—even nuclear missiles. The crisis is diverting billions in information technology resources worldwide. Unless they're fixed, all computer programs, everywhere in the world, are expected to stop working at the stroke of midnight, January 1, 2000.

Tick, tick, tick.

—JCM, 1998

"We are all competing in a race against time to avert an impending computer catastrophe and, unless something is done, when we're in the year 2000 . . . millions of computers, billions of dollars, and just about every human on the planet may be affected."

**Representative Constance Morella,
Republican from Maryland, to Congress**

"We can't have the American people looking to a new century and a new millennium with their computers—the very symbol of modernity in the modern age—holding them back and we are determined to see that it doesn't happen."

President Bill Clinton, August 1997

THE MILLENNIUM PROJECT

You now have only 4 days,
7 hours, 49 minutes,
10 seconds to prepare.

Day One
Monday, December 27, 1999

"I have traveled the length and breadth of this country and talked with the best people, and I can assure you that data processing is a fad that won't last out the year."

**Editor in charge of business books for
Prentice Hall, 1957**

Prologue
Flight 256

155 miles outside Dulles International Airport
Altitude 30,000 feet
Monday, December 27, 1999
1610 Hours

"What the hell is that?" said Al Kingery, the fifty-two-year-old pilot of Transcarrier Airlines Flight 256.

During his twenty-two years as a commercial pilot, Kingery had never seen this particular warning light during a flight, essentially telling him that his aircraft was overdue for a federally mandated inspection.

"Probably a short," said First Officer Peter Savage. "Has to be a short."

Kingery let out a laugh of agreement and reset the Master Caution light. But it was a nervous laugh, with a hint of ubiquitous concern for the integrity of his aircraft. He would not tolerate a warning light of any kind, short or not, aboard his aircraft. The Boeing 767 was easy to handle. Perhaps too easy. Her computer-managed engine thrust and advanced wing design made her rate of descent breathtaking and her landings quick. One hundred forty-three computers in the electronics rack belowdecks monitored every flight detail. Her designers joked that pilots seemed almost superfluous.

The Master Caution light came on again, and another amber light began flashing on the cockpit's annunciator panel, this one

15

accompanied by four sharp beeps. Both men's dismissive grins vanished. The warning light indicated a starboard engine malfunction.

"I don't get it," Savage said, studying the VDU. "All readouts are normal."

There were a lot of things he didn't get inside this cockpit. In fact, Savage had completed his 767 flight training only eight weeks earlier and had hardly flown since. His lack of experience worried Kingery, and he questioned the officer's proficiency.

Kingery rearmed the Master Caution light. "Talk to me, Pete. Tell me what's happening with that engine."

Savage scanned the readouts on the video display and checked the numbers twice against those in the Quick Reference Handbook. "Normal," he said. "Everything's normal. Temperature. Oil pressure. Hydraulics. Hell if I can find anything wrong."

Suddenly the port engine warning light came on, followed by another series of sharp beeps. The chorus of the two alarms was frightening.

"Pete, goddammit," Kingery spat, *"tell me what's happening!"*

Savage felt the pressure to give the captain information, reliable information, which he simply couldn't produce. He set and reset the aircraft's diagnostic system, and scanned the flight deck's eight-color CRT displays, searching for a reason for the warnings.

Savage's mouth dried, making it difficult to speak. "Nothing, Al. I can't find anything."

"Jesus H.," Kingery spat. He keyed his headset's microphone. "Dulles, this is TCA 256 on final approach. We may have a problem. Requesting emergency priority landing. I've got warning lights on both engines!"

Control Tower
Dulles International Airport

Arrival air traffic controller Douglas Sheridan logged Flight 256's request for emergency priority landing. He read off the triangle of data superimposed on his radar screen, which identified the aircraft, its altitude, and its ground speed. He checked the airliner's information against traffic in the area before issuing clearance for Flight 256 to land, Priority One.

"TCA 256, you're cleared for direct Dulles on Runway Two. Maintain six thousand, descend at your discretion. Do you need fire equipment or ambulances?"

"Negative," Kingery replied. "I've got port and starboard engine warning lights. Can't confirm. Readouts are normal. This is precautionary."

"Roger."

As the 767 sank toward the cloud cover below, Kingery could already feel beads of perspiration accumulating on his forehead. It was an automatic reaction, like those of Pavlov's dog. The sound of a cockpit alarm automatically tightened the muscles in his back and made him perspire. There was nothing he could do about it, and he knew it was just a matter of time before the first bead rolled down his temple and forged a tributary to his eye.

He keyed the intercom to the cabin. "Ladies and gentlemen," he said to his 167 passengers and five attendants. "This is Captain Kingery. We're making our final approach to Dulles International. We have reports of some bumpy air around ten thousand feet. I need you all to return to your seats, fasten your seat belts, and secure any loose objects. Thanks."

"What's going on? Why the rush?" It was Sandra Cummings, the in-charge flight attendant, standing in the doorway. She noted Kingery's vexed look, heard the beeps, and saw amber lights on the annunciator panel. Her eyes widened. Although she didn't know what they meant, she had spent enough years on commercial airline flights to know they had a potential emergency here.

"Warning system's gone nuts," Kingery said over his shoulder. "Damn if I can find anything wrong, though. Probably nothing. Do me a favor—brief your flight attendants for a possible emergency landing. Be discreet; I don't want the passengers alarmed."

"Of course," she said, and withdrew, closing the bulkhead door securely behind her.

Four more warning beeps screeched through the cockpit's increasingly anxiety-laden atmosphere. More amber lights glowed on the annunciator panel. Kingery's anxiety turned to genuine fear. He disengaged the autopilot and took the controls. He would hand-fly the remainder of the flight, landing at Dulles on a straight-in approach. For the first time in his life, Al Kingery wanted to be on the ground—*now!*

"Please stow all belongings and fasten your seat belts," Cummings instructed each row of passengers. Her mind was spinning. What if Kingery was wrong? What if it wasn't "nothing"? The snug aisle leading aft seemed to shrink around her, making her feel claustrophobic. She ordered herself to remain calm, to attend to her passengers.

In the coach cabin, two other flight attendants were working their way back, clearing away littered dinner trays and chatting with the passengers. Cummings noticed the aisle floor beneath her tilting forward as the aircraft began to descend. She thought about her family and her friends as she staggered aft as briskly as possible without alerting anyone. Most of the passengers seemed to be vaguely uneasy, she noticed. She thought about her husband, who didn't care for her flying.

"Please put away your belongings and fasten your seat belts," she told each row of business-class passengers.

"It's time to put that away," Nora Lloyd told her daughter, Gina.

The eleven-year-old gave a sulking expression and reluctantly began powering down her dad's ThinkPad computer. She enjoyed playing solitaire and landmine on it, and her dad, Senator Michael Lloyd, was gratified the device worked so well as a baby-sitter, especially on these long flights from the West Coast. Gina reluctantly gave the computer back to her dad, then put on a pair of headphones to listen to the pilot talk with the tower as they landed.

The senator checked his watch. "It's going to be tight."

"You're driving me nuts with this meeting," Nora said. "Stop worrying about it. You won't be late."

The senator checked his watch again. On one level he knew his wife was right; there still was plenty of time. Deeper, though, his emotions wouldn't let him relax. How could anyone relax on their way to a meeting with the President of the United States, especially when air travel was involved? Flights were too unpredictable; too many variables out of his control. He hated not being in control.

Perhaps it was the subject matter: asking the President to shut down Wall Street was no trivial matter. It was imperative for the U.S. economy, he kept telling himself. Representing Congress's Finance Committee, Senator Lloyd would recommend a moratorium on financial trading. Every hour closer to the new millennium brought increased risks of computer complications and malfunctions, some with deep financial consequences, a few with catastrophic implications. In this fragile, suspicious environment, a single computer error in the wrong place at the wrong time could literally topple the U.S. economy. White House computer consultants had certified Wall Street's systems to be Year 2000 compliant more than six months before. But there was no predicting whether the computers of other traders, other companies, other brokerage houses would be every bit as reliable. No one would be sure until the clocks actually changed. And no one was willing to issue a guarantee.

Now he possessed information about a new threat. It was highly confidential, and he was on strict instructions from his congressional subcommittee to brief the President personally.

As an eleventh-hour favor, the President had cleared a half hour to meet with him. A very generous time allotment, and precious little time to convince the President of the extreme importance of this matter. With luck the President would see it his way and issue the moratorium. And the sooner he acted, the better.

The senator looked at his watch again. "We'll probably circle the airport for two more hours."

Nora looked across her daughter and out the cabin's window. "You're in luck; so far we haven't turned. Perhaps we won't need to circle."

Inside the cockpit, Captain Kingery wiped the bead of perspiration stinging his right eye. The annunciator panel's warning lights were lit up like a Christmas tree, telling him to get his aircraft down fast. The controls had become sluggish and unresponsive in his hands. He could feel a vibration in the yoke that, over the course of several minutes, had grown steadily worse.

This was no short circuit. Whatever the source, it was causing real control problems.

"We're losing the hydraulics," Kingery said. "Raise the flaps."

Savage pulled the flap lever. Nothing. "Oh, Jesus." He tried it again. Still nothing. The ADC and VGR annunciator lights came on, something Savage had never seen before. He knew only that they monitored the computers that created the flight instrument displays; he didn't have time to get clarification from his handbook. His hands were shaking. He glanced at Kingery, wrestling with the controls. *I'm not going to help anyone by being afraid*, he thought. He willed his hands to stop shaking.

"I'm powering down," Kingery said. He grabbed the throttles and, with white knuckles, pulled back the levers. The whine of the twin turbine jet engines didn't vary. The RPM indicators remained stubbornly unchanged.

"I don't believe this," Kingery said. "How can this be happening?" He pulled back the throttles even farther, much farther than safety would allow. Still there was no change in the engines' RPMs.

Four more beeps sounded, followed by moments of stark silence, then four more beeps. Eight seemingly endless minutes had passed since the first alarm. Now the two men were being assailed by eerie warning sounds and foreboding amber lights.

"I need drag," Kingery said. "Put down the landing gear."

Savage engaged the landing gear; there was no response. "Negative."

"Well, that makes it unanimous," Kingery said. "Reboot the computer."

"Jesus—"

"Just do it!" Kingery snapped.

Savage reached for the keypad and, with shaking fingers, initiated the master computer reboot sequence. The color readouts on the CRTs blinked off and were replaced with the phrase PLEASE WAIT . . .

Suddenly, the cockpit plunged into darkness. The bank of digital readouts that reported airspeed, altitude, compass direction, pressure, and temperature vanished. Savage waited an interminable five seconds for the main computer to power up, but there still were no signs of life on the displays. He was too frightened to speak.

"Where are my instruments?" Kingery demanded.

Savage checked and rechecked the position of the switches. The computers controlled the aircraft and, like a stubborn child, they wouldn't allow humans to intervene. *How is that possible?* "The computers," he concluded. "They're shutting down this aircraft."

"Nonsense," Kingery said. "There are redundancies."

Savage tried different reboot configurations, all with the same effect. Nothing. To the young copilot, the cockpit had become the darkest place in the world.

Dulles International

Air controller Sheridan searched the black radar screen in vain for Flight 256. He radioed in frustration, "TCA 256, I've lost your transponder." He swept the radar back and forth over the area where Flight 256 should have been. He watched the screen intently, but the plane remained invisible.

Sheridan lifted the phone receiver and punched in the airport's command center. "Dulles, I've got an emergency for you. Got a TCA aircraft coming in. Apparently he's lost all power. He may be having a hard time controlling the aircraft. He's out of nine thousand right now, descending to Dulles. Recommend having equipment standing by."

Kingery and Savage heard the sound they had dreaded—a single, sharp bang. "We've lost the right engine," Savage gasped.

"Power and gear," Kingery said.

"Check."

"Throttle closed, auto throttle disengage."

"Disengaged."

Kingery keyed his headset. "Dulles, we've lost our Number One engine. We need all trucks out."

When he received no acknowledgment, he repeated the message. Still only silence. Then the realization struck him. No power. The right engine had failed also, halting the generators, stopping production of electricity. Without power, there would be no hydraulic pressure. The pilots could no longer control the rudder, elevators, wing flaps, and ailerons that steered the jet.

In the cabin, Sandra Cummings heard a low but unmistakable *ding!* and saw the emergency lighting system activate, turning on red and white lights along the aisle floors. There came a rush of questions from passengers.

"Unlock the RAT," Kingery ordered.

Savage used a manual lever to drop the ram air turbine from its housing next to the right wheel well. Scooping up wind power, the RAT's four-foot propeller would provide enough electricity to maintain a minimal level of hydraulic control.

Kingery summoned Cummings to the flight deck. No sooner had she opened the bulkhead door than Kingery, his voice desperate, said, "We've lost all power. We're going straight into Dulles. Brief the passengers and crew for a full emergency landing."

Cummings felt a rush of adrenaline surge through her, producing a momentary wave of dizziness. There were no lights in the cockpit, and the console appeared dead. Her hands began shaking violently. She sprinted aft past Senator Lloyd and his family, avoiding the questioning stares of her passengers.

"Someone probably puked," Gina said, watching the flight attendant race by.

"Probably," Nora agreed. But every instinct in her shouted that this was not the case. She was very frightened, and she fought to hide her fear from her daughter.

Senator Lloyd did not notice the palpable fear spreading through the cabin. His mind was already in Washington, inside the White House. He didn't see the team of flight attendants positioning themselves at even intervals throughout the aircraft.

Cummings grasped the intercom microphone and began to speak, but there was no amplified sound, no power. She put down the microphone and shouted through cupped hands, "I want everyone to listen carefully. Remove your shoes, glasses, false teeth, and anything sharp from your pockets."

Senator Lloyd looked up, puzzled. He asked his wife, "What's going on? What's happening?"

"Prepare for an emergency landing . . . remove shoes . . . sharp objects . . ."

Gina, visibly alarmed, asked, "Mom, is this for real?"

"Just do what they tell you, honey, and hold my hand," Nora said, forcing her voice to remain steady, adding almost in a whisper, "And say a prayer."

Senator Lloyd watched the flight attendants move through the cabin, talking with passengers, explaining the emergency "brace" position: heads down, hands grasping ankles. Some responded with anger, others appeared anguished over their impotence. Some cried softly.

"This is absurd," the senator said. He felt a growing sense of helplessness and a numbness spreading through his body. He was going into physical shock. Voices seemed muffled and oddly remote. He no longer heard his wife's voice, nor did he feel her hand reach across the aisle to grasp his own. His breathing became shallow and fast; he felt oddly cold.

Savage watched Kingery, his jaw set, working the controls like a rodeo stuntman hanging on to a bull. "We're too high," the copilot said. "At this glide angle we'll be going in too fast."

"Can you think of anything we haven't done?" Kingery asked.

"No, I can't, Al."

Kingery's mind raced with questions. *Okay, what's the best speed here for descent?* Nothing in the pilot's manual dealt with gliding a powerless 767 safely to earth. If not done correctly, he could let the aircraft go down too quickly or too slowly—both would be fatal mistakes—and he could only guess how fast he was descending. "I'm no fucking *glider* pilot," he said aloud.

With the cloud cover now above them, Kingery and Savage could see the familiar straight line of runway Number Three at twelve o'clock.

"Maybe seven miles," Savage estimated.

They were coming in fast with no trailing-edge flaps to slow their speed. Flight 256 would be attempting to land without anti-skid control on the brakes, and without engines to provide maneuverability. There would be no circling; they had one chance.

*   *   *

Joseph Massucci

Senator Lloyd glanced out the window and saw snow-covered fields drawing closer and closer. The plane began bouncing more erratically. He looked to his wife for strength and found her expression a mask of bewilderment and fear. As he removed the pens from his shirt pocket, he noticed the businessman one row back with a rosary reciting the Act of Contrition aloud. He wished he carried a cross. He looked across at his daughter, Gina, sitting rigid against the window, sobbing.

"Holy angels, protect us," he heard her pray.

Dazed, he said to no one in particular, "Everything will be all right, honey. We're just going to land. And then we'll be all right."

The plane continued to drop at an alarmingly steep angle. Kingery knew that unless he acted immediately, they would overshoot the runway. If only they could lower the landing gear to create drag.

"Gear down."

"Al, what's the point—"

"*Gear down!*" Kingery demanded.

Savage pulled the lever to the down position. Both pilots waited breathlessly for the reassuring *whoosh* and *boom* of the gear dropping. Nothing.

"This should be interesting. Hold on." Kingery turned the yoke to his right and jammed his foot against the left rudder pedal. Outside, the wing's left aileron swung up, while the right one dropped. The opposing forces created by the crossed controls turned the plane sharply onto its right side, creating severe drag, resulting in a drop in airspeed and altitude. The move also created considerable stress on the airframe.

Senator Lloyd felt the plane lurch suddenly to the right and settle at a precarious angle, and then he felt the sensation of falling. The airframe began to oscillate—shaking, bouncing, and rattling. He looked out the window. They were low enough to jump down.

Every ounce of Kingery's energy was channeled to his effort to maintain the sideslip. Perspiration flowed down his temples. *C'mon, honey. Slow down. Put us down safely.*

Kingery turned the yoke to the left to straighten but was unable to level the plane. The right wing dipped sharply as the fuselage rolled violently to the right like some scary ride in an amusement park, the right wingtip pointing straight at the ground.

Savage gasped, "My God—"

A sickening, crunching thud filled the cabin as the wing dug into the ground. There came two small explosions, then a large bang at the front of the aircraft. An orange fireball rushed through the cabin.

Senator Lloyd reached for his daughter. The flames engulfed and incinerated him.

Sarah Cummings watched transfixed as the fire roared toward her and felt as though she were sitting on the doorstep of hell. She closed her eyes. *Burning is the worst way to die. Sweet Jesus,* Cummings prayed. *I'm ready. Please don't let it hurt.*

In a gruesome somersault, the 151-foot plane slammed into the ground, flipped over twice, and began a long, grinding skid. An unremitting crescendo of crunching and scraping filled the cabin— a noise as shattering in its power as that of a derailed freight train. Cummings flew violently against her seat belt in a whirlwind of gravel, smoke, and flying metal. The plane broke into smaller pieces as its fuselage hurtled across the snow-covered field.

She could feel snow, dirt, and gravel digging into her face and body as the smashed fuselage tore apart at its seams.

Chapter One
Alexander Skile

Willard, Colorado
Monday, December 27
1830 Hours

Judith wasn't alone in her bedroom this evening. On the contrary, tonight she entertained two male visitors, as was her twice-weekly routine. These young men were not suitors, for she was already married; instead, they had the enviable task of "servicing" her. Twin brothers of Latin descent, the two boasted tall, lean, and virile bodies—qualities any woman would find attractive. As they were brothers, Rolando's and Felipe's tools were shaped and sized similarly, and both knew how to use them to her utter satisfaction.

Judith had uncommon energy in the bedroom. Although she was twice their age, in the course of an evening she would exhaust them both.

Why Judith invited studs into her bedroom twice a week was no mystery to the few who knew her. Her husband had long been impotent, and no therapy or clinic could offer him much help. Most men considered Judith an attractive, voluptuous woman, with ample breasts, strawberry-blond hair, a shapely figure, and legs that extended up to her neck.

Her husband, Alexander, adored her. He considered her the most beautiful woman in the world, and her marvelous counsel and common sense more than compensated for his own eccentricities. Rather than forsake his Judith, he allowed her to indulge in any manner she desired, however peculiar.

On the balcony deck outside the bedroom, magic of another sort was unfolding. Alexander Skile, wearing only his terry-cloth housecoat and slippers, paced the six-foot-wide deck that encircled their perfectly symmetrical house. Skile was a tall, slender man in the shallow end of his forties who, to many, looked worn and frail. Nearly bald, he wore his hair long and pulled back in a ponytail with a diamond clip. Everyone knew him to be an elusive intellectual, and he had built his impressive fortune as an entrepreneur developing microprocessors chiefly for the military and the aviation industry.

Their chateau had two-story glass panels on all sides that afforded every room a magnificent view of the mountains. The panorama from the deck on this clear December night was spectacular, and Skile appeared to be absorbed deeply in its splendor. He gazed down across a great valley. At the bottom sat the small town of Willard; its delicate nest of festive lights sparked like distant jewels. A forest of snow-covered evergreens blanketed the hills leading down to it, and the full moon turned it all into a remarkable winter quilt.

A rare grin stretched Skile's sullen features. He knew this scene would soon change forever. In five days the world would usher in a new millennium—an era in which Alexander Skile would be emperor, ruler of everything material. Judith would be his queen, and he would endow her with every excess she desired.

The soft ring of the portable digital phone roused Skile from his musing. He ceased his pacing. He reached into his robe's pocket and withdrew the phone, opened the mouthpiece, and listened.

A voice of a younger man on the other end said one word: "Bravo."

He nodded. "I'm very glad to hear you say that."

"It's working beautifully," said the caller. "Today's installment is all over the news. You should see it."

"I don't own a television," Skile said.

"You're a friggin' genius," the voice said, his excitement mounting. "A fucking *king*."

27

"Save the commentary," Skile said. "We'll discuss it in the morning."

"Yes, sir. Have a great night."

Skile switched off the phone and returned it to his pocket. Still grinning, he slid open the glass door and slipped into his bedroom. By the glow of the six scented candles that surrounded their canopy bed, he could see that his wife's session was nearly finished.

"I can see you'll be skipping dinner again," Skile said.

Judith pulled away and looked at him, half startled. "Alex, so you finally decided to join us. I thought you had frozen and died out there."

He stepped into the glow surrounding the bed and said, "Bravo."

The look of astonishment on her face was unmistakable. She released Felipe and crawled off his brother. "Are you serious, honey?"

Skile reached into his pocket and held up the phone. "Henry just told me. It's all so incredible."

"Honey, that's wonderful!" Judith slid off the bed and hugged him. "You're a genius, Alex. I love you so much." She kissed him passionately on the lips.

When they finally broke their embrace he said, "You taste like Felipe."

She laughed. "Isn't he delicious? You should try him. Maybe he's just what you need." She felt the front of his housecoat and reached in to give his member a lover's squeeze. He was fully erect.

"*Alex!?*" Incredulous, she opened the front of his robe and stared in awe. "Alex . . . I've never seen you so aroused."

Rolando swung his legs over the side of the bed. "What's all this talk of 'Bravo'?" He waved his massive member at Skile. "Bravo on this for a while." He grinned at his brother. "I think we found what turns on *Alejandro* Skile."

The brothers enjoyed a hearty laugh.

Skile closed his robe and moved to his desk. "You will forget you ever heard the word 'Bravo' tonight." He snatched a switch-blade from the desk—a handsomely carved, ivory-handled utensil he used as a letter opener—and tossed it to his wife.

"I believe you still remember how to open this," he said.

Judith caught the knife and looked at him, questioning its necessity with her eyes.

Skile inserted a key into the desk, turned it, and slid open the top drawer. He stared down at a Walther PPK, fully loaded, a slim-bore silencer attached to its muzzle. He picked up the handgun and felt the power in its weight.

"Bravo," said Rolando, still shaking his penis. "Well, do you want it? Or shall I put it back inside your wife?"

Skile whirled on his heels, thrust the handgun before him, and squeezed off a single round. The bullet struck Rolando square in the groin, spattering blood across the satin sheets and over his brother. Judith screamed in surprise.

"My God—" Felipe gasped.

Rolando's jaw dropped in shock. He stared wide-eyed at the stump at his groin, then looked at Skile, who still stood with the handgun pointed at him.

"Thanks for the offer," Skile said. "Why don't you keep it— or at least what's left of it."

Skile raised the barrel a few inches and fired another round. The bullet tore through Rolando's chest and hurled him backward onto the bed.

Felipe leapt from the bed. *"You bastard!"*

The blade in Judith's knife sprung from its handle.

Skile turned his back and threw the handgun onto his desk. Felipe lunged at him. Before he could take two steps, Judith plunged the knife's blade solidly into the side of Felipe's neck, burying it to the handle. The young man whipped around and looked at her, his eyes wide with surprise. Blood spilled from his lips. Before he could collapse, Skile grabbed him under the arms and held him upright. The youth smelled of sex and sweat.

"He would have killed you," Judith said.

"I wanted to see if you still had the instinct." He pulled the knife from Felipe's neck, closed the blade, and tossed it to her. She caught it in her bloodied hands.

Felipe moaned softly.

"My dear Judith," Skile said, feigning surprise. "You missed his carotid artery. He's still alive." He whispered into Felipe's ear, "But not for long."

Skile dragged him to the glass door, slid it open, and carried him out onto the deck. He laid him facedown over the balcony's snow-covered rail.

"See you in the spring."

Felipe moaned again and tried unsuccessfully to focus his eyes. Skile lifted his legs, hurled him over the rail, and watched Felipe's body fall two hundred feet before it plunged into a deep snowdrift at the base of the chateau's foundation. The body vanished completely. Skile returned to the bedroom, slid shut the glass door behind him, and locked it.

"What about him?" Judith asked, gesturing to Rolando's body on their bed.

"I thought you might want to sleep with him tonight."

She whirled away from him, her large breasts bouncing. Smiling, she said, "You are downright gruesome sometimes."

Skile bowed curtly to her. "Ever at your humble service."

Day Two
Tuesday, December 28, 1999

"I think there is a world market for maybe five computers."

Thomas Watson, chairman of IBM, 1943

Chapter Two
FAA

Cause of Washington Plane Crash
Under Investigation

WASHINGTON, D.C., Dec. 28 (*The Associated Press*)—Investigators are "working around the clock" to determine the cause of the crash of the TCA Flight 256 Monday afternoon, Rita Nichols of the National Transportation Safety Board (NTSB) said yesterday. The plane, a 767 passenger jet, apparently lost power as it attempted to land at Dulles International Airport, overturned and skidded nearly a half mile before bursting into flames. One hundred and sixty passengers died and seven are in critical condition at Walter Reed Hospital.

Nichols told a news conference the plane had no history of mechanical problems, "and we are searching for a reason, whether it be human or mechanical, on why this plane crashed," she said. Nichols would not comment about whether the millennium computer bug may have played a role.

Investigators searched the wreckage Monday for clues. A preliminary report on the cause of the crash may be available later today, Nichols said.

Joseph Massucci

National Transportation Safety Board investigator-in-charge Rita Nichols hurried through the parking lot next to the agency's headquarters on L'Enfant Plaza. The charred wreckage that had once been Flight 256 still sat where it had come to a stop in the field adjacent to the runway of one of the nation's busiest airports, and Nichols hadn't slept in twenty-seven hours because of it. Her "go team" had taken half-hour shifts throughout the night, picking through wreckage in minus-five-degree winds. She had returned home briefly this morning for a shower and a change of clothes. Besides choreographing dozens of investigators working on this case—and delivering four progress reports a day to her boss— Nichols knew she would be working around the clock, sending home for clothes and allowing herself only occasional catnaps on her office sofa. Hopefully, there would be a fast-food breakfast and lots of coffee waiting for her in the team's conference room.

A group of reporters and camera crews had formed a line along the plaza in front of James Spangler, the agency's media relations director. She pursed her lips when she saw the circus. *Bloody hell.* Usually composed and controlled, Spangler looked rattled this morning, Nichols noted. Operating on about two hours' sleep, he was making his way from one interview to another, taking questions from ABC, NBC, Fox, and CNN about the deadly crash of Flight 256. He had few answers for them.

"That's something we're looking into," she could hear him say. "We don't have those details yet . . . Our investigators will be studying those factors."

Better you than me, Nichols thought. She waved to him as she sidestepped the crowd on her way to the side entrance. Another television crew had set up outside the door she planned to use. A woman news anchor looked directly into the camera and began her report: "Rescuers are still pulling charred bodies from the wreckage of a TCA jet that crashed in a field next to Dulles International Airport in a ball of fire. Four FBI agents arrived during the night to identify body parts, which were placed in refrigerated trucks donated by a local grocery chain . . ."

Nichols became a backdrop by walking briskly behind the reporter and entering the building. On the elevator ride to the fourteenth floor, she reviewed in her mind what few facts her team had gathered, her thoughts consumed by the puzzle. Her report thus far was unacceptably lean. She noted that on a day with moderate wind and cloudy conditions, the plane, commissioned in 1991, lost power, rolled to the right, flipped over when the right wing touched the runway, broke apart, and burst into flames. The key question: What caused the plane to suddenly, inexplicably, lose power? She had called in one of the best technicians in the country, who had worked throughout the night to analyze the flight and voice recorder data, and she was eager to find out what he had learned. Still, barring some miracle, it would probably take months to figure out what went wrong, she conceded.

"People want instant answers to complex problems, but usually the instant answers aren't there," she found herself saying aloud. Two elevator passengers glanced up in surprise, then, embarrassed for her, avoided her gaze while pretending they hadn't heard her. She was thankful when the door opened on her floor, and she stepped off, basking in a wave of self-consciousness.

"Dietrich's waiting for you in the observation room," the floor receptionist called after her as she rushed past. Nichols waved an acknowledgment.

Three of the four interrogation rooms were still in use. Nichols slipped into the darkened observation lounge, where she found an aeronautics engineer, a contractor she had met briefly the night before, engaged in an intense discussion with the NTSB vice chairman, Robert Dietrich. Despite the volume of their voices, the soundproof padding muffled their conversation.

"It wasn't a bomb," the engineer was saying. "I examined the engines and pieces of the airplane near the engines. This one has all the earmarks of a crash caused by an error on someone's part—"

"Did you want to see me? We can always talk later," she offered.

Both men turned as she spoke.

"I need to talk to you before I leave," Dietrich said. "Give me one minute."

While she waited for them to finish, Nichols stepped to one of the room's four two-way mirrors. Her mind was already numb, bordering on useless. She struggled to focus her eyes on a woman and a six-year-old boy sitting in the first room across the table from one of her investigators. She raised the volume on the panel below the mirror to listen in.

". . . I heard a loud, low noise," the woman was saying. "We were close enough to see the TCA logo on the side of the plane as it fell. We were close enough to feel the explosion. Then I smelled an awful odor—like grease on an electric burner . . ."

Nichols lowered the volume, moved to the next mirror, and raised the volume.

"I could see there wouldn't be many survivors," said a middle-aged man whose face was seared from the heat of a blaze. "The front section was still reasonably intact. But after that, there was nothing that even looked like a plane."

Nichols lowered the volume as the man she was waiting for finished his discussion with the contractor.

"Gotta run back to Dulles, Bob," the engineer said, picking up his down-filled coat. "I'll catch up with you later."

Dietrich nodded. When he and Nichols were alone, Dietrich, a stocky, fifty-six-year-old former Marine captain, reached for her hand. Instead of a shake, he held her hand with both of his as though she were a close friend. She was surprised by his intimacy. In fact, they hardly were acquaintances at all; she knew him only from the monthly bureau meetings, and he had a poor attendance record at that.

"I'm on my way over to the FAA to see our friend John Tutora," he said. "I have to give him something. What do you have for me so far?"

He expects instant answers to complex problems popped into her head. "Not much."

"Not much," Dietrich repeated, then nodded knowingly. He of all people knew the deep frustration that accompanies air-crash investigations at this stage. Crashes are usually solved, even in cases where a jet explodes over the open seas. It's usually just a matter of time. Unfortunately, in this case he had no time.

"The President's good friend, Senator Mike Lloyd, was killed on that plane," Dietrich said. "Tutora will brief the President today at lunch, and he's waiting for whatever you have."

"If you're going to ask me to make a snap judgment to appease politics—"

Dietrich waved away any such notion. "Of course I don't want you to do that. A lot is riding on what you learn today. Personally, your theory of this millennium computer bug bringing down so many aircraft—let alone a 767—is the biggest fairy tale I've ever heard. Christ, TCA already spent a hundred and fifty million to bring its fleet of one hundred aircraft and other systems into compliance." He squeezed her hand a bit harder than he intended.

She wiggled her hand free of his. "So many things are upside down and backwards in this case. This crash couldn't possibly have happened. And yet . . ."

Dietrich's expression hardened. "The FAA demands to know if this crash and the others have anything to do with your Millennium Bug. Tutora is so confident that the bug won't affect air traffic that he's publicly committed to flying cross-country at midnight this Friday. If you're right, the repercussions for the airline industry will be staggering. Everyone is demanding information. In the unlikely event that this plays out as you suspect, the President will be pressured for an immediate decision. We don't have weeks. I need to know something *now.*"

The last thing she needed now was this kind of pressure. Nichols sighed; she couldn't win this debate. "You can tell Tutora that we're ready to rule out a number of possible explanations. The FBI hasn't found any traces of explosives or other signs of physical sabotage. Meteorologists confirmed that wind shear wasn't a factor. Ornithologists from the Smithsonian helped rule out bird strikes; they said feathers found in the wreckage came from a bird that flies no higher than one hundred feet."

Dietrich was searching for something—anything—but birds wouldn't cut it. "What's the status of the simulations?"

"We've duplicated Flight 256's movements in three flight-simulator tests since midnight, and so far haven't found anything a pilot couldn't correct. Another team is conducting test simulations of the aircraft's computers and related systems, a hundred and sixty of which are date-sensitive."

Dietrich, clearly not satisfied at her progress, picked up his overcoat and ran a hand over his thin, polished hair. When he spoke, his voice had a hard tone of finality. "I'll be back in two hours to review your report on the flight data. There are planes up there with people on them. If computers are to blame and we do nothing, there's going to be another crash tomorrow and another the next day.''

Chapter Three
Drafted

Atlanta, Georgia
Centers for Disease Control
Tuesday, December 28
0620 Hours

In the golden light just before dawn, three military helicopters appeared out of the sky over Atlanta and headed for the forested campus belonging to the Centers for Disease Control. The December sky was crisp and clear, the wind mild. The choppers' high-intensity carbon-arc spotlights swept over the campus. Their pilots had no trouble finding the helipad and set down in an orderly, precise manner, whipping the foliage of the pines into a torrid frenzy. Each of the three pilots reduced his chopper's engines to idle and left its rotors turning. The first two choppers were Sikorsky UH-60A Black Hawk transports, sleek, well-oiled, and spit-polished. The third was a smaller Vietnam-era Huey UH-1H utility helicopter, oddly out of place in the company of the two modern choppers. Built in 1959, its single, tired turbine engine whined noisily, protesting its hasty summons back into service.

The Huey's troop compartment door slid open and out stepped

a military officer, satchel in hand. A security officer from the Centers' main administrative building hurried out to meet him.

"Howdy," he called. "You guys made good time. You're ten minutes early."

The military officer introduced himself as Colonel George Beckman. "I was told Dr. Geiger would meet me."

"I'm Dr. Geiger," said a white-haired gentleman jogging after the much younger security guard.

Colonel Beckman gestured back to the choppers. "We've got forty people waiting on us. We're on a very tight schedule. Where are they?"

The colonel looked smug and officious to Dr. Geiger, and he didn't relish the thought of doing business with him. "I told them to be in my office at six-thirty sharp," Dr. Geiger said, catching his breath. "Just as you instructed. You're early. Do you have the paperwork? I'll need the requisitions for my files."

"Of course." The colonel opened his satchel, removed a plain envelope, and handed it to the doctor.

Dr. Geiger unfolded its contents and did his best to organize the government-issued documents under the downdraft of the idling rotor blades. Although he was familiar with government requisitions, he had never seen paperwork like this before, literally drafting two of his employees into the service of the United States Military.

"Has anyone been out here to talk to you about this?" the colonel asked. "Any reporters asking for interviews?"

Dr. Geiger glanced up from the papers. "The press? No. We've kept this confidential, as you instructed. Has there been a leak?"

The colonel shook his head and said, "No, and that's the way I intend to keep it."

"Fill me in on something, Colonel," Dr. Geiger said.

"If I can."

"I'm one of those people who use computers without really understanding or caring how they work," he said. "I'm aware that the military needs all the help it can get to solve this Year 2000 computer date problem. But I fail to grasp why you're drafting two of my best people—biophysicists, no less—for this project of yours. What does biophysics have to do with computing, and why are you taking them to Cheyenne Mountain?"

Colonel Beckman's eyes fluttered uncertainly, and he appeared uncomfortable with the question.

"Of course, if I'm prying into some government secret . . ."

"Dr. Geiger," the colonel said, "two of your biophysicists are also highly trained, highly competent computer programmers. We are very interested in their white paper that brought to light cyber-toxins—a new generation of computer viruses that manipulate data rather than destroy it."

"How much is all this costing us?" the doctor said.

"Year 2000 remediation hasn't been cheap," the colonel said. "By the time all this is over, it will have cost one trillion dollars to rewrite and test all the codes worldwide. And that doesn't account for the legal issues. But time will be more costly. We've got four days left, and there's no way we're going to remediate even our most mission-critical systems."

Dr. Geiger frowned and shook his head. "That's not what I mean. I'm referring to the cost of taking programmers away from institutions like ours. And what about corporate America? With your draft, there're no resources left for U.S. businesses to address the same problems. Everyone's concerned about the economy."

"Corporate America was slow to respond to government warnings, and is now paying the price of procrastination," Beckman said. "We merely took advantage of the available talent pool. Do you have any idea how many chief information officers in the private sector have already been fired for abdication of responsibilities because they were slow to address this problem? Thousands more will be looking for work next week."

"But the draft gives you an unfair advantage—"

"I thought we were meeting in your office," a female voice called over the idling engines.

Dr. Geiger summoned the pair with a wave. "Here come your draftees now, Colonel."

Colonel Beckman watched two women with light luggage walk briskly toward them. The first was a striking woman the colonel guessed to be in her late twenties with penetrating dark eyes and splendid black hair flowing over her shoulders. He was particularly impressed with her attractive figure, delightfully obvious even covered with a waist-length coat. He smiled cordially and made a mental note to get to know her much better.

"This is Dr. Julie Martinelli," Dr. Geiger said. "She's our prize catch."

Julie accepted the colonel's hand. "I'm a real flounder, always eager to help out the jocks in the military," she lied.

She was hauntingly beautiful, the colonel noted, with a nice, throaty quality in her voice that suggested someone accustomed to giving orders. He liked her instantly.

"A pleasure," he said. "Welcome to the special branch of the U.S. military."

"Take good care of her," Geiger said. "I don't know what we would do without her."

The second woman, half again Julie's age, boasted a seasoned yet vibrant complexion, a firm build, and reddish-auburn hair pulled back in a ponytail. More the colonel's age and type, he concluded, but not nearly as interesting as Dr. Martinelli.

"This is Dr. Nancy Shaw," Geiger said, "our chief biochemist and database manager."

Dr. Shaw offered a forced grin as she accepted the colonel's handshake. She had gotten up too early to offer genuine hospitality. "A pleasure."

Julie noticed that some people had disembarked from the choppers to stretch their legs and enjoy the brisk Georgia morning air. Others preferred lungfuls of cigarette smoke, which they consumed like morning coffee.

"Let's get this over with, shall we," Julie said. "I'm not looking forward to celebrating the end of the millennium in a military compound. Who can show us where we sit?"

The pilot of the Huey chopper stepped forward and, checking his clipboard, asked, "Which of you is Shaw?"

"That would be me," Nancy said.

He thrust his pencil at one of the Black Hawks. "You're on Transport Number Two."

Dr. Shaw nodded her approval. "First class."

Another soldier touched Nancy's arm and gestured toward the aircraft. "This way, Doctor." As the two headed for the chopper, the soldier yelled at the small group milling around the aircraft, "I want everybody inside *now!*"

"Dr. Martinelli," said the Huey pilot, "you're on Transport Three."

Julie swung one of her two bags over her shoulder and began walking toward the second Black Hawk.

"No, this way, Doctor," said Colonel Beckman, taking her arm and pointing to the Huey.

Julie studied the antiquated chopper and grimaced. It looked cramped and cold, and reeked of inadequately burned jet fuel.

"Why can't Nancy and I travel together?" she asked.

"Insurance," said Colonel Beckman. "We don't put all our premium eggs in the same basket."

"So we're farm produce—"

"We'll talk once we're airborne," the colonel said. "Right now time is literally against us."

Chapter Four
Black Box

CNN Headline News
Tuesday, December 28
0800 Hours

"It is still too early to say conclusively what mistakes, if any, were made by Captain Kingery, who died on Flight 256 yesterday," said CNN anchor Betty Joslin. "There was speculation that he was overtired and unfamiliar with the Washington route. The airline said he had flown the route only twice before the crash. It also said Kingery had two days off on December 22 and 23, and then flew for three days before the flight to Washington."

ROLL FILM RICHARD MEIRALEITE, VICE PRESIDENT, TRANSCAR-

RIER AIRLINES: "That kind of schedule is very common. It's normal."

CUT TO JOSLIN: "What happened to Flight 256 is far from normal—and disturbing when viewed against growing speculation that the Millennium Bug may be to blame for the crashes of fourteen private, commercial, and military aircraft during the past three weeks. The Millennium Bug refers to a computer's inability to distinguish the year 2000 from 1900. Forty years ago, programmers began using the last two digits to represent the year, ignoring the '19' . . ."

National Transportation Safety Board
Washington, D.C.
0830 Hours

"I'm afraid your time is up" were Rita Nichols's first words of greeting to Richard Velk, arguably the best electrical engineer in the country.

"It's great to see you again, too," he shot back before turning back to his audio console.

Nichols closed the "No Admittance" door behind her. The room was a technician's dream, dark and cluttered with top-of-the-line computer and audio equipment. On the table before her sat the two flight recorders: one for flight data, the other for voice. Unlike the older analog units that used quarter-inch magnetic tape as a storage medium, these units used digital technology and memory chips. More reliable? She only hoped so. Velk had spent the night extracting information from these recorders and translating it into something understandable. With any luck, this data would help her team reconstruct the events leading to the aircraft accident and help determine the probable cause.

"Richard," she said, uncharacteristically humble, "you've had a long, hard night. We all have. But we're out of time."

Velk, looking every bit as old and worn as he felt, rolled his chair around to the table. The forty-seven-year-old engineer had a sizable weight problem, and preferred the ease of movement offered by an office chair on a linoleum floor. "I'm finished."

"Finished? And?"

"Well, almost finished." He slammed his hand onto a stack of papers that made up two reports. "These are still working drafts. I need to run the voice data through the digital spectrum analyzer for more precise timing."

Nichols picked up the first report; it was a written transcript from the cockpit voice recorder. She began thumbing through the pages. The neatly prepared report gave a detailed description of the crew's last conversation among themselves and with Air Traffic Control, as well as a description of other sounds inside the cockpit. Velk described engine noise, warnings, and other clicks and pops. From these sounds he had estimated engine RPM, system failures, and speed, complete with their associated time codes, which he used to help determine the local time for every event during the accident sequence.

"Richard, you're amazing," she said.

And indeed he was. Velk had been one of the FBI's electronic surveillance wizards. He headed up the legendary "second-story men," a Special Operations group who stole into homes and offices in the middle of the night to plant court-ordered phone taps and bugs. Velk once hid a video camera inside a fire hydrant to watch John Gotti's front door.

"Truly amazing," she repeated.

"You won't learn much reading that," Velk said. "This is what your bosses are paying you to find out." He passed her the second report, the summation of the flight data recorder—a log of more than three hundred in-flight characteristics, from flap position to autopilot mode to smoke alarms.

Nichols took the report, but before she opened it asked him, "I want to hear your bottom-line guesstimate."

Velk leaned back in his office chair and locked his fingers behind his head. He looked quite pleased with himself. "The FAA isn't gonna like that report. When this goes public, we're gonna both be on *Oprah*."

She watched him carefully. "Is there a reason you're keeping me in suspense?"

"Bottom line—a computer timing error."

She nodded, opened the report, and stared unseeing at the pages of numerical tables. "Are you certain?"

"I'm going to stake my career on it. The 767 relies heavily— some are gonna say too heavily—on computers to control every aspect of the flight. When Kingery ran into trouble with his master computer, he thought he could save time by rebooting it, thus unlocking and restarting all subsystems. What he didn't know—what no one could have even suspected—was that once the main computer shut down, the bug prevented the system from rebooting until after a federally mandated inspection was performed. They were shit out of luck, unable to restart any of the subsystems.''

"So it *was* the Millennium Bug."

Velk rocked forward in his chair. "Who said anything about the Millennium Bug?"

"But I thought you said—"

"We're talking about a bona fide computer virus—sabotage."

"Sabotage? Do you know what you're implying?"

"I'm not implying anything. I'm saying that the industry is so freaked about whether its aircraft are Year 2000 compliant that no one noticed a deliberately planted routine that made the master computer on Flight 256 think it was one year older than it really was.''

Chapter Five
Comanche

Lincoln, New Mexico
Tuesday, December 28
1130 Hours

"Yowl, I hate long, cross-country train rides," said Special Forces Captain Jillian Larson. She squirmed in her seat, fast approaching her tolerance limit for what promised to be another long, static journey. "Six years of military flight training, and for what? Train rides, that's what. Geez, I should have joined the Navy."

Sitting across the aisle, Special Forces Colonel Joseph Marshall did his best to ignore her and kept his intense brown eyes fixed on the previous day's *Wall Street Journal*. As her commander and military flight instructor, Marshall could put up with her idle prattle, but he wouldn't listen to whining. A mere twenty-four-year-old, Captain Jill Larson was still a precocious youngster in his well-traveled eyes. She was petite and attractive, and her youthful features and shoulder-length brown hair, which she always wore in a single braid, had fooled many of his staff into dismissing her potential. Despite her slight demeanor, however, she was undeniably quite talented; and as a gunship commander—well, she was the best he had ever trained.

Marshall's right-hand man, Gunnery M.Sgt. J. C. Williams, slouched in his seat across from him, his eyes closed. An extraordinary shooter, Williams had taught Jill and a regiment of Special Forces soldiers to put five consecutive rounds from a Remington 40XB sniper rifle through a one-inch washer at one hundred yards.

The powerfully built black man didn't bother to look up as he pushed a cigar into his mouth. "Captain," Williams called across to her, "trains are good for one thing."

Jill swung her legs up onto her seat so she could face the aisle. "Oh, and what could that possibly be, Sergeant?"

"Sleeping," he said. "And I can't indulge as long as you keep squealing about how much you hate train rides."

Jill frowned. "Well, I can't sleep in moving vehicles."

"You can always do something useful like disassembling and cleaning your Heckler and Koch," the sergeant suggested.

"It's clean already," she insisted. "I finished that chore a half hour outside of El Paso."

Marshall's hard, thirty-nine-year-old facial lines lengthened with a frown. "Please find something to do, Captain," he said without missing a word of his newspaper article. "Otherwise, this is going to be one long-winded trip."

Jill fidgeted some more before finally settling back into her seat and pretending to be interested in the scenery. The view out the window of this three-car United States Army train was harsh and glaring and monotonous. There hadn't been a shred of interesting landscape for the last two hundred miles. Just endless, flat prairie. Okay, there was an occasional ranch to admire. And, if she was patient—and lucky—she might catch a glimpse of a few cows mating. So much fun, she thought.

The view inside the troop compartment offered even less visual stimulation. A third of the seats were taken by overly muscular soldiers, all of them male, all of them jocks from the same dull unit. Jill didn't care for the type: rock-hard torsos and little intellect that they could share in interesting ways. And, like the sergeant, most of them were napping. *Why do men always sleep when they travel?* she wondered. *Are they actually tired or just dealing with their boredom?* Well, she was bored too, but she couldn't do a thing about it.

Besides, Jill couldn't stop thinking about the aircraft buttoned down on the flatbed car behind them—a Boeing-Sikorsky RAH-66 Comanche armed reconnaissance helicopter. A brand-new, still-in-the-box prototype. This twin-turbine, two-seat-tandem aircraft was the next-generation Army gunship, with a fully retractable missile armament system. It boasted one-sixth the radar return of the Apache and an ingenious cold-air exhaust that greatly reduced its infrared print. And it was all hers—well, figuratively. A Special Forces aviation captain, Jill alone had been assigned to take it through a series of intense combat simulations. But not this year—the Comanche was grounded until after January 1. Those were the orders from the very top. With its triple-redundant, fly-by-wire flight-control system and 1.6 million lines of computer code for mission-critical functions, the brass wasn't taking any chances of letting the millennium computer bug transform the $30 million aircraft into a black crater.

Jill's role on this task force was simply to assist Marshall in escorting the aircraft from Fort Bliss out of El Paso to the National Training Center at Fort Irwin in California for final assembly and testing. That meant she had little to do until the techies declared the Comanche airworthy. *A baby-sitter*, she mused. *A highly trained, Special Forces baby-sitter!* There would be plenty of time to fly, she kept telling herself. She sank deeper into her vinyl seat, closed her eyes, and pretended to sleep—maybe she'd be lucky this time and drift off.

"Colonel Marshall," called Dr. Douglas Redmond, Sikorsky's VP of military aeronautical engineering and Comanche's chief designer. He was standing in the car's open vestibule, staring across the flatbed railcar behind them. Just one year shy of his sixtieth birthday, Redmond was a tall, though frail, engineer in a constant state of agitation. "Come look at this, please."

"I'll pass, if you don't mind," Marshall replied. "I've seen it a hundred times." Some of the men sleeping in front of him stirred at the extra noise. Several just sat there watching Redmond vacantly.

"Humor me, please," Redmond insisted.

The colonel threw aside his newspaper, stood, and stretched before making his way aft. He stepped beside Redmond and looked out the rear train door. He could see nothing unusual about the fifty-foot, six-axle flatcar, nor could he spot anything amiss with the cables securing the huge tarpaulin over the aircraft. Their special cargo was one-hundred-percent secure.

"Fascinating, Dr. Redmond," Marshall said, then turned to leave. "Thanks for bringing this to my attention—"

The white-haired aeronautical engineer grabbed the colonel's arm and yanked him back with a force that signaled panic.

Marshall looked questioningly at the engineer. "What are you trying to tell me, Redmond?"

"We're not the only ones on this track, Colonel," he said, pointing to the track behind them.

Marshall squinted at the glare off the desert and saw another train several miles behind them. His features tightened. He couldn't make out much at this distance. But one thing was certain—it shouldn't be there.

"It's been steadily gaining on us," Redmond said. "You told me there wouldn't be other trains on this track."

Marshall put a pensive finger on his lip. "We should have at least a fifty-mile buffer behind us until we connect with the Southern Pacific line. No exceptions."

"Then it must be commercial," Redmond offered, his voice beginning to waver. "The engineer has his schedule screwed up."

Marshall winced and shook his head. "There's no commercial traffic permitted on this track at any time."

"Then what's it doing there?"

Indeed, what?

Marshall turned to head forward to talk to the engineer. "I want you to take your seat—"

A large soldier with broad shoulders and deep-set eyes stood directly before the colonel, blocking his way. His arms were crossed over his chest, and Marshall noticed on his fat wrist a tattoo of what appeared to be the sun.

The colonel's solid, eternally serious face drew taut. "Pardon me." He attempted to step around him.

The soldier threw out his beefy arm and pushed the colonel roughly back. "I don't think so."

The other soldiers in the compartment were no longer sleeping. Several were now on their feet, filling in behind the soldier, while the others watched from their seats. Whatever was going on, they were all in it together.

Redmond turned around and frowned when he saw the troops gathering. "What's this?"

"We're not the only ones escorting the Comanche," Marshall said. The only personnel aboard this transport he knew were Redmond, Williams, and Jill. The other soldiers were strangers—all from the Third Armored Cavalry Regiment hitching a ride to Fort Irwin. Or at least that's what he had been told at the last minute. But there had been no way to verify anything with communications down.

"This is absurd." Redmond's voice was too shaky to command any real authority. He sounded less convincing when he uttered, "I demand an explanation!"

Marshall looked piercingly at the large soldier blocking his way. "Now, what would you boys do with a piece of hardware like the Comanche?"

The soldier withdrew a Browning 9mm and drove it into Marshall's gut. "Oh, we have grand plans," he sneered. "Firepower like that can defeat an army of assholes like you. And that's exactly what we intend to do with it." He stood close enough for Marshall to smell breakfast onions on his breath. "Turn around and face the window. Both of you."

Redmond, his eyes and mouth opened wide, complied immediately. When Marshall didn't move, the soldier added, *"Now*, or we will kill your friends in their sleep. I promise you."

Chapter Six
In Flight

Colorado Rockies
Tuesday, December 28
1140 Hours

The trio of military troop helicopters ascended to 11,000 feet in perfect formation as they approached the foothills of the Colorado Rockies. In the Huey chopper, comfort was a privilege reserved to those clever enough to find or create it. Julie Martinelli wasn't among those fortunate few. She hated getting up so early and was tired and irritated. The compartment was cold and smelled of diesel fuel, and the rumble from the chopper's less-than-tuned rotor blades did its best to annoy and keep her awake. Despite the arrangements, she persisted in her plan to cop a couple of hours of sleep en route to Cheyenne Mountain. And she nearly succeeded, drifting unevenly between shallow sleep and vague awareness of her miserable, smelly surroundings.

She had no idea of the time when a voice, loud enough to get her attention, said, "You're missing the best part of the flight."

Julie opened her eyes with a start and saw Colonel Beckman leaning over her, staring, an unbecoming grin of greeting on his lips.

"What time is it? Where are we?"

"It's zero-nine-forty-two hours," the colonel said.

"Huh?"

"We're about two hundred miles from Cheyenne." He peered

out the port window. "You really should see this."

Julie struggled to sit upright in her metal fold-down seat. Her neck and back ached from her contorted sleeping position. "See what?"

Colonel Beckman gestured out the window. "That."

Julie squinted out the porthole at the harsh morning light. "That" was indeed a magnificent view—beyond the Colorado foothills loomed a backdrop of immense, dark mountains. Rugged, inhospitable terrain, to be sure. She stared for a few seconds, letting her eyes adjust, then pressed her cheek against the Plexiglas to see one of the two Black Hawks off the chopper's starboard quarter. All she could think about was how much sleep its passengers must be getting, stretching out in that slick helicopter. She wondered how Nancy Shaw was faring over there right now. She hoped she was enjoying herself.

"Terrific," Julie said, settling back into her seat. She allowed a huge yawn. "Now, if you'll excuse me, I want to finish something."

The colonel settled back into his seat. "I was hoping we could talk."

"Not now."

"This probably will be our best chance."

Julie, her eyes half open, said nothing and listened to the drone of the engines and the squawky radio communication coming from the cockpit. The half-dozen other people in the cabin, most wearing uniforms, were either sleeping or reading what looked like officially prepared material organized in folders. Her sleepy gaze shifted back to the colonel. There was something about him that made her uncomfortable. He was middle-aged, very lean, probably worked out to obsession, with closely cropped, pointed hair and a decidedly solid, bland face. All military, she concluded; the type who probably didn't spend much time in the company of women.

"So can we talk?" he pressed.

Julie knew she wouldn't get much sleep and, stretching, sat straight in her seat. She yawned again. "I'll need some coffee."

"Of course." He reached under his seat and produced a stainless-steel Eddie Bauer thermos, crowned with several poly-

51

styrene foam cups. He poured a cup and passed it to her. "I hope black is all right."

"It'll do," she said, accepting the cup.

The lights sputtered out, and the cabin fell dark except for the morning rays streaming in through the windows. Those reading muttered their objections.

The colonel was on his feet in an instant, yelling into the cockpit, "Ken, damn it. I thought you said this was fixed."

"The altitude is putting a strain on the electrics," Ken called back. "Wiring's overheating. Blew a fuse in Bay Four, sir."

"So put in a new one."

"Working on it, sir."

Colonel Beckman returned to his seat and smiled at Julie. "I suppose he's doing the best he can under the circumstances. We're just asking too much from this old aircraft. I'll put up with a few inconveniences, just as long the blades keep spinning."

The colonel let out a grandiose laugh that made Julie's head pound. The lights flickered on. "Ah—you see, we're back in business."

"So what are we going to talk about?"

Colonel Beckman settled back into his seat and stretched out his legs until his shoes were touching hers. "I'm intrigued by your background," he began. "Your résumé is quite impressive. Is it true that you could program in three machine languages when you were eight years old?"

"Seven."

"Ahhh. Tell me about your interest in mathematics. Your file says you mastered algebra, geometry, trigonometry, and calculus on your own."

Julie took a tentative sip of coffee; it was strong and stale, but at least it was hot. "That was a long time ago, before I had any sense."

"I read the report on your virus catastrophe a few years back. Genetic engineering. Biological warfare. Nasty stuff—"

"Please, I'm in no mood to talk about myself right now," she said. "Maybe later."

"Are you still seeing Major Joseph Marshall? Or is he a colonel now? I heard you haven't seen him in a while."

She glared at him. "You're way out of line."

A wave of disappointment passed over his expression. "Then tell me about your colleague, Dr. Shaw. I understand she was once your academic adviser."

Julie took another sip. "Nancy is my best friend. We met several years ago at Stanford when she stuck her neck out and agreed to be my Ph.D. thesis adviser." Julie allowed herself a smile, an expression the colonel immediately fell in love with. "I'm sure she thought I was a wild woman at first, at least academically. She didn't approve of my original thesis."

"Tell me about it."

Julie, her eyes downcast, took another sip of coffee. "I was an intern at Fort Detrick. I proposed to genetically engineer a microorganism that might prove useful as a biological weapon."

"Wouldn't that be illegal?"

She frowned. "We shouldn't be talking about this."

The colonel sat upright. "Let me finish your story. You proposed to splice the most potent neurotoxin protein known to man onto the RNA strand of a Group A virus. You succeeded in creating an airborne virus hundreds of times more deadly than any other known neurotoxin. I read the reports. Very lethal stuff. And quite fascinating."

"I didn't create anything," she said. "Dr. Shaw convinced me of the risks, so I decided not to go through with the experiment."

"Whatever. But the Detrick lab you worked at produced the organism. And you let it escape."

Julie was bored with this conversation. "Please, Colonel. I'm tired and haven't had any breakfast yet. You seem to know all the answers anyway. So let's change the subject and let me ask you questions."

Colonel Beckman shrugged with a grin; he, alone, seemed to be enjoying their chat. "Fair enough."

"How many computer programmers have you drafted?" she asked.

"Me personally?"

"The military."

"Eight hundred thousand," the colonel responded without much thought. "About five hundred thousand more volunteered, mostly from overseas—Ireland, India, China. That's where most of the COBOL programmers are these days. A lot of army old-timers are even coming out of retirement."

"Drafting programmers and hiring from overseas. Sounds suspiciously like you're looking for cheap labor."

"Whatever; it's happening. The U.S. government pays top dollar, so it brings out the best programmers from all over the world to work on systems that are of national strategic importance—the military and the Federal Reserve Banks."

"Without any concern about how many of my tax dollars you spend?"

"The military has a simple motto, Doctor: Performance at Any Cost. Every other governmental system is on hold until after the New Year."

Julie finished her coffee. The colonel offered to pour her another, but she declined. "This trip isn't about the Millennium Bug, is it?"

Colonel Beckman's arrogant expression withered. "What do you mean?"

"I smell a snow job. You're bringing in too many specialists. And Cheyenne Mountain isn't exactly the hub of military computing. You've got a nasty little problem on your hands that hasn't been made public—yet. And you need a whole lot more than programmers to fix it. Am I getting warm, Colonel?"

The other officers in the compartment looked up from their folders and watched them, a reaction Julie was quick to notice. The ones who were sleeping stirred noticeably.

"Drop it, Doctor," Beckman said.

"Seems I've aroused some attention," she said, then addressed the others. "I suppose you're all in this little secret conspiracy together."

The colonel's voice turned dark and cold. "Let me remind you, Dr. Martinelli, that you're now in the United States Army, subject to the same rules of conduct as any enlisted man or woman. Insubordination is an imprisonable offense. I told you to drop it, and this will be my last warning."

"Oooooh, you're scaring me," she mocked. Then her tone turned serious. "So put me in the brig right now, Colonel. I promised myself I would cripple the next military officer who bullshitted me. It almost got me killed once. Never again."

Colonel Beckman glanced at his colleagues, who just watched him with stone faces. They would let him handle Julie Martinelli alone.

"Doctor—"

One of the officers, a large black man slumped in his seat, his eyes closed, said in a deep voice that commanded everyone's attention, "Tell her."

All eyes shifted to him. For several long moments, the only sound was the uneven rumble of the chopper's rotor blades. Finally, the colonel shrugged. "Okay, Doctor. We'll play this your way. I can tell you this much: We're going to Cheyenne Mountain, but not to huddle over terminals and rewrite lines of computer code. We've already done that, and our systems have all been tested and certified to be Year 2000 compliant."

Julie looked at him, uncomprehending. "Then why do you need me? Why do you need any programmers, for that matter?"

Colonel Beckman fidgeted in his seat, crossing, then uncrossing his leg, before uttering a single word: "Eclipse."

Julie waited for him to say more, but he appeared to be finished. "I beg your pardon, Colonel?"

Beckman scowled at her, as though the single word would explain everything. "Eclipse is a network of forty-seven military satellites, the likes of which you've never even dreamed. The ultimate surveillance and intelligence-gathering system, it's made modern warfare obsolete. Eclipse is this country's primary defense against aggression from the air, sea, or land. Very top secret, and very high tech."

"I still don't understand what Big Brother, or whatever you call it, has to do with me. If your systems have been tested and certified Year 2000 compliant, then you've got everything under control."

"Not quite, Dr. Martinelli," said the black officer who had been trying to sleep. He threw aside his overcoat, which he had been using as a blanket, sat up groggily, and let out a cavernous yawn. He was built like a football linebacker. Julie saw by his uniform that he was a general.

"Everything is *not* under control," he said, his voice deep and resonant. "Last Friday, Christmas Eve, at midnight—exactly one week before the clocks strike midnight for the last time this millennium—Eclipse shut itself down. Yes, Doctor, what this country doesn't know, what I hope no country ever knows, is we're blind and deaf to any number of growing international threats.''

He looked directly into her eyes with a gaze set in steel. ''And no one has a clue why.''

Chapter Seven
Derailed

Lincoln, New Mexico
Tuesday, December 28
1150 Hours

Special Forces Colonel Joseph Marshall did as the gun-wielding soldier ordered and faced the rear of the troop compartment. His jaw stiffened as he watched a second locomotive rapidly closing the distance between them. It was a common eighty-ton with a center cab, and the engine was more than capable of towing the Comanche's flatbed railcar down any number of sidetracks.

''We're slowing, Colonel,'' Dr. Redmond said, staring out the back window. ''The engineer must be in on this too.''

Marshall said over his shoulder, ''Can I ask how you managed to slip through security?''

The soldier let out a hoot of laughter. ''What security? Fort Bliss's mainframes have been down all night thanks to a lost satellite hookup. All the MP asked before we boarded were our ID numbers, which he dutifully noted on a pad of paper.''

The other soldiers shared his amusement.

''May I ask who you people are?'' Marshall pressed.

The beefy soldier's tone grew serious. "No, you may not." He put the Browning to the back of the colonel's head, while more soldiers rose from their seats to assist. "You'll know everything soon enough—in another life—"

"The only man gonna need another life is you," came a booming voice from behind them. The group of soldiers whirled to see Sergeant J. C. Williams pointing a Smith & Wesson forty-caliber handgun at them with both hands.

For several moments no one in the compartment moved or uttered a sound. The rogue soldiers watched the muscular black sergeant, a cigar clenched between his teeth; he looked as though he could tear apart a forklift with his bare hands. However, it was his satin-black handgun that commanded their undivided attention.

Williams pulled back the hammer with a no-nonsense click. "I wanna see everyone's hands. You in front—I want that gun on the floor *NOW*."

The lead soldier refused to comply. "You don't know what you're doing," he hissed, his bloated features strained with anger. "You're compromising a classified military operation."

"Sorry I spoiled your fun." Williams's tone turned icy. "If that gun isn't at your feet in two seconds, I'm putting a bullet through that cement forehead of yours."

Jill stirred sleepily. "You're too loud."

"Get out your Heckler and Koch," Williams told her.

The beefy soldier raised his Browning slightly. "If you won't listen to reason, perhaps you'll consider your instincts. I'm prepared to offer you a hundred thousand in gold to put down that gun."

"One," Williams announced, the word ringing out like a shot.

The soldier's eyes widened. "Think what a colored man can do with that kind of money!"

"Two."

The soldier brought up his handgun. There came a single blast from Williams's Smith & Wesson. The soldier's sudden movement compromised the sergeant's aim for his forehead and the round exploded through the side of his neck. The soldier gasped and choked as Marshall wrapped his arm around his torso and used him as a shield. The colonel grabbed his gun-wielding hand, raised the Browning, and jerked the soldier's finger. The bullet struck the closest soldier in the center of his chest. Marshall moved the soldier's limp hand and squeezed off a second round at the next soldier, then aimed at another and fired again.

The other soldiers were scrambling for their weapons. Redmond shrank into the corner, his hands pressed against his temples. Jill reached under her seat and opened her bag.

A soldier lunged for Williams's gun, grabbed it, and drove the sergeant's arm straight into the air. A round discharged through the roof. The sergeant rammed his knee solidly into the soldier's groin with enough force to shatter marble. The soldier's mouth opened, but before he could utter a sound, Williams brought his right elbow down hard onto the bridge of his nose, shattering the front of his skull. The soldier's head flew backward with a snap, his neck broken.

Jill stood up suddenly.

"*Sit down*," Williams commanded.

"Hardly."

She brought up her Heckler & Koch submachine gun and squeezed the trigger. Scores of tungsten bullets spat from the weapon's stubby barrel as she swept it across the field of scrambling soldiers. Amid a whirlwind of smoke and blood, the hapless soldiers spun like puppets, flailed backward, and dumped heavily onto the floor.

A round ripped past her face and shattered the window beside her. Jill lost her balance and stumbled backward onto the seat, feeling her face for a wound. There wasn't any. Indiscriminate rounds tore through the seat in front of her, throwing up a spray of fabric.

The shooter came charging at her. Williams grabbed him by the collar as he dove for her and, using his momentum, lifted him off his feet and hurled him bodily through what was left of the window. The soldier flew from the railcar and slammed gracelessly into the rocks beside the tracks at seventy miles an hour.

Three remaining soldiers took modest cover behind their seats. Marshall raced down the aisle. The soldiers fired as he charged past, their rounds tearing into the seats millimeters behind him. One of them stood for a sure aim at his back. Williams emptied his clip into the soldier's upper chest and chin, hurling him back against the side panel with a dull thump.

Jill struggled to rise.

"Keep down!" Williams shouted, crouching to replace his clip.

Marshall dove onto the floor below his seat. He unzipped his duffel bag and withdrew a customized Franchi SPAS-12 semi-automatic military shotgun. He pressed his face against the floor and spotted the soldiers' boots several rows in front of him. He slid his Franchi forward and pumped two quick rounds at them. The men spilled over and howled.

Marshall rolled into the aisle on his knees, the opened shotgun stock braced firmly against his hip. He pumped round after round into the back of the seats, tearing them apart in a flurry of flying metal and fabric. He continued pumping rounds at them through the storm of fabric until his Franchi was empty.

A full three seconds passed before the compartment grew quiet, save for the even rumble of the train's wheels on the tracks.

"Anyone hit?" Marshall said, rising.

Williams slid his handgun into the holster behind his back. "Couldn't possibly be better." He looked at Jill. "What about you?"

"I'm still in one piece." She stood, fumbling with her Heckler & Koch with shaking hands.

"Congratulations on your first kill," Williams said.

She glanced up at him, her face drawn, not at all comfortable with that honor.

Marshall pushed more cartridges into his Franchi. "Redmond, are you all right?"

The doctor stood uneasily. "Yes, I think so. What just happened here?"

Marshall stomped to the front of the compartment. "We stopped a hijacking of United States military property and technology."

Redmond ran a pair of shaking hands through his white wisps of hair while staring trancelike at the carnage strewn like rubbish throughout the compartment. The smell of death was everywhere. A river of blood formed a creek down the center of the aisle, collecting in puddles where the floor panels had been punched through.

"Who were they?" Redmond asked, his voice weak.

"Terrorists, assholes, take your pick," Marshall said. He tried the door leading to the locomotive. It was locked. The door was made of reinforced steel to make sure the engine was inaccessible.

"There's no way you're getting through there," Williams said. He knelt to examine one of the slain soldiers.

"Then how will we stop this train?" Jill asked.

No one had an answer for her.

"This one's still alive," Williams said. He grabbed the soldier's wrist, causing him to stir, and pointed with his cigar. "Take a look at this tattoo."

Marshall crouched next to him and examined the soldier's tattoo of the sun. "Interesting. He's not the only one wearing that sign."

Williams crawled to another soldier, then checked another. "You're right. They all have one, Joe. What's it mean?"

"Damned if I know," Marshall said. "Maybe they all belong to some paramilitary boys' club."

"It's Sirius," Jill said, "a doomsday symbol." She slipped from her seat and knelt next to Williams. "It was in the news last year. These sons of bitches think it's the end of the world. *Newsweek* even featured a cover story on that very symbol."

"Doesn't make sense," Williams said. "If you thought tomorrow was Judgment Day, why steal hardware like the Comanche?"

Marshall grabbed the live soldier by the front of his shirt and pulled him roughly into a sitting position. "Who are you people?"

The soldier stared warily at the colonel. Blood was oozing from the side of his lips from a wound that had pierced his lungs.

"I asked you a question," Marshall demanded, shaking him.

The soldier's lips stretched into a grin, but the lines on his face betrayed his agony. "Dark Star," he spat, "the end of the likes of you." His accent was British.

"What's with this doomsday business?" Marshall pressed. "And why do you want the Comanche?"

"Four more days . . . till the end . . ." He was unable to catch his breath. "Firepower . . . the general wants more firepower . . .

planning grand end of the world . . .'' He began heaving, struggling to breathe.

Jill moved closer to hear him. ''What's he babbling—?''

A sudden jolt knocked each of them off their feet. Jill shouted in surprise. Dr. Redmond flew into the first seat on top of the slain soldier.

''What the hell was that?'' Williams said, sitting up.

''The locomotive behind us just rammed us in the ass,'' Redmond shouted, pulling himself up and wiping his hands on his trousers.

He threw open the rear door—the second locomotive was jammed solidly against the flatbed car, pushing them. Four men in workmen's coveralls appeared on the engine's catwalk and began climbing down onto the flatcar.

Redmond whipped around. ''They're taking the—''

A *crack* from a high-velocity sniper's rifle bore a neat hole through the back of Redmond's head, taking off the front of his cranium.

''*Oh, God!*'' Jill screamed, and huddled down behind a seat.

''*Goddammit* . . . where'd that come from?'' Williams shouted.

Marshall stormed down the aisle and crouched beside Redmond's body. He chanced a look outside. Four railmen had climbed down onto the flatbed. He watched bitterly as two men began working on the rear coupling to attach the flatcar to their engine. The other two were making their way around the tarp-covered chopper toward them, one wielding a belt-fed automatic weapon.

''I don't think so.'' Marshall rolled onto his stomach and pumped several blasts through the doorway at the two approaching workmen. He caught the closest in the leg, tearing the extremity clear off. The man went down with a roar and rolled off the side of the car. The second man, the one with the weapon, dove behind the mountainous tarp covering the chopper.

Marshall slid more rounds into his Franchi. ''They mean to pin us in here while they lock the flatbed to their engine. If they finish, we've lost it.''

''I hear ya.'' Williams opened a hard-shell, military-grade case under his seat and withdrew a custom-made Israeli Galil sniper's rifle. He crawled down the aisle on his belly and lay spread-eagled on the floor beside Marshall. He brought the Galil's scope to his eye but couldn't get a clear shot from his vantage.

Another high-powered round ripped into the compartment, then another.

"Can you see where those shots are coming from?" Marshall asked.

"The engineer's cabin," Williams said, sighting one of the locomotive's narrow windscreens. "The asshole's in the cabin."

The rear locomotive's cabin glass had been removed, and he could see a man leaning out, taking aim with a heavy-barrel, bolt-action sniper's rifle. The sergeant positioned the crosshairs of his rifle's precision scope over the man's face and squeezed the trigger. The sniper heaved backward and disappeared. Williams moved his rifle slightly to the right and sighted a second figure huddled over the controls. He squeezed off another round. The windscreen shattered and the figure vanished.

Williams rose to his knees. "I can't see jack from down here. I'm going up top."

He sprinted to the compartment's blown-out window and found Jill crouched behind the seat. "Can you cover me?"

She stood with her Heckler & Koch cocked and ready. "Of course."

Williams slung the Galil over his shoulder, hefted himself out the window, and began climbing. Several seconds later, he lay on the roof. He glanced forward at the 120-ton locomotive pulling them, then behind at the smaller engine that meant to haul away their flatcar. The hijackers weren't about to make this easy for them. Both trains were roaring in tandem down the tracks at more than seventy miles an hour.

Suddenly, dozens of rounds began hammering the compartment below.

"*Get down!*" Marshall rolled away from the rear wall and tackled Jill onto the floor.

"What is it?" she shouted as the rounds tore apart the walls.

Marshall glanced around the seat. He saw the workman standing beside the tarpaulins hefting a belt-fed SAW combat machine gun. Marshall looked toward the ceiling—Williams was effectively pinned up there.

Marshall rolled across the aisle, reached into Williams's canvas bag, and grabbed one of four hockey-puck-shaped concussion grenades with enough C3 plastique to blow off the rear wall. He pulled the pin and hurled the grenade toward the back wall. The disk's flat magnetized surface slapped against the metal panel and held.

"Keep your head down!" he warned.

Marshall watched the rear wall intensely. The grenade detonated with a deafening concussion, hurling a blizzard of shrapnel and debris over their heads. The blast tore off the rear wall and flung several panels across the flatbed. One of the panels bounced before the gunner. He swung sideways to deflect its impact with his shoulder.

Jill leapt to her feet and ran toward the flatbed with her submachine gun.

"What do you think you're doing?" Marshall hollered after her.

"They're not taking *my* Comanche."

Jill jumped out onto the flatcar and stumbled awkwardly several feet in front of the gunner. He struggled to reposition his weapon. Before he could bring the machine gun to bear, Jill thrust her Heckler & Koch before her with one hand and squeezed the trigger, spraying him with bullets. She emptied the clip into him. His flailing body fell backward in a heap with the weapon in his lap.

Jill felt her jumpsuit for another clip, while the two men working on the rear coupling scrambled to protect themselves. They didn't get far. Each dropped as a bubble of blood leapt from their chests. Jill spun and saw Williams lying at the edge of the troop compartment roof, covering her. He raised his Galil in an "all clear" sign.

Marshall joined Jill on the flatcar and asked, "Are you sure this is your first fireflight?"

"They would've taken my Comanche," she said.

Marshall and Jill could feel the train accelerating with the rush of wind in their faces. They inspected the car's rear coupling. The cables were attached, but the main link hadn't been secured, a difficult task at best with the train moving.

Marshall couldn't see anyone in the second locomotive's center cab. "She's a runaway."

"Can we undo this coupling?" Jill asked.

"The question is, do we want to—"

Two rounds ricocheted off the troop-compartment roof behind Williams. Jill and Marshall whirled. The sergeant screwed his neck around and saw a man in coveralls standing on the lead engine's catwalk, pointing a handgun. His position in front of the engine was awkward, but he still had the advantage. Another man in overalls was leaning out the side window of the engineer's cab, shouting instructions at him.

Williams yelled down to Marshall, "There're two more up here, barricaded inside the cab."

"That means they still control the flatbed," Jill said to the colonel.

"Leave them," Marshall shouted up to the sergeant. "I'll need your help to uncouple the bastards."

Williams acknowledged. He scrambled down into the troop compartment, retrieved both their bags, and joined Marshall out on the flatbed.

"Let's do it," the colonel said.

They climbed down between the cars and stood on either side of the coupling that attached the flatbed to the forward troop car. The speed of the lead engine was uneven, and it alternately pulled and pushed against the coupling. They removed the pins and cables, grabbed the coupling lever, and heaved together. When the stress eased, they lifted the joint and separated the flatbed from the troop car. The lead train pulled steadily away from them.

"Piece of cake," Williams said.

They scrambled up onto the flatbed. Williams emptied one of their bags and placed the remaining three concussion grenades inside.

"Thirty seconds," Marshall instructed.

Williams adjusted the timer on one of the explosives. He pulled the pin, tucked it into the bag, and hurled the package into the troop compartment as it sped away.

"*Move it!*" Jill yelled across to them.

Both men raced to the rear of the flatcar and followed Jill up the second locomotive's catwalk, which led into the engineer's cab. Inside, they found a pair of dead men lying one on top of the other—two rounds from Williams's Galil had effectively removed each of their faces.

"I could have done without seeing this," Jill said. She inspected the compartment's smashed instrumentation. "The radio's gone. So is most of the security equipment."

Without the weight of the flatbed, the lead engine had already pulled several hundred yards ahead of them.

"You've got ten seconds to stop this train, Joe," Williams said.

Marshall grabbed the engine's throttle lever and pulled back the metal bar, producing a hiss. The locomotive jerked and began slowing.

The grenades detonated well ahead of them. The troop car exploded in an impressive fireball that blew it from the track and dragged the lead locomotive with it. The engine twisted ninety degrees, tipped over, and began skidding with 120 tons of momentum. The running tracks ahead of it tore free in an impressive spray of rails and timber. The locomotive left the tracks and slammed into a dune. It bounced end over end like a cartwheel, disintegrating in an appalling roar of twisting, flying metal.

The second train's speed was still much too fast as they raced toward the damaged tracks.

"*Stop this thing!*" Jill shouted.

Marshall put his full weight on the brake pedal, producing a scream of metal against metal. Each of them grabbed a secure handhold as the dramatic deceleration hurled them backward against the steel wall. The locomotive became unstable and began to sway and oscillate with the hiss of ruptured hydraulic lines.

The locomotive's rapid deceleration caused the flatcar in front to burst through its tenuous coupling and continue down the track on its own momentum.

"*Noooooo!*" Jill yelled.

"Son of a bitch," Williams spat. "We lost it!"

They watched helplessly as the fifty-foot flat railcar carried the Comanche unchecked down the tracks at thirty miles an hour. When the flatcar reached the damaged section of tracks, it left the rails and skidded over the hard, flat prairie. Miraculously, it didn't overturn. Instead, its low center of gravity pushed its wheels into the clay, tearing up the soil like a bulldozer while steadying her. Its velocity greatly reduced, the flatbed spun 360 degrees before skidding to a stop.

"Sweet Mary . . ." Williams said breathlessly.

Jill watched speechless.

Marshall moved the eighty-ton locomotive ahead slowly until it reached the edge of the undamaged section of tracks. He engaged the brakes.

"The Comanche's ours," Williams decided. "We earned it."

Chapter Eight
Uplink

Willard, Colorado
Tuesday, December 28
1215 Hours

Alexander Skile checked his watch, then turned to his business associate and raised his arms like an orchestra conductor. "Shall we begin?"

Henry Princeton, Skile's chief microprocessor engineer, sank comfortably into the deep sofa and shrugged, a mischievous grin pasted on his youthful features.

"Go for it," Henry said.

Skile, wearing only a robe as was his custom until noon when working at home, spun around to the computer terminal in his lower-level office. He keyed in a command to update the position of the USLF 1267 satellite, then fed its coordinates to the thirty-foot satellite dish mounted in a clearing above his mountain estate. Outside, electric motors nudged the dish six degrees north latitude and twenty-seven degrees longitude. WAIT appeared at the bottom of the screen while his system and the military command network exchanged communication protocols. A moment later, a green READY light began blinking, signaling that they had a viable connection to the U.S. Strategic Defense network's special-purpose channel transponder for secure data communication.

"That was easy," Skile said in mock surprise.

Henry offered his boss a tip of his imaginary hat.

"Now the fun begins," Skile said.

Henry drew in a deep breath and held it while Skile keyed in another command. The signal uploaded a set of encrypted instructions, a message only a Black Hawk military helicopter could decode.

Finished, Skile leaned back into his leather chair, stuck his skinny bare feet up on his desk, and waited, his eyes locked on the display in rapt attention. The screen remained blank except for a blinking red cursor in the lower left corner. Neither he nor Henry uttered a word for the next thirty seconds.

Finally, the light turned green and a page of information scrolled down the display. Skile leaned forward and read the numbers carefully. A grin broke his sullen features. He spun around to Henry and slapped his hands together with a *crack*. "One of them is ours!"

Henry let out his breath in an abrupt laugh. "And the other?"

Skile squinted at the display and shook his head. "No confirmation. This should prove very interesting."

"Are we interrupting something?" asked Judith Skile from the doorway.

Both men turned in unison. Skile's wife, dressed only in a long transparent negligee that concealed nothing, looked seductively at the two of them. She was eager to play.

Henry sat up with keen interest, his eyes riveted on Judith's abundant breasts, which pushed out the fabric impressively. He had always wanted to see her undressed. Beside her, holding a nearly empty glass of Bloody Mary, stood Henry's wife, Renee, a tall, slender, beautiful woman in her own right. She wore only a short white robe, which barely covered her thighs. Her long black hair was wrapped in a towel.

Renee and Judi had just stepped out of the Jacuzzi and felt hot and revitalized. The women exchanged interested glances, then, sharing some private amusement, offered Skile a pair of alluring smiles.

Judith strolled behind her husband's chair, reached around the front, and untied his robe. She slipped her hands inside and slid them down to his loins.

"Renee, he needs our help," she said over her shoulder. She turned and whispered into his ear, "We've devised a few tricks while you were working. Now we're eager to see if our sorcery will arouse you." She gave the inside of his ear a gentle lick.

Skile pulled his wife's hand away and kissed it, then looked into her eyes. "You're always full of surprises."

Judith gave his hand a gentle yet firm pull until he rose from his chair. He looked at them both curiously as she and Renee led him down the hallway to one of their lower-level bedrooms. Henry, his breathing intensifying, followed a safe distance behind.

Once inside the bedroom, Judi pushed her husband gently onto the king-size canopy bed. The curtains were drawn, but the dimness still afforded Henry sufficient light to see Judi remove Skile's robe and lay him on his back, prone, exposing his long, slender, ropelike member. Henry watched fascinated from the doorway while Judi pulled and stretched it. Despite her expert coaxing, his penis refused to grow to its full aroused length.

She signaled her companion with a nod.

Renee finished her Bloody Mary in a single swallow, then slid off her tiny robe. She pulled the towel from her head and shook free her long black hair. Standing gloriously naked in front of Skile, she felt her own perfect breasts, then ran a hand down over her tight stomach. Smiling, she rolled onto the bed and curled up beside him.

Henry watched her, astonished. He'd never seen his wife with another man. How far would she go? How far would he let this go? Tumultuous emotions churned inside him, and he was unable to discern if he enjoyed these feelings or not. He had his answer shortly. His loins stirred, and within seconds his pants became extraordinarily uncomfortable.

"Let her show you a trick, Alex," Judith said.

Before Skile could respond, Renee crawled over Skile and took his penis into her mouth. Skile moaned with surprise and delight.

Judith slipped off her negligee and positioned herself on all fours behind Renee. She slid her huge breasts over Renee's back and rubbed them over her limber curves. Renee purred while she continued to work on Skile, producing deep, exquisite sounds with her tongue.

Henry, delirious with desire, began unbuckling his shirt as though in a trance.

Skile rose onto his elbows and leveled a stern gaze at him. "What do you think you're doing?"

He shook his vapid stare and said, a note of timidity in his voice, "I wish to join you."

Skile thrust a bony finger at him. "Have you forgotten there's a helicopter waiting for you? Yet here you stand. You'll be lucky to make the briefing."

Henry, his eyes averted as though embarrassed, began rebuttoning his shirt.

Judith continued caressing his wife's back and shoulders with increasingly eager movements. She looked at Henry with sad, apologetic eyes and shrugged.

Chapter Nine
Survivor

Walter Reed Army Medical Center
Washington, D.C.
Tuesday, December 28
1420 Hours

The President and his entourage marched down the first-floor corridor of Washington's Walter Reed Hospital. Instead of a sterile, somber hallway, the passage was loud and animated. A dozen elite newsmen and newswomen, their photographers beside them, formed a gauntlet around the President's procession. They were allowed limited access to the hospital's first floor, an arrangement not uncommon considering the hospital's proximity to the White House.

"Mr. President . . . !"

"Mr. President . . . !"

"Mr. President . . . !"

"Mr. President, do you intend to shut down the airlines?"

Another roar of additional questioning ensued.

"Mr. President, what about military aircraft? Is any plane safe to fly?"

"What about utilities, Mr. President? Are the nuclear reactors safe?"

"Will you put a limited ban on manufacturing? Chemical plants, refineries, and other volatile processes?"

A stern-faced President revealed nothing and continued his march down the corridor with urgency and purpose. When his party reached the end of the hallway, they encountered a pair of closed elevator doors. There were no elevators waiting. An oversight. They would later learn that a surgeon on an emergency call, a Republican, had overridden the elevator with his passkey.

"Well, this is awkward," the President mocked to his aides.

One of the Secret Service agents jammed his huge thumb into the Up button to summon the elevator. When the President realized he was trapped with the reporters, he shed his aloof manner, turned to face them, and raised his hands, his good-natured eyes alive and affable. The reporters fell silent.

"All I can tell you," the President said, "is that any service or process whose malfunction causes a risk to public safety is under close scrutiny. I'm making an announcement this evening at eight o'clock. You and your colleagues can ask questions at that time."

Mercifully, the elevator doors opened and the President's entourage moved quickly inside. The press was forbidden beyond this point. A Secret Service agent hit the button for the third-floor intensive-care ward.

The collective assemblage roared after him, *"Mr. President—"*

The doors slid shut, diminishing the noise and the volley of questions to which the President had few answers.

"I can see it's going to be a very long week," the President said. "I'll be very happy when this millennium is over."

None of his aides offered any comment.

The doors opened on the third-floor intensive-care wing, where a party of doctors and other white-frocked dignitaries stood waiting. They stared at him in awe—or perhaps curiosity—as he stepped off the elevator.

"How is she?" were the President's first words to no one in particular.

"Her injuries are not life-threatening," said one of the doctors, stepping forward. He was a large man with broad shoulders and gray hair. "I'm Dr. Leroy, chief neurosurgeon."

The President shook the doctor's hand in a political gesture of gratitude for the good news. Despite the doctor's size, his hands were soft and delicate.

"She's this way," Dr. Leroy said, gesturing to the critical-care row of cubicles on the opposite end of the hallway.

The others fell in behind them as the President followed the doctor past several intensive-care bays, some with their curtains drawn, others with their patients thrashing about for a glimpse of the procession.

"She received quite a beating," Dr. Leroy explained. "She's got three broken ribs and a collapsed lung. Plus about two dozen assorted bruises and lacerations, most on her upper torso. With luck, she could be out of here in two weeks. Emotionally . . . well, that's a different matter. Long term she'll need a lot of friends after losing her family that way. She's still in shock, and we've kept her sedated through the night. When she heard you were coming she insisted on being alert."

The party stopped in front of a critical unit bay where a woman attached to tubes and wires lay on a bed. Beside her sat the hospital's psychiatrist, a woman who specialized in counseling trauma victims. The President motioned the psychiatrist away, then put up his hand, signaling the others to remain behind. He approached the side of the bed alone and beheld a sight he knew he would never forget. He hardly recognized the senator's wife through the bandages, the discoloration, and the swelling. The scars would be deep and permanent, the President could see, a cruel fate for such a lovely and lively woman.

Her eyes were swollen shut and she looked as though she were asleep. He touched her arm.

"Nora?"

She stirred, and the President thought he detected the slightest smile. "Nora, it's Bill. I'm so sorry about your family. I'm praying for them. It's unconscionable what happened and what you're going through."

She reached blindly for him, and the President took her hand into his own.

"My poor Gina and Michael," she sobbed. "What will I do without them? She was so young . . . so full of life. I heard her screaming for me in the fire. I couldn't see her . . . I tried to help her, but I couldn't see her . . . there was too much fire." A stream of tears spilled down her right temple.

The President squeezed her hand. "Nora—"

"I would have died too . . . the flight attendant pulled me into the snow. I think she said her name was Sandy . . . Cummings. She saved my life. It would mean so much if you could meet her on your way out."

"Of course."

"Thank you so much, Bill."

The President's voice broke. "We're all here for you, Nora. I wish I could make your pain go away. But I know that's not possible. But there are things I can do. Just tell me, and if it's in my power . . ."

She squeezed his hand in a serious grip and opened her eyes as wide as the swelling would allow. "Bill . . . you must stop this. It was Michael's wish that you act to prevent this sort of thing from happening. People are going to keep getting on planes unless you do something."

The President nodded; he knew what he had to do. *God forgive us if we remain ignorant as politicians of what we know as feeling men and women.* "Nora, I promise I'll do everything in my power. I'll have every person in my administration working to make sure this type of tragedy never happens again."

Chapter Ten
Altitude

High over the Colorado Rockies, the unthinkable happened aboard the Number Two Black Hawk. The aircraft's eight EA warning lights blinked on at once, followed by an unsettling screech that filled the cockpit.

"*Jesus*, there she goes," said Brad Madison, the chopper's copilot. "System failure."

The cyclical control grew stiff and unresponsive in Captain Ben Saratoga's hands. "You know what to do," the pilot said.

Madison threw three switches that would transfer control of the chopper's critical systems from the main computer to the backup unit installed in anticipation of this emergency. The warning screeches fell silent, but the indicator lights remained lit.

"Oh, boy," said Madison. He repeated the sequence, but the results were the same—the warning lights remained stubbornly lit. "Here's one we didn't expect, Ben. I can't engage the backup."

"That's unacceptable," Saratoga spat. "All my systems are locked. I've got total failure here, Brad. *Get me on that backup*."

Madison reinitiated the sequence. But it was no use. The microprocessors that controlled the aircraft's critical systems were

73

frozen and, incredibly, wouldn't allow them to manually override to an emergency backup.

"We're screwed big-time, Ben," Madison said, a notable strain in his voice. "What's Plan C?"

Saratoga opened a channel to the other choppers and keyed his headset's microphone. "Mayday. Mayday. This is Five Zero Seven Charlie. I've got complete computer failure. All systems locked. Can't switch to backup."

The pilot from the Number One Black Hawk replied, "Roger, Bravo Five Zero Seven. What's your plan?"

"I have no choice—I'm putting her down."

"I copy you."

"What about you?" Saratoga said. "What's your status?"

"Normal," the pilot responded. "We've experienced no computer abnormality. All systems green. Do what you have to do, Ben. And good luck."

"I hear you." Saratoga drew in a deep breath and grabbed the cyclic control with both hands. The control stick felt as though it were a solid metal spike driven into cement. With steel determination, he pulled on the stick and worked the pedals, attempting to change the angle of the rotors to reduce the chopper's forward motion.

"What do you want me to do, Ben?" Madison asked.

"I want you to watch those engines," Saratoga said. "I need a consistent sixty-eight hundred RPMs. Let me know the second it varies."

"What else?"

"Nothing. Don't touch a *goddamned* thing."

The Black Hawk gave a sudden lurch to the right. In the troop compartment below the flight deck, the twenty passengers, mostly civilians, let out a collective gasp. Everyone reached for something solid to hold on to.

"A little turbulence," said Captain Dwayne Chan, an Asian intelligence officer with the highest IQ in his graduating class at Yale. He adjusted his wire-framed glasses. "An updraft from the mountains."

There was more turbulence accompanied by a chronic, low-level vibration. This wasn't right. Dr. Nancy Shaw felt a sudden drop in altitude and touched her seat belt, which was reassuringly still buckled. She always flew fastened to her seat, as though this would save her in the event the aircraft struck the ground at two hundred miles an hour.

The chopper jerked violently as it pulled into a hover. The outbursts from the passengers bordered on panic.

"What is it, Captain?" Nancy asked. "What's going on?"

Captain Chan spun around to his window. "Hell if I know. Something's up, though. Ben's trying to stabilize a hover. Doesn't look like he's got full control of the rotors."

Besides the turbulence, there was something else—Nancy could smell burning metal. She looked out the window. She estimated their altitude at about 12,000 feet, with enough room to maneuver between the massive Rocky Mountains that stretched in every direction as far as she could see.

A chorus of questions erupted from the passengers. Captain Chan rose unsteadily to his feet, reaching up for the overhead handrail for support. "Everyone stay in your seat and secure all loose items," his voice boomed across the troop compartment as he began making his way forward.

"What are the pilot's options?" Nancy called after him. "What are we going to do?"

Chan didn't answer.

A distinguished-looking gentleman, middle-aged with pure white hair, sat in the fold-down seat next to her. "If he can't regain control, he'll have to put her down," he said.

She looked at him, puzzled, then glanced out the window again. "Here? On top of a mountain?"

He shrugged. "He may have no other option."

Nancy looked at him closely. "What do you know about flying?"

His lips curled into a proud grin. "I've been a helicopter pilot for thirty-two years. Class B license. I flew the CH-46 Seaknight for the Marines in Vietnam." He extended his hand. "My name's McNeil. Terry McNeil. I'm a systems process engineer for Bell Labs."

Nancy took his hand and felt a strong, confident grip. "I don't know if I'm glad you're sitting next to me or not."

*   *   *

Saratoga managed to bring the aircraft to a hover, but he could not stop the yaw-and-pitch motion that swung the aircraft like the gondola of a windswept hot-air balloon. Captain Chan climbed into the flight deck. What he saw there—two seasoned pilots failing to gain control of the aircraft and a console full of warning lights—caused him to bite his lower lip until he tasted blood. Without saying a word, he slipped back into the passenger compartment.

"Everyone in crash positions," Chan shouted. "NOW!"

"What's wrong?" Nancy said. She looked at McNeil, her civilian companion. "Why is this happening?"

"Do as you're told," Chan shouted. "I want everyone to grab their ankles—"

"So we can kiss our asses goodbye," McNeil said with a laugh.

Captain Chan thrust a finger at him. "Stow it, mister."

"Captain," McNeil said. "I understand there are parachutes aboard this helicopter. I suggest we prepare to use them. Ask the pilot if he can stabilize a hover for about three minutes so we can bail out, if necessary."

"Parachutes?" Nancy said.

"Out of the question," Chan said. "I can't let civilians who've never done a parachute jump bail out over the Rockies."

"I'm deeply touched by your concern for our safety," Nancy said. "But—"

"I've parachuted before," someone called from the back.

"So have I," McNeil said. "We can show the others."

"Captain," Nancy said, "if it comes to that, why not leave the choice to each of us—jump or take our chances aboard."

There were shouts of unanimous agreement. The bucking of the aircraft grew alarmingly worse by the moment. Chan clawed forward to the flight deck. He found Saratoga wrestling with the cyclic, trying to keep the chopper level while working the collective to descend.

Copilot Madison glanced at the engine readouts. "She's red hot, Ben. The cooling pumps are out. Set her down *now*."

"That's exactly what I intend to do."

"Captain," Chan said. "Some of the passengers want to try

jumping. I need you to bring the aircraft to a hover at ten thousand feet.''

"Can't do it," Saratoga said.

"We're going down too fast, Ben," Madison said. "Ease up."

"Captain?" Chan said.

"We've got two minutes tops at those RPMs before the engines fail," Saratoga shouted over his shoulder at Chan. "Get the others strapped to their seats and pray there's a flat spot below us."

"*Shit.*" Chan swung about and returned to the passenger compartment.

Aboard the Huey chopper, Julie felt their aircraft pull into a hover. She looked at Colonel Beckman questioningly. "We're here already?"

"Negative." The colonel unbuckled his seat belt and headed forward. "What's going on?" he asked his pilot.

"The Number Two Black Hawk is in trouble," he said, pointing out his windscreen. "A computer lockup. He's losing power as his engines heat up. Saratoga's going to try to set her down."

"Damn," the colonel spat. "What about his backup? Did he say anything about the backup?"

"Didn't work," the pilot said.

"What's the status of Number One?"

"Slavney hasn't reported any abnormalities. He's already switched to backup as a precaution." The pilot gestured out his windscreen at the huge columns of black smoke pouring from each of the Black Hawk's two engines. "He's going to lose both engines in about thirty seconds. He won't make it."

"What do you hope to do for him now?" Beckman asked.

The pilot shook his head. "I suppose there's nothing we can do. I'll get an exact fix on his position when he goes down and relay the coordinates to Cheyenne."

"What's our ETA?"

"Fifteen minutes."

Beckman nodded. "Don't waste time here. I want these choppers down at Cheyenne before anything else happens."

"Yes, sir."

Colonel Beckman returned to his seat and found the others pressed against their windows.

Julie swung around to him. "That's Nancy's helicopter! What are we going to do?"

"We're going to Cheyenne as planned," Beckman said.

"What are you talking about?" Julie said, incredulous. "We can't leave them here."

All eyes shifted to Beckman.

The colonel shook his head. "It was a computer lockup. There's nothing we can do to help them. Peterson Air Field will send out a rescue party."

The general turned away from his window and said to her, "We were concerned something like this would happen, so we installed a backup unit in each Black Hawk to allow the pilot enough control to reach Cheyenne. Unfortunately for Chopper Number Two, it didn't work. You're a computer programmer. You should understand this."

Julie stared at him. The general reminded her of a large, unmovable mountain. "I understand exactly what's going on here," she said. "You're flying a lot more people to Cheyenne than necessary."

"Doctor—"

"You knew all of them wouldn't make it. You're deliberately risking our lives . . ." Julie's eyes narrowed as the realization sunk in, ". . . except for your own lives." Julie glared at the colonel. "I get it. We're all safe in this chopper, aren't we, Colonel? You brought this ancient machine back into service because it doesn't have any computers. I understand; you sacrificed a little comfort to save your own necks. Very smart." She turned toward the general. "What about the others? What are you going to do about the people trapped down there?"

There was silence. The other officers had returned to the windows.

The general took a step toward her. "Doctor, I know you're upset—"

"You don't know how I feel," she shouted. Julie glared at the general for several long moments and saw nothing that could pass for compassion.

"I can see I'm wasting my time." She returned to the window, dreading what she might see.

Nancy's chopper was well below them. All Julie could

see were massive black clouds billowing upward.

"Good luck, Nancy," she whispered, "and God help you."

Inside the Black Hawk, Saratoga continued his desperate battle to keep the aircraft from plunging too rapidly. It was a noble but futile effort. His back was drenched with sweat and both his hands were locked in a death grip around the cyclical stick.

He didn't have the luxury of searching for a suitable landing spot, not that he could have maneuvered even if he saw one. "Why is this happening?" he shouted. "This shouldn't be happening."

"What do you want me to do, Ben?" Madison asked.

"Just keep your mouth shut and your hands in your lap," Saratoga hissed.

Madison activated the VDU display and scanned the rugged terrain below with the belly-mounted cameras. He switched the display to radar image and saw below only the contours of jagged peaks and steep slopes.

"Ben, there's no place to set down."

"Tell me something I don't already know." Saratoga keyed the passengers' intercom. All he said was "Prepare for impact."

The chopper still was plummeting much too fast. Saratoga pulled up hard on the collective with white knuckles and raised the throttle to full. The engines screamed their final protest.

Madison watched in anguish. Never before had he heard sounds like these coming from an aircraft's engines. He grabbed the sides of his seat with a grip equal to any hydraulic clamp's.

"Have mercy—"

One hundred feet . . . twenty-five . . .

The twin engines gave a final, agonized cry of defeat a second before the turbine blades disintegrated in a spiraling tangle of metal. An explosion sent ribbons of razor-sharp steel through the fuselage, tearing apart the flight deck. Saratoga's and Madison's severed limbs painted the controls with blood.

Inside the troop compartment, the passengers let out a collective cry of terror as ribbons of red-hot steel ripped through the cabin. Captain Chan, his face a mask of fear, reached forward and grabbed his ankles. In the seat next to Nancy, McNeil let out a gargled cough. Nancy thought he was turning to look at her, then realized he had been hit. Blood spewed out his neck stump as his head spilled sideways, rolled down his left arm, and dumped into her lap.

The chopper's rotors were the next casualties. Reaching beyond the fuselage, they struck the sheer face of the mountain and shattered. Pieces of rotor flew down the mountainside at five hundred miles per hour.

The chopper's fuselage slammed into solid rock, buckled in two, and tumbled end over end into a deep ravine.

Chapter Eleven
Cheyenne Mountain

Cheyenne Mountain, Colorado
Tuesday, December 28
1250 Hours

The two remaining helicopters approached Cheyenne Mountain from the south. Endless mountain terrain finally gave way to Colorado Springs, a high-tech military town also noted for its awe-inspiring tourist attractions, including, but not exclusively, skiing. The residents of the city were accustomed to military helicopters flying overhead and hardly glanced up as the pair thundered toward the 100-million-year-old mountain twelve miles away. To most eyes, the aircraft appeared to be headed toward 9,600 feet of solid rock. That was hardly the case. As they approached the entrance of the mountain, the choppers pulled up into a hover, the downdraft from their rotors effectively blasting away snow from the four-lane road leading inside the Operations Center's North Portal.

Julie sat gazing out the window, her eyes unfocused, her mind one hundred miles away atop some obscure mountaintop. She could think only of Nancy, and longed to know her fate. Was she still alive? The odds weren't in her favor. Even if Nancy survived the crash, how long could she and the others last in such inhospitable terrain?

The compartment door slid open and Julie ignored Colonel Beckman's order to disembark. As the others filed past her, she chose to remain seated, thinking and staring unseeing at the face of the granite mountainside.

She sat quietly for several moments before a deep, commanding voice from outside called in to her, "We're home, Doctor, in case you haven't noticed."

Julie's eyes shifted to the open door, through which a frigid wind blew. The general stood in the doorway, hands in his pockets, watching her. He wore his overcoat buttoned to the collar and his officer's cap, with its three stars, pushed securely over his closely cropped head.

"Are you going inside or would you prefer to stay out here until you freeze to death?" he asked.

"Did anyone ever mention that you sound just like Barry White?" Julie asked.

He grinned. "Every day. You should hear me in the shower."

Julie smiled, but it was short-lived. Her eyes again grew distant, and the general could see that she was consumed by her thoughts.

"Let me escort you inside," he offered. "It's much warmer in there, I promise you."

Julie nodded; there was nothing more she could do out here. Perhaps inside she could get more information. She stood and grabbed the case from under her fold-down seat that held her notebook computer. The general offered her his huge hand, which she grabbed, and stepped off the aircraft. Once outside she suddenly felt very cold even wearing her heaviest coat, which worked much better in Georgia. Up here it was decidedly inadequate.

The bus transporting the others had already gone inside.

"Sorry I made you miss your ride," she said as they made their way to the entrance of the tunnel.

"No problem. We need to talk."

"I don't even know your name."

"It's General Tyrone Patterson." He removed his glove and held out his hand in formal introduction. "I'm commander of the special op to get Eclipse back on-line."

Julie took his proffered bearlike hand. "Pleased to meet you." His hand was hard and rough, totally in keeping with his line-backer physique.

"You must think I'm one officious prick," he said.

"Not necessarily officious."

The general let out a huff of laughter that turned to a cloud of steam in his face.

Julie shot him a piercing glance. "Leaving those people stranded on top of a mountain is unthinkable."

The general let out a sigh, and when he spoke his voice had a note of sadness. "I know you can't possibly understand that there was nothing we could do to help them, given our situation and type of aircraft. You should take comfort in knowing that even before that chopper went down, we had already radioed Cheyenne with its coordinates, and we have a solid vector on its transponder beacon."

Julie looked at him, her eyes hopeful. "So a rescue helicopter should be there by now."

"Not exactly. A utility chopper from Peterson Air Force Base will dispatch an overland team to the top of the mountain. They'll cover the last miles by foot. I'm told the overland team should reach the site in the morning."

She shook her head in frustration. "Morning? I'll sleep warm and cozy tonight knowing that."

They continued briskly down a jagged tunnel a third of a mile long and high enough to accommodate the tallest freight traffic. Artificial light bathed everything in a yellowish-green glow, and Julie felt a constant rush of air blowing past her from deep inside the mountain.

Julie and General Patterson were the last ones through the mountain's towering forty-foot steel blast doors encased in concrete collars and set flush with the tunnel's rock wall. There came a ringing behind them followed by twin amber rotating lights that signaled to stand clear of the entrance. With a deep rumble, the massive doors, designed to withstand a nuclear blast, began rolling shut. Forty-five seconds later, the doors came to a stop with a pneumatic thump. The bell fell silent and the amber lights extinguished.

Cheyenne Mountain Air Station was again secure.

"I need your help to get Eclipse back on-line," General Patterson said. "When that little task is accomplished, we can all go back home, and I can celebrate the New Year with my family in Boston."

"I'm glad you have so much confidence in me, General. I wish I shared your optimism. Frankly, I don't give us high marks for success in just a couple of days. There must be tens of millions of lines of code controlling a system like Eclipse. And I'll be starting from scratch."

"I always have confidence in my people," he said. "Otherwise, I'd have to do all the work myself." His manner grew stiff, his eyes cold. "Besides, I don't want to think about the consequences if we fail."

"What's the worst that can happen?" Julie asked. "We postpone fighting wars until it's fixed?"

"If only it was that simple." The general looked at her, and she could see that his features were stone serious. Julie's grin vanished.

"If we fail," he said, "you and I will have a ringside seat to a thermonuclear war."

Chapter Twelve
Chasm

Colorado Rockies
Tuesday, December 28
1340 Hours

Nancy Shaw opened her eyes and squinted at the crisp glare reflecting off a section of sheet metal. Her first sensation was numbing cold, so much so that she thought she had lost the use of her extremities to frostbite. Where was she? Her last recollection was the look of terror on Captain Chan's face. Then nothing at all.

Nancy lifted her head and took in the surroundings. She was lying on her side amid debris, some of it recognizable, most of it not. A section of torn fuselage shielded her from a frigid forty-knot wind that howled overheard through what sounded like a cavern. She struggled to sit up before realizing she was still strapped to her seat. She unbuckled herself and sat up slowly. Someone had saved her life by covering her with a heavy down-filled coat. Her right side ached—possibly a cracked rib—as did her left forearm.

"Lovely."

She rolled up her sleeve and inspected her arm; it was discolored and tender, but she had full mobility in her fingers. She felt for a broken bone and detected nothing out of place. Aside from several cuts and bruises, she declared herself miraculously intact.

Nancy's eyes scanned what had once been the passenger compartment of the Black Hawk. There were others here not so fortunate. Several contorted bodies sat upright on their fold-down seats, wedged into pieces of wrinkled fuselage that had crumpled like an accordion on impact. Across from them, along the bulkhead next to where she had been sitting, were mere body parts that had been cut neatly in half and in quarters, the fuselage around them ripped as though thrashed with a sweep of a giant claw.

Nancy felt a wave of nausea sweep through her and looked away. She appeared to be the only one still alive in this museum from hell. She drew in a lungful of frigid air and detected an acrid odor of burning oil. Twisting around, she saw that the forward section of the aircraft had been torn away. The gaping, ragged hole offered her a first glimpse of the outside terrain. All she could make out from this angle were black rocks jutting from the snow. The wreckage was wedged into a chasm with steep walls towering up either side. Twenty yards beyond, black smoke poured from the aircraft's flight deck. A fire, which still burned, had reduced the section to a twisted hulk of black scrap metal. The biggest piece would fit in the back of a pickup. Anyone strapped to that section never stood a chance, she realized.

Nancy let her eyes focus near the fire on what she first thought were two more corpses. But the figures were moving—there were two people huddled next to each other, using the fire for warmth. She stood up and felt dizzy at once as the blood rushed from her head. When the wave subsided, she opened her eyes again, picked up the coat, and slipped her arms into it. The down-filled parka must have belonged to a large man; once inside it she had ample room to spare.

She staggered out of the fuselage. On the ground to her right lay several burned bodies, one of them charred so badly that only a skull and ribs remained. She looked away and continued toward the figures—one of them was Captain Chan. Huddled in the snow next to him was a woman in her mid-twenties, with short, dark hair, attractive features, and wearing glasses, whom Nancy had noticed sitting in the rear of the aircraft. The woman was bundled securely in a parka; Captain Chan, however, sat in the snow with only his uniform jacket for warmth. He didn't seem to notice the subzero air. Behind them lay two zipped-up sleeping bags. A stream of blood still trickled from one of them. An older man

85

squatted next to the sleeping bags, rocking back and forth, his lips moving but emitting no sound. The front of his shirt was covered with blood, and Nancy couldn't tell if it was his own. A piece of torn fabric was wrapped around his eyes, soaked with what she could see was his own blood.

Nancy kneeled before Chan. He had a nasty gash down his right temple that ended at his lip. "Jesus, Chan—"

"It wasn't our fault," he said, his lips quivering. "We took every precaution. The sons of bitches had anticipated what we would do. . . . They had it all figured out—even how to defeat our backup. What are we dealing with here?"

"Who had it all figured out?" she asked.

Chan gazed past her; his eyes couldn't seem to focus on anything. "What are we dealing with here?"

Nancy looked at the woman huddled next to him. One of the lenses of her wire-frame glasses was shattered. "What's he talking about?"

The woman shrugged. "He's been babbling like this since the crash. I suspect he has a concussion."

"They're all dead," Chan said. "I'm the only one who made it."

"What about supplies?" Nancy asked. "What about a radio? Has anyone thought about how we're going to get off this mountain?"

"The radio was trashed with the cockpit," the woman said. "Maybe we can find a handheld in the wreckage."

Nancy looked at the woman's right leg, stretched out before her. "How bad are you hurt?"

"Not serious," the woman said. "I think my leg's broken."

"Do we have first-aid gear?"

"I don't know. We'll have to rummage."

"What's your name?"

"Olin . . . Olin Benson."

"My name's Nancy. And thanks for the coat—you saved my life."

Olin forced a grin. "A pleasure to meet you. I just wish the circumstances were different."

Nancy gestured behind her at the blindfolded man crouching by the sleeping bags. "What's his condition?"

Olin shook her head. "He's got a five-inch sliver of metal buried in his temple. I'm surprise he's still conscious."

Nancy felt something rip past her cheek, then the ground behind her erupted in a small explosion of snow. An instant later, a *crack* she mistook for thunder echoed down the chasm. This was no weather phenomenon; the air was clear and the sky devoid of clouds.

Captain Chan leaned forward, his eyes locked with Nancy's. His mouth opened, but instead of words great bubbles of blood formed on his lips. Startled, Nancy glanced down and saw a massive exit wound on his chest from the bullet of a high-powered rifle.

"What the—?"

The ground around them erupted with several geysers of snow and rock. She heard another *crack*, then another. Chan toppled forward onto her. Who was firing on them up here? How could they be mistaken for anyone other than survivors of a horrid air crash? Nothing made sense to her.

"Nancy," Olin cried, "my leg!"

Nancy scrambled from under Chan, grabbed the front of Olin's parka, and pulled her to her feet. The sound of distant shouting echoed around the canyon. Moments later they saw men dressed in camouflage fatigues and carrying rifles making their way down the chasm.

Nancy stood Olin on her good leg. She half carried, half supported Olin as they staggered toward the wreckage. What they hoped to find there or how it would protect them, Nancy hadn't a clue. She knew only that they were solid targets out here in the open. Olin groaned in agony.

A half-dozen men, hooting and laughing, burst into the wreck area and began firing small arms at anything that even remotely resembled a human shape. Nancy whipped around and saw them shooting countless rounds into Chan's corpse and the sleeping bags.

One of the soldiers put a handgun to the head of the blindfolded man. "Looks like I'm doing this one a favor," he laughed, then squeezed off a round.

The man's body jerked and spilled unceremoniously into the snow.

Another soldier stepped over him and said, "I'll help him too." Laughing, he pumped several rounds into the man's back.

The soldier in the lead, an older man with solid features, pointed at the two women and shouted, "Don't let them get too far!"

Several soldiers bolted after them.

Olin pushed Nancy roughly away from her, then spilled onto her knees. "Get out of here!" she cried.

The soldiers quickly overtook Olin, pushing her face into the snow and pulling off her overcoat.

In a whirlwind of confusion, Nancy scrambled into the twisted airframe as Olin's unheeded cries for help echoed behind her. She looked wildly about for something, anything, with which to protect them. There were no handguns lying about, no cache of ammunition, no weapons of any kinds. Nancy spied a loose piece of steel about three feet long. She dove for it. The rod was bent in the middle and almost too heavy to wield effectively as a weapon.

A soldier lunged at her. She swung the hefty bar like a baseball bat, determined for a home run. The bar connected with the man's chin with a sickening *crack*. He flew backward with a grunt and slammed into the fuselage.

Nancy scrambled to the far end of the fuselage, dragging the bar behind her. The rear of the airframe was twisted, its seams split open. She dropped to her knees and crawled through the slim opening.

Nancy slid out into a snowbank, rolled clear, and rose stiffly to her feet. She heard the unmistakable sound of a handgun being cocked, and then something cold and hard touched the back of her neck.

"Turn around," said a voice with a distinct European accent. "Slowly."

Nancy reluctantly complied. The man in front of her—lean, with solid, almost attractive features and salt-and-pepper hair—was the lead soldier who had ordered the others after them.

He yanked the bar out of her hand and threw it into the snow. When he returned the silver handgun to his side holster, Nancy saw a tattoo of the sun on his wrist.

"I saved your life," he said, "but there are elements at work here even I cannot parry." He offered her his hand. "My name is General Stryker. I believe that you and I are destined to experience the end of the world together."

Chapter Thirteen
Mountain City

Cheyenne Mountain Air Station
Tuesday, December 28
1325 Hours

"This isn't a Florida vacation retreat," Colonel Beckman shouted at Julie as she and General Patterson entered the center's staging area. "I expect you to keep up with the others and not waste the general's or my time."

Julie shot a sideways glance at the general, who just raised his eyebrows and shrugged. The group of new inductees was gathered around the colonel, light luggage in hand, awaiting instructions. Julie and the general were the last to arrive. There were no other officers present; those who had arrived with them were presumably already inside, absorbed into the mountain city.

Colonel Beckman, leaning on a clipboard, addressed the group, but Julie felt he was speaking directly to her. "Let me reemphasize a key point: For the next four days, not one second of time will be your own—that precious resource belongs to the American people, whom you now serve. I am the commander of *time*. Time is our enemy here, and I won't allow it to beat us.

I've been commissioned to ensure that what little time remains in this millennium is spent in the most productive way possible. I will tell you how to use it—when you can rest, when you can eat, and when you can converse with your colleagues. I will not accept failure of our mission here. I will not accept excuses. I will not tolerate wasted time.''

The colonel checked his watch. ''I will give you one half hour to get settled and refreshed. Then I want those of you who have been assigned to special projects to report to your team leaders no later than fourteen hundred hours. Project managers will report to the briefing room on Level C also at fourteen hundred hours. That will be all for now. Sergeant O'Rear will show you to your quarters.''

A woman dressed in a gray flight suit raised her pencil and nodded her greeting to the group. ''Follow me, please.''

A senior gentleman with thin, white hair and a haggard, agitated look, who had been standing aloof from the group, raised his hand. ''Colonel, may I ask a question?''

''No,'' the colonel snapped. ''There isn't time for questions.''

Colonel Beckman spun on his heals and walked briskly from the room.

''This way,'' said Sergeant O'Rear, beckoning the group through a set of double doors. The dozen grim-faced inductees followed her in single file inside.

Julie turned to the general and said, ''Will I see you at the briefing?''

''Of course. We've got lots to do starting right now.''

''And by the way,'' she said, ''I don't think you're a prick, officious or otherwise.''

The general laughed. ''That's refreshing. Now I'll sleep warm and cozy tonight.''

Julie smiled, then turned and followed the others.

Sergeant O'Rear led the group through the beginning of a maze of passageways linking the center's fifteen buildings. As they passed each closed door, the group strained for a glimpse through its wire-mesh window. Several large rooms were filled with the expected high-tech equipment. Others were completely dark.

''Most of the buildings in here are three stories high,'' the sergeant explained as though she were a tour guide. ''Consider this a small military base with the usual offices, a fitness center, barbershop, mess hall, chapel, and a clinic. However, most of those amenities won't be in service while we remain on alert. Only essential personnel are on duty.''

''May we ask *you* a question?'' the white-haired gentleman called to the front.

Sergeant O'Rear answered back over her shoulder, ''Just as long as we keep moving.''

''Are there phones in here?'' he asked.

''Of course,'' she responded. ''Believe it or not, we've managed to enter the nineteenth century.''

''But can we use them?'' someone else asked.

''Yes,'' she said. ''But I must warn you that all phone calls are closely monitored in the interest of national security. Talk to the colonel about authorization and designated times.''

''What about a modem connection for my laptop?'' Julie asked.

''Each room's telephone has an analog line for modems, and the wall outlet has a T1 connection for network communications,'' O'Rear said. ''Also, be aware that all electronic communications in and out of this facility are closely monitored.''

''What about visitors?''

''Cheyenne does allow visitors—normally,'' O'Rear said. ''However, this week is anything but normal. We're under a DEF-CON THREE alert. That means all visits and overnight stays of visitors must be individually approved by Colonel Beckman forty-eight hours in advance.''

''That sounds like a 'no' to me,'' someone snorted.

They entered another wing and marched down a stark hallway lined with offices. The view inside each office revealed an even mix of conservative appointments, which included a computer terminal, a crowded desk, and stacks of reading material. There weren't many administrative personnel at their desks, and most of the offices appeared deserted. Probably on holiday leave, Julie figured. Those few at work today were either glued to their terminal screens or sneaking a peek at the *Colorado Springs Tribune* with their cup of afternoon coffee. They were far from an orderly group, Julie noted, as evidenced by their failure to file foot-high stacks of paperwork on every desk.

They filed through another set of double doors to a third wing, where Sergeant O'Rear began showing each person to his or her room. The handwritten name of each room's occupant was posted on a magnetic strip next to the door frame outside. Julie peered inside the first several rooms. They were more or less identical—humble twelve-foot-by-twelve-foot quarters, each with a twin-size box spring and mattress, military green blankets, a desk with a reading lamp, indoor/outdoor carpeting, and a government-issued painting of a major U.S. city's night skyline. This was no barracks, Julie thought; at least they each had a room to themselves.

"Hey, Sergeant," a heavyset woman hollered from her doorway. "There's no bathroom in here."

Everyone turned and looked questioningly at Sergeant O'Rear.

"Each corridor has its own public showers," she said, pointing down the hallway, "one for the women, the other for men."

"You don't expect me to shower in public!?" the woman scoffed.

Several among the group laughed.

"There's a robe hanging in each closet, in case you didn't bring one," O'Rear advised.

"Terrific," Julie muttered to herself. "Communal bathing."

She found the room with her name outside. She made herself at home, throwing her clothes bag on the bed and setting the case containing her notebook computer on the desk. She opened the closet and inspected the Army-surplus bathrobe, a pale-green affair, slightly tattered from prior users like a communal bath towel that had seen too many scalding washings with strong detergents. A new pair of thong slippers sat neatly on the floor beneath. She slid off her coat and hung it beside the bathrobe.

Julie spotted the telephone on the desk and took a seat before it. She lifted the receiver, but instead of a dial tone, the line started ringing. After a long thirty seconds, the switchboard operator answered.

"Can I help you?"

"I'd like to place a long-distance call, please," Julie said, "to Fort Bragg Army Base, South Carolina."

The woman on the other end responded: "I'm sorry, you have not been authorized to place a phone call, local or long distance."

"I can put it on my credit card," she said.

"Colonel Beckman will authorize all communications going out of this center."

"But—" Julie let out a sigh. "Thank you"—she replaced the receiver—"for nothing."

She leaned back in her chair and surveyed her room with its battleship-gray, windowless walls. Was it day or night? She wouldn't be able to tell in here without her watch. The room had a distinctive prison look and feel, which grew more claustrophobic without free access to an outside line. Perhaps it was worse than a prison—at least in prison you could make a phone call.

Julie spotted the phone's data port. She looked at her watch—seventeen minutes until she was due at the briefing. Plenty of time.

She removed her Compaq Armada notebook computer from its case and opened the lid. On standby mode, it came immediately to life. There were instructions on a laminated card underneath the phone for making a network connection. She plugged the computer's modem into the phone's data port, called up the dial-in network window, and pressed Enter. It took less than a minute to establish a solid TCP/IP connection to NORAD's network. She brought up a simple program she had assembled in Java, typed in a brief message, and entered a pager number in the required field.

Her network browser loaded.

USER ACCESS DENIED
CANNOT AUTHENTICATE PASSWORD

"Go ahead and be difficult," Julie said.

She fished through her bag and produced a cellular phone. She attached it to her laptop's modem port, brought up another program, and pressed Enter to bypass Cheyenne's network "firewall."

She leaned back in her chair, stretched her arms, and ran her hands through her long black hair. "May the best hacker win."

Two minutes. That's how long it took before the program's window disappeared and Julie found herself out on the Internet. She sat up quickly. "Whoa!"

93

Her browser automatically went home to a URL address on her personal server.

"I hope he still remembers me," she said with a grin.

She pressed Enter to load the phone number and message she had keyed in earlier. Several seconds later, her pager message was on its way to Colonel Joseph Marshall.

Chapter Fourteen
Briefing

Cheyenne Mountain Air Station
Tuesday, December 28
1355 Hours

"I want to get rid of her," Colonel Beckman said. "She's an impediment to me, and we can't afford the time she'll waste."

General Patterson rocked back in his conference-room chair, stretched his arms and legs, and let out a slow sigh. He was already very tired and his day had only begun.

"Negative," he said. "I need Dr. Martinelli."

The colonel scowled. "There's nothing special about her. I can get ten people more qualified."

"*I need her,*" the general repeated, the deep tone of his voice signaling that his decision was final. "Sounds like a personal issue between you and her. Deal with it."

A frustrated Colonel Beckman rose from the table and appealed to him. "She's a disruptive element. She's undisciplined and untrainable, and she asks too many questions. She'll be a *liability*."

"Are you suggesting we make her walk home?"

The colonel frowned; he knew when the general was fucking with him. "I'm talking about confining her to quarters," he said, his voice raised.

"Are we interrupting something?" Julie said from the conference room's threshold.

The colonel whirled. Julie and several members of the Project Management team stood in the hallway, hesitant to intrude on what looked like an intense conversation between the center's senior officers.

Colonel Beckman looked at his watch. "You're four minutes early."

"Do we get a time credit?" Julie asked innocently.

The members of her group laughed.

The colonel shot her a cold look. "Take a seat."

General Patterson rocked forward in his chair and decreed, "This discussion is over, the issue closed."

Julie and the others filed into the room and claimed chairs around the oval conference table designed to seat twelve, with extra chairs along the walls. There were two television monitors embedded high up in the walls, several phones on the credenzas, and two computer terminals—a mini crisis room. During the next three minutes, all but one seat was taken.

Julie opened her Franklin day planner to today's date. *Four more days left in this millennium,* she mused. *Then what?* She glanced at the calendars for the coming months and was reminded that the year 2000 was a leap year. Great. *We have to make sure computers recognize not only the correct year but the leap month as well.* Her thoughts drifted to Nancy. She couldn't accept the thought of never seeing her again. How could she start the new millennium without her best friend and mentor? She couldn't focus on anything else until she knew what had happened to her.

"Let's get started," the general said.

The group of information technology professionals around the table fell silent with expectation, their attention riveted on General Patterson.

The colonel checked his notes. "We're short one."

"He's en route," the general said. "He can catch up when he gets here."

General Patterson stood from the table, thrust his hands into his jacket pockets, and stood up before the room's white board. "For those of you I haven't met personally, I'm General Tyrone Patterson, commander of this center until our mission is finished. My background is information systems. Back in the days when I was captain, the Army paid my way through graduate school, where I became the first enlisted African-American to earn a Ph.D. in military information systems management. That's all you need to know about me for the moment."

He paused for several seconds and stared at the carpet, collecting his thoughts. "All of you," he began, "have been inducted into the Armed Forces of the United States to help solve a very critical problem involving national security. I apologize on behalf of the United States government for whatever inconveniences and hardships your hasty summons here undoubtedly has caused you. Let me stress that when a country is faced with extreme challenges it must take extreme measures. I don't believe any of you have had more than forty-eight hours' notice to come here. If what we're facing wasn't so damned critical, we wouldn't be asking you to leave your homes and family at this time of year."

The group around the table shot discreet, sideways glances at one another, trying to determine how much the other knew about the "critical" nature of their assignment.

"I don't have to tell you," the general continued, "that the millennium computer date problem is directly or indirectly impacting every man, woman, and child in this country, perhaps in the world. Every business, industry, institution, family, and individual has been put in a stranglehold that no one can easily loosen. Even those who have had the foresight to put their systems in order have been negatively impacted by those who have not. Despite competent attention, during the last several weeks gross inadequacies in our preparation have become apparent. For every line of code our programmers corrected, there are five others we've missed. For every component we've found, catalogued, and remediated, there are ten others we didn't initially see.

"Clearly, we are at war. The enemy is technology itself, the pillar of our society. We are in a new age of new threats, and it has forced us to think in new ways about our vulnerabilities. I won't presume to debate the wisdom of our reliance on this technology; however, we have been betrayed and must now deal with the consequences. I can only hope and pray that our economy—and the very fabric of our nation—will weather this storm, and doomsday panic will prove unjustified.''

There were puzzled looks around the table; some of his audience winced, not convinced the problem was as severe as the general suggested. *He's overreacting*, Julie thought. Several expressions around the table suggested that others thought so too.

''Most of you were summoned here to help fix lines of computer code that contain date information,'' General Patterson said. ''And, indeed, that was our primary activity here as of late Friday. Some of you already know that the situation changed dramatically at the stroke of midnight Saturday morning. That's when Eclipse went off-line. For those of you not up to speed, let me state that the core of this nation's intelligence-gathering system is a network of forty-seven state-of-the-art, high- and low-Earth-orbit surveillance and communication satellites collectively known as 'Eclipse.' These satellites are our eyes in the sky. They include Photographic Intelligence satellites that use telescopes to take close-up images from high orbit; Signals Intelligence satellites that monitor radio signals, cellular transmissions, and microwaves; and Defense Support Program satellites that use infrared imaging to detect changes in the amount of heat coming from the Earth's surface. They provide strategic intelligence information to the CIA headquarters in Langley, Virginia, the National Reconnaissance Office in Virginia, and the Navy's Fifth Fleet in the Persian Gulf at speeds of up to fifty gigabits, or billions of bits, per second. It's our first line of defense from attack by air, sea, or land.

''For the last two years, Eclipse has performed remarkably well. Now, for reasons unknown, Eclipse shut itself down at midnight two and a half days ago, exactly seven days before the New Year. Since then we've done thousands of man-hours of troubleshooting—rebooted every system and subsystem, and reloaded all software. However, none of this has worked. The systems boot up and perform their routine diagnostics. When finished, the entire network shuts itself down. We can't even get a *ping* returned.''

The white-haired gentleman sitting next to Julie raised his hand.

"General, do you suspect this is the result of a date error in the code?"

General Patterson stopped pacing and faced the man. "I suspect nothing of the sort. At this time we've ruled out nothing. Both the hardware and software were certified Year 2000 compliant before the satellites were launched late in '97. Teams of programmers here at Cheyenne and special government contractors around the world have been poring over more than sixty million lines of computer code looking for possible explanations. So far, they've found nothing."

Colonel Beckman cleared his throat. "With all due respect, sir, we're getting ahead of ourselves."

General Patterson nodded, acknowledging his deviation from the agenda. "The colonel's right. Before we get caught up debating possible causes, Colonel Beckman has divided our resources into teams that will focus on six potential problem areas. Each of these teams will include a project leader and a backup. Each team will have forty-eight hours from the start of this meeting to offer viable explanations in their respective areas."

A few nodded vaguely. The enormity of the task before them hadn't totally sunk in yet. They were all in shock, the general decided. He couldn't blame them.

"Colonel Beckman, please introduce each team leader, his or her alternate, and their assignments."

The colonel stood up from the table, wielding a black three-ring binder that held several inches of paper. "Dr. Terry Burns, IBM?" he asked as though taking roll call.

The white-haired man wearing glasses and a wool turtleneck sweater acknowledged the colonel with a raised hand. "Yes?"

"Doctor, you have the unenviable task of leading the programming group—our largest team. Arlene Levinson from Mylan Laboratories will assist you. Your team will examine each line of code—again—looking for something we've missed. Your task is to find something useful we can test."

The team leaders exchanged wary glances and nodded.

"Dr. Ida Dreyfuss, McBride Research Laboratories?" the colonel called, reading from his binder.

A heavy, graying woman in an unbecoming denim jumpsuit raised her hand.

"Your team is quality assurance. You will support the programming team by testing each software routine and its backup, as well as hardware. You'll have NORAD Hardware Services as your resource. Your coleader is Peter Gott from VisiCom Industries."

Gott, a young wiry man in a flannel shirt, acknowledged his assignment with a nod.

"You'll develop and execute procedures for testing the functionality of every component and subassembly related to Eclipse. This also includes each satellite's bus, including structural framework, power, propulsion, thermal dissipation, and avionics."

Dr. Dreyfuss frowned, apparently uncomfortable with her assignment. "Let me understand something—"

"Terry McCord, Rockwell Engineering? Fred Tyson, NASA?"

The two men raised their hands and offered a collective "here."

"Your team will investigate power supplies. You'll test and retest the way each computer room, each data center, and all embedded hardware receives its power. You'll certify that all power supplies are fully operational and are performing to manufacturer specifications."

The two began scribbling notes onto pages in tablets.

"Rita Quezada, Bell Laboratories; Dr. Jonathan Vershiel, Integrated Systems, Inc.; and Bill Summers, technical evaluation, Central Intelligence Agency. Your team will deal with security. You will review Eclipse's data encryption and digital certificate technology. You'll also look into personnel. The bottom line: I want to know if there has been any breach of security or any sabotage inside or outside of this center."

The three nodded.

"Richard Boyd, ESA Laboratories, and Marlene Staples, EDS Technology—your team will deal with Network Design. You will troubleshoot Eclipse's advanced military network infrastructure. I want you to reassure me that every network system and subsystem, including ground-station transmitters, microwave relays, mission antenna dishes, laser links—the works—are talking to each other clearly and reliably."

Julie was the only one around the table not scribbling notes. While the colonel droned on about assignments, all she could visualize was the black smoke pouring out of Nancy's helicopter as it dropped toward the mountaintops.

"Dr. Julie Martinelli, CDC Atlanta, computer viruses." The colonel glanced up from his binder, and the two's eyes locked. There was genuine hostility in that cold stare of his.

Great—he's pissed at me, Julie thought. Must not have liked the way I challenged his authority on the chopper. Now I've got to deal with a superior who can't stand rejection—

"You will head a special task force to examine the integrity of the satellites' payloads, including the onboard switching systems that move data between satellites on laser beam links."

"I'll need a space shuttle—" Julie mocked.

"You'll examine ground-based counterparts for the satellites' computer microprocessors supplied by the contractor AKS Aeronautics. Assisting you will be Henry Princeton, AKS's VP of development." The colonel glanced around the room. "Where the hell is Henry?"

"I'm right here," came a thin voice from the doorway.

All heads turned toward a young man peeking though the partially opened conference-room door. He still wore his heavy down-filled coat, and a large canvas bag lay at his feet.

The general beckoned him inside. "Please join us. You made excellent time on such short notice."

"Glad I could help out," he said, slipping into the room.

"Henry is AKS's head of microprocessor development for aeronautic and aerospace systems," the general said. "He headed up the team that developed and produced the family of microprocessors that control Eclipse's data-relay systems. He and I have been in contact since Eclipse went off-line, and he graciously volunteered to drop everything to join us."

Not drafted? Julie thought. How does this guy rate?

Henry removed his heavy coat and tossed it into the corner with his duffel bag.

"Meet Dr. Martinelli, your coach," the general said, gesturing to Julie.

Henry dropped into the empty chair next to Julie and appeared pleasantly surprised to meet such an attractive team leader. He offered her his hand. "*Very* pleased to meet you."

Julie took his hand; he reciprocated with a firm and confident grip. Henry Princeton was in his early thirties, with curly blond hair and youthful, affable features that sported a thoroughly genuine smile. His cheeks were flushed and sweating, and he appeared to have done a lot of running in an effort to make the briefing. She could smell the humid vapors venting off him as he caught his breath.

The colonel checked his watch. "At fourteen-thirty hours, you will meet with your teams to begin your Assessment Phase. This group will meet again three hours from now, at which time each of you will present your respective project plans." The colonel's intense gaze scanned each face around the table, looking for signs of dissension. Finding nothing, he said, "I can open this briefing to questions—five minutes, no more."

Richard Boyd from ESA Laboratories raised his hand. "I have a comment and then a question."

"Proceed," Beckman said.

"First, given the complexity of the network and the staggering opportunities for system failure, I don't rate our chances very high to get Eclipse back on-line in the short time frame you've allotted," he said in a smoky, raspy voice without a hint of apology. "This project is much more complex than any needle-in-a-haystack search."

"What's your point?" Beckman spat.

"My point is I don't like to fight a losing battle. I don't work sloppy."

"Duly noted and appreciated," the general said. "And your question?"

"What's the worst that can happen if we fail?" he asked.

General Patterson pushed back his chair, rose, and towered over those around the table like a Herculean wall. "So you folks need motivation."

"I'm talking about practicalities," Boyd huffed.

"Let me share something with you all," the general said, resuming his pacing and sliding his hands into his pockets, "something that's highly classified. For the last two years, several terrorist groups have threatened to take advantage of the window of vulnerability because of computer malfunction. Much of that has been thoroughly documented. However, we've recently gathered convincing evidence from the world intelligence communities that a number of terrorist attacks may be staging right now in Europe and on the U.S. mainland.''

''I don't see how—''

''Wait,'' said the general, thrusting out a hand, ''it gets much better. Just before Eclipse went off-line, we were monitoring a dangerous situation in the Middle East involving our good friends in Iraq. It seems Iraqi aircraft have blatantly crossed into the no-fly zone and may be planning air attacks on Iran and on our bases in Saudi Arabia. We've tightened our flight ban over southern Iraq, and have strategic bombers and Navy ships in the Persian Gulf capable of firing Tomahawk cruise missiles. Also, the Nimitz carrier battle group is steaming toward the Gulf. To make matters worse, there's unconfirmed reports that Iraq now has nuclear capabilities purchased on the black market. Without Eclipse we're blind, our intelligence monitoring capabilities drastically curtailed. God help us if the President orders a military air stand-down.''

''What's our backup?'' asked Dr. Terry Burns.

''Eclipse is our backup,'' the general said. ''The network is the cornerstone of our defense system—a reengineered, Phase IV surveillance and communication satellite network, with twenty-four super-high-frequency transponder channels capable of providing worldwide secure voice and high-rate data communications. One unit goes down, three others fill in. If a quadrant fails, the other three pick up the slack.''

''So communications are down as well?'' Dr. Burns asked.

''Substantially reduced.''

''*Jesus*—''

''So we put all our eggs in one basket,'' said VisiCom's Peter Gott. ''Sounds like we've *fucked* ourselves.''

The general appeared visibly annoyed. ''We're not here to debate military strategy or policy, ladies and gentlemen. It's much too late for that. We're here for one reason—get Eclipse back on-line.''

''What do we know thus far about the possibility of sabotage?'' asked Bell Laboratories' Rita Quezada. ''I suspect this center is vulnerable, especially in these confusing times. There are too many new faces coming in each day. Has each one of them been checked and rechecked?''

"That's exactly what your security team will spend the next forty-eight hours investigating," the general said. "You're absolutely correct. Every day there are hundreds of unauthorized intrusions into all manner of systems, from the Internet to the power-distribution systems, or into defense plants where data is stolen."

"We have to move on," the colonel said, raising his hand. "Just one more question."

Several members of the group asked for the floor.

"Dr. Dreyfuss?"

"When do we sleep?"

Beckman closed his binder with a snap to signal the end of the briefing. "You don't," he said. "No more questions. Your teams are assembling."

Everyone looked at each other with befuddled expressions, not sure what to make of the colonel's plan or the assignments.

"Dismissed," Beckman snapped. *"That's an order."*

Julie stood and began gathering her items.

"We need to talk as soon as possible," said Henry Princeton, standing.

"Of course," she said. "Now?"

General Patterson laid a hand on Princeton's shoulder. "Can I steal her away first for a few minutes?" he asked. "There's something I need to show her."

Julie looked at him, puzzled.

The general offered her a wink. "I promise you'll find what I have to show you extremely interesting."

Chapter Fifteen
Summons

Captain Jill Larson waved the three-foot-long wrench in the air like a club. "If I meet the man responsible for this, I'm taking off his head with this wrench."

She hurled the wrench to the ground in frustration. It struck a football-size sandstone and shattered it.

Jill, Colonel Marshall, and Sergeant Williams had spent the afternoon hoisting the RAH-66 Comanche helicopter from the flatbed railcar and setting it upright onto its wheels on the hard desert clay. They were already hot and thirsty and edgy. Marshall and Williams did the heavy lifting, leaving Jill, with her background in systems engineering, to prep the aircraft's electronics, charge the batteries, and get the radio on-line. The Comanche had been transported mostly assembled. Mostly. They still needed prep time to attach its five main rotor blades, install and calibrate the electronics bays, and make the aircraft flyable.

But flying wasn't Marshall's intention—not yet, anyway, even though train travel was no longer an option, with the nearest road fifty miles away. Nor did he expect another military train to come along on this remote track, which was off-limits to commercial traffic. Most of their equipment was lost in the wreck. That, coupled with the smashed instrumentation in the surviving locomotive, had prevented them from contacting Fort Irwin. Something else kept gnawing at him: Why hadn't the base sent a reconnaissance aircraft searching for them? Surely they were reported overdue by now.

Marshall needed to find out what was going on, and the only serviceable radio was installed in the Comanche. The last estimate Jill had given Marshall for attempting a transmission was 1800 hours—at the earliest. That meant it would be dark before they were able to make contact with the Army base. They all made peace with the fact that tonight they would be sleeping under the stars of the New Mexico desert.

"I can't guarantee these components will work after the rattle they just took," Jill said. Sitting inside the Comanche's armament bay, she examined one of the circuit cards before pushing it into a motherboard.

Williams sat atop the main rotor shaft to remove the transport cowlings from the two LHTEC T800 turboshaft jet engines. He hollered down to her, "So what are you saying?"

"I'm telling you," she said, "be prepared to walk home if I can't get the electronics on-line."

"She's griping again," Williams called to Marshall, who was sitting in the forward gunner's cockpit.

"I like to hear myself gripe," Jill said. "It keeps my mind focused."

"I have every confidence that you'll get the radio working," Marshall said. He looked back at her and grinned. "Besides, that's an order."

"We ought to be down on our knees thanking the Lord this aircraft stayed in one piece," Williams said. "I thought for sure we'd be pulling a Jimmy Stewart and building a new chopper out of salvaged parts to fly out of here."

"What are you talking about?" Jill said.

"Flight of the Phoenix," Williams spat.

She shook her head. "I don't get it."

"It's a movie," Marshall said.

"Oh . . . didn't see it."

Williams jabbed his cigar at her. "Why, child, I suggest you drop what you're doing and rent a copy right now."

She shrugged. "OK. Pick up a copy for me. And while you're

at the store, get me the VOR, TACAN, and ILS navigation radios. Do you think you can heave them up here to me, muscles?''

"I can heave anything anywhere," he said, wiping his hand on his ever-present towel and climbing down from the chopper.

Williams scanned the olive-green military crates stacked beside the Comanche until he found one about a meter wide and half again that deep, stenciled: VOR, TACAN. The metal box was dented just below the latch as though someone had kicked in the front with a giant, steel-tipped boot.

"I hope we have spares," he muttered, squatting next to it.

No amount of coaxing would budge the latch. Williams withdrew an industrial-size screwdriver from his back pocket, stuck it into one of the back hinges, and snapped it off with a flex of his wrist. He did the same with the second hinge. He pulled back the lid until it snapped off at the latch and tossed it aside. He removed one of the black boxes and examined it closely. It didn't appear damaged; however, he couldn't vouch for the circuits inside.

Williams heard a faint beeping. He grew still and listened. Although the sound was teasingly near, he couldn't determine its source.

"Hey," Jill shouted, "am I going to get those boxes today?'' Williams raised his hand. *"Quiet."*

She and Marshall watched him curiously.

It took several seconds for Williams to determine the source—Marshall's utility bag. He grabbed the bag and held it up.

"Hey, Joe," he called. "Your bag's beeping."

"The pager," Marshall called, scrambling from the cockpit. Why hadn't it occur to him earlier to check it? It had to be the Brass trying to contact him.

"I need those bays," Jill shouted after him.

Marshall climbed down from the chopper and grabbed his bag from Williams.

"Give the lady her bays," Marshall said. He rummaged through his utility bag until he found his palm-size Motorola message pager. How long ago had it been activated? he wondered.

Marshall pressed the Retrieve button and read the message as it scrolled across the tiny, sixteen-character display:

03:45 PM: "NANCY'S BLACK HAWK CRASHED IN COLORADO
MOUNTAINS 150 MILES SOUTH OF CHEYENNE . . . DON'T KNOW IF
SHE SURVIVED . . . CAN'T GET ANYONE'S ATTENTION HERE . . .
CAN YOU PLEASE HELP??? . . . JULIE"

Chapter Sixteen
Anthony

Cheyenne Mountain
Tuesday, December 28
1435 Hours

General Patterson led Julie down a long, dim corridor that took
them deep into the mountain. There was no other foot traffic in
this remote wing of the center, and it looked to Julie like they
were heading for some storage area in the bowels of the rock.
The common fluorescent lighting quickly yielded to an entirely
different scheme, which favored the red spectrum. The illumination reminded Julie of emergency lighting, though darker, making
it dangerous to find their way. She also noted a dramatic drop in
temperature the farther they proceeded, until the cold air became
downright uncomfortable.

At the end of the corridor, they were greeted by two metal
doors with wire-meshed windows. Strange glows of blue and red
glowed from within.

"What's with the lights?" she asked.

The general opened a small, hinged compartment embedded
into the wall to reveal a softly lit keypad. "Normal lighting in-

troduces a toxin that interferes with the biological processes in ways we don't completely understand.''

''I think I missed something.''

He grinned, realizing how cryptic he must sound. ''I hope it becomes clear to you in a moment.''

He punched in his access code, which produced a soft buzzing. The general pushed open one of the doors with a magnetic *snap* and beckoned her inside.

If Julie thought the corridor's atmosphere was strange, it didn't prepare her for the ethereal world inside. The huge room, devoid of furnishings, was as high as it was wide, and stretched away into corners that became totally black. A lone terminal sat against the far wall. The only light came from unusual wall panels that offered hues of red and blue. It wouldn't be safe to walk though here unassisted, she concluded.

''Wear these,'' the general said.

He handed her tight-fitting goggles she thought were a pair of skiing glasses. The large lenses were completely opaque, like sunglasses, and she wondered how she would see with them at all. But Julie did as the general instructed and fitted them over her eyes, the elastic band stretched tightly around her head. To her surprise the room brightened, still far from normal, but much clearer than without them.

''They amplify light along the infrared spectrum,'' the general explained, fitting a pair over his own huge features. ''Without them, you'll need a seeing-eye dog in here.''

Julie let out a huff of laughter and watched her breath turn to steam. She had felt more than heard a deep rumble of the overhead blowers when they entered. Now she understood why. The room's cooling system had driven down the room temperature to near freezing.

''You'll also want one of these,'' the general said, handing Julie a heavy polyester coat roughly her size from among several hanging on a rack next to the doors. ''We maintain this room at five degrees Celsius, plus or minus one degree.''

''Bless you.'' She slipped her arms into the coat. ''Where is everyone?''

''This is a 'clean' room and we keep foot traffic to a minimum,'' he said, selecting one of the larger coats and slipping it on. "People interfere with the operation—too much noise, excess vibration, and body heat." He gestured toward the middle of the room. "Besides, it doesn't need tending to."

Julie squinted through the goggles at a black box rising from the middle of the room that reminded her of a large Egyptian sarcophagus. It looked completely enclosed. She couldn't tell if it was made of metal or marble.

"Is it a vault of some kind?" Julie asked.

The general chuckled. "Sure, you could call it a vault. Follow me—and please don't touch anything."

Julie nodded and, curious to find out what this was all about, followed the general to the monolithic box. It stood about six feet high and ten feet long, made of polished black metal, with no visible exterior markings. She moved around it, occasionally catching dim glimpses of herself off its smooth surface. The general watched her closely, his knowing grin about to break into a party-size smile.

"If it's a vault," she said, "what are you guarding so carefully?"

"DNA molecules."

Julie was more confused than ever. "Molecules? Is this some sort of a specimen lab?"

"No. This is a computer room."

Julie froze. In a single, torrid rush it became clear to her—what this room was all about . . . the contents of this box . . . and why she had been summoned so hastily to Cheyenne. *Incredible, if it's true. But it couldn't possibly be.*

She looked at him, incredulous. "Is this a molecular computer?"

"Yes it is."

"I don't understand. What does this have to do with Eclipse?"

"Everything and more," the general said.

Julie took a step closer to the monolith and touched its side. The metal was cold and felt solid.

"What do you call it?"

"During construction its code name was Citadel," the general explained. "When it became operational, the programmers and technical folks started referring to it as 'Sweet Julie.' Doesn't have an official name yet." He directed his oversized goggles at her. "That honor rightly belongs to you—its mother."

She looked at him, unsure what to make of his offer. "I don't deserve that."

General Patterson scoffed away Julie's humility. "Of course you do. It's going to make you famous. This concept has ramifications far beyond the invention of the transistor or the first computer. It has already revolutionized the way we think about both computer science and molecular biology."

Julie shook her head. "Countless people must have been responsible for fleshing out this concept—my God, to actually build a prototype—"

"It was *your* concept—to use chemical units of DNA molecules as computing symbols. Frankly, when I first heard about it, I thought it was science fiction. 'Not possible,' I told the Joint Chiefs."

Julie just stared at him, expecting him to burst out laughing and tell her this was all a big joke on the nerd community. Instead his features grew solemn.

"I was wrong—dead wrong."

Her excitement began building as a thousand possibilities occurred to her. "Let me see it."

"There's not much to see." The general walked to the narrow end of the box and lifted a waist-level access panel.

Julie stepped next to him, leaned over, and peered within. She saw a cylinder deep inside, perhaps one meter around, mounted on a single column. A thin amber light, hardly visible even with the light-amplified goggles, illuminated the vessel.

"Is that the liquid?" she asked.

"Correct," the general said. "One pound of DNA molecules in one thousand quarts of fluid. It holds more memory than all the computers ever made."

"If it's what you say it is," she said.

He let out a sigh that bore a note of frustration. "It's the biotechnology that escapes me. There's reams about the biochemical process I wish I understood."

The general looked at her, and she noted a trace of timidity on his features even through his goggles. He said almost in a whisper, "Would you please explain it to me?"

Julie smiled. This concept had more to do with biology than

computer science, and even a seasoned molecular biochemist might scratch her head at the very idea. Besides, she enjoyed lecturing. "It's not terribly difficult to grasp—at least in theory. DNA—the basic stuff of life—and computers work the same way. DNA essentially is digital, which means it can count. Using a four-letter alphabet, DNA stores information that all living organisms manipulate the same way computers work through strings of 1s and 0s. Both systems are equally good for encoding information. It's just a matter of putting them together in the right sequence."

The general nodded. "I'm with you so far."

"Nature," she continued, "has created an extraordinary, special-purpose computing system. DNA and the genetic machinery that processes it store and retrieve an astounding amount of information—everything you need to design and maintain every kind of living organism. All well and good for nature. But what if we could get the same genetic machinery that generates living organisms to work for us to solve mathematical problems?"

"Yes, yes," the general said, impatient, "but *how* does it work?"

Julie interpreted the general's frustration—no, eagerness—as an indication that he was as on the verge of grasping the notion. "Electronic computers think sequentially," she said. "They're good at solving long, thin problems that require a large number of operations, one after the other. Molecular computers, on the other hand, are good at solving problems that are wide and short and can be broken into a huge number of tasks, each one needing just a few steps to solve."

"But *how?*"

"By simple chemical reactions," she said. "Chemical reactions occur very fast and in parallel. If the DNA molecules are synthesized with a chemical structure that represents numerical information, we can accomplish a vast amount of number crunching as the reaction proceeds. Because of the massively parallel reactions we see in biochemistry—"

"You're losing me."

"Molecules working together at the same time—"

"I see."

"A DNA computer, in terms of the number of operations performed by its trillions of molecules, would be a hundred times faster than today's fastest serial supercomputers.''

The general couldn't control his enthusiasm, and it came out as laughter. ''So DNA computers are 'massively parallel.' ''

''*Exactly!* And that means that when billions or trillions of DNA molecules undergo the chemical reactions, we can perform more operations at once than all the computers in the world working together could ever accomplish. Best of all, DNA runs virtually on its own power, so its energy consumption would be a billion times more efficient than electronic computers, and its storage capabilities a trillion times denser than the best of today's magnetic storage media.''

The general was bordering on giddy. ''Incredible,'' he said, laughing. ''Absolutely incredible. So one day we may actually create a living, thinking machine?''

Julie ran her hand along the side of the box. ''Even though they're made of DNA, what's in this box is not in any sense a living thing.'' She rose to her feet. ''Now it's your turn to explain something to me.''

''Name it.''

''With all due respect, why is it here? Why Cheyenne Mountain of all places?''

''Why not?'' the general said, replacing the access panel. ''When it comes to speed, the military is always looking for better and faster computing power to control its networks, hardware, and processes. National security depends on it. My bosses were convinced that Eclipse would be the ideal project to see what Citadel could do. If there were no insurmountable problems, we would begin employing the speed of molecular computers to solve some of today's unsolvable problems, everything from architectural design and the invention of new drugs to cryptography and quantum mechanics. Its power is truly awesome. The impact this will have on the military and our society in the long term will be staggering.''

''It's too new,'' Julie said. ''There are countless bugs we need to troubleshoot first. Perhaps that can explain Eclipse's failure. It's too risky to keep on-line.''

''It's not controlling anything—yet,'' the general said. ''In practical terms it's only a backup to our current supercomputers.

We use Citadel for diagnostics based on data we mirror from Eclipse's main memory. It performs all tests as though it was on-line, checking and cross-checking every system and subsystem, monitoring our entire communication and surveillance network. It controls nothing and provides nothing we don't already have—except for astonishing processing speed.''

"So it's a brain without a body. It has no extremities to control, no way to realize its potential."

"It's an incredible brain," the general offered. "And one day it will have extremities. When I said at the briefing that we've culled through sixty million lines of code four times since Sunday, that wasn't exactly true. Sweet Julie actually has checked, debugged, recompiled, and tested that code four thousand times since then."

"This will be a great boon for our Programming Team," Julie said.

"I'm afraid it won't. In fact, the team won't even know about it. No one will—for now."

"Why?"

"The Programming Team will go through the process by hand, again and again, checking and rechecking, seeing if the calculations from Citadel are in any way flawed."

"But—"

"This project is highly *classified*. Can you imagine what this technology would be worth on the international black market? Can you imagine what even a test tube of that fluid would be worth? A rudimentary lab could determine its chemical makeup and then synthesize it with biotechnology. The chemicals are inexpensive, and the soup, with a little splicing, can be reused from one experiment to the next."

"But there must be countless engineering hurdles to overcome before the system could be of any use to anyone," she said. "We're years away."

"I assure you it's all doable—most of it with off-the-shelf technology."

Julie looked astonished. "You must show me the development report."

"There will be time for that later," the general said. "Consider yourself in the loop on this project. Use it in your work with

113

Henry Princeton. He brought with him samples of each satellite's microprocessor. I want you to look closely at that hardware—its architecture and design, its BIOS coding, flash memory, and how they execute programs. It's just a hunch, mind you, but I believe therein lie the answers we're looking for.''

A long pause followed as Julie stared vacantly into a dark corner of the strange room as though she had slipped into a trance.

"Anthony," she said finally.

"Excuse me?"

"I would like to name this prototype 'Anthony.' "

The general, unsure, shook his head. "Who the heck is Anthony?"

She looked at him through her goggles and hoped he could see her sincerity. "He was my father."

Chapter Seventeen
Desert Night

New Mexico
Tuesday, December 28
1930 Hours

"I've got us live via satellite!" Jill called to the others.

Marshall wiped his hands on a rag. "It's about time."

Jill sat in the Comanche's cockpit, admiring her ability to light up the consoles like a Christmas tree. She said confidently, "Give me another half hour and I'll have everything on-line—global positioning, long and short radar, the works."

Marshall climbed up the side of the Comanche and put on a headset.

"Patch me through to Fort Irwin."

Jill punched in a series of numbers on her communications keypad. Marshall's headset crackled and emitted an unearthly warbling sound until the scramble synchronized. Her VDR display flashed READY.

"Done," she said. "You're on-line."

Marshall adjusted the headset's microphone over the corner of his mouth. "This is Alpha-Moon-Two-Seven to Mother. Over."

Jill slid on her headset to listen in.

The voice of a seasoned soldier on the other end crackled, "You've got Mother. Go ahead, Alpha-Moon-Two-Seven. Give me your coordinates."

"New Mexico—exact location unknown," Marshall said. "We're not yet fully functional. Our transport crashed in an attempted hijacking."

"We copy, Alpha-Moon. Please stand by."

A lengthy silence followed, and Marshall motioned Jill to check the signal. She affirmed that they still had a connection.

Finally, a voice filled Marshall's headphones. "This is General Medlock at Fort Bragg. You were starting to worry me. What's the condition of the Comanche?"

"Nice to hear you're safe and sound too," Marshall said.

"Stow the crap—"

"She's intact," Marshall said. "Our train derailed during a hijacking, but the Comanche sustained no debilitating damage. We're still inspecting her."

"Hijacking?" Medlock asked. "Who were these sons of bitches? Are they still a threat to you?"

"Negative. We counted eleven, including the train engineer, all Caucasian male. I detected an accent on one of them—European. They appeared to be a paramilitary brigade, extremely well equipped and trained. Their intelligence capabilities are top-notch. They were able to get a train undetected on the tracks behind us."

"That fits," General Medlock said. "The entire power grid on that line shut down at zero-seven-hundred this morning, blinding us. All traffic on that track has been suspended. I need some answers. I want you to question one of those bastards."

"There are no survivors," Marshall said.

"You play too rough," the general said. "I'm looking forward to my retirement next month. No more justifying your out-of-the-box behavior to the Pentagon."

"There's one other interesting note," Marshall offered. "Each one of them wore a tattoo on his wrist."

"Tattoo?" Medlock said. "What kind of tattoo?"

"A sun—possibly Sirius. All of them were identical, like some gang symbol. Jill says it's a doomsday cult that may have been written up last year."

"I'll have it checked out," General Medlock said. "Meanwhile, stay put and defend the Comanche."

"When can we expect an extraction?" Marshall asked. "I need an ETA."

"I can't give you one. In less than an hour, the President will ground all military aircraft, including rescue flights."

"Excuse me," Marshall said. "It must be desert shock. For a moment I thought you were implying we were stuck out here."

"I don't like it any more than you," the general said. "He's effectively crippled us. But the situation is deteriorating by the hour, and he feels he doesn't have a choice."

"What about the Comanche?" Marshall said. "She's airworthy."

"Absolutely not," Medlock said. "That aircraft is grounded until further notice. If you have to, you'll sit out the rest of the week right where you are. Thank God you're alive, for chrissake!"

When there came no reply, the general said, "Do you understand me, Colonel?"

"I hear you."

"Let's agree that our next communication will be at zero-six-hundred hours tomorrow," Medlock said.

"I copy."

Marshall reached into the cockpit and disconnected his headset. He looked at Jill, who just shrugged. The situation was unacceptable. The last thing he intended to do was spend the rest of the millennium on an expensive camping outing in the New Mexican desert, not when Nancy's fate was still unknown. He reached into the pocket of his khakis, withdrew the pager, and reread part of Julie's message: ". . . DON'T KNOW IF SHE SURVIVED . . . CAN'T GET ANYONE'S ATTENTION HERE . . . CAN YOU PLEASE HELP???"

He had to do *something!*

Williams stepped into the light of the carbon-arc work lamps and called up to them, "What's the scoop? When are we gonna see some cavalry?"

"We won't," Marshall said, "at least not for a while. There's a nationwide flight stand-down effective tonight. Medlock wants us to secure the Comanche and stay put."

Williams let out a low whistle.

Jill removed her headset and shook out her hair. "Well, that means we can turn in."

Williams thrust a cigar into his mouth and bit down hard. "That's not the best use of our collective talents. What about your page, Joe? What about Nancy?"

"What page?" Jill asked. "Who's Nancy?"

"Show her," Williams urged

Marshall withdrew his pager, keyed the message, and tossed it up to her. Jill read it with interest. "I still don't get it. Who's Nancy and what does this have to do with us?"

"Nancy Shaw," Marshall said, climbing down from the Comanche, "is a good friend and a great lady. A few years ago she helped save our lives and, in the process, a whole lot of others. She helped prevent a catastrophe that could have infected our entire eastern seaboard with a plague the likes of which you've never even dreamed. The military refused to listen to her warnings about messing with artificial neurotoxins and created a monster virus through bioengineering. Guess who they enlisted to help contain this virus when terrorists stole it from a U.S. Army maximum-containment laboratory?"

"Nancy?" Jill offered.

"You got it," Marshall said.

"She'll tell you to this day that the Army used and coerced her to help contain this thing," Williams added. "Goddammit, the Brass owes her, Joe."

"How deadly was this . . . this plague?" Jill asked.

"Remember your history books about the Black Death that wiped out half of Europe and Asia in the fourteenth century?" Williams quizzed.

Jill shrugged. "Sure."

"This stuff made bubonic plague look like a sore throat," he said. "Hemorrhaging, convulsions, madness—death."

Marshall was pacing now. The adrenaline surging through him made it difficult to stand still. "The last thing I'm prepared to do is sit here while there's a chance she's still alive and dying on top of a mountain."

"Are you suggesting we fly the Comanche to Colorado and find her?" Jill asked.

"That's exactly what I'm going to do," Marshall decided.

"You can stay here if you're worried about your career," Williams said.

"Aren't you guys worried?"

Williams bit down on his cigar and threw a glance at Marshall. "What career?" He riveted Jill with his most serious stare. "Do you think we do this for the money and our careers?"

"You're going to make Medlock one very unhappy general," Jill warned.

"He's never happy anyway," Marshall said. "The general and I have a special relationship. I think we understand each other. How long until this aircraft is operational?"

Jill wiped a hand across her greased forehead, trying to make sense of the situation. "We need at least five more hours of prep time."

"The gunship will seat only two of us," Williams noted, then said to Jill, "That's only a problem if you're going."

"Two can double up in the forward weapon's cockpit," Marshall said. "Cramped but workable. What's our range with the external fuel tanks?"

"Eighteen hundred miles," Jill said. "More than enough to get us to the Colorado Rockies. But where specifically?"

"We'll download the exact coordinates from the COMSAT network once we're airborne," Marshall said.

"So are you in?" Williams pressed.

"I'm in," Jill said. "Besides, I wouldn't miss the maiden flight for anything."

Williams's hard expression melted with a grin.

"Then get some rest." Marshall checked his mountain wrist chronometer.

"We'll start back to work in two hours."

Chapter Eighteen
Real, Serious, Important

U.S. Warns Americans Abroad

WASHINGTON (AP)—Americans in all parts of the world were warned by the State Department today "to exercise great caution" because of a growing threat of anti-U.S. violence. The department went so far as to advise Americans to avoid travel. It said the security of U.S. citizens, business operations and military installations overseas could be affected by a rumored U.S. inability to retaliate. . . .

White House
Tuesday, December 28
2100 Hours

The White House Press Secretary stepped to the lectern and announced, "Ladies and gentlemen, the President of the United States."

A side door opened and in walked the President followed by several members of his staff. The White House briefing room was packed with members of the press and their camera crews, eager to hear arguably the most controversial decision of the President's career. A current of expectation filled the air. The press secretary stepped away from the lectern to make room for the President, who set down several sheets of paper he had brought with him. Behind him sat FAA's John Tutora and NTSB investigator-in-charge Rita Nichols.

"Good evening, ladies and gentlemen," the President said, his eyes scanning familiar and unfamiliar faces alike in the audience. "Because of the urgent nature of this announcement and the crisis in which our country, indeed the world, now finds itself, I ask you, the members of the press and the American people, for your patience. I will read a brief statement and then can answer only a few questions. I apologize for this brevity; however, I must return to a session with the Joint Chiefs, which is still in progress."

The President's eyes dropped to the paper on the lectern and remained there for an interminable several seconds as he summoned the courage to begin.

"As many of you undoubtedly are aware," he said, "my good friend Senator Mike Lloyd was killed last night in an airplane crash not far from here. He died along with one hundred fifty-nine other people, including his daughter, Gina. His wife, Nora, is in serious but stable condition at Walter Reed Medical Center. My purpose here is not to eulogize the senator, but rather to realize his legacy as chairman of a special congressional subcommittee investigating the ramifications of the millennium computer problem on our nation's critical institutions and infrastructures.

"The exact cause of the crash of Flight 256 is still under investigation and will probably take several weeks to determine. However, in a preliminary report, investigators have cited that computer failure of the aircraft's critical systems rendered the plane inoperable. Although both the aircraft's manufacturer, Boeing, and Transcarrier Airways both independently certified the 767 as Year 2000 compliant, evidence from Flight 256's data recorder show that the unrecoverable error was due, at least partially, to the systems' inability to distinguish the correct date. This disaster brings the number of military and civilian air crashes over the last three weeks to fourteen."

Members of the President's audience scribbled furiously in their notepads while he paused, a visible expression of frustration rippling over his features. "Over the last two years," he read, "my administration has been aggressive in confronting and minimizing the Year 2000 problem, which has required a major technology and management effort. I have said repeatedly that this issue is real, it's serious, it's important. But, apparently, this warning has not been heeded. Independent White House security consultants have concluded that government agencies and businesses have failed to take the fundamental steps to ensure that proper date information is passed between systems. There has been little sharing of Year 2000 knowledge, problems, and solutions with one another. We are investigating numerous charges that some members of the airline industry even kept critical information to themselves to use competitively.

"These are abhorrent charges and, if true, have created the worst threat to public and national security in this century. There are dire consequences even for companies that have remediated their systems. I understand that there have been resource allocation problems across this nation and around the world, in business as well as in government. These are mere excuses in the midst of a crisis of global proportions.

"And now people are dying."

The President paused for effect and could hear the scratching of pens in the reporters' notebooks.

"The American people deserve better. Accordingly, to prevent farther loss of life, by the authority vested in me as President by the Constitution and the laws of the United States of America, I hereby declare a national emergency and issue an Executive Order to ground all private, commercial, and military flights. This ban will go into effect immediately and will continue until forty-eight hours after the clocks strike midnight January 1. In the meantime, we will continue to review every facet of every process across the spectrum of industries.

"Thank you, ladies and gentlemen. I will take a few questions."

There came a roar as every press member jumped to his or her feet and asked the President for the floor.

"Yes, Dana," the President shouted over the din.

"You have singled out the airline industry for this ban," said Dana Priest of the *Washington Post* as the sea of reporters around her settled back into their seats to write. "Your statement is unclear about other industries with volatile processes that rely on microprocessors. Are they not also at risk of failure? And what do you plan to do about them?''

"Dana," the President answered, "every system controlled by a microprocessor is at risk until a change is made. At this time we have issued this ban on air travel because of serious safety consequences. When I return to the session with the Joint Chiefs, we will resume our discussions. If we determine there is a risk to public safety and property, we will not hesitate to issue a similar ban on that industry or process."

"*MR. PRESIDENT . . .*" came a collective shout.

"Yes, Wolf," the President said, pointing.

Wolf Blitzer, CNN's senior White House correspondent, called to the front, "How will you respond to charges that you did not act soon enough in grounding air travel? That you waited until there were fatalities?"

The President appeared visibly angered. "I want to assure the American people that this administration has taken this problem very seriously from the beginning. Our first priority is and will remain public safety. Our second priority is the viability of the U.S. and world economy. It has not been an easy task to balance those two objectives. All decisions were made to the best of our ability based on information we had at the time."

There came more shouting, more questions.

"I'll answer one more," the President said.

"Will you subsidize businesses that rely on air transportation during this ban," someone shouted, "or let them go out of business?"

"What about emergency flights for organ transplants?" another reporter called.

"What about Air Force One?"

The President raised his hands for control of the room. "Air Force One is officially grounded. I promise to keep you informed as this situation develops. Thank you."

"Mr. President, one more question . . . *Mr. President . . .*"

The President stepped away from the lectern and exited by way of the side door through which he had come, leaving a clamor for more information behind him.

Chapter Nineteen
All-Nighter

New Mexico
Tuesday, December 28
2210 Hours

Captain Jill Larson engaged the Comanche's rotor clutch and caused the five rotor blades overhead to begin turning. The twin turboshaft engines purred evenly as the blades spooled. An adrenaline rush coursed through her. *This is it—I'm actually going to fly this thing!* She couldn't help breaking into a broad grin as she moved the throttle forward to increase engine torque.

Jill switched on the outside loudspeaker and said into her helmet's mouthpiece, "Sergeant, heft your butt into this aircraft before I leave you here!"

Williams stored the last of their gear in the weapons bay and climbed up to the forward cockpit. Joseph Marshall was already seated inside, absorbed in the tedious business of typing a message into a SkyPager with his thumbs. He looked like he was playing a Game Boy.

Williams eyed the slender cockpit and said, "I got news for you. There isn't room in there for both of us."

"Sure there is." Without looking up from his pager, Marshall slid as far to the left as possible. "Otherwise you walk."

Williams climbed into the cockpit and squeezed beside Marshall.

"Isn't this cozy," he said, pulling down and securing the canopy. He watched Marshall work the pager. "What the heck are you doing?"

"Writing a love letter," Marshall responded.

"Ahhhh," Williams said, nodding. "I was wondering when you'd get in touch with her."

Marshall ignored him and finished his message.

"Everybody secure up there?" Jill asked over the intercom.

Marshall gave her a thumbs-up signal.

Jill increased the throttle and waited for the engine torque to reach seventy-five percent. The rotor blades formed a dishlike blur. When the torque reached 90 percent, she slowly added collective. They hardly felt the aircraft leave the ground. She let the aircraft rise to one hundred feet before retracting the landing gear.

"I'm walking on a cloud, Colonel." She giggled through the intercom.

Marshall keyed his microphone. "I knew you'd like it."

Jill pitched the main rotors to drive the thrust and lift to the rear. The helicopter moved forward. She quickly found the proper mix of pitch angle and collective input and soon had the Comanche moving at seventy knots.

She banked the aircraft northeasterly and said to the others, "Buckle in for a long night, boys. Next stop, Colorado."

Cheyenne Mountain
Tuesday, December 28
2220 Hours

There came a soft knock on the door to the computer lab. Before Julie could respond, Henry Princeton slipped inside. She glanced over her shoulder at him, then returned her full attention to the terminal in front of her.

"I've been looking everywhere for you," Henry said. "It finally occurred to me to look in here."

"Now you found me," she said, continuing her work on the keyboard.

"We need to talk," Henry said. "I don't think the colonel and the general are going to find jack turning over these stones. Just the same worms."

Julie only half listened to him. "Maybe. It's not our jobs to question that. What did you need to talk about?"

Henry sat on the edge of her desk and said softly, "I want to get to know you. I want to learn how you tick so I can support you better. I want to know your background. I want to pick your brain."

Julie scowled and rolled her eyes. "Not now. I'm not in any position to have my brain picked. Later."

"When?"

"How about February?"

Henry let out a huff of laughter and peered over her shoulder at the oversized display. "So what are you working on?"

"I'm entering the simulation results the team put your micro-processors through. Someone's got to do it."

He squinted at her display. "Hmmm. That doesn't look like NORAD's network."

It suddenly occurred to her that Henry was getting a good look at Anthony's experimental interface in direct conflict with General Patterson's orders. "It's not," she said slowly. "I'm patched into the Crays."

"But that's not UNIX either," he pointed out.

"It's brand-new," she said.

Henry's tone changed abruptly. "Why are you screwing around with a new operating system at a time like this?"

Julie blanked the screen and whirled around to Henry. "Do you need something to do? Because I've got enough *friggin'* work here to keep you busy all night long."

"Well, as a matter of fact—"

"Have you finished inputting the circuit schematics for your RAJ277 chips?"

"No, I haven't—"

"And you're waiting for *what?*"

"I thought we should talk first."

Julie stood up and faced him eye to eye. "Talk about *what?*"

When he didn't answer immediately, she said, "Ever since I arrived here, all everyone wants to do is *talk* to me. Well, I didn't come here to talk to you or to anyone else. I'd just be wasting my time. Let's get one thing straight: I was drafted to do a job, and I intend to finish it and go back home, thank you very much.

Please leave me alone so I can get though this and enjoy at least one hour's sleep tonight."

Henry's surprised look melted into his best lady-charming smile. "Anyone ever tell you that you're absolutely lovely when you get angry?"

"Get out of here!" she shouted, pointing at the door.

He offered her a wink and, still smiling, left her alone in the computer lab.

When he was gone, Julie let out a sigh and sank back into her chair. She stared at her terminal's blank screen and ran her hands through her long hair. "Some people just don't get it," she found herself saying aloud.

Julie tried to push Henry and his arrogant interruption out of her mind, called up the screen, and focused on finishing the entries. Satisfied that they were complete, she hit the Enter key. The word PROCESSING began blinking on the lower left corner of her screen. She leaned back into her chair, folded her arms, and watched. Normally, this routine and the answers she was seeking would have taken days to process on the Army's fastest Cray supercomputers. How long would Anthony take? she wondered.

"I'll be back in a little while, Dad," she said to the screen. "Meanwhile, show me what you can do."

2340 Hours

Julie set a stack of notebooks on the desk beside her laptop computer and sprawled out onto her room's twin-size bed. She looked at her watch. "Jeez, almost midnight."

She'd been working constantly since arriving at Cheyenne and wanted only to close her eyes for eight hours to let her psyche heal. But it wasn't to be, nor would Colonel Beckman allow it.

She and her team were given a break only until 1:00 A.M. An hour's sleep, if she was lucky. Not nearly enough. *There's no faster way to make a bitch out of me then to deprive me of sleep.*

Julie had planned to check her mail before dozing off—just in case there was a message from *him*. She dragged herself from the bed, sat at the desk, and turned on her notebook computer. It booted quickly and brought up her off-line e-mail files that she'd automatically downloaded earlier. Her eyes quickly scanned the new mail. Most of it was the usual governmental spam and academic memorandums. She was on countless mailing lists.

One note—a pager response—caused her heart to jump. It was an e-mail from Colonel Joseph Marshall. New energy consumed her. She ignored the other messages and opened Marshall's:

Address: jcmarshall@usm.com, time 22:15

Ran into trouble in New Mexico on our way to Ft. Irwin.

We were stranded here in the middle of nowhere with a first-class RAH-66 Comanche. Just got it operational. We should reach Nancy's crash site at first light. Take care and try not to worry.

Joe.

Julie smiled and breathed a sigh of relief. Now perhaps Nancy had a fighting chance.

God, I miss you, Joe, she thought. *I wish you were here with me now*.

The two hadn't seen each other since Christmas a year before, which, like a pocket veto, had signaled the end of their relationship. Careers. A full year apart thanks to their demanding careers. Another sunk relationship. Julie turned off the desk lamp and rolled onto her bed. The alarm on her watch would go off in one hour, which would give her just ten minutes to drag her weary butt up to meet with Henry Princeton and other team members. *Am I having fun yet?*

"What am I doing here?" she said to the darkness.

Julie closed her eyes and, with the thought of Joe Marshall still on her mind, slipped into a restless sleep.

Day Three
Wednesday, December 29, 1999

"Computers in the future may weigh no more than 1.5 tons."

Popular Mechanics, 1949

Chapter Twenty
First Light

Colorado Rockies
Wednesday, December 29
0635 Hours

"I don't want anybody falling behind," First Lieutenant Richard Gravel shouted back to his five-member rescue team. "Keep in sight of each other."

It was first light when the group made their way down the steep chasm between granite walls as sheer as the side of two buildings. Gravel, his eyes locked on the handheld GPS tracking unit in his gloved hand, took the lead. He was a tall, seasoned soldier with a passion for mountain climbing. He sported a dark mustache and deep rigid features that appeared to be carved from the same mountain surface he so enjoyed climbing.

Not much farther now, he thought. They were closing in on the vector coordinates drawn from the Black Hawk's transponder signal, which had grown fainter throughout the night. By noon, he estimated, its batteries would be dead, its signal lost. Expressions were grim as they proceeded, their expectations nil. They had received no voice transmission of any kind. And it had been a cold night, even for the mountains. Gravel knew, however, that deep inside they were eager to a man and woman. There was always the anticipation of the unknown—an equal blend of the excitement of the search and the dread of finding corpses. What they would find today when they reached the site, no one would presume to even guess.

The last mile of their hike had been the longest—or at least it always seemed that way. Perhaps it was the smell of burning fuel, laced with the unmistakable order of burnt flesh, carried on the canyon breeze.

"We're home," said Sergeant Vicki Mayfield, pointing.

They all looked up at once. About a quarter mile farther lay the wreckage site—several pieces of black, twisted metal that still smoldered.

Lieutenant Gravel waved the others forward. "Double time."

The six of them broke into a jog and covered the final quarter mile in three minutes. The black, acrid smoke burned their eyes. What they found wasn't promising. A steady wind throughout the night had dusted everything with a thin layer of snow. Human-shaped mounds looked as though they were covered with white shrouds.

"You all know what to do," the lieutenant said grimly.

His team nodded somberly and broke up to scour the wreckage for anyone who had managed to stay alive overnight, however remote that possibility now appeared.

Lieutenant Gravel climbed into the aft fuselage, the only section that still resembled an aircraft. It offered a modest barrier from the cold wind. The early-morning light filtering into the chasm created deep shadows that hid clues to this disaster. There were vague, humanlike forms scattered throughout the compartment. He slipped out his flashlight and played the beam into the shadows along the wall. What he saw made him wince. There were bodies, lots of them, several still sitting upright and fastened to the seats on which they had died. The nightlong wind had relentlessly hammered the flesh with ice crystals, turning the corpses into porcelain statues. Gravel directed his light from one waxy expression to another. The ones with their eyes still open seemed to be pleading to release them from this horror. It was as though he had reached the final level of Dante's *Inferno*.

Lieutenant Gravel's flashlight beam found the corpse of a man who looked more like a foot soldier than a helicopter passenger. He was dressed in camouflage fatigues, cold-weather garments, and climbing gear. The right side of his face was bloodied and disfigured from a severe blow. A high-powered rifle lay beside him. What exactly happened here? he wondered.

Outside, Sergeant Vicki Mayfield surveyed the bodies strewn around her. She hardly knew where to start. She noticed that the snow around two of the mounds was soaked with blood that had frozen into solid pools. She secured her shoulder-length blond hair behind her head with a small hair band, knelt beside the first, and brushed aside the snow with her gloves. Several wounds on the corpse's back had produced massive bleeding. She ran a gloved hand over them.

"*Jesus.*" She pulled out her radio. "Lieutenant?"

Inside the fuselage, Gravel responded into the radio, "What do you have?"

"I'm looking at a guy who's taken at least four bullets in the back," she said.

"Bullets?" Gravel frowned. "Is it shrapnel from the engine?"

"Negative. I'm turning him over." Mayfield set down her radio, wedged her fingers underneath the corpse, and attempted to lift it. The body was frozen to the ground.

"Hargitay," Mayfield called to her corporal. "Give me a hand."

Corporal Roger Hargitay knelt beside her.

Mayfield and Hargitay jammed their fingers under the corpse.

"Lift on my command," she said. "Ready? *Lift!*"

The corpse tore free with a *rip*, and they flipped it over. It was an Asian male wearing a U.S. Air Force officer's uniform. A metal cylinder was pressed against the corpse's chest. *What the heck—?* Mayfield knelt forward for a closer look.

Lieutenant Gravel looked up suddenly from his investigation inside the wreck. He roared through the fuselage, yelling into his radio, "Don't touch anything! *Don't touch anything!*"

Mayfield's eyes widened with astonishment. "A grenade—!"

She pushed Corporal Hargitay backward with all her strength. An earsplitting concussion tore them both apart.

Lieutenant Gravel rushed outside and saw smoke billowing from a crater where only a moment before Mayfield and Hargitay had been working.

Specialist Neil Anderson ran toward the blast. "Oh my God. Lieutenant, *they blew up!*"

Another explosion, much stronger than the first, erupted under Anderson's feet and tore him viciously apart. Lieutenant Gravel was too stunned to move. This was no antipersonnel land mine designed to cripple a soldier. The force of this blast was intended to take out a tank.

"LAND MINES!" Gravel shouted through cupped hands. "This site is mined. I want everyone to stand absolutely still."

"Lieutenant," called Specialist Steven Lowe, one of the two remaining members of the party. He took a step forward. "Oh my God. . . . *Oh my God!*"

"DON'T MOVE!" the lieutenant ordered.

There came a crack, and a plum-size hole appeared across Johnson's chest. He toppled backward into the snow. Several more cracks echoed hollowly down the chasm. The ground around Lieutenant Gravel erupted with bullets.

He withdrew his side arm, squatted, and scanned the ridges above for signs of the sniper. He saw nothing among the rock formations.

"*Lieutenant,*" called Specialist Holly Jefferson, "I'm coming to you. Cover me."

Gavel didn't know what to tell her. She was an easy target for the sniper if she stayed there. Make a run for it, and she could step on a mine. He fired several rounds up into the chasm's ridges. The blasts echoed loudly back.

"Holly," he called. "Walk slowly and carefully toward me." She took a tentative step toward him.

"Look for telltale mounds of snow about the size of—"

Suddenly her head flew apart.

"*Holly!*"

Her torso buckled and she collapsed like a rag doll.

Several geysers of snow and rock exploded around him. He was the only target left—an easy one out here alone. Lieutenant Gravel dove inside the fuselage and kicked himself into the wreckage's darkest corner. He pressed his back against one of the fold-down seats and thrust his handgun before him. Anyone who stepped through that opening was a dead man, he decided.

He touched a pair of boots on the floor beside him. *I'm leaning against someone!*

Startled, he thrust his gun up into the porcelain face of a woman's frozen corpse.

Chapter Twenty-one
Blackbird

Cheyenne Mountain
Wednesday, December 29
0730 Hours

"So what do you have for me?" Colonel Beckman asked Julie as he took a seat at the conference table.

The impromptu meeting had officially begun. Beckman sat back and folded his arms in a manner that signaled that he was the single judge and jury of the merit of any idea presented.

General Patterson, a withdrawn look of fatigue pasted on his features, dumped himself into a chair at the head of the table. He opened his mouth impossibly wide and let out a yawn that made up for the previous night's lack of sleep. He buried his eyes into his palms and began rubbing life into them for another demanding day.

Julie watched him sympathetically, imagining the pressure he alone must bear. Although the general often made exaggerated gestures about his personal discomfort, she learned not to be fooled by any seeming weakness of his body, especially lack of sleep. She knew that his mind was still as sharp as a Ginsu. And he possessed an uncanny ability to take in the minutest detail and provide the appropriate decision, all in the time it would take the colonel to ask the speaker to rephrase the question.

"Nothing conclusive," said Henry Princeton, the fourth and final participant of the meeting. In stark contrast to the others,

Henry appeared groomed and fresh this morning.

The colonel hunched over slightly like a vulture, staring at him with oversized eyes, ready to pounce on his carcass if he rolled over and played dead. "But you do have *something* for me?"

"Yes, we do," Julie volunteered. She placed a hand atop a stack of printouts at least six inches deep. "If you look through these reports—"

"Negative," Beckman spat. "I don't have time to read through details and guess what might be important. And I certainly won't scan through pages of numbers. Just tell me what I need to know."

Julie's eyes narrowed and she nodded. "I've completed the first round of tests on the AKS's microprocessors. The samples Henry provided are architecturally perfect, and all of them performed flawlessly as designed in our simulation."

Henry thrust out his chest and raised his chin like a proud second-grader. As the chief architect for the series of microprocessors that controlled Eclipse, he was accustomed to taking bows in recognition of the work.

"So why are we meeting?" Beckman asked, emphasizing the irritation in his voice.

"Because—" She drew in her breath and held it for a moment, letting the word hang in the air until she could summon strength for what she knew would be a controversial statement. "—the chips performed too perfectly."

The general dropped the palm of his right hand so he could see her. She shot him a look with a raised eyebrow she hoped would signal that there were aspects of this best not discussed in front of the others.

Henry was on his feet in an instant. "No, this is not what we agreed to report. Our tests found no operational errors, and phase two of our testing is anything but conclusive. To offer anything else at this time would be pure speculation and irresponsible. We need time to do a thorough investigation."

A crash came as Beckman slammed his fist against the table, rattling their coffee mugs. He looked at Henry, livid with anger. "You will not get more *time*, mister. None of us will."

Henry gestured to Julie and blurted, "For the record, I want to state my dissatisfaction with my team leader."

"We're not keeping an official record of this project," the general said.

"Dr. Martinelli and I have had very little face time together," Henry said, his voice taking a decidedly exasperated tone. "She's difficult to work with. She ignored my repeated requests for meetings and spent most of the night in front of her terminal, playing with a prototype interface, no less."

The general noted Henry's groomed, well-rested appearance. "Doesn't look like you've lost much sleep over it."

Henry's mouth opened, but no words came.

Colonel Beckman looked at Julie, his expression dropping into a sour frown. "Will you please restate your point in a manner that has some relevance here?"

Julie's eyes fluttered. "Of course." She stood and stepped in front of the whiteboard, a finger on her lip. "The chip's architecture is ingenious," she began; "however, there is an area in the circuit that appears to be in conflict with its original design. The circuit takes its instructions from a volatile area of flash memory, which suggests the microprocessor can potentially be programmed for other tasks."

She had gotten the general's undivided attention. "Show me," he said.

Julie stepped to the table, unfolded a tablecloth-size sheet of paper, and attached it to the conference room's metal wall with bottle-cap-size magnets. Henry, refusing to assist, took his seat and watched her, his face flushed.

"Here." She pressed her finger on a tiny area of the circuit diagram. "There are similar circuits in Eclipse's other microprocessors as well. This particular chip is installed in Eclipse's seven Blackbird recon satellites."

"Wait a minute," Beckman said, paging through his binder. "Where are my notes on the Blackbirds?"

"The Blackbirds are seven very low-profile surveillance satellites built by Lockheed Martin Missiles and Space," the general said, spinning his class ring around his pinky—the only finger on which it still fit. "Their specialty is night reconnaissance, using infrared and advanced light-intensifying optics. Each carries six surveillance instruments, mounted at the ends of four eight-foot-long masts."

"Yes, I'm well aware," Beckman said. He stopped paging through his binder and addressed Henry. "Tell me about this circuit, Princeton."

Henry spread his hands disarmingly. "The circuit isn't in use. We include them in all our microprocessors to load onboard diagnostic routines before burning them into memory."

The colonel shot a glance at Julie. "Henry says the circuit isn't in use. Do you have anything that suggests otherwise?"

Julie started to face Henry but caught herself; she didn't want him intimidating her.

"Please speak freely," the general said, noting her trepidation. "This meeting may be your only chance to follow this line of investigation."

Julie nodded. "The circuit is an encryption decoder—fully functional. An advanced, 128-bit security scheme. Simply stated, the circuit takes instructions from signals uploaded into flash memory and decodes them."

"*It what!?*" Beckman said.

"This is pure speculation," Henry complained. "She can't possibly know its purpose."

"Decodes what?" the general asked, looking at Henry.

"As I've told you," he said, "it tests diagnostic routines. Very standard. It hasn't been used since launch."

"There is a way to find out conclusively," Julie said. "Each satellite logs every uploaded instruction it receives. Those commands are archived in the satellite's nonvolatile storage, which can hold four gigabytes of data. There should also be a mirror of those records at each ground station."

"I want a look at them," the general said.

Colonel Beckman let out a frustrated sigh. "Normally that wouldn't be a problem. But the array isn't behaving normally. There are no ground records because we haven't been able to download system information since it went down."

"So I take it we can't manually download the files from the satellites either," the general said.

Beckman shook his head. "The network won't talk to us. There's no way it'll return a downloading command. But the point is finally moot. Even if we found encrypted instructions, it would take all our supercomputers working in parallel months to decode a 128-bit encryption scheme.''

Julie noted a hint of satisfaction on Henry's face. She looked at the general, her eyes narrowing. ''There might be a faster way.''

The general nodded and stretched his tree-trunk-size limbs. ''I want to see every one of Eclipse's diagnostic instruction sets. And I want them within the hour.''

Henry, his expression hardening, agreed with a nod. ''I'll download them from our corporate server.''

''Excuse me, General,'' Julie said. ''The files we get from Henry and the code actually uploaded to the satellites won't necessarily be the same.''

''She's right,'' Beckman said. ''He could feed us anything.''

''What are you suggesting?'' Henry said, standing. ''That AKS has deliberately sabotaged the entire U.S. strategic military network?'' He shook his head and began pacing by his chair. ''This is preposterous.'' He thrust a finger at Julie. ''This is a very dangerous charge you're peddling.''

''Calm down,'' the colonel said. ''No one is accusing anyone of anything. We're just trying to gather some facts. Besides, it doesn't look like we're going to access any code stored aboard those satellites.''

''With all due respect, gentlemen,'' Julie said, ''you're overlooking the obvious.''

Beckman leaned back in his chair. ''Oh, and what might that be?''

''The Blackbird,'' she said, ''is mounted on a bus designed so that in extreme circumstances it can be retrieved from orbit. Its recording devices are recoverable.''

Henry threw his hands into the air and mocked, ''Oh, now I've heard it all.''

She unrolled a large, three-dimensional cutaway diagram of Blackbird over the table and put a finger on its midsection. ''This barrel at the center houses the spacecraft's operating equipment, including its backup storage module.'' She slid her finger down to its ''bus''—a drab-looking cylindrical platform that carried the satellite into space and maneuvered it in orbit. ''Its maneuvering jets can take it out of orbit. You see, it's even equipped with a reentry parachute.''

"We can't communicate with those satellites," the general said. "What's the point—"

"Yes, we can," Beckman said.

"The colonel is right," Julie said. "This bus receives its orbital maneuvering instructions independent of the arrays' relay command set on its own uplink frequency of 2093.0541 MHz." She looked at the colonel. "I believe the receivers are still fully functional.''

Beckman nodded.

"This is absurd," Henry said. "Are you suggesting we pull a sixty-three-million-dollar satellite out of orbit so we can check out your far-fetched theory?"

"That's exactly what I'm recommending," Julie said. She flashed him an accusing stare that she wasn't able to conceal. "It shouldn't be an issue—unless someone is doing something wrong."

Henry's eyes widened.

Julie began rolling up the schematic. "What do you gentlemen say? Shall we bring home a Blackbird and find out what it has to tell us?"

The general, grinning, nodded. "Let's do it."

Chapter Twenty-two
Wreckage

Colorado Rockies
Wednesday, December 29
0905 Hours

"ETA five minutes, gentlemen," Jill said over the Comanche's intercom. "We've got some weather coming in. Count on pea soup for visibility."

Marshall, seated in the gunnery cockpit in front of her, keyed his helmet microphone. "I copy that. Five minutes," he said to Williams, who was squeezed into the seat beside him.

Jill worked the controls of the Comanche as though she had slipped from the womb right into its cockpit. Flying a helicopter is at best a difficult task, but she was a natural—her father had given her chopper lessons as her fourteenth birthday gift. For the rest of her teens she spent more time in cockpits than most girls her age talked on telephones. Captain Jill Larson was born to fly choppers.

"The simulators don't do her justice," she said over the intercom. "You've got to try this, Colonel."

Marshall grinned; he could well understand Jill's excitement. In fact, he had already flown the Comanche, although not this particular aircraft. More than two years before he had trained on the original RAH-66 prototype at Boeing's Helicopter Division in Philadelphia and declared the stealth aircraft the premier

141

twenty-first-century reconnaissance/attack helicopter. Now it was her turn to discover that thrill firsthand.

Jill brought the Comanche up over a ridge and sank down into a valley punctuated with deep ridges and caverns. A thick cloud cover obscured the higher ridges and made the landscape look like the surface of Venus. She switched her TSD to topography mode to keep an eye on the terrain contours and relief.

Williams let out a whistle. "The wreck could be anywhere. There's no way a chopper's gonna stay in once piece trying to land down there."

"Agreed," Marshall said. "I'm not betting my pension on finding anyone alive."

"I have a lock on the beacon," Jill said over the intercom. "Its transmitter is down to one-eighth power. If we got here much later, we'd have lost the signal. I'm changing our heading to one-zero-niner."

She banked the Comanche into a mountain slipstream and glided across several canyons, honing in on the Black Hawk's transponder signal.

"We're almost at the vector," she said. "I've locked the cameras on the coordinates. We should be getting a visual any sec."

They rode in silence, each of them watching their respective displays for anything that resembled wreckage.

"Got it," she said. "Watch your TSD."

Jill brought the Comanche to a hover and zoomed into a deep canyon. Marshall switched his left tactical monitor to low-light magnification and panned the wreck site. He could make out several pieces of the fuselage, some of it still smoldering. There were also unmistakable shapes of several bodies.

"Can't tell a goddamned thing from up here," Williams said, watching the display.

"I don't see any activity," Marshall said. "There's no evidence that the rescue party even made it here." He keyed his intercom. "Put us down so we can take a look."

"Can't do it," Jill responded. "The canyon's too narrow."

"We've got about three hundred feet of nylon cord," Marshall said. "Take us down as far as you can and I'll rappel the rest of the way."

"I'll go," Williams said. "Rappelling is my forte."

Marshall acquiesced. Jill put the Comanche into an auto-hover and, working the collective like a surgeon, let the aircraft sink into the canyon until the clearance around the rotors diminished to a mere ten feet.

"That's as far as we go," she said. "You're on your own."

"Roger," Marshall said.

"And one more thing," she said.

"What's that?"

"You guys are nuts."

Marshall grinned. "You're just noticing?"

Williams pushed open the canopy and was accosted by a frigid blast from the rotor's downwash. He secured one end of the nylon cord to the side of the cockpit and let the spool drop into the canyon. The area below looked like a graveyard—inhospitable and unsettling. The sergeant zipped up his flight jacket and slipped on his gloves.

"Take this," Marshall said, handing him a palm-size Motorola VHF radio. "Its range is two miles. Normally it would be useless in these mountains. But we should be able to maintain a line of sight."

Williams slid the radio into a pocket inside his jacket. "I'm not dressed for this," he said. "I'll be back in a jiff."

Williams stuck an unlit cigar into his mouth and disappeared over the side. It took him thirty seconds to rappel to the ground into knee-deep snow not a hundred feet from the first piece of wreckage. He trudged to the closest human-shaped mound, knelt down, and dusted off the snow with his gloved hand. The body underneath was burned far beyond his ability to tell if it was a man or a woman.

Frowning, he slid his hands into his pockets and moved on. He passed several more mounds and, stopping by each, cleared some snow away for a brief inspection. More bodies. None was in much better shape than the first.

Williams saw something distinctly out of place—a body dressed in an orange jumpsuit, minus the layer of snow that obscured the others. There was something terribly wrong here. Even from a distance of several yards he could see that this was not an air-crash victim. He'd found his first member of the rescue party. Williams spotted two more bodies dressed in orange jumpsuits

143

adorned with mountain-climbing gear. Each had been shot with a high-powered rifle.

He pulled out his pocket radio. "Joe, are you listening?"

His radio crackled. "I hear you. The signal's not ideal."

"This isn't a crash site," Williams said. "It's a massacre."

"Explain."

"The rescue team's been murdered," he said into his radio. "Their death can't be more than a couple hours old."

"Murdered?" Marshall said. "What the hell for? Any chance you'll be able to find Nancy's corpse?"

"Negative. I could be looking right at her and wouldn't know it."

Marshall nodded, well aware of the futility of this search. His eyes dropped to his lap and he said a silent prayer for his friend. He knew Julie would take this news hard.

Williams continued his search. The snow several yards beyond was splashed with blood and scattered with material that, upon closer scrutiny, revealed pieces of orange fiber and what could be body parts. Williams's eyes followed the trail of blood to a crater several feet across and deep enough to unearth a good-size section of granite.

"A crater, Joe," he said into his radio. "There was an explosion—a direct hit on some poor bastard."

The sergeant spotted a second crater, also rimmed with blood and human remains. "There are two of them."

"*Sweet Jessie,*" Marshall said. "I want you out of there now. Retrace your steps *exactly*."

A round tore diagonally through the front of Williams's jacket, ripping the fabric and plowing into the ground beside him. He rolled for cover.

Williams thrust the radio to his mouth. "*Sniper fire!* Where the hell is it coming from?"

Marshall's eyes scanned the chasm walls on either side of the Comanche, then up along the ridge. He thought he spotted movement.

"We've got company," Marshall said. "Possibly along the ridge."

A round struck the canyon wall and ricocheted off his bulletproof windshield. Marshall flinched instinctively. "Get above them!"

"Roger that," Jill said.

She pulled on the collective and brought the Comanche above the canyon walls.

"Do you see them?" Marshall said.

"Negative."

Williams took refuge inside the rear section of the Black Hawk's fuselage. "Talk to me, people."

Neither responded. Their undivided attention was focused on the jagged terrain above the rim. Jill scanned the ridge with the aircraft's electro-optical camera and saw nothing but rocks on her Helmet Mounted Display.

"I'm switching to Forward Looking Infrared."

Once in thermal-imaging mode, it took her only seconds to locate the heat signatures.

"Got them," she said. "Locked. I'm putting the thermal scan on your TADS display."

Jill switched the image on Marshall's left multifunction display and showed him a veritable snipers' nest.

"I count four," he said, "perhaps more hidden among the rocks."

One of the humanlike shapes carried a rifle, its thermal signature indicating it had recently been fired.

"Give us some distance," Marshall instructed Jill.

She manipulated the throttles and moved the Comanche several hundred yards away.

"I have a strong lock," she said. "TRGT Priority. Distance to target: two hundred yards."

"I'm taking them out," Marshall said.

He opened the aircraft's weapons bay doors and the Comanche sprouted two winglike EFAMS. He selected and armed a single AGM-114 Hellfire.

"Firing," he said.

The laser-guided missile ignited and roared away from the Comanche's left armament wing. It headed straight up, covered two hundred yards in just over three seconds, then plunged downward, scoring a direct hit on the snipers' cove. There came a flash and their displays momentarily went white as the nine-kilogram antipersonnel fragmentation warhead detonated. Through their canopies they watched a fireball rise over the grotto where the snipers had taken refuge. Rock fragments spewed forth like a volcano.

Down below them, Williams watched the fireball roll into a black cloud over the rim of the canyon. "Now you guys are talking business—"

Another round from a high-velocity rifle pierced the blackened sheet metal in front of him.

"They don't quit," he hollered into his radio. "There's at least one more. I'm still pinned down."

Jill eased down the Comanche's nose and moved the aircraft forward while scanning for another thermal signature. It didn't take long to find what she was looking for—a human-shaped infrared signature lying flat by the edge of the ridge.

Marshall watched the target through his helmet. "Locked."

Jill brought the chopper steadily forward. The crimson signature on Marshall's helmet display spun around and pointed a rifle at the Comanche. The figure fired, cocked, then fired again. The rounds ricocheted off the aircraft's armor plating. Marshall put the chain-cannon mounted beneath his cockpit in priority mode. The figure on the display, realizing he was severely outgunned, bolted away from them. Marshall pressed the trigger. The chain-cannon's three barrels began spinning and spitting dozens of twenty-millimeter rounds. The figure collapsed and went into spasms as the ground around him erupted with shards of granite and ice.

Marshall released the trigger, and the gun fell silent.

"I'd say you got him, Colonel," Jill said.

"Are you through fooling around up there?" Williams's voice crackled over their headsets.

"The area's clean," Marshall confirmed.

"I'm freezing my ass off down here," Williams hollered. "Would you please lower that line and hoist me out of this friggin' graveyard?"

Chapter Twenty-three
Reentry

"Our burn will begin in t-minus twenty seconds," announced Mission Commander Thomas LaGrange.

A skeleton crew, just enough personnel to oversee the reentry, had assembled in NORAD's dimly lit Air Defense Operations Center. Two of the four huge projection screens at the front of the room offered a second-by-second display of the mission. The right active screen showed the coordinates and flight paths of Eclipse's array of forty-seven orbiting satellites. The left screen showed the position of a single six-foot, 850-pound Blackbird spacecraft. The crew had targeted this particular bird for orbital extraction, and a team from Peterson Air Base would recover it from the Nevada desert approximately forty-four minutes from now. They would then bring it back to Cheyenne Mountain for analysis.

LaGrange, a slight middle-aged man with wire-rimmed glasses, crew cut, and a loud voice, liked to run his ops precisely by the book. He announced over the intercom, "Burn in minus five seconds ... four ... three ... two ... one ... I can confirm a burn."

Two columns of numbers began scrolling down the left display, documenting each millisecond of the engine's reverse thrust designed to slow this Blackbird enough to drop it gently out of its circular orbit. General Patterson gave Julie a hopeful, thumbs-up signal. She acknowledged the success of Phase One with a cautious nod.

LaGrange sat back comfortably in an overstuffed chair that looked as if it belonged in a personal study. "It is a joy to fly this spacecraft. It really is child's play."

For the next seven minutes of the burn no one said a word. Colonel Beckman, standing stiffly aloof with his arms folded, quietly watched the activities in NORAD's war room. To his right, Henry Princeton sat at an empty console while biting the nail of his pinky.

Nine hundred miles over South Carolina, the thrusters on the Number Four Blackbird RAJ277 satellite bus continued to slow the spacecraft to suborbital velocity. In seven minutes, its fuel would be exhausted, its thrusters burned beyond any reasonable hope of repair. However, it hardly mattered. This particular bird would never fly again. Its fuel spent, the satellite would enter a narrow window that would take it through earth's atmosphere without disintegrating.

The program was straightforward for satellite recovery. Once inside the atmosphere, the bus would act as a heat shield to protect the onboard data units. Fourteen miles above the earth's surface, the first parachute would deploy, slowing the satellite to seven hundred miles an hour. Four minutes later, at sixty thousand feet, after the main parachute had been sufficiently destroyed and ejected, a trio of parachutes would deploy and carry Blackbird RAJ277 to the recovery crew waiting below it. At least that was the plan.

Only, this particular bird didn't follow the book.

Six minutes and thirty-three seconds into the seven-minute burn, the thrusters on Blackbird bus RAJ277 suddenly and mysteriously extinguished. A dozen warning lights accompanied by a cacophony of buzzers went off in NORAD's operations room. Mission Commander LaGrange sat bolt upright, almost knocking the swivel chair out from under him. All eyes shifted to the projection screens.

"We have a malfunction," LaGrange said. "Full stop at six minutes and thirty-three seconds into the burn. Orbital extraction unlikely."

Beckman slammed his binder onto the console in front of him. *"Goddammit!"* Henry Princeton jumped at his outburst.

General Patterson, standing away from the group with his hands locked behind his back, stared at the floor and shook his head.

Julie whirled. "What does this mean?"

"It means, Doctor," Colonel Beckman said, "we're going to lose the Blackbird."

"Lose it?" she said. "You mean it will stay in orbit?"

"On the contrary," Henry said. "It's going to enter the atmosphere at an angle too steep for its heat shields. It'll burn up and take with it everything it has to tell us."

She appealed to the mission commander. "Is there anything we can do?"

LaGrange scowled. "Not a thing. The ionization from heat buildup is too severe. All communications with the satellite bus have terminated."

Julie looked at the huge screens on the wall above her. "How long until it disintegrates?"

"About forty-five seconds," LaGrange said. He punched a key on his terminal, and the left projection screen filled with a curve that described the satellite's reentry slope next to another that compared it with the intended trajectory. It didn't look good.

"Fifteen seconds," LaGrange said.

"You can find me in the briefing room," the general said. "I've got people waiting on me." He headed for the room's double doors.

Julie stepped next to LaGrange's console for a better view of the satellite's final moments.

"Five seconds," LaGrange said. "Four ... three ... two ..." There was a pause while he watched his terminal screen. "Now, this is interesting."

"Is it gone?" Julie asked.

LaGrange checked the readouts against new information pouring into the tracking system. Finally, he said, "No, it is *not* gone."

Henry whirled at the news. General Patterson was halfway out the double doors when he heard LaGrange's prognosis. He turned to watch.

"Believe it or not, folks," LaGrange said, "Blackbird RAJ277 is still alive."

Colonel Beckman, Henry, and the general joined Julie at the console. They watched intently as LaGrange zoomed in on the graphic of the reentry glide slope.

"Well, I'll be damned," LaGrange said, his deep-set eyes opened wide. "She could just make it."

"Rephrase the situation for me," Beckman demanded.

"I'm saying the satellite's reentry is not steep enough to destroy it," LaGrange said. "Three seconds. If those thrusters had extinguished three seconds earlier, we would've lost her for sure. Now she has a fighting chance."

"But will the data be of any use to us?" Henry said. "Will the storage medium be destroyed by the extra heat?"

"I don't see a problem," LaGrange said, returning to his terminal. "The bus should deflect the heat. There is a small chance the initial parachute deployment won't hold. Still, I give it better than a seventy-percent chance of recovery. The odds in its favor grow exponentially each second. Uh-oh . . ."

"What is it?" Beckman asked.

LaGrange watched more numbers scroll down his screen. "If it survives, it's going to touch down about three hundred miles from here." He pulled up a three-state topographical map. "I'll be able to give you its exact coordinates in about two minutes."

"Alert the recovery team of the new target location," the general ordered.

"Forget the Nevada team," LaGrange said. "You'll need to prepare for a different type of recovery."

"And what would that be?" Beckman asked.

LaGrange stepped around his desk, took off his glasses, and stared up at the topographical map of the Colorado Rockies on the large projection screen. "You're going to need mountain climbers."

Chapter Twenty-four
The Pit

"He want see you," boomed a voice from the blackness.

An incandescent lightbulb hanging high above flared on and blinded Nancy with its harsh glare. She placed a muddy hand over her eyes until they could adjust, and remained on an icy stone floor where she had spent the night without the warmth of her parka, which had been taken on her arrival. The air was damp and frigid, and smelled of excrement. This wasn't a cell, but a twelve-foot-deep pit with granite block walls and narrow mortar spacing to discourage climbing. Nevertheless, she had spent half the night trying before settling back into this black corner, exhausted, with no sense of time.

And there she waited. When sitting in the cold dampness proved too much, Nancy took to squatting for the remainder of the night, and now found it nearly impossible to stand.

A chain ladder dropped into the pit beside her. Nancy struggled to stand and let out a cry as a sharp pain pierced her cramped calves. Without questioning, she grabbed the ladder and pulled herself out. A peculiar man—a large, overweight brute peering at her over the rim—made no move to assist. His head was clean-shaven, and he looked like an overgrown baby with features and manners that indicated a brain abnormality. She forced herself not to stare at him. He was dressed like a combat soldier in olive-green camouflage fatigues that were several sizes too small. He watched her climb out of the pit with dark, vacant eyes that suggested a killer. She dismissed any notion of trying to escape from him.

She emerged into a cellar with walls carved from the mountain. A few tools, worn and rusted, lined the walls, and two mossy benches held heaps of spare parts and other rubbish.

The brute tilted his head and beckoned her up a narrow stone staircase.

"Whatever you say," she said, anxious to be out of this hell-hole.

Nancy braced her hands on both walls and staggered up the stone steps. Once through a pair of storm cellar doors, she stumbled into the knee-deep snow. The morning sunlight, amplified by its reflection off the snow, bore painfully into her retinas. She found herself on a splendid wooded mountainside, meticulously manicured even in its dormant winter state. Through the leafless trees, she could see that their elevation was at least 10,000 feet, a vantage that afforded a breathtaking view of a steep valley.

As she trudged up the path clad only in boots, jeans, and a flannel shirt, Nancy folded her arms across her chest but felt no warmth. If she thought it was cold in the pit, the mountain air was more severe, below freezing without windchill. Probably great skiing weather, she thought. Nancy never cared much for the great outdoors. Sure, it was wonderful to frolic in. But she hated camping, and had no survival skills. She had been a Girl Scout dropout after one year. Even if she managed to get away, she would be dead of exposure on this mountainside within minutes.

They passed through a grove of Douglas firs and entered a lightly wooded clearing. Before them stood an awesome chateau that resembled a mountain ski resort made of hand-carved stone, natural wood beams, and huge two-story windows on all sides. A steady stream of smoke drifted from its chimney and filled the air with the aroma of freshly burned timber. What a grand weekend retreat this would make under different circumstances, she thought. Instead of its beauty, Nancy saw the chateau as another part of this nightmare prison in which she found herself.

Milling about the property were a dozen or so men dressed in snow fatigues and climbing gear. Most carried military-style assault rifles. Stations with kegs of beer had been set up around the estate, and the men were imbibing freely. Some were laughing and roughnecking, while others remained to themselves checking and cleaning their weapons. A few were engaged in an elite shooting competition at the edge of the estate. Two men and a woman hung by elongated necks from a barren tree, swaying in rhythm to the shots the soldiers were pumping into them.

Nancy looked away in revulsion and followed the brute toward the house. A bearded soldier, a foaming beer mug splashing in his hand, stumbled forward and reached for her.

"What have you brought for me, bonehead?" he bellowed.

Nancy recoiled, terrified. Before he could lay a hand on her, the brute brought up his forearm fast and caught him on the jaw. The man cartwheeled backward into the snow, out cold.

The brute led her to the back of the house, slid open the heavy glass door, and beckoned her inside. The warm air inside had just the right amount of humidity and flowed over her like a huge, quilted comforter. They walked through an office area with several desks, each with its own computer terminal. One entire wall hosted a built-in, floor-to-ceiling oak bookcase filled with hardbound volumes and an impressive collection of paperback novels. Nancy read a few titles, trying to get a sense of their owner, and saw only manuals about computer languages. The well-worn paperbacks were mostly romances.

They entered a much larger sitting room with a plush, wraparound couch, a wet bar, and a health-club-size collection of exercise equipment in a mirrored corner. In the center of the room sat a magnificent pool table. Several men dressed in camouflage fatigues were drinking beer and shouting at each other. Two were playing pool, the rest watching and laughing. The air was thick with smoke from their cigars.

The room fell quiet when Nancy entered. Finally, one of them blurted, "Well, well, what do you have this time, Tim, my friend?"

One of the pool players glanced up, shook his head, and resumed his shot. "She's all yours, Frank. I don't quark women who are the same age as my mother."

153

The other men laughed, spitting out jokes about having their way with his mother.

The brute pointed up a flight of rosewood-beam steps. Nancy did as he directed, while rubbing warmth back into her arms. The upper level was even more impressive. Everything about the house was first class, from its high-vaulted oak-beamed ceiling, two-story glass windows offering a heavenly view, to impeccable taste in furniture and fixtures. A massive, circular fireplace in the center of a great room hosted a cozy fire that warmed the half-dozen soldiers sitting around it, mugs in hand.

"Well, hello, my lovely," one of them called. Another stood for a better look at her and began barking like a dog.

"Who's here?" came a female voice.

A lovely woman with blond hair and smart makeup appeared from the kitchen, dressed for travel in a fur coat and carrying a leather shoulder bag. The two locked awkward stares for several moments. Nancy saw something beyond her questioning gaze: It was the look of desire.

The woman looked away and hollered down the hallway behind Nancy. "Alex, honey, I'm off. I'll see you tonight." Without waiting for a response, she headed for what Nancy assumed was the front door, where a man in a suit stood waiting for her. A limo driver, perhaps?

Nancy turned and followed the brute in the opposite direction down a long hallway. Several doors along the corridor stood open. Nancy stole a glance into each room as she passed. The first two—neatly appointed bedrooms, each with its own bath—didn't appear to be in use. The third bedroom, however, stood in disarray, the bed unmade.

It took Nancy a moment to realize that there was someone lying among the soiled sheets. A woman. Something told her that this person wasn't just a late riser. Nancy stared into the bedroom while the brute continued down the hallway. Her eyes widened. It was Olin—the only other survivor of the chopper crash.

"Oh my God!" Nancy rushed to the side of the bed.

Olin, covered with sweat and bruises, lay completely naked and appeared to be unconscious. Her hands were handcuffed over her head, the chain looped through the metal-grilled headboard. Her feet were tied with nylon cord and bound to the sides of the footboard to spread her legs wide. Her broken lower leg was bruised and lumpy, and no medical attention appeared to have been given. Nancy could see abundant evidence that she had been raped repeatedly.

Nancy pulled a sheet up around her and turned Olin's head slightly to examine her face. Her eyes were swollen shut.

Olin stirred and frowned when Nancy touched her. "No . . . no," she groaned.

"Olin, it's Nancy Shaw."

She stopped struggling and said weakly, "Nancy?"

"Yes."

"Please don't let them touch me again." Olin's voice rose in volume. "Oh God, don't let them *touch me!*"

"Don't give up, Olin," Nancy said, brushing back her blood-matted pixie hair. "I'll think of something."

"Are you my guardian angel?"

Nancy smiled. "You never know. Maybe I'm supposed to protect you—"

A large hand clamped around Nancy's arm and whipped her around.

"He want see you," the brute said.

"How dare you treat her this way," Nancy roared. *"How dare you!"*

When he showed no emotion of any kind, Nancy lunged at him and brought both fists down with all her strength onto his chest.

"You ANIMALS!"

He didn't flinch—she might as well have pounded a half-ton bag of cement. He pulled Nancy's flannel shirt into his huge fist, yanked her viciously out into the hallway, and threw her like a rag doll into the wall. His expression bore no trace of anger, contempt, or amusement. The ferocity of his strength stunned her. Nancy thought she would black out, and supported herself with both hands on the wall. He grabbed the back of her shirt and hurled her headlong down the hallway. She spilled facedown on the black slate floor.

"He want see you," he repeated.

Nancy heard his boots clomping down the corridor after her. She scrambled onto her hands and knees and struggled to keep beyond his reach.

"What is all this about?" demanded a voice with a European accent.

Nancy glanced up. In the doorway above her stood General Stryker.

He thrust an angry finger at the brute. "I don't want you in the house. Where are the others?"

The brute cocked his head, indicating behind him.

"I'll deal with them later," Stryker said. "Meanwhile, I want you out of here."

The brute turned and stomped down the hallway from which he came.

Nancy scrambled into a sitting position, cradling her arm, bracing herself for a blow she thought would come. Instead, Stryker extended a hand and said in a tone intended to calm her, "Come with me."

Surprised, Nancy took his hand, and he helped her to her feet. They locked eyes, and she was taken aback by a look that could have passed for respect.

Stryker released her hand. "I won't harm you."

Was she crazy, Nancy thought, or did that look of his mean something more? Could it be genuine compassion—or passion? She believed that whatever fueled it probably had saved her life.

Nancy followed Stryker into an incredible world-class media room. A comfortable living area with a wraparound sofa and plush chairs surrounded a majestic oak coffee table with a television monitor built into the top. The centerpiece of the room was a state-of-the-art, eighty-inch projection television, tuned to CNN Financial News with scrolling ticker tape, its sound muted. Built into the wall to the left of the screen were three racks of audio gear behind twin glass doors, topped by two smaller video monitors.

The room's only other occupant sat behind a mahogany desk in the far corner, typing undistracted at a computer.

Stryker led Nancy across the room and waved her into one of the two overstuffed chairs in front of the desk. She sank into the chair's plush cushions. The man working the terminal did not bother to look up or otherwise acknowledge the pair. He was tall and slender, in his early forties, with skeletal features, balding, with long, graying hair pulled back into a trendy ponytail and held in place by a diamond hair clip that, if genuine, would be worth her entire year's salary. She thought of a sixties hippie years later with money—lots of it. She was about to speak, until Stryker shook his head and placed an index finger across his lips.

They waited several minutes before Alexander Skile finished his work. Finally, he pressed the Enter key to send off his e-mail, then spun around in his chair and looked directly at Nancy. He scrutinized her through squinting eyes, then reclined in his huge office chair that formed a comfortable cushion around him.

"I trust General Stryker hasn't made your stay here comfortable," he said. "I prefer that special guests don't become too attached to my hospitality, or I can never get rid of them." He grinned broadly, a smug expression she immediately detested.

"My name is Dr. Nancy Shaw. I'm a biophysicist by education. I manage the database for the Centers for Disease Control in Atlanta."

"Name, rank, and serial number." Skile shook his grin away. "I know full well who you are. Do you have any idea who I am, or why I brought you here instead of leaving you to die a slow, frozen death on a godforsaken mountaintop?"

"I know *what* you are," Nancy said, glaring at him. "You're a murderer and a commander of rapists who masquerade as soldiers. I'm not sure I want to know more."

"My name is Alexander Skile," he said. "I founded AKS Technologies fifteen years ago. My firm designs and manufactures highly specialized microprocessors primarily for the aerospace industry. Thanks mainly to highly sensitive military contracts, AKS at its peak was an eight-billion-dollar private company."

"Congratulations," she said. "I'm sure you must feel very proud."

"Do you know how much I earned on military contracts this year?"

"I'm sure it's impressive."

"Zero," he said. "Zero. At the end of 'ninety-eight, AKS lost its military contracts to a low bidder who can't possibly match our quality." There was strained bitterness in his voice. "Now my company's future is not so bright."

"Damn that free enterprise," she mocked.

Skile lifted his feet up onto the desk and put the tips of his fingers together. "Let's talk about why you're here. You and thirty-five equally qualified information technology professionals were destined for Cheyenne Mountain Air Station, about two hundred–odd miles from here. Unfortunately, your aircraft suffered a mishap en route and some of you didn't make it. Why do you think that happened?"

"Please," she said, "if you want me to play some morbid game—"

"Why do you think that mishap occurred?" he pressed.

Nancy shook her head. "Engine fatigue? A missile? Bad directions?"

"Computer failure," Skile said, a hint of pride in his voice. "A computer failure I engineered."

"*You?*" Nancy gasped.

Skile nodded. "It was an attack every bit as effective and lethal as a surface-to-air missile. I'm surprised anyone survived at all—a tribute to your pilot's skill, I'm sure. Too bad he didn't make it; I would have put him on my payroll. The passengers in the second Black Hawk weren't supposed to reach the mountain either. They are extremely fortunate, thanks to a clever backup computer I hadn't anticipated."

Nancy looked at him, incredulous. "You killed fourteen people. . . . Why?"

Skile shrugged as though the answer was obvious. "So they wouldn't reach Cheyenne. You and the others were the hand-picked best in this area. I can't allow that sort of brainpower to assemble to sniff through my circuits and pry into my secrets. Who can say? You might have been lucky and actually found something."

Nancy closed her eyes and shook her throbbing head. "I don't understand. Found what?"

Skile waved away the question. "It doesn't matter."

She opened her eyes. "What do you want from me that you can't simply take?"

"I have a very simple request," Skile said. "I need you to log into Stanford's mainframe and circumvent the security firewall so I can access the university's personnel records. I'd do it myself, but I can't risk leaving my cyber-fingerprints."

"Then what?"

"Then I will print off the résumés of several individuals I know are on file there. You see, it's very simple."

"If this is about taking sick revenge over lost government contracts because you're poor again . . ."

General Stryker leaned forward in his chair and appealed to her. "Dr. Shaw, you must do as he says. Otherwise I cannot protect you."

"Who are you people?" she demanded. "What is this circus about, anyway?"

Skile let out a squeal of laughter that sent shudders through Nancy. "No circus, Doctor," he said. "The general commands an army of very devoted soldiers with ties to the Order of the Dark Star, doomsday's most violent movement. Your timing is fortunate. Tonight they will begin three days of celebration. And then they will be gone."

"Celebrate what?"

"The end of the world," Skile said. He gestured to the general. "Tell her."

General Stryker took Nancy's hand into his own. "God has given us indisputable signs that Armageddon will commence in three days. He said that 'those of us who have faith shall rule in my kingdom as my soldiers. Captivity for those who are destined for captivity; the sword for those who are to die by the sword.' " Stryker shook his head in amazement. "We are about to leave this earth to find a new dimension of truth and absolution, far from the hypocrisies of this world. It is a wondrous time."

Nancy looked at Skile, who sat there grinning. "You're incredibly mad—both of you."

The general gently squeezed her hand. "I know this is extremely difficult for you to comprehend. There is little time left to properly orientate you. Nevertheless, I want you to bear witness to it—with me."

She brushed away his hand. "What difference does it make if I die today or in three days?"

"Death does not exist, Doctor; it is pure illusion," General Stryker said.

"What the hell is he talking about?" Nancy asked Skile.

Skile rocked forward in his chair and set his feet on the floor. "Allow me to offer an explanation that may mean more to you.

General Stryker leads a contingent of well-armed, highly trained, highly motivated soldiers. Because they believe Armageddon is upon us, life and death no longer have meaning to them. They believe that their brand of violence is sanctioned and blessed by the universe's highest Authority. They say each of us is standing at the edge of the world, facing oblivion. To them Heaven is Sirius—the brightest star in the sky—in the constellation Canis Major, about eight and a half light-years from here. When they awaken moments after their deaths, they will join a growing force that shares their faith. Meanwhile, they have no intention of leaving this world quietly."

Skile rose from his chair. "And, unfortunately, we have a few hangers-on who are just plain psychotic."

"Careful, Alex," the general began.

Skile raised a hand in apology. "Whatever you say, General. The point is," he said, his narrow eyes focused on Nancy, "you have no choice at all in this matter. Refuse to work with me, and I will order his soldiers to make the remainder of your short life a living hell."

Nancy shook her head violently. "You're crazy for belonging to this . . . this gang."

"The general respects the fact that I do not follow his beliefs," Skile said. "Our association is simply a business partnership. He serves my needs, and in return I finance his army. I couldn't ask for a better resource to deal with my very special needs."

"You mean do your killing," Nancy said.

Skile shrugged. "Sometimes killing is necessary."

"So you invite these monsters into your home."

"I've already given this modest property to the general," Skile said. "I no longer need it. Later today I will join my wife in Chicago, where we will celebrate the end of the millennium together. For the remainder of this week the general and his men can do with this place as they please."

Skile stepped around his desk and grabbed a long overcoat draped over the wraparound couch. "Come. I want to show you something."

General Stryker stood and offered Nancy his hand.

She refused it. "These dossiers you need, whose are they?"

Skile slipped on his coat and squeezed his long, skinny hands into a pair of tight, leather gloves. "People who at this moment are at Cheyenne Mountain straying too close to my business. People who could potentially ruin my plan and me along with it. I need to know exactly how good they are."

"*Who*, for chrissake?" she demanded.

"At the top of my list is a woman named Dr. Julie Martinelli."

Chapter Twenty-five
Down

Cheyenne Mountain
Wednesday, December 29
1030 Hours

"I found it," said Eclipse Mission Commander Thomas La-Grange.

Julie, Colonel Beckman, and Henry Princeton each jumped from their respective chairs, where they had settled into a silent, melancholy stupor. They pushed in around his console.

LaGrange refined the coordinates scrolling down the side of his screen, while the colored image from the display in the darkened war room reflected in his glasses. "I should have figured as much."

"Where is it?" Beckman demanded.

"The satellite came down about three hundred miles from here," he said, "elevation ten thousand feet." LaGrange pulled up a topographical map of Colorado and put it on one of the large projection screens. He zoomed into the southwest corner of the state. "You couldn't get more remote. The closest road is through a town called Washington Peak, population one hundred twenty-seven.''

"How far is our site from the closest road?" Beckman asked.

LaGrange keyed more numbers into his terminal. "Approximately one hundred eleven miles, all mountain terrain."

Beckman whirled away from the console. "*Jesus.* That'll take a week to reach by overland trails, assuming there are trails through that terrain."

"Give it up, Colonel," Henry said. "It just isn't meant to be."

"*Bullshit.*" Beckman appealed to General Patterson, who had been sitting aloof from the others in an office chair against the wall, twisting his class ring around his pinkie. "We need to get a chopper into that area."

"Can't do it," the general decided. "All aircraft are grounded, including military flights. That's straight from the White House."

"Sir, this is an *emergency*," Beckman said. "We can get an exception."

"Everything this week is an emergency," the general said. "I've been on the phone to the Pentagon twice already this morning. They're not going to budge. There have already been four military crashes since the stand-down began. All of them violated the order. No business case in the world, no emergency scenario you can construct, is going to get you authorization for a flight."

Colonel Beckman swung his arm in frustration. "That's unacceptable. We *need* this."

"As I said," Henry said, gathering up his notebooks to leave, "it isn't meant to be."

"Gentlemen," Julie said, looking straight up at the topographical map on the overhead screen, "that satellite went down in the same set of ridges where Nancy's Black Hawk crashed."

"Are you saying there's some connection?" the colonel asked. Henry watched her closely.

"Perhaps," she said. "What if there is already an aircraft airborne in that area?"

"There isn't," Beckman snapped. "So stop wasting our time."

"If you're going to do any wishing," Henry said, snickering, "then wish it was this time next week."

Julie appealed confidently to the general. "It's no wish, sir. I know for a fact that there's an aircraft airborne in that area. And the people flying are just crazy enough to ignore the stand-down.''

Colorado Rockies
1040 Hours

''Tell me you didn't deliberately disobey my order and fly the Comanche out of New Mexico,'' General Medlock said, his voice thin and angry over Marshall's headset.

Marshall gave Williams a sideways glance and mouthed *He's pissed.*

Williams put an unlit cigar between his teeth. ''What else is new?''

Marshall keyed his microphone and said over the secure channel to Fort Bragg, ''What makes you think we left New Mexico, sir?''

''Don't push it, Colonel,'' Medlock said. ''I know your every move before it even occurs to you.''

''General—''

''Now listen to me carefully,'' Medlock said. ''The Comanche was involved in a train derailment in the thwarting of a hijacking. Am I correct?''

''Yes, sir.''

''The aircraft sustained some damage,'' Medlock said, ''and you weren't able to get your radio operational. So you've been out of touch with us since then. Correct?''

''General,'' Marshall said, ''our radio is working fine thanks to—''

''You're not listening to me,'' Medlock spat. ''I'll ask you again: You were not able to get your radio operational. Correct?''

''Yes, General,'' Marshall said.

''So you have no knowledge at this time of the military aircraft stand-down,'' Medlock said.

''What's this all about?'' Marshall asked.

''You have no knowledge of the military aircraft stand-down,'' he repeated.

''Correct.''

''Thank you,'' Medlock said. ''In about ten minutes, I'll send you via COMSAT a set of coordinates for a piece of military hardware you are to recover. I'll also send you the frequency of a ping signal you can home in on. You're to go to those coordinates, retrieve the hardware, then deliver it immediately to Cheyenne Mountain.''

"What hardware?" Marshall asked. "What's going on?"

"You'll be recovering a module from the world's most sophisticated military surveillance satellite," the general said. "You'll also allow me to return a favor to a certain General Patterson, who needs a miracle right now."

Chapter Twenty-six
Persuasion

Willard, Colorado
Wednesday, December 29
1050 Hours

"It's quite beautiful up here this time of year," Skile said. "Don't you agree?"

Nancy said nothing.

Skile, dressed comfortably in a long camel-hair coat, led the way through a grove of pines deep into the woods behind his chateau. Nancy shuffled through the snow behind him, while General Stryker followed. No one had offered her a coat. She was rapidly losing body heat and shivering so severely that she thought she might collapse in a convulsive fit.

Skile led them to what first appeared to be a shed. He opened the door to reveal a set of dimly lit steps not unlike those leading to the cellar in which she had spent the night. They descended in single file. The stone walls on either side felt like blocks of ice on Nancy's bare hands. They entered a small chamber at the bottom, perhaps a hundred feet square; the darkness made it impossible to determine its exact dimensions. Skile snapped on a pocket light and directed its thin beam into a corner, illuminating a heap of chains fastened to the stone floor with a heavy O-ring.

Skile beckoned her. "Over here."

Nancy wrapped her arms tightly around her chest and began shaking uncontrollably. Skile grabbed her arm and yanked her into the corner.

"I haven't got much *time*," he said.

Skile fastened a pair of leg irons around each of her ankles and locked them. He directed the light at the face of his watch. "I'm leaving here by helicopter promptly at three. I'll have with me those dossiers I've asked you for. If for any reason I don't . . . well, there will be consequences."

Skile nodded to General Stryker, who lifted an oil lantern from the floor by the wall, produced a lighter, and lit its wick. The flame, smoky and pungent, offered the cell modest illumination. Skile took the lantern and, raising it over his head, allowed its light to fall upon another figure chained to the floor across from Nancy. At first she didn't recognize the form as anything human. But it was a man. Both his legs and his right hand had been amputated, leaving only his left wrist around which to attach a single metal cuff. A pointless precaution; this man wasn't going anywhere. The stumps had been crudely cauterized with what appeared to be tar. He lay there naked, and Nancy could see that even his genitals had been removed. His face was bloodied and swollen, and she could distinguish a mustache, but little else. The man was perhaps in his thirties—she couldn't be certain through his permanent mask of anguish.

Nancy looked away. "What have you done?"

General Stryker stepped into the light of Skile's lantern, and his tone when he spoke was apologetic. "We do not condone this action. The soldier who did this is an imbecile with the intelligence of a six-year-old. He thought it necessary for the man's own salvation. I know this must look terrible to you but, you see, this man's body is merely a shell—"

"*Shut up!*" she screamed.

General Stryker fell silent and just looked at her, dejected that he could not make her understand.

"They found him at your chopper's wreckage site this morning," Skile said. "His name is Richard. He told us he is a skier and a mountain climber, but I don't think he'll be doing either anytime soon. What do you think?"

Nancy, her eyes downcast, said nothing.

"He's been given regular injections of antibiotics for infection, fluids, and an amphetamine to keep him awake," Skile said.

He removed a small bottle of ammonia from his pocket, uncorked it, and squatted beside the man. He waved the opened bottle under his prisoner's nose. Richard shook himself awake with a start and began choking.

When he saw it was Skile, he turned his head away. "Leave me alone."

"I need something from you," Skile said.

The man shook his head vehemently. "I will give you *nothing*. You have already killed me."

"Not so fast," Skile said. "I want you to meet your new cellmate. May I present to you Dr. Nancy Shaw." Skile raised the lantern to her.

Richard was barely able to open one swollen eye to look at her. He shook his head. "No . . . no more."

Skile put his face close to the man's ear. "You will convince her to work with me. You understand the consequences of resisting."

"No!" he shouted. "This must stop."

Skile slapped the man's face with a sharp brush of his hand. "If you are unsuccessful, you will watch the same fate befall her."

Richard began to weep bitterly. *"Please . . . no more . . . no more!"*

Chapter Twenty-seven
Deep Six

Colorado Rockies
Wednesday, December 29
1205 Hours

"Cool your jets, gentlemen. We're nearly there."

Jill brought the Comanche up over a peak and sunk into a quarrylike canyon as deep as it was wide. A huge lake filled the canyon like water in a bowl.

"Uh-oh," Jill said. "You guys see this?"

"We see it," Marshall said. He put a pair of small binoculars to his eyes and scanned the slim bank for a possible landing site. There was little foliage at this altitude and the crag looked like red clay.

Williams shook his head. "That bird sure doesn't want to get found."

Jill brought the Comanche down to within one hundred feet of the lake's surface. "The transponder signal is approximately two hundred yards from shore. I'll need to triangulate its exact vector."

"Depth?" Marshall asked.

"About one hundred fifty feet."

"Salvageable," Marshall declared.

"Don't dive in yet," she said. "It gets a whole lot deeper toward the middle."

"What does a whole lot mean?" Marshall asked.

"More than a thousand feet," she said.

Williams bit down hard on his cigar stub. "Do you get the feeling someone's messing with us?"

"Hello," Jill announced. "We just flew past it."

Jill banked the chopper ninety degrees and brought it around on a reciprocal heading. "Our baby's in ninety feet of water!"

"I can deal with that," Williams said.

"Who's the lucky guy who gets to go down for it?" Jill asked.

"I will," Marshall said.

"No you won't," Williams said. "I'll do it. Ninety feet is a walk in the park."

"You're both nuts," Jill said. "You're forgetting I took the Illinois State Swimming Championship in 'ninety-four. I'm going."

They set the Comanche down on a gravel beach on the northern shore and kept the turboshaft engines at idle. Jill stood by the surf dressed in a heavy nylon flight suit, which she hoped would offer modest insulation from the near-freezing water.

Williams handed her a quart-size tank of compressed air. "This should give you a couple of breaths. If you need more, get your butt back to shore."

Jill accepted the container. It looked like a small hospital respirator with a flexible tube attached to its nozzle. "How do I use it?"

Williams held up the end of the tube. "Keep this in your mouth and put your tongue on the end to keep a seal. Each time you need a breath, exhale from the side of your mouth, turn this valve to full, and let the air fill your lungs. Be careful, though; as the air starts running out, the pressure at ninety feet will play some weird tricks on you."

Jill nodded and threaded the tank onto her utility belt.

Marshall withdrew a section of winch cable and stretched it out toward them. "The weight of this cable will take you to the bottom. Hook the end wherever you can. Pull twice when it's secure, and I'll haul you and it out."

"This is your last chance to give me this assignment," Williams said to Jill.

A cheery smile spread over her lips. "This should be fun. After this, I may just join the SEALs."

Marshall didn't share her amusement; there were too many aspects of this operation he didn't like. He said somberly, "Let's get this over with."

The colonel climbed into the Comanche's cockpit and advanced the throttles. When the torque reached seventy-five percent he pulled up on the collective and lifted the aircraft to twenty-five feet. He engaged the hoist's motor and let the cable feed until the hook nearly touched the ground.

Williams said into his VHF radio, "Far enough."

The cable stopped.

Jill tied her sandy hair back and put on a pair of goggles she hoped would offer a seal around her eyes. She stuck her right foot into the cable's curved hook and grabbed the winch cable. She gave Williams a thumbs-up.

"She's ready," the sergeant said into the radio.

Marshall eased Jill off the ground and allowed her a moment to distribute her weight onto the hook. She gave Williams another "ready" hand signal.

"Take her away, Joe," Williams said.

Marshall pitched the rotors slightly and carried Jill slowly over the lake. He watched the readouts through his Helmet Mounted Display and maneuvered the chopper to the coordinates Jill had preprogrammed. Marshall opened the Comanche's external loudspeaker and said to her, "We're almost there."

She waved at the camera on the Comanche's underbelly.

Several dozen yards farther, Marshall put the Comanche into a programmed hover at twenty-five feet and switched the rotors to whisper mode to minimize the downwash.

"I'm going to lower you at five feet per second," he said through the loudspeaker. "The ball and hook will take you down."

She waved her acknowledgment.

Marshall activated the winch. The cable played out slowly and lowered Jill into the water. When she was fully submerged, Marshall increased the rate of descent to get her to the bottom as quickly as possible.

The cold water struck Jill like a cruel blow, and she fought the urge to draw in a great lungful of air. The lake was dark and murky. She had only the vaguest sense of her frightening surroundings. She couldn't see the bottom, and it was impossible to determine how deep she was sinking.

Above her, Marshall illuminated the Comanche's belly-mounted dual twelve-hundred-watt halogen spot lamps. The murky world around Jill suddenly lit up and glowed a strange gold, like light though a honey jar. She could see the lake bed about ten feet below rising steadily to meet her. Seconds later, she touched the ground with a soft squash that sent up a cloud of snowy sediment.

The cable stopped. Marshall's gauge of the water's depth was impeccably accurate thanks to the Comanche's topographical radar.

Jill's first task was to breathe. She let out the spent air in her lungs, then turned the valve of her belt-mounted tank of compressed air. A rush of air poured into her lungs. She had to work quickly to close the valve before spilling precious air from her lips. The sensation of artificial breathing was peculiar, but she conceded that it worked well. She noticed a tiny stream of water seeping into her goggles. In a minute or two they would be completely filled. *Let's get to work*, she thought.

Jill made a slow turn, scrutinizing every shadow and shape across the lake bed for anything that resembled a satellite. It didn't take her long to spot this particular bird—the size and shape of the spacecraft was unmistakable. About twenty yards from her, a five-foot-high, drum-shaped spacecraft stood tilted on its end like the Leaning Tower of Pisa. Its three melted, eight-foot-long equipment masts stretched and twisted outward like alien arms.

Jill gave the cable a hard tug and began swimming awkwardly through the murk toward the spacecraft.

Williams, standing onshore with the binoculars pressed against his eyes, said into his radio, "She sees it."

In response to her signal, Marshall slowly played out more cable in pace with her movements. When she reached the satellite, she paused to take another breath from the tank. Perhaps it was just her imagination, but the air pressure seemed less than the first time.

Don't even think of panicking, she warned herself.

The water was still seeping inside her goggles and now covered the lower third of her eyes. She tilted her head slightly to let the water flow forward and momentarily give her clear vision—a quick fix good for another few seconds.

Jill quickly inspected the satellite. It was nothing like she imagined. The Blackbird appeared to be constructed from three distinct modules. One-third was the base, which had few features on it and fewer places to connect the cable.

Jill pulled out a watertight flashlight and circled the satellite, searching for a place to secure the winch's hook. She was aware of the changing angle and texture of Marshall's spotlights as he followed her movements on the radar and repositioned the Comanche over her. Every bit helped. She allowed herself another generous breath. She was now certain that the air from the tank did not expel with the same force as it had for her previous breaths.

She moved her flashlight's beam along the face of the satellite and spotted something odd—an opening that had once held a module. It didn't make sense to her that a satellite would be launched minus some of its parts. She directed the beam along the lake bed and found no pieces of wreckage or other signs that a crash landing had jarred the unit free. She returned her light beam to the empty equipment bay and ran a finger over the mounting surface. Someone with the right tools had expertly removed the screws and clips. Who could have taken it? And, more important, to where?

Jill needed air more frequently and turned the tank's valve to full. It took a disturbing amount of time for the air to fill her lungs. Her hands were stiff from the cold, and maneuvering the cable was becoming increasingly difficult. She was rapidly running out of time.

She decided to attach the hook to a handlelike protrusion jutting from the base of the satellite. She hadn't a clue of the handle's original purpose and imagined a space-shuttle astronaut grabbing it to haul the satellite into the ship's cargo bay. She wished she had the luxury of a warm space suit.

Jill gave the cable two hard pulls to signal Marshall. She opened the valve and drew in greedily what she knew would be her last breath from the tank. *Time to go.*

171

With a deep grinding sound, the Comanche pulled the satellite free of the sucking mud and dragged it through clouds of sediment. It moved faster than Jill expected. She grabbed for the base, but her stiff hands couldn't find a secure hold. The satellite slid from her grasp and began its ascent without her.

Jill raced after it, kicking and thrashing her legs. But common sense quickly prevailed—she realized there was no way to catch up with it. Instead of exhausting the precious little air in her lungs on an adrenaline rush, she followed the satellite at a distance and ascended at a calm, steady rate.

Marshall hoisted the satellite out of the lake and watched the water cascade off it. Where was Jill? He switched to infrared to look for her heat signature.

The satellite suddenly exploded in a great fireball. Marshall's helmet display went white. He struggled with the controls as the shock wave nearly knocked the Comanche from the air.

Williams watched the flaming debris fall back into the lake. *"Fuck me."*

Thirty feet below the surface, the blast's concussion forced the last of the air from Jill's lungs. The turbulence swept her along head over heels through the falling debris like a leaf in a windstorm. She fumbled with the tank's valve and sucked greedily. But there was no air left to draw. She spat out the tube and began swimming toward the surface with great strokes and kicks. Her limbs were unresponsive, the water heavy. Her lungs ached and threatened to collapse.

Jill lost all sense of direction. She fought the reflex to breathe deeply and knew that in a matter of moments she would black out. *Focus*, she told herself. *Focus on surviving*.

Suddenly, her head broke the surface.

Jill inhaled great lungfuls of air between fits of coughing. Her throat and sinuses burned. She tore off her goggles and tossed them away from her. Through clouded vision, she saw the Comanche hovering over her, its downwash punishing her. She didn't care—it looked wonderful!

The winch cable had been sheared off in the blast, leaving nothing for Jill to grab. Marshall lowered the Comanche's landing gear and descended to the surface of the water. Jill grabbed its undercarriage. She tried to hoist herself up but had no strength left.

With the Comanche's wheel in the water, Marshall pitched the aircraft forward and began moving toward shore at a steady fourteen knots. He watched Jill on his display. She appeared unconscious, but her grip on the undercarriage remained firm.

Williams watched her through binoculars. "Hold on, honey. Hold on just a little longer."

Marshall reached the surf and brought the aircraft to a hover rather than risk dragging Jill over the rocks on the beach. She let her arms slip through the undercarriage and set herself down in waist-deep water. Her legs collapsed and her head vanished beneath the surface. Williams bolted into the surf after her. He lifted her up into his arms and carried her to shore.

Her skin was pale, her lips blue. He set her down on the gravel beach and lightly slapped each of her cheeks. "C'mon, sweetie. Stay with me."

He snapped off her gloves and rubbed her hands to restore the circulation. "C'mon, baby, wake up. Talk to me."

Jill's eyes fluttered open.

Williams smiled. "That's right, sweetie. Talk to me."

"I'm cold," she said, "very cold. I can't feel my legs."

"I'm gonna build you the biggest bonfire right out here on this beach."

She forced a smile. "Just tell the colonel to direct the exhaust this way and throttle up to six hundred RPMs. That'll be toasty."

Williams's expression turned grim. "Sorry you went through all that for nothing. The satellite's gone. Looks like it was boobytrapped."

She closed her eyes. "We did good. Its cargo is safe."

"Say what?"

"We weren't the first to find it. Someone with a good deal of knowledge about that satellite removed a module, then threw the rest of it into the lake. They were counting on us eventually finding it, so they mined it and put it in shallow water."

Williams put a cigar into his mouth and bit down hard. "Well, I'll be a son of a bitch. Looks like our little rescue op isn't over yet."

* * *

"This is Alpha One Two Five to Mother," Marshall said into his headset's mouthpiece.

"You've got Mother," a voice squawked back. "Please stand by."

There followed an annoying silence during which time Marshall looked questioningly at Williams, who folded his arms impatiently, then at Jill, who stood nearby with a blanket wrapped around her. She was still shivering.

"Medlock here," said a voice from Fort Bragg. "Give me an update."

"Someone reached the satellite before us," Marshall said. "We found it on the bottom of a lake. A charge destroyed it when we tried to raise her."

"*Damn!*" Medlock spat. "That was valuable evidence."

"What we need may not have been destroyed," Marshall said. "Jill says a module had been removed by someone who knew what he was doing."

"Removed?" said Medlock. "That's interesting."

"Finding it will be difficult, though," Marshall said. "The unit could be out of the country by now."

"If the module is still intact," Medlock countered, "I can tell you exactly where it is."

Marshall looked at the others quizzically. Williams continued chewing the end of his unlit cigar, and Jill just shrugged. "How do you figure?"

"Each one of the Blackbird's storage units is equipped with its own homing beacon embedded right onto its circuit board," Medlock explained. "In the unlikely event the unit ever falls into enemy hands, we can find it. Stand by, and I'll have the signal activated."

A full minute passed before the general came back on-line. "The beacon is now operational. Scan on frequency one-double-oh-four-eight."

Marshall keyed in the military frequency per the general's instruction. A blip appeared on the aircraft's GPS screen.

"Well, I'll be damned," Marshall said, zooming in on the coordinates. "The son of a bitch works! The signal is less than one hundred miles from here."

"I've got something else for you," Medlock said. "Army Intelligence has linked the tattoo you found and the hijacking of the Comanche to a paramilitary brigade who claim a loose allegiance to Dark Star.''

"Come again?''

"The tattoo you saw is the star Sirius, which a lot of folks believe is heaven,'' Medlock explained. "Members of this renegade group are very well-equipped doomsday militants who have officially and unofficially been connected to dozens of bombings and massacres in Europe and the United States during the past year. Their latest party in Madrid two weeks ago claimed twenty-three lives. Nasty stuff. Watch this gang, Joe.''

"Perhaps we've seen the last of them,'' Marshall said.

"Don't count on it,'' the general said. "They're well infiltrated in this country. Army Intelligence has confirmed their presence in your area—those mountains may even be their base. We can't track them without satellite reconnaissance and aircraft surveillance.''

Marshall's mind was reeling. "Is there a connection with this group and this lost satellite?''

"It's very possible. So watch your backs. Fortunately, you've got the Army's best reconnaissance aircraft. See that you don't lose it.''

"Are we still officially grounded?''

"Bet your ass,'' Medlock said. "And your radio is still busted. Now find that unit and take it to Cheyenne before the President personally roasts my hide.''

"Anything else?'' Marshall asked.

"Yeah, don't let anybody see you.''

Chapter Twenty-eight
Martyr

Willard, Colorado
Wednesday, December 29
1430 Hours

The door to the shed flew open and a frigid blast poured down the stone steps. Enveloped in its icy fingers, Nancy shivered involuntarily.

"Don't . . ." a hoarse voice managed from the darkened corner. "Don't be a martyr." It was Richard.

"What are you talking about?" she whispered.

"Our moral sensibilities . . . they don't mean a thing up here," he said. "They'll inflict a living death on you . . . don't let them. *Save yourself.*"

"I still don't understand—"

Someone began descending the steps. When the figure reached the bottom, an electric lamp flared on and threw off an even light that filled every corner.

Its bearer was Alexander Skile, holding a notebook computer in his left hand. Another figure—the large, dumpy soldier who had taken Nancy to the house earlier—descended the staircase behind him. He carried a rusty chain saw in one hand and a rolled-up leather satchel in the other.

Skile crouched before Nancy. The strong light cast an otherworldly aura over his skeletal features as they stretched into a grin she had come to loathe. She turned away from him.

"You know why I'm here," he said. "You can either give me what I want now, or five minutes from now after you lose your first limb."

"Screw you!" she spat. "It makes me physically ill to look at you."

"Do as he asks," Richard sighed. "He'll take what he wants anyway. Your sacrifice . . . will be for nothing."

Skile glanced over his shoulder and said to the brute, "Tim, I'm pressed for time. Please begin."

Tim unrolled his leather pouch, revealing several long needles and coarse, black thread.

"We convinced Tim that using tar to cauterize wounds is right out of the Dark Ages," Skile said. "Severe wounds are sewn closed, not tarred or burned. Isn't that right, Tim?"

The brute glanced up from his tools. "No tar . . . I sew . . ."

"You see," Skile laughed, "Tim learns very well."

Tears flowed from Nancy eyes, and she was trembling terribly. Skile waved his notebook computer at her. "Do you know what this is?"

She was too frightened to speak.

When she didn't answer, he explained, "It's a wireless terminal that connects to a network by a digital cellular phone. We can log into Stanford's network from right down here. What can be more convenient?"

He opened the lid of his portable Compaq Armada and the screen immediately blinked to life. He pressed the Enter key. Nancy heard a modem dialing, followed by a high whine as the machine made a network connection. In a moment, Stanford's main menu popped up onto the screen.

"That part was easy." Skile set the computer at her feet. "The next step is yours. I need you to log into Stanford's personnel records. Once you're in, I can proceed."

"But," she managed, "I don't have a password—"

Skile raised a quick hand to silence her. "You are a database manager by profession. I believe you will have little difficulty accessing a system belonging to an institution with which you've had an affiliation for the past seventeen years. I could do it easily, but the process would leave traces pointing back to me."

Nancy made no attempt to comply with his request.

"Do what he asks," Richard urged. "There's no honor in this martyrdom."

Skile stood and sighed. "I'm going outside for some air. When I return in five minutes, you will be missing a leg, and good Tim here will have sewn you up. Each time I ask you to assist me and you refuse—or your password fails—you will lose another limb."

Nancy felt dizzy, and she thought she might slip into shock. Don't pass out now, she warned herself. Stay coherent. *Stay alive!*

Skile nodded to Tim. The brute picked up his rusty chain saw and pulled the cord. The machine sputtered and coughed, and finally gave out, leaving behind a smelly residue of smoke. The brute tried again, with the same result.

Skile buttoned his long, camel-hair coat and began climbing the steps.

"Okay!" Nancy yelled after him, her voice bordering on hysteria. "I'll do what you want!"

Skile stopped midstride and mocked, "Are you sure? I can give you five minutes to think about it."

She extended a trembling hand over the computer and keyed in several commands, including her password. Grinning, Skile put his hands in his pockets and strolled over to watch her.

Nancy pressed Enter and drew back, loathing to be near the machine. "There. You're in. Does that make you happy?"

Skile stooped down, removed his hands from his pockets, and picked up the computer. On the screen was the main menu to Stanford's personnel files. He was now free to call up the file of any individual in Stanford's database by simply entering a last name or social security number. All activity would be logged to her ID.

He offered her a smile of gratitude. "You're a very smart woman."

Skile carried the computer with its display still open across the cell and vanished smartly up the steps. The brute, however, made no overtures to follow him. Instead, he pulled the cord of the chain saw. This time it caught, sputtering and smoking, and began whining unevenly.

Nancy's eyes widened. "What do you think you're doing!?"

The brute tweaked the choke until the chain saw whined evenly. He throttled it several times as he lumbered toward her.

178

"Noooooo!" Richard shrieked.

Nancy shrank into the corner. "Keep away from me! KEEP AWAY!"

Tim thrust the chain saw's blade to within a breath of her face. Its roar in the confined, solid space so near to her was deafening. Nancy stared at it, utterly paralyzed.

A hand encircled the brute's wrist and firmly pulled him away from her. General Stryker, appearing as if from nowhere, shook his head as a father might scold a misbehaving son. "Don't do it."

The whining of the chain saw continued unabated. Stryker reached down, closed the choke, and let the machine die. The brute looked at Stryker, and for the first time Nancy saw emotion in those dead eyes of his—it was genuine fear. The soldier gestured in her direction and grunted a few unintelligible words, incapable of offering any coherent explanation.

Stryker cocked his head. "Leave here."

The soldier brushed past him and, his tools in hand, began a slow ascent up the stairs.

Stryker stooped in front of Nancy. "I am sorry. Truly I am." He raised a hand to touch her face, but she turned away and, weeping, buried her face into the corner.

"What have I done?"

Stryker shook his head in regret, grabbed the electric lamp Skile had left, and retreated up the stone staircase.

"Oh God!" she sobbed. "What have I done?"

"There is no shame," Richard reassured her from the darkness. "You had no choice . . . no choice at all."

Chapter Twenty-nine
Darkness

Willard, Colorado
Wednesday, December 29
1445 Hours

The Hummer all-terrain vehicle rolled out of the remote garage and headed up the snowy road toward the airfield. Alexander Skile sat in the passenger seat with his notebook computer in his lap searching through Stanford's on-line personnel database. He pulled up the dossier of Dr. Julie Martinelli and read it with keen interest. Very impressive. Here was the story of a gifted woman who seemingly could accomplish anything. In her youthful life she had accomplished more in several diverse fields than most narrowly focused scientists achieved in a lifetime. She was indeed extraordinary.

Skile stared at the file's two-year-old color portrait of Julie, whose image radiated with intelligence and self-confidence. Quite beautiful, he admitted. And dangerous. He withdrew a cellular phone from inside his suit coat and punched a preprogrammed number. The call bounced to Henry Princeton's voice mail.

At the beep, Skile said, "You're definitely outclassed, my friend. Begin Clean Sweep immediately."

The Millennium Project

A loud clanging jarred Julie from a deep sleep. She sat bolt upright, her heart racing, her eyes open wide to the room's blackness. The desk phone emitted another jarring ring—the room's previous user had set it to full volume. At first she thought she'd overslept. She looked at the indigo readout of her watch—just after 3:00 P.M. Still another twenty minutes left to this break.

The phone rang again. *No rest for the war weary.* She popped from the bed, snapped on the desk lamp, and sat down before the phone.

Julie lifted the receiver and expelled a hoarse "Martinelli."

"Beckman here."

Julie rolled her eyes and shook her head. "What can I do for you, Colonel?"

"Stop by my quarters before you go off break?"

Julie put a hand on her forehead to stem the pounding that had begun the moment she sat up. "Am I getting another reprimand?"

"Negative," Beckman said. "I owe you a favor. Your friends found the satellite at the bottom of a mountain lake."

Her interest was suddenly piqued. "That's wonderful! Can they salvage it?"

"They're already finished. But there was a problem."

Her heart missed a beat. "Are they all right?"

"They're fine," Beckman said. "But some son of a bitch booby-trapped the satellite and destroyed it. The explosives were intended to kill whoever salvaged it. Fortunately, none of our people were hurt."

"Thank God. But that puts us right back where we started."

"Maybe not," Beckman said. "Before the satellite was destroyed, the diver was able to determine that the storage module had already been removed."

"Removed? By whom?"

"Don't know. There aren't many clues left."

"What else do we know?" she asked.

"The missing module has a built-in transponder, and we've vectored its location," Beckman said. "Your friends are heading for it right now. They should be there in minutes."

181

"So where is it?"

"That's what I need to discuss with you, and I'd rather not do it over the phone. It's extremely confidential."

"Interesting." Julie looked at her watch. "Give me ten minutes to step under the shower and change."

1512 Hours

Julie burst through the double doors and moved briskly down the elite apartment wing for officers stationed at Cheyenne Mountain. Surprisingly, the corridor was empty. The schedules of the various teams had become so erratic that at all hours she expected to see people on their way to meetings or heading back to their rooms to cop a nap. *Did someone not tell me about a town hall?*

The corridor lights extinguished with a sudden bang that made Julie jump. Red safety lights clicked on.

DING! DING! DING!

"*Attention all personnel,*" a metallic voice echoed down the hallway. "*Attention all personnel.*"

Julie stopped to listen.

"*There has been an unscheduled interruption to Cheyenne Mountain Air Station's power grid. For safety reasons, you are instructed to remain where you are. Repeat. For safety reasons, you are instructed to remain where you are. You will be noti- fieeeeeeddddddddddd . . .*"

The voice wound to a stop as though someone had pulled the plug on a tape machine. Then the crimson emergency lights blinked off, leaving only barely adequate local battery backups. Julie waited an impatient thirty seconds for the lights to return. They didn't. Finally, the even background rumble of the ventilation system stopped. In the vacuum of silence that followed, Julie thought she heard someone running up a flight of steps. Was there even a staircase nearby? She stared into the dimness but saw no one.

"This is too creepy," she muttered to herself.

Julie hurried along the corridor, her eyes struggling to make out the nameplates beside each door, searching for the colonel's. It didn't take her long to find "Beckman." She knocked and waited anxiously for a reply. No one came. Were the officers' quarters so large he couldn't hear her?

Annoyed, Julie knocked again, this time much harder. "Colonel Beckman?"

Again, no answer. *But he's expecting me.* She tried the doorknob and, to her surprise, found the door unlocked. She peered inside.

"Colonel?"

Silence.

Julie slipped into the colonel's apartment. The living room was dark and still except for a lone safety light glowing in the kitchen area. She took a tentative step toward it.

Something she saw startled her—a silhouette sitting in a reclining chair.

"Colonel Beckman . . ." she began, "I'm sorry, but when you didn't answer . . . the door was unlocked . . ."

The figure didn't move. Certainly the colonel was exhausted, she thought, and like her, he probably could fall asleep anywhere, anytime, during any stolen moment.

"Colonel!" she shouted.

He didn't stir.

Julie slipped into the tiny kitchen and unplugged the emergency safety light—the kind that sat unobtrusively, always recharging. When power was interrupted, the low-wattage unit came on automatically.

Julie carried it into the living room and directed its beam at the figure in the chair. She nearly dropped the light.

"Oh my God!"

Colonel Beckman stared back at her from the comfort of his chair. A large-caliber handgun had put a bullet at close range through the side of his head. The wall beside him was spattered with bone and brain matter, and a long string of bloody drool hung from his lower lip and draped down the front of his T-shirt. An army-issued Colt .45 dangled from his right index finger.

A buzzing filled Julie's ears and her stomach gave an involuntary heave. Her head felt extremely light. She eased herself onto the colonel's sofa and put her head between her knees.

"Colonel," she gasped. "What do you think you're doing?"

When the nausea eased, she raised her head and spotted a hastily scribbled note on the low table before the colonel. She grabbed it and read:

> Forgive my haste, but I now must leave this earth and enter a new dimension of truth where I shall rule in His kingdom as soldier. I leave nothing behind of value. My work here has been hypocritical and will serve no useful end. My only regret is not taking you all with me on this passage. But there is no time. I am leaving that task to others here who share my vision and my conviction to support this extraordinary event. "Captivity for those destined for captivity; the sword for those who are to die by the sword."
> Beckman

The note slipped from Julie's hand and fluttered to the floor.

Chapter Thirty
Mountain Chateau

Willard, Colorado
Wednesday, December 29
1520 Hours

"If I'd known we'd be climbing mountains, I'd have put on extra socks," Williams said to Marshall as they made their way up the steep, snow-covered path. "We're not dressed for this weather."

The colonel agreed. Their flight jackets worked well in moderate weather but were far from adequate at this altitude in winter. Nor were their field boots warm enough. If they didn't get out of the snow soon, there would be a serious issue of frostbite to deal with.

The sky was overcast, the wind, gratefully, calm. They had little trouble following the telltale signs in the snow of heavy foot traffic that had passed this way earlier. According to Marshall's handheld GPS unit, the satellite module was just ahead of them. The signal hadn't moved since they'd acquired it, suggesting the unit had reached its ultimate destination. But why bring it up here? And who was responsible?

As they approached the top of the hill, there came shouting and laughing ahead beyond a line of Douglas firs. They moved forward, staying well hidden behind the fir branches. In the clearing beyond, they saw people milling about an impressive piece of property that looked like a posh ski resort. A huge, multilevel house rose into the winter sky like a fortress. The cozy aroma of burning wood drifted passed them. Whoever owned this estate had lots of money and knew how to spend it in style.

Marshall raised his binoculars. He counted about a dozen men, each armed with a fully automatic, military-issue M16 or a Russian-made AK-47 assault rifle, and dressed in similar white parkas with hoods. On the far side of the estate Marshall spotted a trio of mutilated corpses hanging from a tree by their necks. He refocused on a group of soldiers using the bodies for target practice.

Marshall removed the binoculars from his eyes. "We've found ourselves a paramilitary brigade," he said to Williams. "And they like to play rough."

A mile east of them, Jill Larson sat comfortably in the Comanche's heated cockpit. She had hidden the chopper behind a row of pine trees at the end of a tiny airstrip to keep close surveillance on the site's lone hangar, radio hut, and transmission tower. Two men had arrived in a Hummer several minutes earlier. One of them was tall and thin, dressed stylishly in a long, beige coat. His companion, dressed in a flight jacket, was much shorter and noticeably stockier.

The smaller of the two slid open the hangar door and revealed two commercial helicopters—identical five-seat, single-engine Boeing MD 520Ns, one painted bright blue, the other red. Jill raised her eyebrows agreeably. She had flown an MD 500 series chopper in law-enforcement training and loved every minute of it. Its NOTAR anti-torque system was markedly quieter and allowed more maneuverability than conventional tail rotors.

Jill keyed in the frequency of the portable VHF units. "Got a helicopter getting ready to take off."

"Who's leaving?" Marshall asked.

"Two men who look like they own the goddamn world," she said. "Apparently the flight stand-down doesn't apply to them either."

"I copy," Marshall said. "Relay this information to Medlock. Find out who owns this property."

"Will do."

The shorter man positioned and prepped the blue 520N and soon had its rotors spooling at flight idle. The taller man waited inside the hangar, a cellular phone to his ear. Jill scanned all frequencies for the call and found only the buzz of a scrambled digital telephone signal. When the aircraft was ready, the tall man, still clinging to his phone, climbed into the chopper while the pilot throttled up. Finally, the chopper lifted into the thin mountain air, banked eastward, and vanished over the treetops.

Jill followed its northeast heading until it disappeared from the Comanche's radar.

Marshall and Williams heard someone approaching behind them. They rolled away in opposite directions and disappeared into the snowy underbrush. A soldier appeared on the path, thermos in hand, a Kalashnikov assault rifle slung over his shoulder. His dark hair was closely cropped in a military style, except in front, where a small crop of longer hair flopped down across his nose like a whisk broom. He unscrewed his thermos as he strolled and raised it to his lips.

Williams slid from the bramble and lunged at him. A streak of sunlight reflected off his knife as he buried its blade into the soldier's throat beneath his raised thermos. The soldier dropped the thermos with a splash and stared at Williams, stunned, while a mixture of blood and beer poured out his neck wound. Marshall was at his side in an instant, and together they lowered the soldier facedown into the snow. Marshall wasted no time retrieving his parka and slipped it over his flight jacket.

Williams knelt beside the corpse. "Check this out, Joe." He held up the soldier's wrist. "Recognize this?"

Marshall squatted next to him and examined the familiar tattoo of a sun. "Well, if it isn't our old friend Sirius. Medlock was right—our paths are destined to cross."

Williams shook his head. "I don't like what I see up here. There are too many of them, well-armed and using the house as a fortress. If they find us, we're screwed."

"I want you to cover me," Marshall said, standing and adjusting the soldier's sunglasses over his eyes. He took a grenade from Williams's pack and attached it to his utility belt. "If you spot any trouble, deal with these assholes with extreme prejudice."

Marshall slung his Franchi over his shoulder and walked briskly through the grove of pines into the clearing. He passed several soldiers, each holding a beer mug.

"Hey, Stu!" one of them called to him.

Marshall spun and saw a bearded soldier, cradling a rifle, waving to him.

"It's about *fucking* time!" the soldier hollered.

Marshall returned the wave, then resumed his brisk walk toward the house This was hardly a good start. How well did this group know each of its members? he wondered. For all he knew, he stood out as an intruder and had already been marked as a dead man. He noticed a stream of blood down the front of his parka that belonged to its previous owner—a conspicuous stain on white fabric. He walked smartly to a beer station, helped himself to a mug on a table beside the keg, and filled it with brew. As he moved away, Marshall spilled part of the beer over the stain and rubbed it with his glove. The diluted stain turned the front of his coat pink.

Williams lay spread-eagled under a patch of bramble and watched him through the scope of his Galil, a suppressor screwed to its chromed bore muzzle. The shadows were lengthening. He figured in about a half hour the sun would sink behind the mountains and bring an early dusk. He already had his gear meticulously laid out, ready to replace the scope with a light-intensifying system.

Marshall stepped onto a low, decklike porch leading to a pair of sliding glass doors. He grabbed the handle. Before he could pull it open, a heavy hand grabbed his arm.

"You're not Stu," said the bearded soldier, discharging a beer burp into his face.

"Never said I was," Marshall responded, then broke the soldier's grip with a jerk of his arm. The two's eyes locked in intense stares like the eyes of duelers before the draw.

The soldier spotted the blood on the front of Marshall's parka. "What's this? What have you done with him?"

"Piss off," Marshall said.

The soldier grabbed the front of Marshall's coat in his bear fists. "I'm gonna break your *fucking*—!"

A round from Williams's silenced Galil ripped through the soldier's chest and struck with a *chunk* into the wooden beams next to the glass door. Marshall grabbed the soldier before he could fall and eased him into a sitting position on a snow-covered wooden chair. He pushed the man's head down between his knees to conceal the wound, then offered a subtle nod of gratitude in Williams's direction.

Marshall slid open the double glass door and slipped inside. He found himself in an office with several desks, computer terminals, filing cabinets, and lots of books. Nowhere in this neatly appointed office did he see anything that resembled a satellite module. He could hear voices and boisterous laughter coming from the next room. There also was the thick, oily smell of cigar smoke.

He slipped out his radio and said to Williams and Jill, "I'm leaving this on transmit in the unlikely event I can't respond."

There came a crackle of acknowledgment.

Marshall unzipped his parka and fastened the radio onto his belt. He slipped past a recreation room where several men, drunk and rowdy, were roughnecking around a game of pool. They ignored Marshall as he headed for a large wooden staircase leading to the house's second level. He mounted the first steps. Suddenly, a pair of soldiers hefting a metal beer keg began descending.

Marshall froze as they stormed down the steps toward him.

"These stairs are in use," one of them hollered down to him.

Marshall retreated to the bottom just ahead of them. They carried the keg through the office and headed outside with it. With the steps again clear, Marshall bounded up them two at a time. The main floor's hallway opened to a great sitting room where soldiers in increasing numbers were gathering about a mammoth fireplace. It looked like a party of urban guerrillas.

Marshall turned and headed down the long hallway away from the crowd. He heard voices coming from an open doorway at the opposite end. A man shouted, "You're an asshole, Farrell. You've disobeyed Stryker's orders. You were told to destroy it, not bring it here, for *chrissake*."

The silhouette of a soldier appeared in the doorway. Marshall grabbed the nearest doorknob and slipped inside a bedroom, then listened at the door as a soldier stormed past the room. People were wrestling on a bed behind him. He whirled and saw a couple engaged in furious intercourse.

"You wait your turn," growled the man on the bed with his pants wrapped around his boots. "Obviously Stryker didn't give you a proper orientation."

The woman was not a willing partner. Her arms and feet were bound to the bed, which appeared to have seen a lot of use lately. Marshall slid out a stiletto from his utility belt as he approached the bed.

The soldier flared, "I'm not going to tell you again, foghead—"

Marshall lunged forward, grabbed his black burly locks of hair, and placed the serrated blade against the flesh under his chin. The colonel looked into a grizzled face that sported a thick mustache and an uneven goatee that looked as if he were drooling chocolate pudding.

"What are you doing, man?" the soldier gasped.

"You should be thrilled," Marshall said. "I'm giving you a one-way express ticket to Sirius." Marshall snapped back the soldier's head by his hair. "Someone, possibly several people, brought a piece of electronic gear here today—a thin, rack-mounted unit from a satellite. Do you know what I'm talking about?"

The soldier spat at him in contempt and succeeded only in

189

spreading foam over his goatee. "What's it to you?"

"I've made it *my* business," Marshall sneered. He pressed the stiletto's tip into the soldier's flesh and let him feel a drop of blood trickle down his neck.

"Okay! Okay! Yeah, I know whatchur talkin' about. Farrell brought it here. He'll get his when Stryker finds out."

"Where?"

"In the mess . . . two doors down."

"Anything else you want to tell me?" Marshall asked.

"That's all I know. I swear."

"I believe you."

Marshall pushed the knife into the soldier's throat and twisted the blade. The soldier, his eyes wide in shock, vomited a quart of blood in a single cough. Marshall dragged him off the woman by his hair and dumped him heavily onto the floor as a fountain of blood leapt from his throat wound.

Marshall wiped the blade across the sheets and cut the nylon cords binding the woman's feet to the bed. He inspected the metal cuffs on her wrists. These weren't standard handcuffs, but rather maximum-security nickel leg irons used to transport dangerous prisoners. He searched the soldier's pockets for a key and found none.

"So we do this the hard way," he said to the soldier, whose corpse returned a vacant stare.

Marshall withdrew an electronic lock pick from his belt, extended the probe, stuck it into the cuff's keyhole, and turned on its tiny motor. Seconds later, he had both cuffs open and the chain off her wrists.

The woman groaned. Marshall helped her into a sitting position. She was young and attractive, with short, black hair and a slender figure. He examined her face. She had taken quite a beating, and those lovely features of hers would need stitches.

"Who are you?" he asked.

When she didn't respond, he grabbed her chin and shook it gently. "Can you hear me?"

The woman's swollen eyes flared open. When she saw him dressed like one of Stryker's soldiers, she closed her eyes tight. "Just kill me. Please. Do it now and be done with it."

"I'm not going to hurt you," Marshall said. "My name is

Colonel Joseph Marshall, United States Special Forces.''

Her eyes opened tentatively and looked up at him. Suddenly she yelled, "They raped me!"

Marshall put a finger to her lips. "Just tell me who you are."

"Olin Benson . . . computer applications designer for Digital Equipment. I was on my way to Cheyenne Mountain on a special assignment when our helicopter crashed. Soldiers brought us here . . . animals—"

"Are you saying there are other survivors?"

"Just Nancy and me. No one else."

"Nancy?" Marshall asked. "Nancy Shaw?"

She looked quizzically at him. "Yes. Do you know her?"

"Very well. Where is she?"

Olin shook her head. "I don't know . . . most likely back in one of the cellars. She talked to me very briefly this morning before they took her away."

Marshall helped Olin to the edge of the bed. She kept the sheets wrapped around her.

"We don't have much time." He noticed her bruised and swollen leg. "Are you able to walk?"

She nodded.

Marshall carefully felt her lower left leg. Olin winced. The inner and larger of the two bones was fractured. "Your tibia is broken. It's going to hurt like hell when you put weight on it."

"I don't care."

Marshall's eyes scanned the room for her belongings. "Where are your clothes?"

"They're long gone. I really miss my glasses."

Marshall found scattered pieces of men's clothing on the floor and gathered them into a pile on the bed beside her. "Get dressed. I'll be back in two minutes."

Olin forced a smile and looked at him closely. Despite her nearsightedness, she liked what she saw and immediately trusted him. *"Yes, sir."*

Marshall pulled out his Beretta and twisted on a suppressor. He chambered a round, stood, and cracked open the bedroom door. He could hear more voices from the great room at the far end of the hallway as soldiers in increasing numbers began gathering inside. He slipped into the hallway.

A huge soldier stormed down the hallway. "We'll see what Stryker has to say—" He spotted Marshall and sneered, "What the fuck do you want?"

The colonel offered his best disarming grin. "I'm just the cable guy."

"Fuck you—"

Marshall brought up his stiletto and, with a quick, deep slice, severed the man's jugular and larynx like a surgeon. He grabbed the soldier around his torso, pushed him into an empty room, and rolled him neatly onto the bed. He returned to the hallway and shut the door behind him.

Marshall peered into an open room at the end of the hallway—it was a snack area with several circular tables, a sink, and a seven-foot stainless-steel refrigerator. Three men around a table were arguing over an electronic component the size and shape of a squat safety-deposit box. Marshall's eyes narrowed; this was what he had come for. He checked the hallway behind for foot traffic. Satisfied he was alone, he concealed the Beretta behind him and stepped into the room.

One of the soldiers yelled at him, "Get the fuck out of here, you moron! This is private business."

Marshall approached the table. "I want to know which of you geniuses brought that satellite module into this house."

Surprised by the question and unsure how to answer, the soldiers eyed each other, their eyebrows cocked at various angles of uncertainty. Finally, one of them shoved a finger at the man across from him. *"He did!"*

Marshall thrust his Beretta in front of him and discharged a single round. The bullet caught the accused soldier in the chest and hurled him backward onto another table.

The other two stood and stared in mute surprise.

"That's from Stryker," Marshall said, keeping his gun pointed at the pair. "Do you stooges know there's a homing transmitter in that box? While you sat here playing with yourselves, U.S. Commandos vectored this location."

One of them signaled a time-out with his hands. "Hold on right there. Even if this is so, there ain't no military flights. It'd take days till someone could get here."

"You didn't answer my question," Marshall said. "Why haven't you destroyed this unit?"

"Because it's worth money," the other soldier sneered. "A lot of money."

"Do you intend to sell it?" Marshall asked.

"Maybe."

"Wrong answer." Marshall discharged another bullet that struck the soldier square in his chest. His body looped backward onto the floor.

"Okay . . . okay," said the remaining soldier, his shaking hands outstretched. "I'll help you get rid of this thing."

"You're too late," Marshall said. "Federal troops are already here."

He looked at Marshall, puzzled. "How would you know that?"

"Because I'm one of them. Covert Operations. Antiterrorism."

The soldier's hand raced for his holstered gun. Marshall fired. The silenced bullet hit the soldier in the center of his forehead. His eyes rolled up into his head and he fell with the others.

Marshall quickly examined the box. Someone had tried to force it open with a screwdriver, but otherwise it appeared undamaged. The module wasn't particularly weighty—perhaps seven pounds. He slid it under his left arm.

"Don't you move, asshole!" ordered a voice from the doorway.

Marshall, his expression grim, crouched and spun on his heels. At the same moment he brought up his Beretta and fired without the benefit of a solid aim. The soldier spilled backward and slammed into the door across the hallway. It flew open to reveal a room in which another soldier sat on the bed lacing up his boots. He jumped to his feet. Marshall fired a round that caught him on the chin. He whirled and landed facedown over the bed.

Marshall moved cautiously into the hallway. He could hear boisterous laughter from the great room but no general alert; there were no indications his presence had been discovered. He slipped into Olin's room.

She looked up with a start as he entered and sighed when she recognized him. "Thank God."

Olin sat at the edge of the bed clumsily dressed in a sweatshirt and pair of jeans too large for her. She had nearly finished tying up a pair of men's boots. The bedsheet she had been wearing now covered the corpse of the last man who raped her.

Marshall checked her clothing. "At least you'll be warm."

Olin, her eyes moist, looked up at him. "I'm afraid I might get you killed trying to help me. I don't want that to happen."

"It won't."

Marshall helped her to her feet. She cried out in pain as her leg accepted even modest weight.

"Put your weight on me," he instructed. He unclipped the radio from his belt. "Jill, do you copy?" He released the Send button.

Jill crackled an acknowledgment. "I'm right here."

"I need your diversion," he said. "Give me bursts of cannon fire all around the house. Put the rounds right through the windows. I need enough time to clear out. Williams?"

"Right here."

"I'm coming out the same door. I'll have a woman with me, and she's wounded."

"Go for it," he said. "No one's gonna get close to you."

One mile away, Jill felt the chopper shudder. There were brief power losses a fraction of a second each.

She felt an unmistakable vibration that wasn't there before. Her knuckles turned white from an overprotective grip on the cyclic lever. *I don't need this right now, thank you very much.*

The RPMs dipped notably with each power interruption, and she inched the throttles forward to compensate. She switched the screen in her helmet to damage control. Nothing apparent. The Millennium Bug? she wondered. Was it there all along, finally awakening and rearing its ugly head?

"Please," she said aloud, "stay with me for one more hour."

Outside, at the far end of the estate, General Stryker stood with several soldiers by a blazing bonfire. The heat in the mountain air at dusk felt wonderful, and some of the men had removed their hoods and gloves for full appreciation.

A soldier, no older than a teen, ran up to the general waving a portable radio. "Sir! You've got to hear this!"

General Stryker, intrigued by the youth's excitement, accepted the radio and put it to his ear. He heard static and crackles, then a female voice—very clear and very close—blared over the channel, "I'm in whisper mode . . . coming up on the house now. Stand by."

Stryker tossed the radio back to the teen and said to the others, his voice remarkably calm, "Gentlemen, I suggest we get out of the open. We are under attack."

Chapter Thirty-one
Poison

Cheyenne Mountain
Wednesday, December 29
1530 Hours

"Help me! *Somebody please help me!*"

Julie, her heart pounding, her lungs heaving, stumbled into the corridor. The door across from the colonel's apartment stood ajar; its doorway nameplate read "Dwight." She burst inside.

"Can someone help me?" she called into the darkness.

Julie swept her light across the apartment's living area. The room appeared deserted. Her hands were shaking as she directed her light through the open bedroom doorway. Two men in officers' uniforms lay on the bed, their arms around each other. She crept forward and scanned them with her light. Their throats were cut, the light-colored comforter under them soaked a deep maroon.

Julie raised her light slightly to the wall above the bed. Scrawled in blood was the word *Sirius*. One of the men's hands, still stretched across the pillow over his head, was painted with blood.

What madness had possessed these people? Julie couldn't believe that they would submit so readily to suicide—especially the colonel—simply over a date change. Something besides the senselessness of these deaths was dreadfully wrong. There must have been some intervention. But by whom or what?

Julie left the apartment and rushed down the corridor, her eyes scanning each nameplate beside every door she passed. She stopped before the one labeled "Patterson." Like the others, the door opened easily.

"General?"

There was no response. She swept her light across the main living area, then checked the bedroom. The apartment was empty.

She returned to the hallway and whispered, "Thank God."

Julie ran through a set of double doors and entered Cheyenne's administrative wing, where she continued down another dark corridor toward her team's conference room. Julie burst inside. She found her seven team members all present and accounted for—all of them dead. The conference room had become a morgue. She stared, unbelieving, at the bodies of her teammates. Several were slumped at the oval table, some with fingers still hooked through coffee-mug handles. The rest were curled on the floor in fetal positions. There were no obvious signs of a struggle or violence. She directed her light into each face. They appeared to have died peacefully enough, their serene expressions resembling that of sleep.

Julie picked up a coffee mug, sniffed its contents, and detected a slightly medicinal odor. She inspected the room's credenza with its of drug paraphernalia, including syringes, cotton balls, rubbing alcohol, and several small bottles of liquid. She picked up one of the bottles and recognized the label's pharmaceutical name as an industrial-grade heroin. Only a small amount of fluid remained in the bottle. Among the items sat an unlabeled bottle with several capsules filled with powder. She slid two into her palm.

"It's cyanide," came a voice.

Julie whipped around and aimed her light into the corner. Henry Princeton sat slumped in an office chair, a hypodermic needle nested between two fingers.

"In case you were wondering, most of them took cyanide," he said.

Henry looked disheveled and sleepy. His left shirtsleeve was rolled up and a rubber tourniquet was wrapped around his upper arm.

She rushed to him. "Henry, for God's sake, what's happened here?"

He said dreamily, "The Great Shout has spoken."

She doubted his glazed eyes could focus on her. "Henry, stay with me. Tell me what this is all about."

"The Second Coming has come," he slurred. "We've all seen it . . . you will too. A great light came down from heaven and touched us all. The sensation was indescribable."

"Henry—"

"We were all singing. You should have been here ten minutes ago, Dr. Julie. It was beautiful . . . it was beautiful . . ." He started drifting away.

Julie grabbed the front of his shirt and shook him severely. "Henry! *Wake up!* Stay with me. I want to save your life."

He shook his head. "Oh no, Dr. Julie. Please don't. I'm already in heaven . . . and I don't want you or anybody else spoiling it."

She inspected his arm below the rubber tourniquet and found a single needle bruise. "How much heroin did you take?"

He smiled broadly. "Not quite heroin. Close, though. A synthetic compound, industrial grade . . . much more powerful. I could have taken cyanide . . . it would have been quicker." He raised his syringe. "But one hundred CC's of this yields a much more interesting death. And slowly, so I can enjoy."

He offered her the syringe. She looked closely at it—half its contents still remained.

"Henry," she said, "you haven't taken a lethal dose."

He shoved the syringe at her. "I've saved some for you. Try this rush. I've never felt anything like it. It's given me the largest erection of my life. What we could do together—"

She pushed his hand away in disgust and looked across the field of bodies. Most were young and highly educated. She'd worked very closely with these people over the last forty-eight hours and found them stable individuals, not susceptible to brainwash.

Julie looked closely at Henry. "These people didn't commit suicide, did they?"

His bemused expression evaporated, replaced with an ugly look she had never seen before. "Some were doubters . . . I had to put cyanide in their coffee. They're always drinking coffee. They eventually thanked me."

"*You killed them?* Why, you murdering son of a—"

Henry lashed out and plunged the needle into her neck. She screamed in surprise. He giggled uncontrollably as he watched her scramble away from him, tripping over bodies, knocking over half-filled coffee mugs. Henry collapsed onto the floor behind her, laughing heartily.

Julie stumbled into the hallway. She pulled the syringe out of her neck with a groan. She already felt light-headed. There wasn't enough light in the corridor to determine how much he had injected, and she had left her light in the conference room.

"Somebody help me!"

Her tongue grew numb and heavy. A peculiar euphoria enveloped her, and she felt as though her mind's eye had somehow slipped outside her body.

"Some . . . one . . . help . . . meeeeeeee . . ."

A shower of colors burst before her eyes. She grabbed the wall for support, found nothing, and crumpled to the floor. Her heart raced and her breathing increased to the point of hyperventilation. She could still hear Henry's mad laughter, like a far-off echo in a dream. The parade of colors blended into a deep red and quickly faded.

Finally, there was only blackness.

Chapter Thirty-two
Precarious

Willard, Colorado
Wednesday, December 29
1630 Hours

Suddenly, and without a sound, the Comanche rose from behind the Douglas firs and headed straight for Skile's chateau.

General Stryker, his eyes riveted on the aircraft not fifty feet above his head, whispered, "Don't do it. In the name of our God, don't do it."

Jill activated the Comanche's chain cannon. The weapon's turret, mounted beneath the fuselage directly below the gunner's position, swiveled left to right on its hydraulic actuator. Soldiers scattered from its path.

"Get down!" Stryker shouted to his men.

Jill pressed the Fire trigger, and the cannon, slaved to Jill's helmet, roared to life. Each second, dozens of 20mm high-explosive shells on an electrically driven chain ripped from the cannon's three muzzles and began hammering the chateau's two-story windows.

Inside, the world truly was ending for the unsuspecting soldiers. The huge windows around the house systematically exploded in a devastating fury. Glass splinters whirled about the rooms at tornado force. The shells' liners collapsed on impact into jets of molten metal capable of penetrating more than two inches of armor. Others disintegrated into shrapnel. The exploding rounds

199

caught dozens of scrambling men and turned their flesh into liquid.

Wherever Jill looked, whoever she spotted disintegrated instantly.

General Stryker tuned his UHF radio to channel four and shouted, "Hangar, this is Stryker. Answer me, dammit!"

One mile east of the chateau, a lone soldier working Skile's personal airfield swiveled his chair around to the radio console and grabbed the microphone. "Sir, I hear shooting. What's your status?"

"We're under attack," Stryker spat. "I want you to jam all frequencies."

"What about—"

"Do it now!"

"Yes, sir!"

The soldier wheeled his chair to another console and powered up a rack of gear. One by one the units blinked to life. When the master control blinked READY, the soldier engaged the transmitter and pumped a powerful signal through the antenna tower beside his control room. The signal was wide enough and strong enough to obliterate all radio traffic within a twenty-five-mile radius. Its effect wasn't limited to military radio traffic. The residents of Willard, Colorado, lost their televisions, AM/FM radios, and cellular phones.

Jill released the chain-cannon trigger when a shrill screech filled her ears. "Criminy . . . now what?" Jill decreased the gain of her headset. "Colonel, do you copy?"

She received only the jamming signal in response.

Jill nodded knowingly. "I bet I know where you're coming from."

She engaged the chain cannon's trigger until the round indicator reached zero. The chain cannon fell silent, its five-hundred-round magazine exhausted.

Jill banked the chopper away from the house and flew over a contingent of soldiers with assault rifles scrambling to rally a defense against her. She didn't give them a chance.

"Milquetoasts."

Before they could fire a round, Jill *whump*ed over them all and vanished behind a grove of pines toward the airfield.

Marshall holstered his Beretta and threw the slain soldier's down-filled parka over Olin's shoulders. She slipped her arms into its sleeves.

He slid the satellite module under his left arm. "Ready?"

She slipped an arm around his waist for support and held him tightly. Tears of pain spilled down her bruised cheeks. "Get me out of here."

Marshall half carried, half supported Olin into the hallway. The damage to the house was severe. The colonel hid her face from the carnage as they waded through the rubble to the house's great room. Bodies, some of them unrecognizable, lay strewn everywhere. Those who weren't severely wounded were crawling to help those who were.

No one paid Marshall and Olin the slightest notice as they moved toward the rosewood staircase and began descending. The hurried clicks of assault weapons below brought Marshall to a halt. Stryker's soldiers were gathering down in the recreation room, hastily putting on winter gear and checking their weapons. Marshall didn't intend to wait until they cleared out. He detached the only grenade from his utility belt, pulled the pin, and released the handle. He counted four seconds before dropping it. The grenade bounced off the bottom steps and rolled into the room.

Marshall shielded Olin's face.

"*Jesus*, who lost a gr—"

The grenade detonated and took out every lower-level window that had managed to survive the Comanche's chain cannon. He took Olin down the rest of the stairs, letting the smoke and small fires from the explosion mask their movements. Several soldiers caught by the grenade's shrapnel lay lifeless. One was on his knees, crawling toward a weapon.

Marshall raised his Beretta and fired a silenced round into his back. He spun and collapsed.

"I can see your lethal skills have become second nature to you," Olin said.

"Close your eyes," Marshall told her.

"No. I want to see this."

They made their way into Skile's office, where two more soldiers were barricaded beside the sliding glass doors. Marshall fired two quick rounds. Both soldiers crashed headlong through the ceiling-high windows.

Marshall spotted a walking stick with a hand-carved mallard's head in a bucket of umbrellas by the open doors. He grabbed it for Olin.

"Use this to help distribute your weight," he said.

She readily accepted it. Marshall pulled Olin's hood up over her head and covered his own as well.

"Just act like another wounded soldier," he instructed.

"Who has to act?"

Marshall allowed himself a smile as he led her out onto the deck. There was little to suggest that they weren't as they appeared—one soldier helping a wounded comrade. It was nearly dark now, save for the uneven light of a dozen unintentional fires inside and out.

A harried soldier charged down the deck toward them. There wasn't time for Marshall to determine whether the soldier had any interest in them. He released Olin, drew his Beretta, and squeezed off a silenced round. The soldier flew backward off the deck.

Marshall holstered his handgun and brought the radio to his lips. "Jill? What's your position?"

He took his finger off the Send button and was assailed by the whine of a jamming signal.

"That's just great." He slipped the radio into one of his parka's pockets.

He felt Olin tighten her grip around his waist and urge him forward; she was anxious to leave the grounds. They stepped off the deck into the snow and began crossing the estate.

Jill swung the Comanche in a wide arch around Skile's airfield to complete the triangulation of the signal, then swooped down toward the airfield's radio shack. She circled the tall radio tower once to reconfirm the source.

"You're history," she said.

Jill brought the Comanche into a hover at the edge of the airfield one hundred feet off the ground. She opened the weapons canopy wings and target-locked both the radio shack and its companion antenna tower. She armed two hellfire missiles.

"I'm canceling your license," she said.

Suddenly, a damage-control alarm blared in her headset. She punched up the display. The Number One turboshaft was overheating, its RPMs dipping unevenly.

"Dammit," she yelled. "There's no reason for this."

She ignored the engine warning and pressed Fire.

The laser-guided rockets ignited and roared from the chopper at Mach 1.4. Inside the radio shack, the soldier glanced up in time to see two flaming streaks boring straight toward his window. He swiveled around in his chair and reached for the microphone.

"Stryker—"

The last thing he heard was the squeal of his own jamming signal as the first rocket tore through the wall and detonated. The radio shack and its tower disintegrated in a magnificent display of fire and metal that lit up the mountain and showered unrecognizable pieces of burning debris over the airfield. The squeal of the jamming signal fell silent in Jill's ears.

Twenty-five miles away, the residents of Willard were curious about a rare earthquake that rattled their windows.

Marshall and Olin trudged through the trampled snow toward the grove of pines behind the estate. Stryker's soldiers, many of them wounded, staggered next to them in an attempt to find even modest cover.

A soldier rushed toward them, his M-16 raised and pointed. Marshall resisted the urge to draw his Beretta in the open and give away their identity. The soldier stopped suddenly and collapsed into the snow in front of them, a round from Williams's sniper rifle through his back.

They pressed on.

Another soldier slung his assault weapon over his shoulder as he ran up to them. "You're heading the wrong way. Let me help you before you get lost—"

His head jerked and he, too, collapsed in the snow, the back of his skull cleanly removed by a sniper's round. The walk was taking its toll on Olin. She was moaning continuously by the time they reached the row of conifers at the edge of the clearing.

One hundred yards away, nearly obscured in the line of trees, another soldier watched them. He made no move to either help or attack them. He just stood there staring with piercing eyes that seemed to miss nothing. He had his hood down, and Marshall noted his salt-and-pepper hair and a solid, angular chin. This wasn't another "grunt." He was a leader of men, Marshall surmised, not a follower.

With Olin secured firmly on his arm, Marshall disappeared into the grove of conifers.

General Stryker called two of his soldiers. "Come with me. I want your weapons ready."

The soldiers unshouldered and cocked their M16s while Stryker chambered a round into his silver-plated 9mm Mauser. The trio began marching along the edge of the trees toward the path where Marshall and Olin had disappeared.

Williams grabbed Olin and eased her into a sitting position in the snow. She cried out in pain and threw down her cane.

Marshall set the module next to her. "I know it's hard, but try not to shout. A woman's voice doesn't blend in well out here."

"I can't go any farther," she said, her expression one of agony. "Leave me."

"We're not leaving anybody here," Marshall said. "Olin, meet your new best friend, Gunnery Master Sergeant J. C. Williams."

Williams tipped his baseball cap and finished disassembling and packing his Galil. "Ma'am."

Marshall noted the sergeant's mountain parka. "I'm curious where you found that."

"Its owner won't need it anymore," Williams said.

He lifted some conifer branches in the underbrush to reveal two bodies. Williams dragged out the first corpse, which Marshall recognized as "Stu," the soldier whose coat he was now wearing. He didn't recognize the second soldier, also minus a coat.

Williams set them up in the snow, back to back. "There's a garage at the end of that path—"

"Anybody care to talk to me?" Jill's voice blared out of both their radios.

Marshall retrieved his radio and pressed Send. "Marshall here. How did you get through?"

"I took the liberty of taking out the airfield's radio tower," Jill said. "I was beginning to miss you guys."

Williams threw his rifle pack over his shoulder. "Tell her she's becoming a bad ass like her mentors—"

"Someone's coming!" Olin hissed, pointing.

Marshall and Williams whirled. Through the branches they could see the outlines of three soldiers making their way along the grove of trees toward them.

Marshall put his radio to his lips. "We've got a situation. I need you right now."

"I've got the Comanche in whisper mode about one hundred yards south-southeast of the house," she said. "Damage control indicates—"

"I want you to put a Sidewinder into the living room," Marshall said. "Do it *now!*"

"You got it," Jill replied.

Marshall lifted Olin into his arms and said to Williams, "Tell me more about those garages."

Jill raised the Comanche two hundred feet until she had a clear line of sight to Skile's chateau. She ignored the engine warning buzzers, opened the aircraft's armament bay doors, and armed a single Sidewinder.

TARGET PRIORITY LOCKED

She pressed Fire and watched a Sidewinder roar out from under her and sail over the treetops.

General Stryker heard voices just ahead accompanied by the squawking of a radio. He beckoned his two soldiers to hasten their pace.

Suddenly a missile shrieked overhead. Stryker turned to see it soar straight into the chateau's upper story. The flash of its detonation ruined his night vision as the front of Skile's mountain chateau disappeared in a great fireball.

General Stryker whirled away from the blast and charged through the bramble, his Mauser thrust before him. Spots from the afterimage paraded before his eyes. They came upon two men sitting back to back in the snow. Stryker raised his handgun and discharged several rounds into each of them. The two soldiers stepped from behind him and added a spray of bullets from their M-16s.

Stryker put up his hand. He stepped over the corpses and looked down bitterly at the bullet-ridden bodies of two of his soldiers stripped of their coats.

Marshall carried Olin in his arms down the path toward Skile's remote garages.

"Nancy's out here somewhere," Marshall called back to his sergeant.

"She's what!?" Williams asked.

Marshall stopped and said to him, "Olin saw her this morning."

"When we first arrived," Olin said, "they kept us in a cellar in these woods. The entrance looks like a toolshed."

Williams drew his Smith & Wesson. "Take Olin away from here, Joe. If Nancy's here, I'll find her."

Williams turned and vanished through the bramble.

Chapter Thirty-three
Escape

"Make friends with the angels, who though invisible are always with you. . . ."

Saint Francis de Sales

The Millennium Project

Williams pressed through the layers of pine branches until he saw something that brought him to a wavering halt. A man, his back to him, stood at the edge of the path, staring into the darkness. His appearance gave Williams pause. The soldier was grossly overweight, his bare arms huge and flabby, his bloated body forced into a pair of unbecoming camouflage fatigues.

Williams moved nimbly forward. He pressed his Smith & Wesson's cold, steel muzzle against the base of the soldier's neck and pulled back the hammer with his thumb.

"Any tick from you I don't like and I'll put a bullet through that fat head of yours," the sergeant said. "Now turn around very slowly."

The soldier didn't move.

"Are you deaf?" Williams hissed. "I said turn around NOW."

When he failed to respond a second time, Williams placed the muzzle against the soldier's right calf and discharged a round. The bullet tore through the fabric of his tight khakis and bore a groove along the flesh. The wound wasn't deep enough to rip an artery or to split a bone; the sergeant just wanted to get his attention.

And it worked. The soldier slowly turned until he faced him. Williams directed the beam of his pencil flashlight into the soldier's face.

"You've got to be kidding."

The soldier reminded him of an infant on hormones and steroids. His head was clean-shaven, his eyes vague and droopy. He returned Williams's gaze with a cold, glassy stare that seemed permanently fixed on a point sixteen inches before him. Those dead eyes warned Williams he could probably kill cold-bloodedly without the distraction of conscience.

"Looks like I found me the village idiot," the sergeant said. "Let's be buddies. I'll buy you a shiny, red bicycle if you tell me where I can find a woman who, I'm told, you have under lock and key around here. Something about a cellar. She's in her for-

207

ties, with auburn hair a little longer than her shoulders, and a great face. Seen anybody like that lately?"

Williams watched the soldier closely for any sign of comprehension. There was nothing to suggest he would get anything from him. "I'm wasting my time—"

The brute suddenly turned and began lumbering down the path.

Williams put a cigar between his teeth. "That's more like it."

The sergeant followed three paces behind, his handgun pointed at the soldier, whose gait seemed unaffected by the gunshot wound.

"If you're taking me on a wild-goose chase—"

They broke through a layer of conifers that hid what Williams first took for a toolshed. The brute opened the door, revealing a pair of stone steps leading into blackness. He cocked his head.

"After you," Williams said, gesturing inside. "I insist."

The brute began an awkward descent down the steps. Williams followed. When the soldier reached the bottom, Williams heard a female voice shout, "*Keep away from me!*"

It was Nancy.

Williams scurried to the bottom of the steps and found himself in a dark, concrete cell. He hollered to the mute soldier, "Give me some light down here!"

"*J.C.?*" Nancy asked.

The beam of Williams's pocket light found Nancy huddled and chained to the floor in the far corner. "What the—"

She stood up quickly. "It *is* you, isn't it?"

Williams played the beam around the small room and spotted another prisoner chained to the floor across from her. "Sweet Mary, Mother of God . . ."

The man lay naked, mutilated beyond anything Williams had encountered in his two decades as a commando. How was it humanly possible?

"*J.C.!*" Nancy shouted.

Williams spun and deflected a blow to the side of his head that drove him hard against the stone wall. His handgun and flashlight clattered across the floor. The brute was on him in an instant. He wrapped his treelike arms around Williams's chest and plucked him from the floor as though he were a toy. The soldier's strength was astounding. The sergeant let out a cry of agony, the blood pounding in his ears.

Nancy reached for Williams's handgun, but the chain stopped her several feet short. She frantically pulled at the chain, trying to rip the links from the stone floor. It was an act of futility bordering on madness.

The last breath of air shot from Williams's lungs. The brute applied enough pressure to Williams's chest to kill him in seconds.

"Help!" Nancy screamed. *"Someone please help us!"*

Several cracks echoed off the room's solid walls. The brute's grip slackened. Williams slid free of the death grip and fell to his knees, laboring to draw a breath.

A silhouetted figure, a silenced Beretta thrust before him, descended the remaining steps. Marshall snapped on his flashlight. Three distinct streams of blood flowed down the brute's back. He turned around and faced the colonel with his blank stare.

Marshall directed his light's beam at Nancy in the corner, then over to Williams still struggling on his hands and knees.

The brute took an awkward step toward the colonel.

"Don't let him get near you," Nancy warned.

Marshall discharged two quick rounds, one into the soldier's gut, another into his chest to get him down. He staggered back a step, regained his balance, then resumed his slow gait forward. He raised a bearlike paw for him.

Marshall discharged a round into the center of his forehead. The brute's eyes rolled up into his head and blood spilled from the side of his mouth. He let out a snort as he dropped heavily onto the stone floor.

"You don't know how glad I am to see you," Williams gasped, rising unsteadily to his feet.

"Not as happy as I am," Nancy said. "Joe, I've got volumes to tell you!"

Marshall inspected her chains, then said to Williams, "See if that asshole has the key."

The sergeant felt through the brute's pockets until he found a ring with two keys. He tossed them to Marshall. The first one worked, and he quickly released Nancy from her shackles.

She fell into his arms. "Joe, thank God . . . *thank God!*"

She held him tightly and kissed his cheeks. She pulled away from him, her eyes anxious. "Julie's in great danger. And I'm responsible."

Marshall began leading her out of the dismal cellar. "Tell me about it on the way. A young lady is waiting on us."

"*Olin!?*"

"Yes. She told us where we might find you."

"Wait." She pulled him to a stop and gestured to Richard, still chained to the floor. "We can't leave him."

Marshall knelt beside the man and examined him under his light beam. "My God . . ."

"His name is Richard," Nancy said. "He was part of the rescue party at our crash site." She pointed to the dead brute. "That animal did this to him."

Marshall reached under and raised Richard's head slightly so he could speak to him. His eyes were open and he seemed to be fully aware of what was occurring.

"I'll get you to a hospital," Marshall said.

Richard, his breathing labored, shook his head. "I've had enough pain for one lifetime. I'm already dead. Now I'd just like to sleep. Would you mind helping me sleep? You see, there's no way I can do it myself."

Marshall looked up at Williams. "What do we have for his pain?"

Williams produced a cigar-size metal tube from his utility belt, opened it, and slid out an ampoule and syringe. "Morphine."

Nancy took them from him. "Let me do it."

She filled the syringe and knelt beside Richard.

His eyes were pleading. "Yes . . ."

Richard closed his eyes as she injected him. His labored breathing calmed noticeably, and for the first time she saw a slight smile on his lips. Nancy filled the syringe and injected him a second time. She repeated this procedure until the ampoule was empty. His breathing was barely noticeable.

Nancy stroked his forehead. "Now you can sleep." He could no longer hear her.

She stood and put a hand over her mouth.

Marshall looked curiously at her. "That morphine was concentrated. How much did you give him?"

Tears flowed down her cheeks. "All of it . . . he needed all of it to be lethal."

He nodded and holstered his Beretta. "It's finished. Let's leave here."

Williams was the first up the steps. When he neared the top he signaled the others to stop. "I see movement."

He slid off his parka, heaved it over the shed's threshold, and quickly withdrew. Bullets from several automatic assault rifles tore into the coat and ricocheted around the stone walls at the top of the steps. The three retreated to the bottom.

"They've got us pinned down here," Nancy said, her voice reflecting her hopelessness.

Williams riveted Marshall with an eager look. "Where's our cavalry?"

Marshall removed the VHF radio from his belt and pressed Send. "Captain, I need you."

Nancy looked questioningly at Williams. He patted her arm reassuringly.

Jill's voice crackled back, "Your signal's breaking up. Sounds like you're in a sewer."

Marshall moved halfway up the steps. "Better?"

"Much. I'm getting a vector on your position. I see a shed. Is that you?"

"Yes." Marshall's eyes scanned the woody area outside. There were men with rifles moving around, jockeying for better positions. "Captain Larson, are you able to clear a path for us?"

"Yes, sir," Jill said.

The Comanche appeared suddenly over the grove of pines behind the shed. Marshall scrambled to the bottom of the steps. Jill opened the weapons bay door, armed two Sidewinder missiles, and targeted two points—one in front of the shed, one behind, two hundred feet apart.

"Heads down," she warned, then pressed Fire.

The pair of missiles roared from the aircraft's armament bay and plunged into their marks. The fireball uprooted and snapped forty-foot trees like twigs and spewed antipersonnel fragments in a spiral pattern. Men caught by the shrapnel began yelling and dropping.

Fragments tore into the shed and ripped its boards from the frame.

Marshall said into the radio, "Captain, we're out of here. Watch over us like a good guardian angel."

"Just call me Gabriel."

He took Nancy's hand. "I'm taking you home."

The three raced to the top of the steps and scrambled outside. The air was smoky with burning pine mixed with the stench of burnt flesh. Nancy, shuddering, wrapped her arms around her chest as they ran.

Marshall whipped off his parka and swung it over her shoulders. He led the way through the bramble toward Skile's remote garages. Jill followed one hundred feet above them, the chopper's low-light camera scanning the area beyond them for other signs of activity.

"You're clear," she informed them. "Just don't stop to pick up any pinecones."

General Stryker led several soldiers down the steps of the demolished shed like a flurry of ants on attack. Stryker's flashlight beam found the face of the fallen brute. The soldier's eyes were open and staring, and bore the same glazed, disinterested look they had exhibited in life. He swept his light over the empty chains in Nancy's corner.

Stryker swung his arm in defeat. *"Find her!"*

Marshall, Williams, and Nancy ran down the snow-covered road to Skile's remote barrackslike garage. All four of its doors were closed.

"What about Olin?" Nancy asked.

"She's behind door number three." Marshall grabbed the handle at its base and lifted, revealing a Hummer all-terrain vehicle. "Olin?" he called.

Olin raised her head from the back seat of the Hummer. "You guys were beginning to worry me."

Nancy opened the vehicle's back door and slid in beside her. "Olin, thank God!"

Williams climbed into the passenger seat while Marshall got behind the wheel. The satellite module lay on the floor between them. The colonel had already disconnected the ignition wires beneath the dash and left them dangling.

"Uh-oh," Williams said. "More company."

A half-dozen soldiers, their weapons drawn and ready, were making their way down the road toward them.

Williams grabbed his Galil and opened the passenger door. "I'll handle them."

Marshall grabbed his arm. "We'll stay together."

The colonel twisted together the two ends of the dangling wires. The Hummer roared to life. He put the vehicle in first gear and eased out the clutch. The vehicle rolled from the garage. The soldiers broke into a dead run, their automatic weapons braced in a firing position. In the backseat, Nancy wrapped her arm around Olin's shoulder for warmth. Olin moved closer to her.

Marshall put the radio to his lips. "Okay, team. Let's see how cohesive we've become."

Marshall dropped the Hummer into second gear and jammed the accelerator, sending up a spray of gravel and snow in their wake. The Comanche *whump*ed overhead. A second later, the soldiers vanished in a flash of a warhead's fireball.

The Hummer plowed through the section of road where the soldiers had marched only moments before. All that remained were patches of fire, loose gravel, and blackened snow.

At the road's next intersection, Marshall maneuvered the corner on two wheels and sped due west toward Skile's personal airfield.

Chapter Thirty-four
Airfield

"You took your time getting here," Jill chided Marshall as he climbed out of the Hummer. She had arrived only minutes before them, after making sure the road to the airfield was clear.

Marshall opened the Hummer's back door and helped Nancy and Olin out. "I'm putting you in charge of the others," he informed Jill. He indicated the Boeing helicopter in the hangar. "Take the civilian aircraft and get them both to an emergency room. Forget this town, though; it may be connected to this militia. Take them to Colorado Springs."

"Yes, sir."

"Did you find out who owns this estate?" Marshall added.

"It belongs to Alexander Skile of AKS Industries. Lots of tight connections. He probably wouldn't appreciate us taking one of his choppers."

"Screw him," Nancy yelled. "Skile's a murderer and a terrorist. He's crippled the North American Aerospace Defense infrastructure. He has the military community by the balls and is blackmailing them with his damn microprocessors."

"What could possibly be in it for him?" Williams asked.

"Maybe he's in cahoots with a foreign power that wants to kick some serious butt," Jill offered.

Marshall removed the satellite unit from the Hummer's front seat. "That could explain why he's been working so hard to keep this from us. It must be very incriminating evidence."

"I must tell you something, Joe," Nancy said. "Julie's in great danger at Cheyenne. And it's my fault—I gave her to that son of a bitch."

Marshall looked severely at her. "What do you mean?"

"Skile forced me to give him access to the Stanford personnel database," she said. "Now I know he wanted to study Julie's background to see if she and her team are capable of breaking some code of his. When he sees how much of a threat she is, he'll kill her."

"Let's go." Marshall slapped Williams's shoulder and they began making their way to the hangar.

"Take me with you," Nancy said, keeping up with them.

"Stay with Olin," Marshall said. "The sergeant and I will handle this."

Marshall stowed the satellite module inside the Comanche, which Jill had left idling on the helipad, while Williams and Jill prepped the Boeing helicopter. Finished, Marshall checked Olin in the backseat of the Boeing and positioned her leg for maximum comfort.

"You're a very dangerous man," Olin said to him.

"I have my gentler moments," he reassured her.

Olin's smile faded, and she took his hand. "You saved me from something far worse than death. I don't know how I'll ever—"

"Joe, we've got company," Williams hollered.

Olin squeezed his hand before he could slip away. "Thank you . . . for everything."

He returned her squeeze. "Gotta go."

Marshall joined Williams in front of the Comanche. The sergeant had his Galil out and fully assembled, its light-intensifying scope mounted on top. Jill appeared beside them. The night sky over Skile's chateau glowed an eerie red.

"Two rough-terrain vehicles and about a dozen men on foot coming straight for us," Williams said, pointing.

The vague shapes of the approaching contingent looked like

ghosts in the night. Marshall said to Jill, "I want you to get going."

"With all due respect, Colonel, the Comanche's misbehaving," Jill said. "Her flight-control systems are unreliable. You might not be able to take off. I suspect it's all computer related, but there's no way to tell without thorough diagnostics. I'd hate to leave it here just as much as you, but there's room for all of us in the N520."

Marshall shook his head. "I'll take my chances. I can't leave the Comanche on this mountain for them."

"They're coming," Williams warned.

Two utility vehicles raced ahead of the line of soldiers and sped straight for them.

"Get moving," Marshall ordered.

Jill climbed into the pilot's seat of the Boeing chopper. Nancy was already buckled in and secure beside her.

"Can you slow them down?" Marshall asked his sergeant.

"Yep." Williams brought his Galil to bear. He targeted one of the two rough-terrain vehicles leading the advance. He put the crosshair of his scope directly over the windshield on the driver's side and fired a single round. The vehicle lurched forward, careened sharply ninety degrees, and flipped over onto its side.

Marshall gave Jill a hurried "go" signal. She throttled up and lifted the chopper's collective. The Boeing N520 lifted easily, banked, and vanished into the night sky.

Marshall climbed into the pilot's seat of the Comanche, throttled up, and engaged the clutch. The main rotor began turning. He put on his flight helmet.

The second vehicle accelerated toward them. Williams fixed his scope's crosshairs over the driver's side of the windshield and squeezed off another round. The windshield shattered. The vehicle continued to speed toward them, unaffected by the round.

Williams positioned his crosshairs over the engine compartment and fired. The hood flew up and out billowed a pillar of steam. The vehicle spun around and slid to a stop not three hundred feet in front of him.

The foot soldiers broke into a dead run, firing their weapons. Williams shouldered his rifle and climbed up into the Comanche's gunnery cockpit. Round after round from automatic gunfire ricocheted off the Comanche's armored plating as Williams secured his canopy. Marshall throttled to full flight, but the engine RPMs would not rise above fifty percent. He needed seventy-five for lift.

Williams grabbed the intercom microphone. "I hope you're not waiting for Santa back there. 'Cause you just missed him."

"The engines want to shut down," Marshall said.

"Say what!?"

"It's part of the aircraft's safety system," Marshall explained, working the keyboard to manually override each critical flight system. "If the sensors detect instability, rather than explode in the red, they keep the RPM at idle so you can't take off and kill yourself. It'll take a few seconds to override."

Several of Stryker's soldiers rushed onto the helipad. Williams activated the chain-cannon turret under the fuselage. The ammunition display read zero-zero-zero. A soldier began climbing up the side. Williams drew his Smith & Wesson, cracked open the canopy, and fired. The man dropped from the aircraft. Williams shoved the handgun's muzzle into the opening on the opposite side of the cockpit and fired several rounds at another soldier attempting to climb aboard.

Williams felt the vibration increase as the engine's RPMs rose. "Whatever you're doing back there," he said, "do more of it and take us out of here."

Marshall worked the throttle, coaxing incremental RPMs from the engines. "C'mon, baby . . . keep going . . ."

Two more soldiers began climbing up opposite sides of the Comanche.

"Hell," Williams said.

When the RPMs reached seventy percent, Marshall engaged the collective. The Comanche gave a shutter and lifted tentatively off the helipad.

A soldier's face appeared through the canopy at Williams's right. The sergeant shouted, "Jesus, you scared the piss out of me!"

The soldier held on precariously as the aircraft gained altitude. Williams cracked open the canopy and shoved the muzzle into the soldier's abdomen. The two exchanged odd glances through the windscreen. Williams fired. The man vanished into the night.

Williams peered down the left side of the aircraft and saw the second soldier clinging for his life onto the landing gear, his left arm locked around the undercarriage. He held a dark, cylindrical object in his right hand. The sergeant switched on his tactical monitor and activated the low-light camera under the chopper's fuselage. He swiveled it for a close-up of the soldier.

Williams engaged the intercom. "We've got one with a grenade on the landing gear."

"Roger."

Marshall retracted the aircraft's wheels and let the hydraulics lift the soldier toward the aircraft. The soldier let out a howl as the retracting mechanism crushed his left arm against the fuselage.

The warning light on Marshall's heads-up display indicated a landing gear malfunction. He lowered the gear.

Williams watched the soldier slip from the undercarriage and fall several hundred feet to the helipad below. An explosion bellowed upward as his grenade detonated.

"Do you think his buddies were happy to see him return?" Williams asked.

Marshall grinned, banked the Comanche northward, and entered the slipstream that would take them off the mountain.

Chapter Thirty-five
Utopia

Cheyenne Mountain
Wednesday, December 29
1935 Hours

Julie woke suddenly. "Ohhhhhh . . ."

She had little awareness of her surroundings and an even vaguer notion of how long she'd been unconscious. Her head pounded terribly—worse than any hangover she could remember. She wanted desperately to close her eyes again and drift back into a long, deep sleep, but some instinct urged her to stay awake at all costs.

Images and memories, all of them disturbing, began seeping back into her brain. Which of them were real and which were fantasies, she couldn't be certain. Perhaps it had all been a dream. *Why am I so damned tired?*

Julie rolled her head to the side and stared across a control room illuminated by inadequate emergency lighting. The air was stuffy and smelled of burning wires. She became aware of someone else in the room with her. She struggled to focus on a man sitting at the controls of the room's only working console. It was General Patterson. He was smoking a cigarette and was dressed casually in shirtsleeves without his jacket.

Get your ass in gear, Martinelli. Julie swung her legs off the bench and sat up. She felt dizzy immediately. Her knees were shaking, and she thought that she might be ill.

"General?" she managed. The word came out only slightly slurred—not bad, she admitted, considering she still didn't have full use of her tongue.

General Patterson whirled and stood up from his chair. "You worried the hell out of me, young lady."

He crushed out his cigarette and weaved among the consoles to her.

"When I carried you in from the hallway," he said, helping her into a sitting position, "your face was beet red." He raised her chin to get a good look at her by the room's dim light. "You were flushed and your heart rate was dangerously high. Looked like someone tried to poison you. Hmmmm. How do you feel?"

She shook her head. "Like I'm going to throw up and die. And not necessarily in that order. What time is it?"

The general glanced up at the wall clock—4:30—it had stopped hours before with the loss of power. He looked at his watch. "Nineteen forty hours."

"I've been out for more than three hours." The fog blanketing Julie's mind began to lift and memories flowed back. "What's going on, General? What happened to Colonel Beckman? I can't believe he would commit suicide."

"He didn't. I suspect we're caught in the middle of a coup led by a bunch of sickos." He gestured toward the single metal door, modestly lit by an amber light over the transom. "One door, one way in. Nobody can sneak up on us." He pulled out his Army-issued .45 from his shoulder holster. "The next person who comes through that door is going to have to talk fast to keep me from putting a bullet through him."

Julie dumped her head into her palms and tried to shake sense and reason back into her brain. Her memories of the afternoon were a whirlwind of confusion.

Henry Princeton!

Her head jerked up with a start. "Where is he?"

"Who?"

"Henry."

"Princeton? With the rest of your team."

"Dead?"

"Just like the others. In his case it looked like an overdose."

"So you examined his body and you're sure he's dead?" she pressed.

The general shrugged. "Well, I didn't perform an autopsy. But he looked like everyone else in the room."

"So you didn't examine him?"

The general's voice took on an irritated tone. "I saw him on the floor with the rest of them—dead!"

"*Jesus Christ!* He probably just passed out. Help me up."

She put out her hand, and the general helped her to her feet. "Why are you so concerned about Henry? There are plenty of others—"

"He tried to kill me." She took a shaky step forward and nearly blacked out as her blood redistributed.

"*Henry?* That makes no sense at all. Why would he do such a thing?"

"Because he's responsible for the deaths of my team. He may have killed Beckman and the others as well."

The general grimaced at the thought. "But why?"

"I can think of at least one reason—he sabotaged Eclipse. His company conspired and succeeded in taking the entire network off-line."

"You're still delirious, Martinelli. That's high treason. What possible motive would they have?"

Julie wobbled to the first console. "I don't know. Maybe I am delusional, but I'm sure about one thing—I didn't inject myself with heroin. That was Henry. He's been lying to us all along."

General Patterson slid out another cigarette from a pack he kept in his shirt pocket. "I hope you're dead wrong. AKS has its processors in every one of our military systems. Telecommunications, surveillance, networking . . . Christ, our most sophisticated strategic and tactical weapons systems. What if he can detonate a nuclear warhead?"

Julie leaned back heavily onto the desk. "Oh God, I think I'm going to be ill. . . ."

General Patterson, an unlit cigarette dangling from his lips, rushed to put his arm around her for support. "You should lie down. The shock's been terrible."

Julie brushed him away. "No! We've got to leave here."

"We're not going anywhere," Patterson said. "The center's

221

power grid has been deliberately shut down. And it's taken all communications with it. There's no way past the blast doors without the generators.''

She looked at him severely. "So we're trapped in here?''

The general lit his cigarette. "I assure you this center is a self-sustained city—four and a half acres. We've got a million gallons of drinking water and plenty of food. We can survive in here for months without any contact from the outside world.''

"It's a death trap in here as long as Henry's still alive," Julie said. "He probably enlisted others to help him.''

The general drew in a lungful of smoke. "You're right. It would take more than one man to shut down this center. It would take a highly trained team with very specific roles, expertise, equipment . . . a major op.''

Julie sat against one of the console tables. "Great. So we can look forward to spending months in here with terrorists and saboteurs.'' She pulled back her long black hair and took a deep breath. "Can you at least do something about the heat and circulation in this utopian city of yours? I can hardly breathe. And that cigarette of yours isn't helping my stomach.''

General Patterson crushed out his cigarette and returned to the active terminal. Frowning, he stared at the screen, his grim expression aglow with the screen's colors. "I'm no engineer, but . . .'' he paused and stared, ". . . this can't . . . possibly be—''

"What's wrong?'' Julie asked.

The general looked at her, his eyes stone serious. "Someone or something is deliberately sucking the air out of this center.''

Chapter Thirty-six
ER

Colorado Springs, Colorado
Wednesday, December 29
1900 Hours

"Someone get us a wheelchair!" Jill's voice blasted through the mostly empty emergency room like a cannon.

Several nurses in the administration area looked up, annoyed.

Jill and Nancy helped Olin into the Silver Cross Hospital's emergency wing, her arms over their shoulders as though they were carrying a wounded football player off the field. Only one other couple sat waiting in the patients' lounge, and no doctors were present.

Jill, hoarse and winded, said to a large nurse seated in the reception cubicle, "We need a wheelchair."

The grooves in the nurse's aged face deepened. "We don't need your kind of noise in here," she scolded. The nurse was old enough to have seen every type of injury that could be carried, dragged, or wheeled through that door. But she could see that this was different, and it spelled trouble. She eyed all three of them, with their distraught expressions and well-traveled clothes—especially Jill in her soiled flight garbs, Yankees baseball cap, and Beretta side arm—and assumed the worst.

"Have a seat and fill out these forms." The nurse pointed her pen at Olin. "And I'll need to make a copy of her insurance card."

"Screw the insurance!" Jill yelled. "This woman's been in a helicopter crash and raped by men who think the world is coming to an end."

The nurse's serious expression remained unimpressed. "Save your stories. You need to fill out these forms."

"I'll take those," Nancy offered.

The nurse gave her the clipboard of papers, picked up the phone receiver, and punched in a number.

An orderly wheeled a gurney toward them. "Someone need help?"

"Bless you," Jill huffed.

Jill and Nancy helped Olin onto the gurney.

Olin screamed when the orderly tried to lift her leg onto the table. "Please!"

"It's broken," Nancy told him. "It happened yesterday in a crash and it hasn't been looked after."

The orderly—a young, clean man barely twenty—scanned Olin's lacerations and bruises. "Jimminy!"

Jill indicated her swollen leg. "You have no idea what she's been—"

A green-frocked doctor burst through the set of double doors to the operating area. "What's going on here?"

"Air-crash victim," Nancy said.

"Looks like she's got a broken leg," the orderly offered. "Multiple lacerations and contusions."

"Severe trauma," Nancy said, adding, "emotional."

The doctor—a tall, lean man with wire-frame glasses and closely cropped hair to camouflage his baldness—gave Olin's face a cursory examination and scowled when he saw the neglected wounds. The delay would make it worse for scarring. He called to one of the nurses behind the reception desk for assistance, then said to the orderly, "Get her down to Radiology. I need a full set of X rays. Then get her cleaned up so I can see what's what."

"You got 'em." The orderly began pushing Olin's gurney down the corridor. A nurse walked alongside, noting Olin's responses to her questions on a page clipped to a board.

Before the doctor could retreat, Nancy grabbed his arm and whispered, "She's been raped."

The doctor looked puzzled. "Before the crash?"

"After. Marauders found her wreck and raped her repeatedly with no regard for her injuries. They meant to kill her."

"*Christ.*" The doctor called for another nurse. The old woman with the deep facial grooves approached them. "Get a crisis counselor over here," he ordered. "And call the sheriff's office."

The nurse threw Jill a wary glance. "The sheriff's already here."

The doctor said to Nancy, "It would help if you stayed with your friend awhile."

Nancy's head bobbed. "Of course."

"Excuse me." The doctor retreated through the double doors.

Jill rushed to Nancy and said, "I need to get to Cheyenne. Do you think you can handle this by yourself?"

"I was hoping to go with you later," Nancy said.

"I can't wait around," Jill said. "Besides, it'll take the rest of the evening to check in here. Cheyenne Mountain's not twelve miles away. Have the doctor check you over and get a good night's sleep. In the morning, call a cab and join us there."

Jill spun and headed for the door.

"But I don't have my wallet," Nancy called after her.

Jill found the sheriff and three of his deputies standing in the doorway.

"That was quick," Jill said. "They just took her into X ray. She's got quite a story to tell you."

The sheriff, a gray, stocky man with a crew cut, removed his John B. Stetson and said, "Are you the pilot of that red chopper sittin' up there on the roof helipad?"

"Yes . . . but it's not mine . . . actually . . . it's on loan."

"Uh-huh. Looks like you've got a story to tell us too." The sheriff turned to his deputies. "Cuff her."

"What!?"

Nancy, watching, took a tentative step toward them.

"I'm Sheriff Sherman Block," he said, "and you're under arrest. First off, you admitted to possessing stolen property. But it gets a whole lot better. You're in violation of a presidential mandate making it illegal to fly an aircraft of any kind in this country. No exceptions. I'm sure you heard all about it."

His three deputies surrounded Jill, removed her side arm, and grabbed her arms.

"Make sure she hears her rights," the sheriff said.

"This is absurd!" Jill said. "I'm a captain in the U.S. Army on active duty. I've got to get to Cheyenne Mountain. I can't be delayed!"

"I'm sure you've got your reasons—all of them in the name of national security," the sheriff mocked. "And you can tell me your story in the mornin'. Meanwhile, my deputies will take you downtown."

When Jill saw Nancy approaching, she signaled her to stay out of this.

"McNitt," the sheriff said to one of his deputies, "I'm going home to my wife and some supper." He winked at him and added, "You'd be doin' me a big favor tonight by seein' I'm not disturbed till mornin'."

"Promise, boss," the deputy said, grinning.

Sheriff Block pushed his John B. over his dome as he walked out the double doors into the night.

Chapter Thirty-seven
Breathless

Cheyenne Mountain
Wednesday, December 29
1900 Hours

"This is impossible," Julie said, looking over General Patterson's shoulder at the display.

"I wish it were," he said. "The fact is we're rapidly losing our air."

"But how?"

"This center requires an enormous ventilation system," the general explained. "It continually pulls out stale air and brings in new. You would assume that if the air intakes were compromised, the outtake vents would stop functioning. But it's clearly not working that way now." He indicated the screen's power grid schematic. "Only one generator is on-line, and it's tied full throttle to the outtakes. Someone with a great deal of knowledge about this center is using the ventilation system to make sure no one leaves here alive."

Julie nudged the general aside so she could have access to the room's only operating terminal. She scanned the readouts. "We're losing ten thousand cubic feet of air every minute. How large is this center?"

"Four and a half acres spread across fifteen buildings," the general said.

"How high are the ceilings?"

"Varies. The war room is a fifty-foot. The corridors and the living quarters are standard eight feet."

"So if the average ceiling height is, say, fifteen feet, times four and a half acres . . ." Julie sat down at the terminal and scribbled the arithmetic on a notepad beside the keyboard. "This center has about three million cubic feet of air. At a loss rate of ten thousand cubic feet per minute, that gives us about four and a half hours. Assuming the loss started when the center's power was compromised," she checked her watch, then looked at the general, "we have twenty-seven minutes left."

The general winced. "And I've been sitting here twiddling my thumbs all this time."

Julie stood up from the terminal. "What about an emergency air supply?"

"None. There is a purification system that scrubs and recycles the air like in a submarine," the general explained. "But it won't help if we can't power it up. Or if the air is being drawn out."

"What about the north entrance's blast doors?" Julie asked. "Is there a manual override?"

"Those doors weigh twenty-five tons each," the general said. "Even if they could move manually, we would need an army to open them."

Julie slowly let out the air in her lungs. Each breath seemed to be harder to draw than the one before. "Then our only chance is to restore power. Even ten seconds would be enough to crack open the north doors."

The general shook his head. "Everything's controlled from the operations center. That area's sealed off tight—I've tried to access it. Doesn't even have emergency lights."

"So there's no one else out there we can count on."

"No one. They're all dead or dying."

Julie returned to the display's power grid. "Where are the power plant generators?"

"In Section C, lower level," the general said. "Easy access."

"May I make a suggestion?" Julie offered, studying the screen. "Please."

She tapped a finger on the schematic. "Go down there and try to manually restart the air intakes by rerouting power from the working generator. If that isn't possible, then take that last generator off-line.''

"Sounds reasonable.'' General Patterson withdrew his .45. "I want you to keep this with you. And stay put in this room.''

"No way. I need to do a little coaxing.''

"Coaxing?'' the general scoffed.

"Anthony's still on-line and patched into the data centers, isn't it?''

The general lifted his eyebrows. "Yes, of course it is. The room is self-powered.''

Julie took the general's .45 and started for the door. "It's time I asked Anthony to help us.''

Chapter Thirty-eight
Off-line

Cheyenne Mountain
Wednesday, December 29
1930 Hours

"This is Alpha Seven-Two-Zero to NORAD Op Center. Acknowledge, please.''

Marshall waited for a response but, as with his other attempts en route, received no reply. The conclusion was clear enough: Cheyenne Air Center's communications had been compromised.

"Every channel is down,'' he said to Williams over the intercom. "All NORAD frequencies.''

"Doesn't make sense,'' the sergeant said. "Is everybody on holiday?''

Marshall didn't offer a theory; they would appraise the situation firsthand soon enough. He brought the Comanche over the final ridge and descended toward Cheyenne's north entrance. They had flown halfway across Colorado without serious incident after shutting down all noncritical flight systems. Throughout the journey, the engine RPMs had remained stubbornly in the red while the telltale odor of burning seals told them of an imminent breakdown.

Marshall set down the Comanche on the road outside the tunnel next to two other choppers: one a modern UH-60A Black Hawk, the other an older Huey UH-1H, a model so archaic he had never actually seen one in service. As soon as the wheels touched the pavement, he extinguished the engines and activated the chopper's automatic fire-control system—just in case.

Williams opened his canopy and surveyed the mountain's entrance, which reminded him of the Bat Cave. The tunnel leading inside stood dark, quiet, and empty. Even the pole lamps were extinguished.

"They're taking cost-containment measures much too far," Williams jested, though every instinct told him not to relax his guard.

They retrieved their gear from the weapons bay and headed for the darkened entrance. Marshall switched on his flashlight and directed its powerful beam into the misty tunnel. This was no holiday shutdown. There had been a fire in here recently.

They proceeded inside.

They hadn't walked far before reaching the first security checkpoint. The two directed their lights through the glass of the tollbooth-size station. The booth was empty.

"Anybody home?" Williams shouted down the tunnel through cupped hands. His voice echoed hollowly back.

Marshall led the way around the gate arm and they continued their investigation of the tunnel. At the second checkpoint, the security room's double glass panels had been shattered. They swept their lights inside and found two soldiers on the floor, one of them still clutching a .45 handgun. Both had been shot in the head.

"A murder-suicide?" Williams offered.

"Hardly," Marshall said. "This station's been hit."

They proceeded to the third checkpoint. A fire had swept through the glass-enclosed room, its huge windows shattered, its beams blackened, its wood charred. An appalling stench consumed the tunnel. Their light beams found several bodies inside too badly burned to determine specifics.

"This place has been cleared to the man," Williams observed.

Marshall's thoughts focused on Julie. All he could think about was her trapped inside. Was she even still alive? he wondered. They covered the tunnel's remaining third of a mile in less than three minutes to the center's towering steel blast doors. Both were closed, the mountain secured.

"A dozen giants with chains and winches aren't going to open these," Williams said. "Any chance of us using explosives?"

Marshall shook his head. "These doors are three feet thick and built to withstand a thermonuclear blast. Someone inside wants to make damn sure the likes of us stay out."

Julie moved past door after unfamiliar door, scanning each of them with the aid of a cigarette-size flashlight General Patterson had found in a desk drawer. Every doorway looked the same to her. The air had grown cold and foul and stale. Breathing was no longer a routine Julie took for granted; it was a strenuous chore requiring concentration and resolve.

Her oxygen-starved mind raced with frightful hallucinations. Every shadow under her light moved as though someone or something were stalking her. She thought she heard footsteps behind her. Then in front. She tightened her already overprotective grip on the handle of the general's .45, while her fear produced waves of adrenaline that threatened to strangle her.

Julie reached the end of the corridor and recognized the familiar crimson glow through the wire-mesh windows of Anthony's computer room. Her heart fluttered when she saw the palm-size keypad beside the double doors, its usual muted-green glow now flashing red. She didn't need to enter the general's code. One of the doors stood ajar—a wedge of wood had been jammed under to keep it from shutting and locking.

Julie transferred the flashlight to her left hand to allow full use of the general's handgun. Her misgivings about this place refused to give her feet the mobility to enter. However, she knew that if she stayed in the hallway, she would be dead in less than twenty minutes.

Julie drew in the deepest breath she could summon, slipped inside the room, and watched. The room's large size rendered her tiny flashlight useless. She looked for signs of an intruder but saw nothing she hadn't seen on her first visit here. The air was cold, like a crisp November evening. She began shivering. Special light panels bounced red and blue hues off the high walls and ceiling, giving the room the ambience of a laser-tag arcade. Her eyes settled on the object she had come for—a dark sarcophagus rising from the center of the room. Anthony was waiting for her.

Julie grabbed a heavy coat from the rack beside the door and slipped her arms into a garment several sizes too large. She immediately felt more comfortable. She unhooked a pair of infrared goggles from a rack and fitted them over her eyes as she made her way to the room's only workstation. She took a seat before the terminal. Doubts about her plan began to percolate. What if this workstation had been installed on its own electrical line to lessen the load of Anthony's power consumption? If so, without power to the terminal her plan was finished.

She drew in another precious lungful of air and pressed the terminal's master power switch. The terminal powered up without incident.

"Thank God . . ."

When its display panel flared on, she let out her breath slowly and slid the infrared goggles onto her forehead before burning her retinas. The CPU booted and presented her with an interface to Anthony's awesome computing capabilities. Julie requested access to the center's computing network. An error message appeared:

UNABLE TO ACCESS NETWORK SERVERS.
SEE ADMINISTRATOR.

"No kidding."

NORAD's computing network was down, and she couldn't restart any part of it from here. Julie requested access to Anthony's experimental microprocessors. Several seconds later, a comforting READY message appeared on the screen's lower left corner.

"Yes!"

Did Anthony need to communicate through the network, she wondered, or did it have its own links to the center's operations? There was only one way to find out; she called up the Cheyenne Mountain's power grid. Anthony searched through its vast inventory of mirrored files and presented her with a graphical map representing key areas and functions that controlled all power produced and consumed within the center.

Julie was in! She and Anthony had lots to talk about.

General Patterson opened the steel door to the center's power station and stepped out onto the catwalk. The area below him was dark and dead. By the dim emergency lighting he could make out the monster shapes of six generators. Normally the decibels emitted by this machinery would have made conversation difficult at best. Now there was only the distant whine of a single generator.

He placed a hand on the railing and the other against the cinder-block wall while descending the dark, steel-mesh steps. At the bottom, he switched on his flashlight and made his way past rows of diesel generators each the size of half a railroad car. He reached the plant's only working unit, its roaring turbines producing 22,000 volts of electricity, or roughly one-fifth of the center's power needs. Coffin-size toolboxes sat against the wall between each generator. Even with the proper tools, he knew he couldn't restore power to these other units without diagrams, schematics, experienced technicians, and lots of time. Their only hope lay in his ability to shut down this single unit—*fast!*

On one side of the working generator he found a panel with several meters and twist-switches devoid of instructions or other markings to assist him. The system's architects did not allow for these machines to be tweaked at the source by someone without the proper credentials and degrees; qualified technicians controlled everything through computers on another level of the center. His light bounced from one switch to another. His first impulse was to turn all of them in the opposite direction. But that course troubled him. If shutting down the generator was that simple, then what would prevent the saboteur from simply coming down here and turning the switches back to the On position? To make that plan work, he would have to be willing and able to guard this station with deadly force.

The general let out a sigh of defeat. The air was almost gone, and with it the last of his hope. He simply didn't know enough about the power station to offer a foolproof solution to their problem. Their only chance lay in permanently disabling this generator, thereby cutting power to all outlet vents. That would at least buy them limited time to consume the stale air still trapped inside.

But how would he accomplish this?

General Patterson investigated the large toolbox against the wall. He opened it and stared vacantly at the selection of huge tools, some of which he could not identify. He wiped the sweat from his eyes and wrapped his fingers around a wrench the size of a baseball bat. He lifted the weighty tool and wondered how he might effectively use it.

"You're becoming quite the handyman."

The general whirled and saw Henry Princeton surrounded by four men wearing technician's frocks whom he recognized from various teams. Henry's clothes and hair were disheveled—the opposite of his usual impeccably groomed appearance—as though he had just risen from a fitful night's sleep.

General Patterson managed, "Henry, you wouldn't by chance know anything about all this?"

Henry's sullen expression melted into a grin. "I will neither confirm nor deny any knowledge of this affair or anything related to the demise of the Eclipse Strategic Defense Satellite Network. Now it's your turn. What are you hoping to accomplish with that wrench?"

"I intend to see that we don't all suffocate," Patterson replied.

Henry laughed uproariously, then blurted, "I don't think so."

"Are you mad?" the general shouted. "Do you want to die in here?"

"I assure you I have no such death wish." Henry signaled the others with a cock of his head. The four technicians surrounded the general.

General Patterson laughed. "You guys need to lighten up. You're taking your jobs way too seriously—" The general took a home-run-size swing with his wrench that caught the closest technician solidly on the bridge of his nose. The blow had all his strength behind it. There came a sickening crack of bone as the technician flew backward, his neck at an odd angle, and dumped heavily on the floor against the generator.

The three remaining technicians quickly subdued the general and twisted his arms severely behind his back to the point of breaking. The wrench clattered noisily to the floor. The general gritted his teeth against the pain.

Henry strolled forward. "Bravo, General. You are the great black warrior after all." He picked up the wrench and, feeling its sheer weight, admired how the general was able to wield it so effortlessly. "So you thought you could shut down the generator with this. What a pathetically meager plan. It wouldn't have worked, I assure you. Let me show you how robust these generators are."

Henry lifted the wrench like a spear and plunged it into the grid between the generator's two electrical terminals. A flurry of sparks poured from the end of the wrench like an electric waterfall. The roar of the turbines did not vary.

"You see, General, no short." Henry beckoned his associates to continue. They dragged the general forward.

"Why are you doing this, Henry?" the general shouted. "What's this all about?"

"It's about a very large sum of money," Henry said, the tone of his voice suggesting the general should have known as much. "And I've worked very hard during the past twenty-four hours to keep my share."

"You've succeeded in shutting down Eclipse. Why not just clear out of here while you can?"

"Eclipse was only a dry run," Henry said. "The technology worked brilliantly—so brilliantly, in fact, that you can't begin to imagine the power we're now wielding. Too bad you won't be around to see us put it to great use. I believe you would have appreciated the intricacies. But, sadly, my job now is to make certain there are no witnesses—like you."

Henry signaled the men to proceed. The trio forced the general down onto his knees before the protruding wrench.

"A witness to what, for God's sake?" the general demanded.

Henry didn't answer him; instead, he instructed his men, "Careful what you touch."

One of the technicians, the largest of the group, grabbed the general by his closely cropped hair and brought his face to within inches of the wrench. The general could hear the electricity crackle over its metallic surface as the cascading sparks flew down his cheeks. He struggled helplessly against the three pairs of strong arms that held him. The technician pulled up on the general's hair.

General Patterson cried out. *"Henry!"*

His men drove the general forward, jamming his mouth into the wrench. Teeth flew everywhere. The men jumped quickly away as 22,000 volts of electricity pumped through the general's spasming body.

Julie completed her "rewiring" of the center's master power grid by moving objects around a flowchart diagram. There were page after page of electronic objects and schematics for her to consider. Every ventilator, every fan, every thermostat, every boiler, every light fed its sensors into a master clock, with which Julie, given enough time, could work out an override scheme. However, *time* was in critically short demand. The foul air was taking its toll on her brain, and she had nearly blacked out twice since sitting down here. If that happened, she knew she would never wake up. If her rewiring worked, it would direct power to the north entrance, where she had set the twin blast doors to Open. That was the best she could do, given the time. Everything, theoretically, was ready.

She heard something, a movement off in the darkness. Or had she imagined it? The center was full of groans and creaks as the pipes and conduits contracted with the drop in temperature. She drew in her breath with difficulty and perched her hand over the keyboard. This would be her only chance.

Shaking, she pressed the Enter key.

The word PROCESSING began blinking at the bottom of her display. *So far, so good.* She gave up trying to breathe and just held her breath. Suddenly, the PROCESSING signal froze and the word ABORTED appeared in its place.

"What the—!"

Julie heard movement to her right—the unmistakable sound of someone walking.

She stood up from the terminal. "General?"

Through the dimness she could see several shadows moving toward her like zombies in the night. She was too terrified to move.

Henry Princeton, his eyes wild and glassy, stepped into the glow cast by her display. Three men whose features she couldn't make out stood behind him like bodyguards.

Henry drew in a deep breath and expelled it in the form of words. "I figured you would be here in this last bastion of our computer-controlled world. Everything else in this center is dormant and dead, but in here there's life—and *thinking*."

Julie couldn't summon the air into her lungs to speak. She stole a glance at the general's handgun sitting on the table next to the terminal, a look Henry quickly noticed.

"But not for long," Henry added. He helped himself to the general's .45. "You too will grow cold and still, your memory centers shut down. For it is my duty to take you off-line."

Chapter Thirty-nine
Thunder

Cheyenne Mountain
Wednesday, December 29
1930 Hours

The north tunnel lights came on with a bang, bathing the walls with its yellow-green illumination. Marshall and Williams were on their feet in an instant.

"That's more like it," Williams said, throwing down his cigar stub.

A buzzer sounded, and several amber lights began rotating. There came a deep rumble as the pneumatic arm began moving the two forty-foot steel blast doors. A great rush of air blew past them as the center greedily sucked the tunnel's air inside.

It was over as suddenly as it began. Seconds later, the tunnel's lights again darkened and the rumble of the doors fell silent. The two men stood in complete darkness, listening. In the eerie silence that followed, all that remained was the sound of the wind blowing past them.

"What the hell just happened?" Williams asked.

Marshall thought of Julie. "Maybe someone with enough knowledge of this place is trying like hell to get out."

They switched on their lights and directed the beams along the edge of the three-foot-thick blast doors. The opening was barely wide enough for a man to squeeze through.

Marshall slipped off his flight jacket and utility belt, and stripped down to his T-shirt. He pressed his body between the doors. It would indeed be a very tight fit. He raised his arms and, stretching, tried to flatten himself like a worm. With a great heave, Marshall pushed himself through the doors, tearing the T-shirt off his back.

He was inside.

"Nice going." Williams passed him his shirt, utility belt, Franchi, and flashlight. Then he, too, began stripping to his waist.

"There's no way you're going to fit through," Marshall said.

"Watch me."

When Williams was naked to the waist, he showed Marshall a tiny ampoule of oil. "Gun lubricant."

He squeezed the tube's contents into his hand and rubbed it over his chest until it resembled oiled mahogany. He raised his arms and attempted to push himself through the opening, but his muscular frame was simply too wide. Williams gave a battle-cry holler and pushed for all he was worth. He succeeded only in pushing his left shoulder through the opening.

"Don't this just beat all," he said.

"Back off," Marshall said. "If these doors decide to close, they'll crush you like a walnut. I'll meet you back here as quick as I can."

"Joe . . . ?"

Marshall disappeared from the opening and played his light across the center's staging area. There was no power apparent anywhere. The security desk stood empty, the area abandoned. He tried the double doors leading into the administrative wing. They were locked. Marshall withdrew his Franchi from his back holster and pumped four consecutive rounds into one of the doors. He thrust his boot against the door and kicked it down.

A corridor, dark and dense, beckoned him. With his Franchi thrust before him, Marshall proceeded down the hallway. The air was stale and cold and required an effort to draw in a modest lungful. He stopped at the first door with a large wire-mesh window, pushed it open, and peered into some sort of control room. He counted four bodies. One was still propped in a chair, the others sprawled across the floor.

Marshall heard gunfire coming from another wing. He returned to the hallway and listened. A shot sounded again—someone was firing a handgun. He hurried toward its source.

Marshall entered another wing of personal quarters. He heard voices behind one of the doors. There was something else, too—a woman crying. Two men were conversing, while a woman whose voice he did not recognize wept. He moved quickly and silently toward the open doorway at the end of the hallway and listened.

"... so she barges in on these two queers and finds them in each other's arms," one of the men was saying. "Angle is everything to make it appear self-inflicted."

Marshall slipped into the room just as a man pulled the trigger. The blast nearly removed half the woman's head. She collapsed on top of two other bodies, also with bullet wounds to their heads. A half-dozen candles lit the room. Marshall could scarcely make out two young men in white robes standing over a woman.

The man who had fired placed the gun in her hand and looped her index finger around the trigger. "She shoots both queers in the head before turning the gun on herself. No forensic investigator would question . . ."

"I've got a question," Marshall said. Both men scrambled to their feet and, when they saw his shotgun, raised their arms in an automatic gesture of capitulation.

"Where did you come from?" the gun-wielding man asked.

"None of your goddamn business," Marshall spat. "I'll give

239

you two seconds to tell me why this woman is dead."

"*Fuck you!*" he said.

Marshall pumped two rounds directly into his chest, transforming the front of his white robe into a bloody mat. The man flew back against the wall as though a truck had hit him.

His friend waved Marshall off. "Don't shoot!"

"I'll give you the same two seconds to tell me what's going on here."

"A ... a death m-masquerade," he stammered. "W-we have orders to execute all personnel in the center. No exceptions. W-we were told to make them look like suicides and murder-suicides ... a ritual—"

"*Who ordered you?*" Marshall shouted.

"I can't tell you that."

Marshall, sneering, fired a round into the young man's knee. He went down with a howl, his lower right leg reduced to a web of hanging flesh and sinew. Marshall jammed the Franchi into his face.

"*Who?*"

"Skile!" he cried, hands on his temples. "Alexander *Fucking* Skile!"

Marshall's face brightened. "See what you can do when you put your mind to it?"

The young man looked up into Marshall's face and saw a soldier consumed with rage to the point of madness for failing to prevent the woman's death. He knew at that moment that he was a dead man.

"Don't—"

The colonel pulled the trigger of his Franchi. The familiar sound of thunder roared through the room.

Henry glanced up from his examination of the general's .45. "It's almost impossible to hit anything with one of these." When Julie didn't respond, he added, "You do realize that your colleagues are all dead, don't you?"

Julie pressed her back against the wall of the cubicle. "Why are you doing this?"

"Even your general is dead. He succumbed to a rather freakish

240

accident while valiantly trying to restore power to the center. Such a tragic end to his brilliant career.''

Julie wouldn't accept that. "You're lying."

Henry, grinning, produced the general's pinkie ring and threw it out onto the table in front of her. "Such a tragedy."

"You bastard . . ." As she moved toward him, the other three stepped in around Henry, effectively protecting him. "No investigators in their right mind will think all this was an accident. Or that these people willingly committed suicide."

"Whatever—it's just not that important," Henry said. "So let me explain why *you're* still alive. The simple fact is, I promised myself that I'd have my way with you before leaving here. Now, is that asking too much?"

"You're talking nonsense," Julie said. "We've only got minutes of air left. Then we'll all die."

Henry didn't appear the least bit concerned about that possibility. "Don't fret it. I assure you we've provided for ourselves in that regard." He threw a glance at his associates, who smiled and nodded.

"Oh, there is one more thing," Henry said. "I promised the others that I would share you. After you and I finish, of course."

Julie slipped to the back of the cubicle and wedged herself into the corner.

Henry followed her. "And even if you do mind, there's not much—"

The crack of a handgun rang through the corridor outside the computer room. All heads turned toward the room's double doors.

Henry scowled. "There isn't supposed to be anybody down here. Paul, find out what's going on."

Henry's most able man bolted for the doors. He pushed them open and shouted, "Henry wants this area cleared—"

The blast from a shotgun at close range hurled him back through the doors with a crash, where his dark shape fell in full sight of the others. The two remaining technicians produced side arms from their frocks.

Henry thrust the general's .45 at Julie and demanded, "Who's out there?"

"How would I know?" she said. "This is *your* little party."

241

Henry drew back the hammer of the .45. "I assure you that the moment my plans change you will be dead."

Julie grew silent. The room's soft red and blue lights blinked out, plunging them into near darkness; the only light came from the glow of colors off the computer monitor. The double doors flew open.

Henry whirled and saw someone charge inside, but couldn't make out anything specific beyond movement. *"Damn!"*

He spun and discharged a round at Julie, but she was gone. The bullet tore a huge hole in the fabric wall. He saw a dark blur as she rushed out of the cubicle. He fired another round after her and succeeded only in putting a bullet through the terminal display, which erupted in sparks. She vanished into the darkness.

Henry's two associates, their handguns held ready, took up defensive positions on either side of the double doors. There was no light for their eyes to adjust.

"What's happening, guys?" Henry hollered after them. "Ray, what do you see?"

"Nothing," Ray said. "This is nuts. Fred, do you see anything?"

Fred didn't answer.

Ray rolled away from the door to his comrade and nearly stumbled over Fred's body. He knelt down and felt his face, which was wet and slippery, and touched a deep gash that stretched halfway around Fred's throat.

"Someone's in here!" Ray hollered into the darkness. "Someone has a knife!"

Ray made his way to the wall and fumbled for a pair of infrared goggles. He sensed someone standing directly behind him.

Ray spun and fired into the darkness.

On the opposite side of the room, Henry thrust the .45 in the direction of the shot and discharged five rounds. When the roar of the gunfire subsided, he waited and watched. Someone staggered toward him. The uneven light from the sparking display washed across the figure. Henry's rounds had put two huge holes in Ray's abdomen. The two exchanged confused glances before Ray collapsed onto his knees and fell facedown before Henry.

Across the room, Julie sat at the base of the steel monolith that contained the brains of Anthony. The casing felt cold and immovable against her back. She slipped the infrared goggles over her eyes and saw Henry's heat signature next to the terminal. He made an easy target, and she cursed herself for letting him take the .45 from her. She scanned the room on this side of the monolith and saw no one else.

Henry moved away from the terminal and headed straight toward her. Julie remained absolutely still. He couldn't possibly see her, she convinced herself. He walked straight into the side of Anthony with enough force to nearly knock him unconscious. She heard the .45 clatter to the floor and saw the heat signature of its muzzle. He cursed to himself.

Henry put a hand on the side for support and ran the other through his curly hair, shaking his throbbing head. The gun lay several feet from Julie. She moved for it without making a sound. The heat signature of another man, larger than Henry, appeared from behind the monolith and began walking straight toward them. She drew in her breath sharply, a noise Henry was quick to notice.

"Ah!" Henry said, turning in her direction. "So I've found my mad scientist."

Julie slid away, her nylon coat brushing the steel side. Henry followed her, keeping a hand on Anthony for bearing.

Suddenly, the muzzle of a Beretta jammed painfully into the base of Henry's neck. At the same instant, an arm wrapped around his neck and locked it in a deadly bear hug. He froze.

Marshall put his lips next to Henry's ear. "Did you touch her?"

Henry was too surprised to answer.

Marshall tightened his hold around Henry's neck. "I won't ask you again."

"S-she's unharmed," Henry stammered. "Ask her yourself."

Julie jumped to her feet. "Joe!?"

"Is he telling the truth?" Marshall asked. "Are you all right?"

"Yes. Be careful, Joe. He's responsible for many deaths here today."

"I'm begging you," Henry sobbed. "Don't kill me. I can offer you information."

Marshall holstered his Beretta, grabbed Henry by his wavy hair, and drove his head into Anthony's steel casing. He didn't care if he smashed his skull like a pumpkin. Henry let out a grunt and, out cold, dropped to the floor at the colonel's feet.

Julie studied Marshall's heat signature and could make out the outline of a pair of infrared goggles, which he had taken from the rack beside the doors. What she saw wasn't a man, per se, but an aura of heat moving and radiating like an angel.

She rushed into his eager arms. "Oh, Joe!"

They held each other for several minutes. Tears flowed freely down Julie's cheeks and collected in a trough at the bottom of her goggles.

Chapter Forty
Good Night

Cheyenne Mountain
Wednesday, December 29
2030 hours

"It's no wonder Skile went to so much trouble to keep this unit from us," Julie said.

After restoring partial power to the center, Julie had disassembled and connected the Blackbird satellite module to a workbench of test equipment, then downloaded its archived files to a workstation. They had hit the jackpot of evidence. For the past half hour she had scanned through one incriminating file after another. High-treason charges were the least of Skile's legal problems.

Marshall folded his arms across his chest and leaned against her worktable to watch her work. "I'm surprised that with all his resources Skile didn't cover his tracks better."

Julie leaned back in her chair and drew in a deep breath of fresh air that had been pouring in since she had opened the blast doors and restarted the ventilation. "The satellite's archiving system wasn't designed to re-encrypt its commands. They're system-management routines that are no longer needed once they're authenticated and executed. So every command Skile uploaded was automatically stored in its native machine language. The likelihood that any satellite would be taken out of orbit so its files could be scrutinized was quite small. Maybe he thought the risks of getting caught were minimal."

"So what you're saying," Marshall noted, "is he didn't count on you being on the investigation team."

Julie accepted the compliment with a smile.

"I still don't get it," Williams said. The sergeant reclined in an office chair in the corner of the computer lab, his hands locked behind his head, a cigar stub between his lips. "So the son of a bitch shuts down our defense satellite network. Good for him. But what's he trying to prove? That he's some kind of Master of the World?"

Julie's frustration was apparent. "That bothers me too. It's going to take weeks for a team to sort through these files and reconstruct exactly what he was up to. Maybe then we'll have some clues."

"So what about Eclipse?" Marshall asked. "How long do you think it will take to get the network back on-line?"

Julie wheeled away from her terminal. "I suspect that once the team gets here, they'll have partial operation reestablished by morning."

"What's the status of the MPs?" Marshall asked his sergeant.

"An investigation team arrived half an hour ago," Williams said. "They've got their work cut out for them."

"Well," Marshall said, stretching, "I, for one, am exhausted. Any chance we can cop a couple hours' sleep before the other teams get here?"

"That's a splendid idea!" Julie said, rising from her chair. She took his hand. "Come. Let me show you my new apartment."

*   *   *

"How long has it been since we made love?" Marshall asked.

"A year ago Christmas Eve," Julie said, running her hands through her long black hair.

Marshall stretched out on Julie's twin-size bed. "It's been an extremely busy time for both of us. This hasn't been an easy year for me. But I should have called you more."

"That's a totally unacceptable excuse," Julie responded. Grinning mischievously, she slipped off her blouse. "I think we should talk about this."

"I think you're right."

The next minutes were a blur to Marshall. He would later tell her that he had no memory of them undressing and snuggling under the sheets together. It was as though some power had miraculously stripped and thrust them together in a passionate embrace. The next thing Marshall remembered was holding Julie in his arms while tucked snugly beneath a quilt. He'd forgotten how gloriously soft and warm her skin felt. He kissed her deeply until his lips were raw.

Finally, Marshall could hold in his passion no longer. He was already painfully aroused. He whipped Julie onto her back. More than ready, she let out a deep moan of satisfaction.

"Joe, I've missed you so much," she whispered.

"So have I. How could I have been so stupid to let you go?"

Julie wrapped her legs around him and pulled him closer and deeper.

Day Four
Thursday, December 30, 1999

*"There are no problems complex enough
that computers are needed."*

**Mathematicians during the unveiling
of the world's first general-purpose computer in 1947**

Chapter Forty-one
Morning

Hackers Break Into
Chicago Exchange Network

CHICAGO (Reuters)—A computer intruder reportedly broke into one of the Chicago Board of Trade's computer links with financial institutions abroad yesterday, forcing the stock exchange to shut down for nearly two hours.

Trade officials discovered that a hacker, using off-the-shelf equipment, had left "digital footprints" in its computers. Government and private experts repaired the breach, but the hacker has not been identified.

The system is reportedly used to carry messages deemed to be sensitive but not proprietary. One official described it as "not major."

Cheyenne Mountain
Thursday, December 30
0430 hours

Colonel Joseph Marshall woke from an exhausted sleep. He sat up in a room that was thick and black. There were no windows to open for some fresh air or to emit even modest illumination. Marshall knew he was inside Cheyenne Mountain, but little else. For several hours his mind had soaked up the healing elixir only the solitude of sleep could provide. The process had temporarily severed his tenuous strands of memory, leaving him confused and disoriented.

He began to check his watch before realizing he wasn't wearing it. In fact, he wasn't wearing anything at all. He felt the sheets beside him.

Julie was gone.

Marshall sprang off the bed and snatched his watch from the desk. Its luminous dial read 4:30—he had slept for five hours. He switched on the desk lamp. His clothes had vanished as well— every last shred. He checked the closet and found only a worn bathrobe hanging over a pair of sandal thongs. He slipped into both. The robe, intended for someone much smaller, barely covered his thighs. He cracked open the door and heard voices and activity of the arriving military investigation teams.

Marshall stepped into the hallway. "Julie?"

This is nuts! he thought. He paraded down the corridor and slipped through the double doors leading to Cheyenne's administrative wing. Dozens of people were gathering here—some in fatigues, most in uniforms—taking over offices and setting up tables in common areas.

A soldier dressed for combat spotted him. "Who are you?"

"Just the live-in maid," Marshall said.

The colonel continued down the hallway and passed a break room where several soldiers were sitting around a table, chatting and sipping coffee. He spotted Williams among them.

"Have you seen Julie?" Marshall called into the kitchenette.

The soldiers turned to look at him. An awkward silence followed as they scrutinized Marshall's nonstandard military attire.

Marshall repeated his question, his tone cold and stern. "Have you seen her?"

Williams cocked his head down the hallway. "She's in the computer lab. I thought you were with her. Nancy's here."

"Nancy? When did she arrive?"

"Just after midnight. A Colorado Springs patrol car drove her up."

Marshall started to withdraw.

Before the colonel could get away, Williams called after him, "I've got one more item for your to-do list."

"What is it?"

"Jill's in jail."

"What!?"

"Nancy said the sheriff grabbed her at the hospital for violating the flight ban with stolen property," Williams said.

Marshall rolled his eyeballs. "Oh, for . . . Get her out of there!"

"The sheriff won't be in for at least another hour," Williams said, checking his watch. "And we'll need some bail money."

Marshall, shaking his head, disappeared from the doorway and headed for the computer lab.

"Now, this is interesting," Nancy said.

Julie wheeled away from her terminal where she had been printing out every piece of data she could find about Alexander Skile and his company, AKS Aeronautics Industries. "What's so interesting?"

Nancy glanced up from the stack of printouts Julie had given her. "Did you know Skile manufacturers microprocessors for another industry besides aerospace?"

"No, I didn't," Julie said.

"His wholly owned subsidiary, Maxim Technologies, makes specialty microprocessors for financial institutions." Nancy scanned the printout's list of applications. "Now this really gets interesting. His clients include hundreds of banks, savings and loans, ATMs, and credit-card bureaus. Guess who his biggest customers are?"

Julie put a hand on her forehead. "I'm afraid to ask."

"Wall Street and the Chicago Mercantile Exchange."

Julie closed her eyes. "Don't tell me that."

" 'Fraid so. The U.S. finance industry spent six billion dollars to upgrade its network of computers," she read from a report. "For that upgrade, seventy percent of Maxim's microprocessors were sold to Tandem and Hewlett-Packard, who provide the refrigerator-sized mainframes for some of the largest financial exchanges in the world."

"You've just given me a very big migraine," Julie said. "Do you know what you're saying?"

"I'm not sure what I'm saying," Nancy admitted. "Do you think that maybe Skile wasn't really interested in Eclipse? That maybe all along he was working on a way to save his failing company?"

"Where are my clothes?" Marshall demanded.

Julie and Nancy turned in unison to see him standing in the computer lab's doorway clad only in a barely adequate bathrobe.

Julie burst into laughter. "Honey, I'm so sorry. I carried your clothes down to the laundry. They desperately needed washing. I intended to have them back before you woke, but I guess I got distracted. I put them in the dryer more than an hour ago. I'm sure they're ready."

"Morning, Colonel," Nancy interjected. "Did you sleep well?"

Marshall closed the door securely behind him. "Yes, thank you. I'm surprised to see you here at all, let alone this early. You must feel like crap."

Nancy shrugged. "I feel a lot better than some others I once knew."

"How's Olin?"

"She spent two hours in surgery last night for her leg, and she should make a good recovery—at least physically. She'll need some plastic surgery."

Marshall nodded.

"Jill's in jail," Nancy added.

"So I heard," he said. "Williams is working on it." He rolled a chair next to Julie's. "You two looked pretty intense a moment ago. I interrupted something."

"As a matter of fact," Julie said, "we may have stumbled onto Skile's motive for shutting down Eclipse. It's just a theory, mind you, without much to back it up."

"Try me."

Julie returned to her terminal and scanned her notes. "Suppose Skile used Eclipse to take everyone's attention away from another threat. He forces Washington to put all its resources into getting its military house back in order in the face of critical security issues in the Middle East and elsewhere. While this is going on, Skile is interested in something much bigger."

"And what might that be?"

"The world's financial infrastructure," Julie announced.

Marshall, unsure what to make of the theory, glanced at Nancy, who concurred with a nod.

"The same technology that ultimately led to Eclipse's erratic behavior and failure," Julie explained, "also controls the nation's largest financial exchanges, banks, and investment houses. And guess what? The technology belongs to Skile. If he can shut down the military's proprietary surveillance and communication network, imagine what he might be able to do to financial systems."

Marshall's expression mirrored his puzzlement. "What would Skile gain by shutting down banks and exchanges?"

"Not shut down," Julie explained. "Manipulate them. It would be child's play for him to transfer millions of dollars from one account to another for personal gain. Suppose he could also change the price of a stock or commodity, erase a loan, devalue foreign currency, destroy records, change interest rates, or credit himself with shares?"

Marshall began snapping his fingers. "What was the name of the senator who died in a plane crash Monday? The President's buddy?"

"Senator Michael Lloyd," Nancy said. "Do you think there's a connection?"

"Maybe," Marshall said. "He chaired a special senate subcommittee investigating a Year 2000 computer problem. But which problem?"

Julie looked up the senator on the Internet and found several articles about him. "He was overseeing the Year 2000 computer impact on the Securities Industry."

"And he died on his way to meet with the President," Marshall said.

"There was speculation the senator intended to propose a moratorium on securities trading," Julie read. "Maybe that move would have messed up Skile's plan."

"Oh my God," Nancy said, standing. She put her fingers to her bottom lip. "Skile killed the senator."

Marshall swiveled in his chair to face her. "How could he possibly do that?"

"The air crash was blamed on computer error," Nancy said. "Somehow Skile arranged it, just as he downed my transport on its way here. He said a computer could crash an aircraft every bit as effectively as a surface-to-air missile."

"Find out if any of Skile's microprocessors are aboard a 767," Julie urged.

"Checking." Nancy began paging through another stack of printouts.

Marshall let out a low whistle. "You're scaring the hell out of me. If people wake up Monday and discover their bank accounts are empty or their assets are devalued, we're going to see a world-wide financial panic. A depression would be the least of our headaches."

"Utter chaos while Skile becomes a very wealthy man," Julie added. "But how?"

"Bingo," Nancy said. "It's here in AKS's own annual report. One hundred forty-three separate computers control a 767. Skile's microprocessors are in eighty-six of them."

"So he killed a hundred sixty innocent people just to silence one man and brought the country's airline industry to a standstill," Marshall said. He sat back, his arms folded across his chest, and added, "Do we know anything about this General Stryker? How does he fit in?"

Nancy handed him a folder. "That's straight from the CIA, highly classified. Stryker's a self-proclaimed general of a brigade of 'Dark Star' militants. A real whacko. He believes God himself has ordained him to be the commander in chief of Heaven's armed forces, and he's been recruiting troops on two continents for a couple of years. While training for Armageddon, they've left a trail of corpses and destruction throughout Europe and across half this country. He and his followers dropped out of sight about nine months ago, probably when he hooked up with Skile and his money."

Marshall, leafing through the folder, stopped to scrutinize an enlarged passport photo of Stryker dressed in a suit and tie. He could pass for a politician better than a military officer.

Julie let out a gasp. "The financial markets will close this afternoon for the remainder of the year. Whatever Skile's planning, he'd have to act today."

"We're going to need more resources," Marshall said, setting the folder aside. "I'm bringing General Medlock into the loop." He rose from his chair. "Is there a phone in here?"

Nancy pointed to a wall phone next to the door. Marshall picked up the receiver and waited for a dial tone. It never came.

"It's probably not back on-line yet," Nancy said.

"I'll need something wireless," Marshall said.

Julie held up her bag. "How about my cell phone?"

"Perfect."

She rummaged through the bag until she found her Motorola flip phone and handed it to Marshall. He punched in the number for Fort Bragg. It took a minute of switchboard connections before General Medlock's home phone began to ring. Marshall glanced at his watch and grimaced when he realized the early hour.

The general answered. "Medlock."

"Marshall here. Sorry about the time, General, but this can't wait."

"Get on with it, then," the general rasped.

"The good news is that Eclipse should be back on-line in a few hours. The teams have started arriving here at Cheyenne. The bad news is Eclipse's shutdown may have been a ruse to take our attention away from something much bigger."

"What's bigger?" the general asked.

"We're not certain," Marshall said, "but it may involve manipulating world financial markets. We believe Alexander Skile is involved. We need every piece of information about him the intelligence community can lay its hands on. His holdings, investments—"

"Slow down, Colonel. It would be a waste of time."

"A waste?" Marshall asked. "Do you know something I don't?"

"Apparently so," the general said. "It was all over the evening news last night. Skile disobeyed the flight stand-down. He and his wife and their pilot were killed in a chopper crash last night about forty-five miles outside of Chicago."

Chapter Forty-two
Master of the World

*"Money . . . ranks with love as man's greatest
source of joy."*

John Kenneth Galbraith

*Colorado Springs
Thursday, December 30
0545 hours*

"Is somebody coming to get me out of here or what?" Jill said
into the phone.

She sat at a stark table in the interrogation room of the Colorado Springs County Jail, still dressed in her well-traveled flight
uniform and wearing a baseball cap to cover her unkempt hair.
She hadn't slept a wink all night and looked it. Two deputies,
sitting at each end of the table, watched and listened to her every
word.

"You'll be bailed out today," Marshall said. "I promise."

"I don't want to be bailed out!" Jill hollered. "I want to walk
out of here a free person. I was on official military business on
orders from you. I don't deserve to be in here!"

"Slow down and listen to me, Captain," Marshall said.

"No, you listen!" Jill yelled. "I don't want to talk to any
policemen and I don't want to be interrogated. I want a friggin'
presidential pardon."

"Calm down, Jill," Marshall said. "That's an order. I promise to get you out of there. In the meantime, it's very important that you listen to me and answer my questions. Time is very short."

Jill drew in a deep breath to calm herself, but her heart continued to race as anger-induced adrenaline coursed through her. "I'll try."

"That's the Jill I know," Marshall said. "You saw two men fly out of Skile's airfield in a chopper."

"Yes, they left in one of the hangar's two Boeing 520Ns," she said.

"Describe these men to me."

"One was the pilot," Jill said. "A short guy dressed in a leather flight jacket, with closely cropped gray hair."

"And the other?" Marshall asked.

"He was the boss—you could tell by the way he carried himself. Middle-aged, very tall, very lean and balding."

Nancy pushed in beside Marshall and leaned over the conference room's speakerphone. "Jill, this is Nancy. What was this man wearing?"

"A long coat."

"What color?"

"Beige," Jill replied.

"That's him!" Nancy said, turning to the others. "That's the way Skile was dressed when I last saw him. He said he was leaving for Chicago at three o'clock to start a new life with his wife. That had to be him."

"What about a woman?" Marshall queried. "Did Skile have a woman with him?"

"Negative," Jill said.

"Maybe he picked her up along the way," Williams offered.

Nancy shook her head. "He spoke as though she had already gone ahead."

"One more question, Jill," Marshall said. "You flew one of Skile's Boeings. Did you experience any trouble on your way to Colorado Springs—component malfunction, computer or otherwise?"

"None whatsoever, Colonel. The Boeing performed flawlessly without even a hint of a computer-related problem."

The door to the interrogation room opened and in walked Sheriff Sherman Block, looking well groomed and morning fresh. He scowled when he saw Jill on the phone and said to his deputies, "So we're running a hotel now?"

"Incoming call from her superior officer," one of the deputies explained. "He said it was urgent."

"I don't give a rat's ass if it's the President of the United States trying to prevent the Second Coming. We're not running this jail for the convenience of any inmate." He thrust a finger at Jill. "I want you off that phone now."

"Colonel, I've got to go," she said.

"I'll have you out today," Marshall said. "I promise."

"*Yessir.*" She hung up the phone.

The sheriff set his hat on the table and dumped his square frame into a chair directly across from Jill. "Let's get started."

Marshall disconnected the speakerphone. "Any more theories?"

Julie, who had been nursing a coffee mug at the far end of the conference table, stood and approached the group. "Who wants to bet that our friend Alexander Skile is very much alive and planning to celebrate New Year's Eve with his wife in Chicago?"

Chicago
0600 Hours

With great fanfare, Skile and Judith burst into the living room of their elite four-bedroom condo on Chicago's Michigan Avenue. He threw up his hands as he entered and announced to his eight friends and colleagues gathered there, "Welcome to the first day of your new lives!"

There was an outburst of spontaneous cheers and applause as his guests surrounded the couple. They were genuinely glad to see them and were equally delighted to be part of Skile's grand plan, even if it meant giving up the conceited lives they had known and often loved.

This wasn't another doomsday bash that would end with a cyanide toast. The life Skile promised his closest friends and brightest associates was not cosmic in scope; instead, it was deeply rooted on this planet and nourished with wealth. Besides new identities, he had given each a new bank account. Fat ones—created and managed by Skile himself. Determined not to lose his friends in the wake of his own rebirth, he had arranged to take them with him like toys on a trip.

"Congratulations on your death, Mr. Fox," Skile said to a white-haired gentleman with a deep tan.

"And on yours as well, Alex," the man replied, toasting with an orange juice. "Most spectacular."

Skile's grin faded and he raised his hands to the group. "May I have quiet for one moment, please?"

It took a half minute for the clamor in the room to die down—their excitement was that fervent. When Skile finally had everyone's attention, he said to them somberly, "It is extremely important that from this moment forward, we embrace our new identities and honor those of our friends and colleagues. We must not let our excitement inadvertently reveal our pasts. Even a small slip now like Mr. Fox's could be catastrophic if uttered in the wrong situation. I well understand how difficult this will be. It will take patience and discipline. But it is necessary; otherwise, everything we have worked so hard for will be lost."

There were sober nods of agreement all around.

Skile's tone lightened. "Tonight we will begin our celebration in earnest. For now, I must ask for your patience; the next several hours will be extremely busy for me. I apologize. Please entertain yourselves until I return later this afternoon."

Judith raised a Bloody Mary. "Enjoy the city. Go shopping. *Spend a lot of money!*"

The jubilant mood of his guests again ignited and spread infectiously through the room as they broke into smaller groups to talk of new lives and vast fortunes. To this special group, today was an incredible dream come true.

"Sorry about that, Jonathan," said "Mr. Fox," the white-haired gentleman Skile had just chastised. Skile had paid cash for this condominium six months before under the name Jonathan Stone. "I don't know what I was thinking."

Skile placed a hand on his friend's shoulder and led him away from the others to the living room's huge picture window, which offered a magnificent view of Chicago's lakefront.

"Don't you give it another thought, Peter," Skile said. "There are too many exciting things happening for us to dwell on a single mistake.''

"Yes, yes, Jon," Fox said. "It will be just as you say. All the way down to the last detail.''

Skile's eyes drifted out the window to the twin Harrison Dever Cribs about two and a half miles from shore, cylindrical-shaped intake towers that supplied raw water from Lake Michigan to Chicago's water-purification plant. He had ordered his seventy-foot yacht moored at the Harrison tower at dusk. It was a precaution, one of many details he had engineered over the preceding months. He had told none of his friends about this arrangement. Not even his wife knew specifics. After the celebration tonight, Skile planned to take Judith aboard the vessel and disappear into the night, never to be seen in this country again. He would unite with his friends in Europe when his fortune was secure. True Masters of the World.

"Excuse me, Peter," Skile said to his friend. "I've got several urgent matters to attend to. We'll talk more tonight and smoke those cigars.''

Mr. Fox gave Skile a friendly hug, punctuated with a pat on the back. "Of course, Jon.''

Skile left Judith to entertain their friends and slipped down a hallway leading to the condo's back bedroom. He waved his wallet in front of a proximity card reader that verified his identity. The remote bedroom door buzzed softly. He moved inside and closed the door behind him. The room was a thousand-square-foot, soundproof, state-of-the-art computer trading room of his own design. His staff already was present and hard at work this morning—in fact, they had spent most of the night here. Seven analysts and computer security technicians were seated at terminals, which were networked into the largest financial institutions and exchanges in the world. Against the far wall, watching over them like a lifeguard, was his personal bodyguard, Steven Gully. The financial specialists and code crackers who controlled the data coming into and out of this self-contained room were the handpicked best Skile ever had the pleasure to work with.

"Good morning," he said to the group. Several returned a smile or offered a courteous nod of greeting. The others remained absorbed in their work, their eyes focused on screens of charts and numbers.

"Jordon?" Skile asked. "What's the status of our networks this morning?"

The middle-aged systems administrator, smoking a pipe and dressed in blue jeans and a sweatshirt, gave Skile an "okay" signal. "We've got three proprietary T3's with solid connections to the backbone. All hubs and Ethernet switches are green. Battery backups are fully charged and on standby."

Skile nodded. "Rita, the status of your team, please."

An attractive woman in her thirties, wearing a business suit and professional wire-rimmed glasses, swiveled around in her chair and said, "I'm on-line with New York, Chase, Mellon, and Citibank. All accounts are green and accessible. We're ready to begin."

"Fredrickson? Your team?"

Paul Fredrickson shifted his troubled eyes from the oversized monitor in front of him. "Still no luck. I've got a solid handshake with the Merc. But we haven't broken GLOBEX's new encryption scheme. Pretty strong stuff."

"How much longer?"

"My guys expect to break the algorithm and reverse-engineer the code by noon."

"That's cutting it very close, Mr. Fredrickson," Skile pointed out.

"It would make things a whole lot easier if we had the password."

Skile nodded. "I understand, Mr. Fredrickson. I will get you your password."

Skile turned to the others in the room and raised his hands for silence. "Could I have everyone's attention for just one moment more? Please. I want everyone's attention."

There were several nudges and pokes among the group until everyone's eyes were on Skile.

"Thank you," Skile said. "In one hour the Chicago exchanges will begin opening for the last time this millennium." His eyes fluttered, and he conceded with a grin, "Perhaps forever. Some markets will conduct business today on a compressed schedule, which will make our timing all the more critical. As each market closes, another phase of our work will be completed. However, until all markets are off-line we must have *perfection*. There can be no mistakes. Let me rephrase that: Failure is not an option.''

Skile looked at each of their brainy expressions; the combined total IQs in this room was staggering. What they could accomplish together absolutely thrilled him. ''I trust you people with all my heart and with all my wealth. I appreciate very much what you have done to set this up and what you are about to do. I wish you only the greatest of success. Tonight we will gather for the grandest of celebrations. It will be my treat and my honor. Meanwhile, I promise to keep your disruptions to a minimum. Thank you very, very much.''

The group watched as Skile bowed his head, blessed himself with the sign of the cross, and left the room to make history.

Chapter Forty-three Depot

Cheyenne Mountain
Thursday, December 30
0620 Hours

''Comin' through,'' the paramedic warned. ''Please stand aside. Let us through.''

A tall, young, responsible-looking paramedic and two of his colleagues pushed the gurney stretcher that held an unconscious Henry Princeton toward an ambulance waiting outside Cheyenne Mountain's steel blast doors. Henry's neck was supported by a brace, and an oxygen mask covered his nose and mouth.

Julie broke away from the group that had gathered in the tunnel and drove a hand into the front of the gurney to bring it to a halt. "Where are you taking this man?"

"To Silver Cross," the paramedic answered. "Now, please step aside and let us do our jobs."

"This man is a criminal," Julie said. "Why isn't he hand-cuffed? Where is his police escort?"

"He's in serious condition with a concussion and perhaps a skull fracture," the paramedic explained. "He's in no condition to get up and go anywhere."

"Listen to the lady," Marshall said, stepping to Julie's side. "I don't care if this man's in two pieces, he's not leaving here unless he's in police custody."

"Someone from the sheriff's office is meeting us at Silver Cross," said the paramedic. "I assure you it will be handled properly."

"What about a military escort in the meantime?" Julie asked.

"I'll go with him," Williams offered.

"No," Marshall said. "I need you here."

"What's going on?" barked an officer. It was Captain Hill, the no-nonsense senior officer in charge of Cheyenne Mountain's military cleanup operation.

Marshall gestured to the gurney. "This man's responsible for the deaths of a lot of good soldiers here yesterday. Yet I don't see an MP anywhere. They're moving him to a civilian hospital unescorted."

"Like hell they are," Captain Hill said. He barked to his second-in-command, "I want two men glued to this scum until he's in police custody."

The lieutenant snapped to attention. *"Yessir!"*

While the paramedics transferred Henry to their truck, the lieutenant enlisted two of his men to ride in the ambulance with him.

"I thought I'd seen everything," the captain said to Marshall. "Yet what I found inside this mountain this morning is worse than any battleground. Maybe the world is coming to an end after all. Wouldn't surprise me anymore. We'll catch every man or woman responsible for this. I promise."

"I'm sure you will, Captain," Marshall said.

Captain Hill threw the colonel a suspicious glance. "Sir, why are you sticking around here anyhow?"

"We're getting ready to head out." Marshall led the captain away from the others. "We need to get to Chicago as quickly as possible. I've got a general who wants to meet me there by noon."

"Better start walking, sir," Captain Hill said.

Marshall laughed politely. "One slight technicality, though. We need to fly."

"That'll be real hard to do with everything grounded," the captain said. "No exceptions, sir."

"Of course," Marshall said. "Wouldn't want to crash because of a damn computer bug."

"You got that right."

"Suppose," Marshall said, "I could find an aircraft—say, an older Vietnam-era Huey utility helicopter—that didn't have computer chips aboard. There wouldn't be a problem flying that aircraft. Right?"

"Wrong," Captain Hill snapped. "Awwww, don't even think about it, Joe. Don't put me in a position of having to arrest you. I don't need that bullshit today."

Marshall grinned broadly. "I was just exploring a possibility, Captain. Acting on it was the furthest thing from my mind."

0630 Hours

Marshall throttled up the Huey UH-1H chopper and watched impatiently as the engine torque rose toward flight idle. Every soldier standing outside Cheyenne's north entrance turned in amazement to watch this blatant violation of the presidential Executive Order. Marshall engaged the rotor clutch. The two main rotor blades began slicing through the air. More curious soldiers began to appear at the mouth of the tunnel.

A soldier in battle gear ran up to the chopper and pounded on the window beside Marshall. His expression was flushed as he mouthed a string of words no one inside could hear.

Williams, sitting in the copilot's seat, said, "He sure looks pissed."

Marshall ignored the soldier and increased the throttle. Soon the rotors were spinning in a dishlike blur. When the yelling soldier realized he couldn't stop them, he backed off and joined others who had gathered to watch.

Marshall's headphones crackled with a voice from the center's control room. "Huey 147B, please state your intentions. You are not, repeat not, to attempt flight. You are in violation of an Executive Order grounding all commercial and military aircraft. Please state your intentions."

Marshall reached for the radio but thought better of it. He couldn't think of a single reason for answering.

Another voice crackled over the headset. "You're not doing what I think you're doing?" It was Captain Hill. "Joe, answer me, please."

"Your call," Williams said.

Marshall keyed the intercom to the troop compartment and said, "Next stop Chicago."

In the compartment behind them, Julie and Nancy secured their seat buckles. Marshall pulled up on the collective and lifted the Huey off the helipad.

"Son of a bitch!" Colonel Hill's voice crackled over his headset.

Marshall peered out his window and saw the captain, transceiver in hand, run from the mouth of the tunnel, his head tilted back to watch them.

Armed soldiers poured from the tunnel entrance and pointed their automatic assault rifles at the chopper.

"Put those down!" Captain Hill screamed. "We've got enough dead bodies here without shooting down an unarmed aircraft."

The captain watched helplessly as the Huey gained altitude, banked northeasterly, and disappeared over the northern ridge.

Chicago
0730 Hours

"You're much too rough," Judith said to her husband, then offered him a mischievous grin. "Just the way I like it!"

"Let me do you from behind," Skile said.

She rolled over on their king-size canopy bed, got up on her hands and knees, and thrust her perfect behind into the air. "Alex, I can't remember when we've had this much fun!"

"Get used to it, you insatiable whore," he said. "Every day for the rest of our lives is going to be as exciting as today." He positioned himself behind her and sunk his long, unusually hard member deep inside of her. She was eager for him.

"Ohhhh, Alex. You're going to have to do me much harder." He complied with her urgent request. "Yes, baby, just like that."

Skile enjoyed this position with its breathtaking view and finished seconds later. They both collapsed into each other's arms.

"I've never seen you so excited," she huffed, exploring his body with her hands. "Tell me what you're taking. Viagra?"

"I've given up on medication," he answered. "It's worthless."

"What you're doing today excites you so, doesn't it?"

Skile rolled onto his back and grabbed the switchblade letter opener Judith kept on the bedstand. "I'm a new man with new energy. Everything I've ever done in my life has led to this day, and I've never felt so exhilarated. One thing is certain. My plan is perfect." He opened the blade with an authoritative snap. "No one's taking that away from me."

She climbed on top of him and, rubbing her abundant breasts across his chest, teased, "I won't dare stop you."

Skile glanced at the luminous readout on the bedside clock—the exchanges were opening. "I best get ready for the Merc. Are you sure you won't join me?"

"No, you go and have your fun," she said. "I've got plans of my own up Michigan Avenue. I intend to be a good wife and spend lots of money today."

Union Station, Chicago
0755 Hours

The Amtrak train from Denver pulled into Chicago's Union Station ahead of schedule. Four men wearing military-style white parkas stood up and gathered their carry-on belongings, which included several elongated fabric gun cases. They looked like a group of hunters who had just spent a long week together in the forest. Their grim expressions suggested that their outing hadn't been successful.

They disembarked and proceeded into the terminal along with the other passengers. As they passed the public phones, General Stryker said to his three men, "Excuse me. I must first make a phone call."

Stryker deposited several coins and punched in a number he knew from memory. The furrows in his brow deepened as he waited for an answer.

Chicago's Michigan Avenue

Skile had just finished showering and was dressing in his navy blue suit when the bedroom phone rang.

He slid on the double-breasted jacket before lifting the receiver. "Jonathan here."

"Alexander," rasped the voice on the other end, "this is Stryker."

"General?" Skile said, surprised. He glanced at the master bath where his Judith was still in the shower. She would be furious if she knew Stryker had called them here.

"Sounds like you weren't expecting to hear from me again," the general said.

"I assumed you would be celebrating."

"There is no celebration. Nor am I a general anymore. I have no army left to lead."

"You're not making any sense," Skile said.

"There are four of us left who can still walk," Stryker said. "The rest of my men were killed or injured in an ambush at your chateau just after you left. You wouldn't know anything about that, would you?"

"Of course not," Skile said. "The very idea is preposterous."

"I don't believe the attack was a sanctioned federal military operation," Stryker said. "Nevertheless, the people who did this were very well financed and had access to serious military hardware. They had top-notch intelligence and were able to walk right into your home. They left in one of your helicopters."

"*Jesus,*" Skile said. "I want you to stay put in Colorado."

"I'm already here at Union Station," Stryker said.

"*What!?*"

"I want some answers," Stryker said. "And I came to get them from you—personally."

"Not now, not today," Skile said. "You're jeopardizing everything by coming here. *I won't have it!*"

The bathroom shower stopped.

"We'll meet face-to-face this morning," Stryker instructed. "I'll come to your apartment."

"*No!* I'm engaged at the Mercantile Exchange this morning, then the Board of Trade this afternoon." Skile looked at his watch. "Meet me at the Merc at noon."

"Ahhhh, so you want to keep it public," Stryker said. "Do you not trust me?"

"Trust has nothing to do with it," Skile snapped. "I have important business there this morning. And come alone. We can't afford to draw attention."

Stryker grinned. "Whatever you say, Alex. There's one more item you should be aware of. It involves your man Henry Princeton."

"What about him?"

"He's in police custody at the hospital. The Colorado Springs sheriff says Cheyenne is crawling with military police. Your plan blew wide open."

"Sounds like Henry fucked up," Skile spat. "It doesn't matter. He's a loose end; I'll deal with him."

"As you wish. I'll meet you at the exchange at noon." Stryker replaced the receiver of the public phone, where his three men had gathered to listen to his side of the conversation.

"What would you like us to do?" one of them asked.

Stryker stood and picked up his bag. "I want you to pay a visit to a friend."

Skile decided he wouldn't be fully dressed today without one more item. He slipped off his suit jacket, opened the drawer of his nightstand, and removed his Walther PPK and shoulder holster.

Iowa, 1,500 feet
0830 Hours

"Skile has no known address in Chicago," Julie said as she hung up her cell phone. "Nor do the deed records indicate he owns property there."

"That got us nowhere," Nancy said.

"The morgue's positively identified Skile's body," Marshall said over the intercom. "He, his wife, and his pilot have all been identified through dental records."

"Let me guess," Nancy said. "Their bodies, or what parts of them they could recover, are burnt beyond recognition."

"You got that right," Marshall said.

Nancy nodded knowingly. "He's a more resourceful and connected bastard than I dared imagine."

Chapter Forty-four
Key to the City

Chicago Mercantile Exchange
Thursday, December 30
1330 Hours

Alexander Skile peered through the doors onto the main trading floor of the Chicago Mercantile Exchange, home of the nation's currency and interest-rate futures and options markets, and the largest trading arena of its kind in the world. There were people in colorful jackets everywhere, like ants marching. Each one of them, it seemed, had a cell phone, and all of them were ringing at the same time. He watched a fax spew out of a man's jacket pocket as he rushed by.

Skile's eyes scaled the steeply tiered trading booths that extended up toward the floor's thirty-two-foot ceiling, where traders and clerks could see into each of the trading "pits" that were jammed with runners. The pace of trading this morning had already reached frantic proportions as the markets responded boisterously to the release of economic indicators and political and technological uncertainty. The huge scoreboards wrapping around the trading floor above told him that investors were rapidly buying and selling shares, constantly watching the competition for ways to make money—or keep from losing too much of it—on the new millennium. Confusion promised to be the order of each hour. He had no doubt that the final day of trading in this millennium would be particularly brutal, with lots of losers.

Skile smiled at the absurdity of it all. Despite everyone's best efforts, none of them had even a modicum of control of their financial destinies. Would the year 2000, with its deeply encoded computer bugs, trigger a recession or worse? Or would fears prove unjustified as some predicted and the economy breathe a sigh of relief with the arrival of an era of prosperity and steep growth?

Only one man could say, and he now stood at the back of the Exchange like a monarch surveying the fuel of his empire.

"Dr. Stone," a voice called to him. Skile turned to see an older man with pure white hair and dressed impeccably in a $2,000 suit walking toward him with both hands extended. It was Ben Ottinger, the Exchange's chairman. "Dr. Stone. What a pleasure. I didn't expect to see you here today."

Skile accepted Ottinger's cordial hand. "I'm not trading today, Ben. In fact, my wife and I are on holiday. I came here to assure myself that we will survive this final day of trading."

Ottinger flashed his expensive and perfectly white teeth. "You never fail to amuse me, Doctor. Of course, we'll be open as usual on Monday morning. That I can assure you."

"Can you? I've heard scenarios that paint a different picture."

Ottinger's golden smile tarnished, and he became uncomfortably aware of the people around them. "Perhaps you'd like to come up to my office where we can talk about this over coffee."

Skile looked at his watch. "I have a few minutes. Yes, I'll take you up on that offer."

Ben Ottinger escorted Skile to the executive floor of the Mercantile Exchange. As chairman, Ottinger enjoyed authority, and his executive office more than ably mirrored that power with its high ceiling and spacious windows. He directed Skile to a comfortable sitting area with sofas surrounding a low coffee table—an impressive fixture chiseled from stone in Nairobi.

"What can I bring you gentlemen?" a woman asked from the doorway.

"You can bring Dr. Stone and me coffee. Thank you, Annette."

She withdrew to carry out his request.

Ottinger waved Skile into one of two facing sofas. "Tell me something, Jonathan," he said as he took a seat across from Skile. "I would have thought you and your wife would celebrate in New York. What keeps you here?"

Skile shrugged. "This is my home. We have big plans with family and friends."

"Of course," Ottinger replied, grinning.

Annette returned with a splendid coffee tray complete with porcelain saucers and cups. She set the impressive affair on the stone table between them and withdrew just as efficiently. The men each helped themselves to a cup.

"I do have a concern about your exchange, as you may have noted," Skile said as he stirred sugar into his freshly brewed coffee.

Ottinger took a tentative sip from his cup. "What is this all about, Jonathan?"

"It's about your system's ability to handle the date change," Skile said.

Ottinger laughed away Skile's concern. "After spending one point two billion to upgrade our networks worldwide, I assure you that this weekend will be no different from any other."

"It's not the hardware that concerns me," Skile said. "It's your software and the final upgrade you intend to install this weekend. You realize even one faulty line of code can do very strange things to simple arithmetic. How can you be certain that, with more than seven million lines of code rewritten, your systems will behave properly when the clocks change to the new millennium?"

Ottinger's jovial expression hardened. Skile had just touched upon the Exchange's single most critical issue and the greatest challenge in Ottinger's thirty-three-year career as a finance officer. The chairman had lost untold nights of sleep because of it over the past two years. "Jonathan, I'm afraid you're going to have to trust me on that issue. In fact, we're going to have to trust each other. This millennium alarm is overblown. I, of all people, should be concerned about the impact of this glitch on my pacemaker. But I trust those who built my unit. The manufacturer has reassured me that the microchip-guided device in my chest will tick uninterrupted into the year 2000."

"I appreciate your situation, Ben," Skile said. "But trust simply isn't good enough for me."

The anxiety reflected in Ottinger's face deepened. "You're putting me in a very awkward situation. If a man of your stature suggests publicly that our systems are incapable of handling the date change, it will significantly devalue our assets. A reckless statement today will create a panic that would cause irreparable harm. These are very fragile times, Jonathan. What can I do to assure you that your fears are not justified?"

Skile raised the porcelain cup to his lips and finished the coffee in a single swallow. It was delightfully fresh. "There is something you can do for me," he said, setting down the cup into its delicate saucer. "You can allow me a look at GLOBEX's registration key."

Ottinger watched him severely over the rim of his cup, not knowing what to make of this odd request. "What will that tell you?"

"It will tell me volumes about the health of your reworked code. If your systems cannot handle the date change, the registry will already show signs of corruption."

The chairman's eyes were deep and dark, and gone were any forced overtures of civility. "So it *is* your intention to trade today."

Skile waved off any such notion. "Allow me that one indulgence, Ben. And I assure you that whatever I find, I will speak to no one about it until after the millennium."

Michigan Avenue, Chicago
0955 Hours

Judith Skile picked up the phone's receiver on the second ring. "Yes?"

"Sorry for the intrusion, Colleen," said Linda, the building's front-desk receptionist.

"No intrusion, Linda," Judith said. "What can I do for you?"

"Three gentlemen are here to see you."

"I'm not expecting anyone," Judith said, adding with a laugh, "In fact, I'm getting ready for a major shopping expedition."

"Should I send them away?"

"Let me speak to one of them first."

Linda, a cheery, capable woman with fluffy, blond hair and a year-round tan, presented the receiver to the three young, muscular men standing before her station. "Who wants to state your business?"

A handsome man with solid features and dark, flowing hair accepted the receiver. "My name is Michael," Stryker's soldier said in his most disarming voice. "Your husband thought you might need company and sent us to entertain you. But if you have other plans, we'll be on our way."

Judith was intrigued. "Thank you very much, Michael. I love the sound of your voice. Could I speak with Linda again, please?"

"Certainly." Michael, grinning, returned the phone to the receptionist.

"Yes, Colleen?" Linda asked.

"Describe them to me," Judith said.

Linda scrutinized the trio with her deep-blue eyes. Young and strong and virile. Any one of them would probably be a dream in bed. Three of them? Well, that was just too much to ask for. "They're hunks," Linda said. "Every one of them."

"I see," Judith said. She looked at her watch and shrugged. "I just decided to delay my shopping. Please send them up."

"Will do," Linda said. She stole a glance at Michael and added, "And let me know if you need any help."

Joseph Massucci

Ben Ottinger led Skile into a secure computer room that served as the nerve hub for GLOBEX, the Mercantile Exchange's international, automated, order-entry and matching system. He closed the door securely behind them until it locked with a magnetic snap.

As a network monitoring station, it offered none of the high-tech trappings to awe the hardware fanatic. There were no refrigerator-size mainframes or network routers or obvious wiring of any kind. That equipment was off site in the basement of a warehouse several miles away. The room offered terminals, dozens of them, each manned by a highly skilled analyst. Skile wondered which ones were on his payroll. Their job was to do nothing but observe and be alert for telltale signs of system failure or other abnormalities. All other functions were automated.

Skile noted the room's Kremlinesque atmosphere: complex, studied, and, of course, secretive. The room also felt chilly, and he assumed the low ambient air temperature kept the terminals from overheating.

"Please have a seat at that table while I call up the records you requested," Ottinger said. "I'll let you know when we're ready."

"Thanks, Ben." Skile took a seat at a small, circular table and watched eagerly as the Exchange's chairman approached the room's supervisor and whispered something to him. The middle-aged man in a turtleneck sweater broke away from his colleagues and moved to the corner for a private huddle with the boss. Skile saw the supervisor steal furtive glances at him as Ottinger explained the situation.

The man nodded, and he and Ottinger disappeared into a cubicle where a lone terminal was set up for confidential access to their proprietary network. Skile waited several long minutes while the network supervisor brought up the appropriate system files, which must have been an unusual request for him. That hardly mattered. The only thing that mattered was the moment Ottinger typed in his password—a cryptic combination of random letters and numbers—to bring up GLOBEX's registry key.

Finally, Ottinger raised his head over the cubicle partition and beckoned him. Skile let out his breath slowly as he stood and strolled among the terminals, careful to feign only modest interest in what Ottinger had to show him.

The system's manager had already left the cubicle to forgo any awkward introduction or explanation. Ottinger's clientele were an eccentric bunch and their requests were often bizarre. The chairman would always attempt to appease them whenever possible, short of breaking the law. Sometimes the law had to be interpreted by Ottinger at a moment's notice. This was one of those cases, but it involved no information Skile could use to trade. Could he profit from it? That was a matter of debate.

The cubicle hosted a single telephone, pencil holder, and paper tablet—nothing else. This wasn't a personal office, nor was it allowed to be used as such.

"The records you wished to see are on the display," Ottinger said. "I can't allow you access for longer than two minutes. Even that is overly generous. Nor can I allow you to make notes."

"I understand." Skile took a seat before the terminal. He peered at the screen and recognized the cumbersome registry, which kept track of the functions of all mission-critical applications installed on the network. He scanned the list to assure himself that the records were genuine, that Ottinger had, in fact, entered his password to access GLOBEX's core. Skile reached for the Page Down key to view the next screen, but before he could touch it, Ottinger placed a hand on his forearm.

"Please don't touch the keyboard," he said. "Allow me." Ottinger pressed the Page Down key and new information filled the screen.

Skile scanned more lines of registry data to assure himself that they were genuine. They appeared so.

"May I ask what you're looking for?" Ottinger queried.

"If GLOBEX could not handle the date change, I would already see an abnormality in the way these records are automatically sorted." Skile rose from his chair. "And I find no problem in that regard." Skile extended his hand. "Congratulations, Ben. You have my complete confidence."

A smile of relief spread over Ottinger's features as he accepted Skile's hand with both of his. "Glad I could assure you."

Ottinger reached over the keyboard and pressed the Escape key to clear the terminal's volatile memory. The registry key vanished and returned the screen to a system prompt.

1050 Hours

Skile stood before the glass window of the Exchange's fourth-floor visitors' gallery and stared unseeing at the mass of swirling red, yellow, and blue jackets on the trading floor below. He opened his cellular phone and punched in a preprogrammed button. The call rang over the secured digital line and answered after the first ring.

"Fredrickson," the voice said.

"Did you get what you needed?" Skile asked.

Fredrickson lowered the receiver and waved to the others in the computer room to be quiet. He put the phone back to his ear and said, "We're in business."

Skile nodded and without acknowledging pressed the End button on his phone to disconnect the call.

In the back room of Skile's penthouse condominium two miles away, Fredrickson replaced the receiver and expelled a long breath of relief. The application he had engineered had performed even better than he had dared hope. He had done nothing while his software scanned the Exchange's network and captured the keystrokes of the password known only to the chairman of the Chicago Mercantile Exchange. The password was a key of sorts—a golden key to the city.

Chapter Forty-five
Loop

Meigs Field, Chicago
Thursday, December 30
1330 Hours

The Huey chopper swooped out over Lake Michigan and continued south along Chicago's skyline toward Meigs Airfield. Williams watched a caravan of police cars below with lights flashing, moving south along Lake Shore Drive. His interest was modest until the cars exited onto the road leading to the airfield.

"Doesn't look like our afternoon is gonna start much better than the morning," he said to Marshall.

In the back, Julie and Nancy leaned against the window for a look below.

"They're not after us, are they?" Nancy asked.

"Us law-abiding citizens?" Williams said. He turned to Marshall. "Who wants to do some fast talking?"

"I will," the colonel volunteered.

Marshall brought the Huey into a hover over to the downtown area's airfield and set it onto the tarmac. If they had any questions about the patrol cars' intentions, it was quickly settled when the procession formed a circle around their chopper. Marshall disengaged the rotor and extinguished the engine. While the blades wound to a stop, uniformed policemen were scrambling from their vehicles, some with their guns drawn.

Williams automatically reached for his Galil case.

"Leave your weapons inside," Marshall ordered. "Ladies," he called to the back. "Same goes for your bags."

"Do they intend shooting us on the spot?" Julie asked as she slid open the troop compartment door.

Marshall didn't offer an explanation. He and the others exited the chopper in silence and formed a line on one side for the inevitable arrest procedure to begin.

A police sergeant, sporting a clean-shaven head and week-old goatee, hollered into a microphone tethered to his car's radio. "Put your hands in the air." His amplified voice boomed across the airfield like a loudspeaker at a carnival. "You're under arrest for violating an Executive Order banning all flight. Lie facedown on the tarmac and put your hands behind your heads."

"They've got to be kidding," Nancy said. "I'm not lying on anything colder than sixty degrees."

The police officers, their weapons drawn, took up defensive positions behind their patrol cars. Some wielded shotguns.

"This is ridiculous," Julie huffed.

"Better do as they say," Williams said.

With their hands in the air, the four got down on their knees and lay facedown on the tarmac as instructed with their hands behind their heads. Marshall saw dozens of black, polished shoes rush forward and fan out around them. The sergeant with the loudspeaker took out his handcuffs and stepped over Marshall.

"I'm a United States Special Forces colonel," Marshall told him. "We have a very dangerous terrorist situation in progress."

"That's not my problem," the sergeant said. "What does concern me is another helicopter falling out of the air. A chopper just like yours took out half a building in the Loop yesterday and killed fourteen people."

"It wasn't like ours," Williams said. "This aircraft doesn't have computers—"

"Shut your mouth!" the police sergeant yelled. "Same goes for all of you. Not another word." He grabbed Marshall's wrist to cuff him.

A black stretch limousine flanked by two Jeeps roared onto the airstrip with its lights flashing and honking its horn.

The police sergeant straightened. "What the . . ."

The limousine worked its way through the line of Chicago po-

lice officers and stopped not five feet from where Marshall and
the others lay. Its rear passenger door opened and out stepped a
distinguished-looking gray-haired gentleman in a long coat. A
high-ranking uniformed military officer exited from the opposite
side of the limousine, while soldiers with assault rifles climbed
out of the Jeeps.

"Who's in charge here?" asked the distinguished civilian.

The police sergeant, still holding the handcuffs, approached the
limo. "I am—" His eyes grew wide. "Governor Boyd!?"

"Would you have a problem releasing these people into my
custody?" the governor asked.

Marshall rose onto his knees to appraise the situation. He
nudged Williams and indicated the officer walking around the
front of the limo. It was General Medlock.

"Well, I'll be." Williams joined Marshall on his feet. Julie and
Nancy likewise stood.

"Will the police cooperate?" Medlock asked, joining the governor.

"I haven't received an answer," Governor Boyd said to the
police sergeant. "These people are part of an FBI counterterror-
ism task force. Will you release them into my custody?"

Williams glanced questioningly at Marshall.

"They endangered lives, sir," the sergeant said. "People could
have been killed."

"No one was at risk," Medlock said. "This military transport
doesn't use computers. It's as safe as a tricycle."

The police sergeant holstered his side arm. "Making exceptions
for the military after yesterday's disaster isn't going to play well
with the people who live and work in the city."

"Tell the media the truth," Medlock instructed. "After taking
the helicopter's crew into custody, you turned them over to senior
military officials for discipline with the governor's approval. My
public affairs people will help you draft a statement about the
nature of this flight and the minimal danger of using this particular
aircraft."

Governor Boyd shook the police officer's hand. "Thank you,
Sergeant. I appreciate your cooperation. As does the President of
the United States."

Medlock allowed Marshall's group to retrieve their belongings from the chopper before directing them into the limo. There was ample room inside for six.

"I only arrived from Fort Bragg by car an hour ago," General Medlock said as they climbed into the back.

"Damn inconvenient not being able to fly," Williams allowed.

"How the hell would you know?" Medlock countered. He turned to Marshall. "We got the President's attention on this one. We're calling it 'well-financed criminal info-warfare.' He promised to support us. Meanwhile, consider yourselves on loan to the FBI's new interagency cyber-crime group."

Marshall asked the governor, "Speaking of Executive decisions, how well do you know the President?"

"Extremely well," Governor Boyd said. "I wouldn't be holding this office without his support."

"I hate to ask favors," Marshall said, "but in this case I need a big one."

Chicago Mercantile Exchange
1355 hours

General Stryker entered the fourth-floor visitors' gallery of the Chicago Exchange and scanned the faces of the people who had come to watch what promised to be an historic day. This was his first visit to a financial trading center, and he knew little about how it worked. He could discern one thing, however: Today was indeed special. Business was booming, the activity on the trading floor below loud and frenetic. No one, not even his highly trained soldiers, he thought, could maintain this level of energy without burning out and becoming a liability to their team—even when the motivator was money.

Despite the large number of visitors, he had little trouble finding Skile seated on a bench at the front of the gallery sucking down a soda. Skile also noted the general's arrival—he was easy to spot by the gift counter, wearing his white mountain parka. As the general approached him, Skile stood up with a cordial smile and an extended hand.

"General," Skile said, "I knew our paths would cross again on this good Earth despite your prediction of the end of the world."

Instead of returning the handshake, General Stryker kept his hand in his coat pocket around the handle of his Mauser. "If I was a suspicious man, I would say that you had arranged that we would never meet again."

"You are a suspicious man." Skile watched the general closely. "Am I still one of your suspects?"

General Stryker gazed at the blur of faces in the gallery. "I suspect everyone and trust no one." Then he riveted his rock-gray eyes on Skile. "I came here on behalf of my men. They needed these three days to prepare themselves for new lives. They never got that chance. I will find the man responsible for the massacre and make him suffer for what he did."

A smile broke Skile's solemn features. "Forget this talk of revenge and doom, General, and plan a different future. I want you to feel the energy here today." Skile placed an arm around his comrade's shoulder and led him to the glass window away from the crowd, where they had a grand view of the trading floor. "Say the word and I will make you part of this. I can give you riches the likes of which you've never dreamed!"

"Personal wealth means nothing to me," General Stryker said. "I am only interested in finding the man responsible for the deaths of my soldiers."

Skile looked at his watch—it was nearly one o'clock. "You must see this." He gestured to the huge electronic board over the trading pit. "In a few minutes all agriculture futures and options trading will cease for the year. It will be the first of many such closings today. However, my interest is not in the market but rather in the computer system that monitors and controls after-hours trading. When the bell sounds at the end of trading, the mainframe computers will be taken off-line so that new software can be installed and tested. Officials will work throughout the weekend to make certain there will be no date-induced malfunctions when this Exchange opens again Monday morning. It's a very critical time for everyone.

"Although the systems will be off-line, the mainframes will remain powered up, waiting for their next command. I will not make them wait long. Embedded inside the microprocessors that control after-hours trading in three major time zones and nine financial centers around the world is a precise set of encrypted commands that will allow trading to continue this weekend—my trading.

"I will feed these computers contracts that will meticulously and correctly credit my accounts with very proper transactions—currency, precious metals, commodity shares, bonds, stakes in financial institutions, and, of course, property. Come Monday morning, I will own entire corporations and control whole industries."

Skile, grinning, looked for an indication that the general was absorbing what he heard. However, he noted no such expression. Clearly, Stryker could not grasp the enormity of what he was telling him.

Finally, General Stryker shook his head. "It cannot work. You will be caught. The fact that your hardware is to blame will raise serious questions and point to you and you alone. In time, you and everyone associated with you will be brought down."

Skile laugh loudly. "The Millennium Bug is to blame, General. A single date change has created an extraordinary opportunity that will bring down this house of cards. Any human complicity will be blamed on Alexander Skile, who, as you're aware, died yesterday in a tragic air disaster. You're talking with a dead man, General."

Stryker wasn't convinced. "They will eventually find you."

"Everything that I was, I leave behind in ruins. The authorities can pick through the rubble of my previous life, but they will find nothing of value. Meanwhile, a new Phoenix will rise from those ashes to command a New World. I am that entity. The world will change, that I promise you."

"She was right," Stryker said.

"Who?" Skile, puzzled, shook his head. "Who's right?"

"Dr. Shaw. We are both madmen."

Skile scoffed away the notion and grabbed the general's shoulder as though to shake sense into him. "On Monday, we will speak. If it happens that we meet on Sirius, I will congratulate you on your prophetic vision and we will toast your heaven. If it turns out you and I are still Earthbound, we'll talk business—"

A bell signaled the end of trading for the agricultural commodity market. A roar rose from the floor below as the final numbers rolled across the huge boards above the trading floor. It had been a very interesting day. In the end, traders of agricultural commodities had lost any courage forged earlier in the session and tried to sell their shares for whatever scarce dollars they could find. An interesting day indeed.

Skile, beaming, said to the general, "That single bell has already made me a wealthy man. And this is only the beginning. More, much more, is coming, my friend."

Colorado Springs County Jail
1310 Hours

Deputy Meyers picked up the phone receiver on the third ring. "Meyers."

The woman on the other end introduced herself and explained the situation. The deputy grew rigid, and his face paled as he listened.

Finally, he said, "You'll have to talk to the sheriff about this. And we'll need a fax. Hold on."

With his hand over the mouthpiece, Deputy Meyers thrust the phone toward Sheriff Block, who was sitting with his feet on the desk reading the *Denver Post*. "It's the White House."

Sheriff Block looked uncertainly over the edge of his newspaper. "If you're pulling my leg . . ."

"It's no joke. She wants to talk with you about releasing one of our prisoners."

Chapter Forty-six
Rough Play

Michigan Avenue
Thursday, December 30
1415 Hours

"I can see you gentlemen like to play rough," said Judith Skile.

Her king-size canopied bed had become very crowded with four—Judith and three of the finest studs she had ever had the pleasure of sitting on. It had been a wild lunch, and tonight, no doubt, she would be a very sore woman.

"We were told you would like to play rough," said Michael. He could have been a bodybuilder, given the size of his muscles and how they rippled perfectly over his body.

"Let's just say I like to play," Judith said. "Rough is just one game."

"We were wondering how much you can really handle," Michael said. "I have a suggestion: We tie you to the bed and each of us tries to break your resilience."

Judith let out a laugh. "I think you've done enough damage for one day. Let's give it a rest."

One of the other soldiers, a young man with flowing blond hair, withdrew a serious set of leg irons from his bag. "My friend's right," he said. "The fun is just starting."

Judith swung her legs over the side of the bed. "I don't think so, boys. It's time you all left."

Before Judith could stand, Michael grabbed her pretty

strawberry-blond hair and yanked her cruelly back onto the bed. He sat astride her and squeezed his strong legs against her sides like a vise, effectively pinning her to the mattress. He draped his semi-tough member between her abundant breasts.

"We haven't even started," he sneered.

She punched and slapped his legs helplessly. "That's enough!" she screamed. "You're hurting me. I want you all out of here!"

Michael let out a throaty laugh, then slapped the palm of his hand viciously across her face. "You're not giving me orders." He raised his hand. "Jeffrey, I'll take those cuffs."

His friend tossed the metal leg irons to him. Judith's left arm flew out and she grabbed the switchblade letter opener on the stand beside her bed. She opened the blade with a snap and plunged it to the handle into Michael's groin. He let out a howl fiercer than any wild animal's.

Enraged, Michael swung the heavy chain downward with both hands. It had all his strength behind it. The chain struck the side of Judith's skull with a solid crack. Her head flew to one side. He repeated the blow to the opposite side of her head. Her hand slipped from the knife's handle and streams of blood spilled from her head onto the pink satin sheet.

Michael couldn't discern if he had killed her. For her sake, he thought, it would be better if she were dead.

Precinct Station Fourteen, Chicago
1420 Hours

General Medlock, Marshall, and the others were shown into an interrogation room, one of the few spaces left in the precinct station not in use on this busy afternoon. There were already people present with official-looking notebooks under their arms and cell phones to their ears. An attractive black woman in her thirties, her hair in braids, approached them, her hand extended. "You must be General Medlock. I'm Acting Special Agent Arlene Love, in charge of the Chicago office's Cyber Emergency Support Team."

"That's a mouthful," Medlock noted, taking her hand. "What does it mean?"

"We're a six-person special FBI cyber-crime squad," she said.

"Think of us as a cyber-SWAT team. We investigate security concerns related to the Internet, the telephone system, electronic banking systems, and the computerized systems that operate the country's oil pipelines, electrical power grids, and other utilities."

"Fine." Medlock threw his overcoat onto a chair. "So where do we start?"

Agent Love indicated the stacks of folders, printouts, and photographs her team had organized over the long interrogation table. "We're going through everything you've sent us about this fellow Skile. Our first priority is to determine his whereabouts."

Medlock faced the room's two-way mirror, which covered half the wall. There was enough light in the room behind it to reveal detail of another conference in progress. "So far my intelligence group hasn't found jack," the general said. "If you can determine his whereabouts, it would make my day a hell of a lot easier."

"Do you have any evidence at all that he's still alive?" she asked.

Medlock deferred the question to Marshall.

"None whatsoever," the colonel said, stepping forward. "Assuming he's alive, he'll most likely be well hidden. He'll probably have a new identity and maybe a new appearance."

Love scowled. "That's worse than nothing to go on." She appealed to the general. "We're going to need a lot more than that."

"We're working on it," Medlock said. "Meanwhile, what's your plan?"

"We're sorting through Skile's holdings and who he might have transferred his assets to during the past year," she said. "Especially any contacts here in Chicago. Did you know that his attorneys filed for bankruptcy yesterday? AKS Industries is officially in Chapter Eleven, which complicates matters. It's going to take time to find the trail from his past to his new identity—"

"*We don't have time!*" Julie hollered. The room fell quiet, and all eyes shifted to her.

"Excuse me," Love said. "Maybe you have a constructive suggestion?"

Julie checked her watch. "Financial exchanges are closing for the year. For all we know, we're already too late."

Williams placed his weight against the interrogation table, his arms folded over his chest. "What we need is a miracle."

"Unfortunately, we don't have a divine entity on the team," Agent Love mocked.

"The sergeant's right," Medlock said. "We need a lucky break, and fast."

"I'd even settle for a long shot," Nancy said. "If I have to, I'll walk the streets trying to spot him getting in or out of a cab."

Julie's eyes fluttered as an idea occurred to her. "Speaking of walks, Nancy, it's getting stuffy in here. How about we bring back some lunch?"

"A great idea," Williams said. "I'm ready to keel over."

"Sure," Nancy said. "Any suggestions?"

Julie picked up her bag and swung it over her shoulder. "I'll bet we can find a sandwich shop at the Chicago Mercantile Exchange or the Board of Trade."

Michigan Avenue
1425 Hours

One of Stryker's three soldiers emerged from Skile's master bedroom wearing nothing at all and carrying a silenced handgun. Somewhere in the spacious apartment, a television was blaring. He checked the other bedrooms. Two were empty; the fourth was locked, its door made of reinforced steel. He saw no key access, only a proximity reader next to the door.

He paraded down the hallway toward the source of the television noise and emerged into an expansive living room where a lone couple in their sixties was watching Jerry Springer on a fifty-inch projection television. The woman spotted him first.

"Peter," she said. "That man is not wearing anything."

Her husband assumed she was referring to the television. "Where?"

She touched his arm. "Peter?"

Peter glanced up from his program and saw Stryker's soldier standing undressed before them. He immediately disliked this brash young man, who he assumed was one of Judith's eccentric guests. *Pretentious prick!*

"If you're running down to the lobby," Peter laughed, "would you mind picking up a newspaper?"

He and his wife enjoyed a hearty laugh. Stryker's soldier wasn't amused. He revealed his handgun and fired repeated rounds into the couple until he was certain they would never recover from their wounds.

Colorado Springs
1334 hours

Jill walked out of the county jailhouse a free woman. A permanent grin was pasted on her face thanks to a release requisition issued by the White House. The colonel actually pulled it off, she thought. "How amazing!"

Her immediate plan was to eat a hearty lunch, then find a bed and do some power sleeping—twelve hours, at least. But first a phone call of thanks was in order.

Jill spotted a mom-and-pop diner across the street and walked smartly over to it. She entered the establishment at the tail end of its lunch hour. All booths were taken, but there was an empty stool at the counter. She saw a pay phone near the rest rooms. She made a detour to it, lifted the receiver, and punched in the access number and identification code that put her on a designated long-distance phone line. Following another dial tone, she punched in the colonel's private forwarded number.

It took several minutes of transfers before the phone began ringing in the interrogation room of the Chicago police station.

The phone answered: "Sergeant Williams."

"Hey, muscles, where did you guys end up?" Jill asked.

Williams smiled and took the cigar out of his mouth. "We're in windy Chicago. Where are you?"

"I'm in a diner across from the county jail. I'm about to have a very large lunch. Is the colonel handy?"

"I'll see if I can tear him away."

Marshall, sitting at the far end of the table between General Medlock and Special Agent Arlene Love, finished drawing a likeness of the Sirius tattoo on his wrist with a blue ballpoint pen. "They look something like this," he said, holding up his wrist. "They're tattooed on the same spot of every soldier we found."

"Let's get that drawing on a piece of paper so I can fax it over the net," said Special Agent Love.

"Colonel," Williams hollered from across the room, waving the phone, "it's Jill."

Marshall returned the pen to Agent Love and grabbed the phone. "Are you a free woman?"

"As a matter of fact, I am," Jill beamed. "I just called to thank you. I didn't realize you had friends in such low places."

"You can thank Illinois' governor for that one. I owe him. How are you holding up?"

"Hungry and tired."

"Take a cab over to Patterson Air Base. They'll feed you and put you up for the night."

"Sounds great. Thanks, Colonel."

"One more thing before you head out," Marshall said. "I need you to make a stop at Silver Cross hospital to check on Olin. Give her one of your pep talks."

"Sure, Colonel. No problem."

"And as long as you're there, check on one more patient for me."

Puzzled, Jill frowned. "Who?"

"His name is Henry Princeton," Marshall said. "He's taken a nasty blow to the head. Make sure he can't do anything foolish like walk out of there."

Michigan Avenue
1440 Hours

In the back bedroom of Skile's apartment, Paul Fredrickson's automated trading script finished executing its commands. He announced to the others: "Agricultural options and futures have been put to bed. All files have been uploaded to GLOBEX. On Monday morning, Mr. Jonathan Stone will be the proud owner of seventy million dollars' worth of cattle, hogs, pork bellies, butter, milk, and lumber."

There was spontaneous applause throughout the condominium's miniature trading room and one shrill whistle. "I'll personally kiss his shoes next time he walks through that door," said Rita, Skile's chief financial analyst.

Laughter erupted throughout the room.

Suddenly, the steel door exploded with a lethal concussion. The massive slab blew inward and violently took out the first desk in its path. The analyst seated at the terminal never knew what hit her, and she died instantly of severe head trauma.

Two men, standing naked to the waist, stepped through the doorway wielding M16 assault rifles. Stryker's two soldiers opened fire. The six remaining analysts and technicians scrambled for cover. But there was no place to hide. Dozens of rounds per second indiscriminately sprayed terminals, desks, and people, turning the room into a whirlwind storm of paper and blood.

The cacophony of gunfire was quickly augmented by a third weapon—the hammering of an Uzi. A trail of bullets raked the pair of assailants, creating a half-dozen plum-size wounds across their naked chests. Their weapons fell silent and their bodies slumped back against the wall.

Steven Gully, Skile's seasoned security officer, ejected the spent Uzi's clip and snapped in a fresh one. However, there were no more targets, nor did he see any activity in the hallway outside.

In the silence that followed, moans and cries arose from the room's rubble. Gully, a tall, lean gentleman in his fifties dressed in a three-piece suit, could pass for a corporate executive. However, as an ex–British SAS commando, Gully had never worked behind a desk in his life. He stepped cautiously into the hallway, his assault weapon braced for firing, and checked the first two bedrooms. When he peered into the master bedroom, he quickly looked away in repulsion. Even a soldier of his experience could not stomach the carnage inside. *Alex will not take lightly to this news*, he thought.

Gully ran a hand through his pure white hair, then shouted down the hallway, "Shut down and prepare to evacuate— *quickly!*"

Inside what was left of the trading room, Fredrickson, dizzy and fending off waves of unconsciousness, struggled to his feet. He'd been shot through his upper left chest and was rapidly losing blood. He eased himself into the nearest office chair, his right hand covering the wound to stem the bleeding.

"Jorgensen," he shouted, his voice phlegmy. "What's the status of our backbone? Are we still on-line?"

"Jorgensen's dead!" Rita shouted. She alone had managed to miss a direct hit from a bullet. Several superficial cuts along her jawline and forehead had marred her perfect complexion, and she was bleeding from a deeper cut on her back that had ruined her white satin blouse. "Oh, God . . . my team is dead. . . ."

"Then *fuck* them," Fredrickson spat. "I need to know if we have an active terminal."

Rita left one of her fallen teammates, a young man who was beyond her help, and began to check for functioning displays. Most were damaged and inoperable. Two of them, miraculously, remained functional, and both screens displayed trading information.

"I'll be damned," Rita said. "We still have the network."

Fredrickson rose shakily to his feet. He pushed her aside and plopped into an office chair before the terminal, almost blacking out from the exertion. He could feel the blood flowing unabated down his arm.

"That needs immediate attention," Rita warned him.

He ignored her. "Get to work. I want everything transferred to Recovery Scheme Three. Auto-start the routines. Defer all execution to our schedule."

Rita sat before the second terminal and began entering the commands per his instructions. Fredrickson did the same with his good hand.

"This is going to be sloppy," Rita said. "Goddammit! Who were those assholes, anyway? Are more coming?"

"Mercenaries," Gully said, returning to the room. "They appear to have acted alone." He crouched between the corpses of the two assailants and spotted their wrist tattoos—blue orbs of light resembling the sun. He knew immediately who they were—Stryker's men. "How much time do you need to finish?"

"A couple of minutes," Rita said. "But we can't be certain—"

"I don't care about the details," Gully spat. "How long specifically?"

"Give me five minutes," Rita said.

"You've got three," Gully said. He withdrew his portable phone and raised the antenna.

Chicago Mercantile Exchange
1445 Hours

Skile heard the soft ring of the portable phone in his coat pocket. He activated it and put the receiver to his ear.

Gully's voice at the other end said, "There's been a breach. Heavy damages and loss of life. We've switched to Recovery Scheme Three. All commands are now on auto. We're shutting down and evacuating."

Gully disconnected the line.

Skile, his face pale and sullen, returned the phone to his pocket and said to General Stryker, "I must go."

Stryker pushed Skile back into his gallery bench. "We still have so much to talk about."

"*Bullshit!*" Skile snapped. "My wife may be in danger."

"I arranged for her to be occupied," General Stryker said. "She is in capable hands."

Skile glared at the general. "What do you mean?"

"I sent three of my men to see her. I suspect that by now your wife is a very satisfied woman."

"*You bastard—*"

"One more thing," General Stryker said. "I instructed my men to put a stop to this nonsense of yours. It is unclean. We must all leave this planet tomorrow as paupers." He withdrew the silver-plated Mauser and, his finger on the trigger, placed it on his lap in the folds of his parka. "You will stay here with me and watch your fortune erode. Think of it as your penance."

Chapter Forty-seven
Trading

Chicago Mercantile Exchange
Thursday, December 30
1500 Hours

"The last place I thought I'd spend my lunch hour today was in an exchange watching market trading," Nancy said to Julie as they rode up the long escalator to the fourth-floor visitors' gallery.

Touring the Exchange hadn't been on Julie's agenda either. She was simply acting on a hunch that Skile might come here to see his handiwork up close. Or might he turn up at the Board of Trade a few streets away? Or was the whole idea pure fantasy? As each hour passed without solid evidence surfacing, Julie began to doubt the sanity of her theory. There were too many "ifs." Still, all her hunch really merited was a quick look around the Exchange. Then she and Nancy could return to the station with a bag full of sandwiches and Cokes for the others.

They entered the visitors' gallery with its limited bench seating, most of which was taken. It was a weeklong holiday for a lot of people, and the Exchange's activities were generating keen interest. If there would be a time-triggered Millennium spectacle, the Chicago Mercantile Exchange was as likely a place as any for something interesting to occur. And folks were turning out in record numbers to see it firsthand.

"This isn't going to work," Julie said, scanning the crowd. "I don't even know what Skile looks like."

"You're right," Nancy admitted. "If he's here, he'll be too deeply buried. We might as well try doing something more productive, like going back to the lobby and getting lunch."

As Nancy turned to leave, something she saw out of the corner of her eye caught her attention. She spun and stared at a white mountain parka.

Her eyes riveted, she began walking around the back of the gallery for a better look. The coat belonged to a man with salt-and-pepper hair seated in the front row of benches with his back to her. Her heart began pounding. She pushed past a group jammed before the displays for a closer look at the coat's owner. She put her hand to her mouth—it was General Stryker. Sitting on the bench next to him was Skile.

Julie pushed in next to her. "What is it?"

Nancy turned away so as to not draw attention to her interest in them. "The man in the dark suit is Alexander Skile . . . he's talking with General Stryker. What are we going to do?"

Julie chanced a good, long stare at the pair before leading Nancy back out of the gallery. When they were in the common area in front of the elevators, Julie said, "Find a phone and call Joe. Tell him to get down here as quickly as possible."

As the elevator doors opened, Nancy said, "Where are you going?"

"They don't know me," Julie said. "I'm getting a closer look."

Julie vanished inside. She pushed through to the front of the gallery where Stryker and Skile were sitting against the far wall. She entered the row behind and, squeezing in front of the occupied seats, made her way down the aisle until she was standing directly behind them. Julie spotted the handgun partially concealed in the general's lap. She hadn't counted on seeing a weapon. She glanced down the aisle—there were too many people filling in after her to make a graceful exit.

General Stryker noticed her standing behind them and slid the gun into his pocket. He was visibly annoyed by her presence. "May I help you?"

"Are either of you gentlemen John Coyne?" Julie asked in her most disarming voice.

"No," the general spat.

Skile glanced up at her, and Julie noticed him do a double take. His eyes narrowed. "Good afternoon, Dr. Martinelli. Never in my wildest dreams did I imagine our paths crossing."

Michigan Avenue
1503 Hours

"I want everyone out of here *now*," Gully ordered.

With his single good hand, Fredrickson struggled to finish keying in the commands that would make Skile's network inaccessible. "I'm not finished." His shaking fingers were coated with his blood, and he swore as he entered error after error.

"Yes you are." Gully fired his handgun into Fredrickson's monitor, causing it to spin off the desk in a shower of sparks. He put another bullet into the CPU box.

"Goddammit!" Fredrickson spat. "I need to erase the drives." He staggered to Rita's terminal, pushed her aside, and fell into the chair.

"I'm outta here," Rita said. She grabbed her purse and coat and rushed down the hallway. "Have nice lives, you guys."

Gully checked his watch. "Leave it."

Fredrickson's eyes couldn't focus on the screen's text, and he began to black out. "For God's sake help me."

"Of course I will," Gully said. He put a round through this monitor as well, then pointed his gun at Fredrickson.

"Help me . . ."

Gully put a single bullet into Fredrickson's forehead. The security analyst toppled backward and became part of the floor's eclectic collection of electronic and human rubbish.

Gully hid the handgun under the jacket of his three-piece suit, donned his overcoat, and exited the apartment with Rita.

Chicago Mercantile Exchange

Nancy rushed down the hallway looking for an open pay phone. There weren't any, and the lines of people waiting to use them were long. It hadn't occurred to her until this moment to borrow Julie's cell phone—

He would know her!

Stanford's personnel files . . . Julie's dossier . . . her photo! If he had paid close attention to her photo, Skile could identify her. She was in a very dangerous situation.

Nancy abandoned her place in line and rushed toward the escalator.

"You can close your mouth and quit gawking, Dr. Martinelli," Skile said.

He rose and faced her, towering over her. His stare was intense, his eyes maniacal. "I've read your dossier with interest and admired your photo. Your face is hauntingly beautiful. How could I not know you?"

Stryker stood and looked cautiously around them. "I forbid you to speak to this woman," he hissed.

Skile spun and thrust his large hand into Stryker's jaw. The shove caught the general unprepared. He lost his balance and toppled over the back of his seat onto the people sitting on the bench behind. His hand flew from his pocket as he fell and brought with it his silver-plated handgun. The row of spectators around him began shouting and pointing.

Skile leapt over his seat and rammed his shoulder into Julie, pushing her aside like a football lineman. She fell backward into the laps of two visitors. Skile stumbled over row after row on his way to the exit. There came more shouting with each row he passed.

General Stryker struggled to his feet. He pointed his gun at Skile but couldn't get a clean shot.

"What do you think you're doing?" roared a man behind him. Stryker swung his handgun around and caught a heavyset businessman solidly on the bridge of his nose. The man's head snapped back and his portly body slammed heavily against the glass partition at the front of the gallery. The force shattered the glass, allowing him to fall back through it. He crashed onto the trading floor below, bringing a shower of shattered glass onto the traders.

Visitors in that corner of the gallery were on their feet roaring about what they had just witnessed. Julie, winded by the blow, scrambled forward but could not squeeze through the hordes of people pushing past her. She stood up on a seat in time to see

Skile tear through the gallery's exit toward the stairs. She began climbing over the seats after him.

Outside the gallery, Skile shoved his way through the crowded hallway. He bolted down one escalator after another, pushing past people and knocking aside anyone who wouldn't move.

A man with long hair beneath a cowboy hat laid a heavy hand on Skile's shoulder and yanked him back. "Where the hell are you going, asshole?"

Skile withdrew his Walther PPK. He whirled and shoved it into the man's gut. There came a crack that drove the man back into the others. Skile turned and vanished into the crowd.

Julie reached the top of the escalator and found it impassable. She heard shouting and screaming from the bottom of the steps, but she couldn't make out the source of the congestion. A red stencil on the door across the hallway read "Emergency Exit Only." Julie abandoned the escalator and burst into the stairwell. An alarm began to wail. She ignored it and ran down the steps.

Skile reached the lobby and, feigning composure, walked toward the Exchange's main entrance. He hadn't bothered to retrieve his garment from the coat check.

Someone touched his arm. "Dr. Stone—"

Skile spun and fired a single shot, which incited more screams. Ben Ottinger stared into Skile's eyes in surprise. His mouth opened—a reaction to shock rather than an attempt to speak. Blood spilled from his lips as he collapsed onto his knees.

Skile slid the handgun into the shoulder holster beneath his jacket and walked briskly through the revolving door out onto Wacker Drive.

Julie burst from the stairwell and rushed through the lobby where a small crowd had formed around someone who had fallen. Skile? she wondered. Julie roughly pushed her way through for a glimpse of an older man lying on his back, the front of his gray suit soaked with blood from a severe chest wound. She quickly withdrew.

People milling about the lobby were gesturing toward the entrances along Wacker Drive and telling others what they had just seen. Julie bolted outside and looked wildly about for Skile. She spotted a tall man in a dark suit climbing into the passenger seat of the first in a short line of cabs.

Julie bolted toward the front of the line. As the cab pulled away into the flow of dense traffic toward Monroe Street, she spotted Skile's telltale ponytail through the back window. Before Julie could reach the next cab in line, a man stepped in front of her and opened the door for his female companion.

"This sucks." Julie backed away and climbed into the next cab.

"Ma'am?" said the cabdriver, a hulky man with a crew cut.

"*Go!*" she instructed him. "I'll tell you when and where to turn."

Inside the Exchange, Nancy searched the faces of the crowd flowing from the visitors' gallery but couldn't spot her friend. Increasing numbers of people jammed into the hallway waiting for elevators, talking animatedly and making it increasingly difficult to find someone. Somewhere below them, an alarm was ringing. She decided she would have to page Julie.

A rough hand grabbed her upper arm and squeezed. Nancy froze.

General Stryker put his lips to her ear and said, "You left so suddenly yesterday. I've missed you."

"Leave me alone," she managed.

"We're going to walk out of here together very calmly," he instructed her. "The last thing I want is to kill you, Dr. Shaw. But at the first sign of trouble, I will not hesitate to hasten your journey to the afterlife."

The traffic along State Street was particularly heavy, complicated by pedestrians who were turning the streets into one large outdoor shopping thoroughfare. A stalled car blocked their lane.

"Get past this crap now!" Skile ordered his driver.

"I cannot do a thing," said the cabbie, a slight, dark-complexioned Iranian with a beard. "I should have gone to Michigan."

"*Fuck* Michigan!" Skile shouted. "Get around this!"

The cabdriver leaned on his horn. When that gesture proved useless, he drove his wheels up onto the sidewalk and began creeping past the stall. He almost succeeded until a Thunderbird, its hazard lights flashing, slid into a "No Stopping" space directly in front of him. The cab drove straight into the T-bird's rear fender panel.

"Shit!" cried the cabbie. He put his cab into park.

"What are you doing?" Skile asked. "We can't stop here."

The cabdriver glared at him in disgust for his role in this accident. "You want me to just drive away?"

"That's exactly what you're going to do," Skile said.

When the cabbie opened his door to leave, Skile grabbed him roughly by the back of his shirt and yanked him back. "I said *move!*"

Shaking visibly, the cabbie put his car into drive. The vehicle lurched forward, careened across the sidewalk out of control, and plowed into several people who had stopped to watch the fender bender. The cabbie cried out as he slammed on his brakes.

"*Christ!*" Skile yelled. He jammed his Walther PPK against the side of the cabdriver's neck and demanded, "*Move.*"

The cabbie looked at the handgun, then at Skile. He saw something sinister in this peculiar man that meant death if he didn't do exactly as instructed. He blessed himself with the sign of Allah, then drove the cab onto State Street, leaving behind a desperate crowd with injured people.

Julie saw Skile's cab roll off the sidewalk and merge into the traffic ahead of the congestion that had now completely blocked State Street. She was about to lose him.

Julie tossed a five-dollar bill onto the front seat and exited her cab. People were rushing to see the sidewalk accident. She weaved between the cars and spotted a cab letting off passengers on the next block. She ran to it and slipped into the backseat as the previous passengers finished paying.

The diver looked at her in the rearview mirror and asked in a thick accent, "Where?"

She couldn't spot Skile's cab anywhere. "Just keep going down this street, please."

"Where?"

"*Just go!*" she hollered, waving her hand toward the road ahead. "Go! *Ondelay!* Godspeed!"

The cabdriver shrugged and headed down State Street, looking every bit the perplexed driver. They pulled behind another cab at a red light at Lake Street. Through the back window, Julie saw Skile leaning over the front seat issuing orders to his driver. When the light changed, his cab made a right onto Lake.

"Turn here," Julie instructed her driver.

They had little trouble following Skile's cab through the thick traffic up Michigan Avenue and across the Chicago River Bridge. Skile's cab stopped in front of a nondescript condominium building sandwiched between a hotel and a clothier business.

Skile burst from his cab and didn't bother to pay his driver before running up the step and disappearing inside.

Julie left a ten-dollar bill with the driver before exiting her cab. Skile's cabdriver, visibly upset, began telling her his saga about what he had just been through. His accent was thick, his speech rushed.

"I'm sorry, I don't understand," she said. "I suggest you call the police."

Julie bounded up the building's steps and entered the building's reception area. There was no other foot traffic in the lobby, a chic area made of polished white marble. Through the double glass doors she saw Skile step into an elevator just as the doors closed behind him. She grabbed one of the silver handles to the door leading to the elevator lobby. It was locked.

"Excuse me," said a smiling young blond-haired woman behind the reception desk. "May I help you?"

"Can you please buzz me in?" Julie asked. "I need to get through."

"I'm afraid I can't do that. Is there someone I can call for you?"

"Who is that man who just got onto that elevator? I need to know his address."

The receptionist's smile faded. "I can't tell you that. If you're not a guest, you're going to have to leave."

Julie watched the needle above the elevator door move steadily to the top floor. That's all she needed to know.

"I must ask you to leave," the receptionist repeated.

Julie ignored her, retrieved the cellular phone from her handbag, and punched in the number to the interrogation room of Chicago's Fourteenth Precinct.

Chapter Forty-eight
Bravo

Michigan Avenue
Thursday, December 30
1520 Hours

The door to the apartment stood open. Skile pulled out his Walther PPK, stepped into the foyer, and listened. The unmistakable smell of gunpowder and burning electronics assailed him.

He moved into his living room, where the bullet-riddled bodies of his longtime friends Betty and Peter Fox lay on the floor in front of the sofa. Oprah Winfrey glared down at them from the large-screen television.

Skile grabbed his chin and settled into the easy chair across from the corpses. The white carpet had soaked up their blood and spread it like an absorbent paper towel. Both bodies bore accusing stares from the moment of death, expressions that demanded to know how this could have happened. The fact was, this shouldn't have happened. He had assured his friends that they would be safe in his haven, with the new lives he had given them. *This shouldn't have happened!*

Skile stood bolt upright. "Judith!"

He ran down the hallway and burst into their bedroom. And there he stood, horrified, staring at the unimaginable. Their king-size canopy bed, once Judith's playground, had become her death-bed. The sheets had been removed and Judith had been laid out on the bare mattress, which now looked like an autopsy table. A crude incision had been made from her sternum to her pelvis.

"Oh, my poor Judith." Skile staggered to the side of the bed, where he collapsed onto his knees. "What have I done?"

A voice behind him gave up a deep, guttural laugh.

Skile whirled. Michael sat hidden in the chair behind the door, laughing at him. He was naked except for a bloody sheet wrapped around his loins. Stryker's soldier whipped his long, flowing hair back over his shoulder, then pointed a blood-drenched finger at Skile.

"I insist that you see her this way. After all, beauty is on the inside." His head flew back and his muscular frame rippled with his laughter.

Skile sprang to his feet and thrust the muzzle of his Walther PPK into Michael's face between his eyes. "Why?"

The soldier did not appear alarmed. He riveted a pair of serious eyes at Skile and said, "She was a fornicator and an adultress. Someone had to cleanse her before the Big Shout. She had everything and threw it away for a few moments of carnal pleasure. I did her a favor and taught her something she will take with her into the afterlife."

"Did she suffer?" Skile asked.

"Unfortunately, no. The blow to the head caused too much brain damage. I would have preferred that she'd been aware."

Skile nodded; there was the smallest hint of a smile on his lips. He squeezed the trigger and put a bullet between the assailant's eyes. Michael's head flew back and he expelled a final, relieved gasp. Skile pumped several more rounds into his face until the handgun was empty. He ejected the spent magazine, removed another from his jacket pocket, and drove it firmly into the handle with the heel of his palm until it locked. He chambered a round and fired it into Michael's wounded groin before replacing the handgun in his shoulder holster.

Chicago Freight Tunnels
1530 Hours

General Stryker forced Nancy at gunpoint down a narrow, poured-concrete tunnel through which miniature electric trains once ferried merchandise, coal, and even mail beneath the city's

Loop area. They had entered Chicago's old freight tunnel system by way of the basement of an abandoned storefront on Dearborn and headed northeast. Nearly a mile later, the beam of Stryker's flashlight hit what appeared to be a solid dead end under Illinois Street.

Nancy eyed the rock wall before her. "Wherever you're taking me, I hope you know a different route."

"This is no mistake," Stryker said. "My men planned this route at the insistence of Mr. Skile so that he and his wife would have a way of leaving the city tonight unobserved. Very unconventional but, he assured us, very necessary."

His beam followed ladderlike rungs up the wall to the ceiling. Instead of stone, there was a circular manhole cover at the top.

"My engineers installed this access panel for him," Stryker said. "A simple project, which we completed in less than four hours."

"Very paranoid behavior," Nancy said. "Wouldn't it have been a lot easier if he'd just taken public transportation out of town?"

"Yes, Mr. Skile is very paranoid," the general said. "He knew there would be no flights, and the highway's jammed. So he insisted on this route." He gestured to the panel. "Unfortunately, I must insist that you climb through first."

Nancy, apprehensive, grasped the narrow rung. It felt cold and wet. "Are you kidding me?"

"I assure you this is no joke. Please proceed. We are running short of time."

"I wish I had worn my Nikes." Nancy used the hand rungs to hoist herself up the side of the wall, while General Stryker assisted with his light beam. When she reached the top of the short climb, she slapped a hand against the solid metal cover, which she could see was a new addition to the old tunnel, just as he had said.

"What now?" she called down to him.

"Push," he said.

Nancy used her free hand to push up on the metal cover. It moved slightly. "I'm going to need help."

"Use your shoulder," Stryker instructed.

Nancy moved up another rung until she could put her shoulder against the steel cover. Pushing with her legs, she moved the plate aside with a screech.

"Very good," Stryker said. "Now climb up into the tunnel above."

Nancy did as the general instructed and found herself squatting in a muddy, circular tunnel, about ten feet in diameter, made of old bricks. The air was foul and damp, the area as black as the inside of her eyelids. The tunnel reeked of death, and she dared not venture out on her own. General Stryker scrambled up the rungs to join her. The addition of his light beam only made matters worse—the ugly tunnel reminded Nancy of an ancient catacomb.

"Where the hell are we?" Nancy asked.

"This tunnel has supplied the city with water for most of this century," the general explained, pushing the access cover back into place. "It is presently under repair."

Nancy scrutinized the mossy bricks and marveled, "My hat's off to the engineers who kept it from caving in."

General Stryker pointed eastward. "The intake tower is two miles in that direction."

"So?"

The general held out his hand, palm up. "After you."

Michigan Avenue
1535 Hours

Marshall led an eager contingent of FBI agents, Hostage-Barricade-Terrorism (HBT) team members, and police officers into the upscale condo building.

Julie met him in the lobby and indicated the elevators through the double glass doors. "He's still on the top floor. No one has gone up there or come down."

The blond-haired woman behind the reception desk stood as the parade of uniformed police officers and people in suits flowed into her lobby. "You can't come in here—"

Special Agent Arlene Love showed the woman her identification. "This building is now under FBI jurisdiction. I suggest you call your managers and get them down here immediately. My agents will question you and all other employees on and off duty."

"It's locked," said the HBT lieutenant over his shoulder, grasping the handle of one of the double glass doors leading into the elevator lobby.

"Open this door," Williams said to the receptionist. "Or I'll open it permanently."

Linda's shaking hands groped across her desk to a button that buzzed them through to the inner lobby. The HBT lieutenant led his team to the elevators. The doors to the first car opened and his squad crowded inside.

"I want you to be our eyes and ears down here," Marshall instructed his sergeant. "Find out if there's any other way out of this building."

"You got it," Williams said.

When the second car came, Marshall and Julie squeezed inside with Agent Love and her team. It was too crowded for conversation, and no one said a word until they reached the penthouse on the sixteenth floor. A HBT officer stood stationed outside Skile's apartment.

"It's secured," he said as they stormed past.

Marshall scanned the living room while Agent Love scribbled notes into her book as she stepped over the two bodies. The colonel's interest shifted to more extensive damage down the hallway. He left Julie with the others and went to the master bedroom, which held particular interest for the HBT team. He slipped inside. His eyes shifted from the carnage on the bed to another body, a male, slumped in a chair behind the door. Half of his head had been shot away at close range. The wounds were fresh, and blood still flowed like a bad leak from the wounds onto the carpet.

Julie pressed into the room behind him. "Oh, God—"

Marshall led her back out into the hallway. "Believe me, you don't want to see this."

"What about Skile?"

"So far there's no sign of him," he said.

More police officers were arriving with each elevator, jamming into the once spacious apartment. Julie moved to the back bedroom, still hazy with smoke. Explosives had removed its door, leaving large swaths of blackened plaster along the walls on either side.

"Find out what the neighbors heard and when," ordered a man in an overcoat, a homicide detective named Theodore Spark.

The detective stepped inside the back bedroom, where police officers were already kneeling over several bodies. Julie followed him inside and surveyed the rows of shattered computer terminals that had been blown off the desktops. Someone wanted to make damn sure no one would work in here again.

Detective Spark put up a hand. "You can't come in here." He pushed her back into the hallway with Marshall.

"Joe, this may be Skile's op center," Julie said. "I need to get in there and determine what he was up to."

Marshall nodded and, placing a hand on her shoulder, led her back inside the room.

"We're in the middle of an investigation," said Detective Spark. "I've already told the woman that this room is off-limits."

Agent Love pushed past them and showed the detective her identification. "There may be other crimes in progress. We need full access to this room to determine the nature of the computer work conducted in here." She surveyed the carnage and damaged machines and added, "That is, if he left us any evidence."

Detective Spark, frowning, waved them through. "Just don't touch anything."

"Find me pieces that still work," Julie said, making her way between the overturned tables and smashed terminals.

"This box doesn't look damaged," said one of the FBI agents, indicating a unit beneath an overturned table.

"Here's a monitor without a bullet through it," said Marshall, picking up the display.

"Let's try to get a system working and on-line," Julie said.

She righted the table while the FBI agent retrieved the CPU box. Together they quickly set up the machine.

"I said don't touch anything!" Detective Spark shouted at them.

"Don't get your shorts bunched," Agent Love insisted. "We're not about to blow what may be our only chance to find this guy."

Julie found a cable and plugged one end into the computer's

network card and the other into the room's common router outlet. They powered up the box and monitor, then waited an interminable two minutes for the setup to boot and automatically log onto the network. A list of options finally popped onto the screen:

A. CHICAGO

B. HONG KONG

C. BRAVO

D. TOKYO

E. BERMUDA

F. SINGAPORE

G. PARIS

H. NEW YORK

J. CAPE TOWN

K. LONDON

"We're in," Julie said, taking a seat in front of the display.

"No surprises so far," Marshall said, reading over her shoulder. "He's on-line with some of the world's largest trading markets."

Julie highlighted the menu option for Chicago and pressed Enter. A first-class proprietary financial trading package booted up. The first window showed trading activity on the Chicago Mercantile Exchange and Board of Trade in real time. Another window graphically plotted the trends of several major commodity, currency, and futures markets in fifteen-minute intervals. The pattern for today showed a decidedly negative bend.

"State of the art," Julie noted. "But nothing illegal about any of this." She exited the program and returned to the main menu.

"What the heck is *Bravo?*" asked Agent Love, pointing at the menu.

"Let's find out." Julie highlighted the word "Bravo" and pressed Enter.

The hefty program took thirty seconds to load before a dialogue box appeared requesting a password.

"Figures," Julie said. "A dead end."

"How long will it take to break that password?" Agent Love asked.

Joseph Massucci

"A lot more time than we have," Julie said.

Agent Love looked across the room at each corpse's face. Whatever these people knew about Skile's operation, they took with them to the grave. "If only we had someone in custody— somebody to question."

"As a matter of fact, we do," Marshall said.

Agent Love turned to him. "Are you going to keep me in suspense?"

"His name is Henry Princeton," Marshall said, "and at last report he was still unconscious in a Colorado Springs hospital."

The building's service elevator doors slid open. Skile stepped off into the utility area beneath the apartment building and proceeded briskly down a narrow alley between the building's boilers and furnaces. He entered the machine shop, where a beefy operator was working a drill press.

When the worker saw Skile, he raised his safety goggles and shouted, "This area is off-limits—"

Skile thrust his Walther PPK at him and fired. The drill-press operator dropped without a sound.

Skile walked to the back of the shop and entered a narrow room full of pipes and cables, the entry point for the building's utility conduits. He proceeded to the back and crouched beside a manhole cover. He fitted his fingers into the handhold grooves and pulled. Its weight, approaching one hundred pounds, surprised him. He let out a cry and, flexing every arm muscle, lifted. The cover yielded, and he rolled it to one side with a bang.

Skile swung his feet into the opening, grabbed the handhold, and began climbing down into the access tunnels beneath the city.

Chapter Forty-nine
Judith-55S

Silver Cross Hospital, Colorado Springs
Thursday, December 30
1434 Hours

The police deputy sitting outside Henry's hospital room rocked his chair forward onto all four of its legs when he saw Jill approaching. "You can't go in there."

"What if I told you he was family?" she asked. "A second cousin once removed."

"Take a hike," the deputy responded. "This wing is off limits to everyone but us and his doctor."

The door to the private room was ajar, and Jill could see two official-looking men in suits interrogating the patient. They had a serious player in custody. It didn't look like he was going anywhere.

"Hey, I know when I'm not wanted." She tipped her Yankees cap and strolled down the corridor from which she had come.

Inside the single-bed hospital room, another deputy stood guard over Henry Princeton, who was handcuffed to the bars of his bed. Henry was awake and coherent, sitting with his back propped against a stack of pillows and talking with two FBI agents standing on either side of his bed. His head bandages resembled a sailor's cap that had weathered one too many storms. For the moment he was lucid and talkative; however, his doctor cautioned that he could slip into bouts of disorientation, or black out without warning.

"I'm eager to cooperate," Henry told them, adding, "for a price."

"Ahhhh, there's always a price tag," said Steven Johnson, his voice deep and commanding. The senior of the two FBI field agents, Johnson was a tall, black gentleman, whose lean body was built to wear a crisp business suit. "We didn't come here to negotiate with you, Mr. Princeton."

"Then you're wasting your time," Henry said. "Nothing I have to say will be free. And what I have to tell you is worth billions. Maybe more."

"What information would be worth that much?" Johnson asked.

"Information that would assure the integrity of our nation's economy. Is that enough for you?"

The two agents didn't respond.

"What time is it, anyway?" Henry asked.

The second agent, a younger man named Beck, glanced at his watch. "Twenty to two."

Henry smiled. "You guys must be in a hurry. He's sucking hundreds of millions of dollars from the economy as we speak while you hold thumbs up your asses pretending not to be interested in negotiating. What horseshit."

"Are you referring to Alexander Skile?" Johnson asked.

"I might be."

"I regret to inform you that Mr. Skile was killed in a plane crash last night along with his wife."

"Of course he was." Henry laughed. "Just like I was supposed to 'die.' Maybe I'm talking about somebody else. Someone who looks and talks like Skile, yet has all the right papers to prove he's— Oops, I almost gave away part of the store."

"He's fucking with us," Agent Beck said. "We're out of time."

Johnson grasped the bed bars with pale knuckles and leaned over Henry. "Suppose I would cut you a deal. Could you give me enough information to find and prosecute Skile, or whatever his name is now?"

"Of course I can," Henry answered. "I'll tell you things that'll blow your slick, nylon socks off. You'll have solved the crime of the century."

"And your price?" Johnson asked.

"Not much," Henry said. "For starters, I want immunity from any alleged criminal activity occurring within the last seventy-two hours, and for any activity associated with Skile Industries. Then there's the matter of payment—"

"*Bullshit!*" Johnson spat, reeling away from the bed in disgust. "You were responsible for the deaths of dozens of people last night at Cheyenne Mountain. No one's going to let you walk out of here."

Henry spread his arms in a surrendering gesture. "The military would love to blame everything on me, the fall guy. Wouldn't that be convenient? But they'll never be able to prove anything conclusively." Henry held out his hand to Johnson. "I can give you reams of evidence to convict the people who were responsible."

"I need to know if you're genuine," Johnson said. "Call it a good-faith down payment."

"Ask me something," Henry offered.

Johnson pulled out a portable phone from his pocket and punched in a number. "We need a computer password. If it works, maybe we'll talk about a deal. If you refuse, I'll take that as your failure to cooperate. If the password doesn't work, I'll regard your information as worthless."

Johnson put the phone to his ear. A woman answered: "Agent Love."

"He says he'll cooperate," Johnson said, adding, "I have my doubts he can deliver." Johnson handed the phone to Henry. "Give her what she needs."

Henry accepted the phone and said, "And you are?"

"I'm FBI Special Agent Arlene Love," she said. "I'm in a Chicago apartment that belongs to a Jonathan Stone. We're attempting to open a software package with the name 'Bravo.' We need a password to proceed."

"Whoa!" Henry laughed. "You guys work fast. You must either have a lot of people in custody by now, or they're all dead. And since you're desperate and resorting to dealing with me, I'm assuming that 'dead' is correct."

"I need the password," Love repeated.

"Who's there with you?" Henry asked.

Agent Love's eyes darted from Julie, then over to Marshall. "I'm not at liberty to say. Can you give me that password or not?"

"I certainly can," he said. "I helped design that friggin' package."

Agent Love leaned over and put the phone next to Julie's ear so she could hear as well. Julie grabbed a pencil.

"Ready?" Henry said. "It's JUDITH-55S, all uppercase—for all the good it will do you."

"What does that mean?" Love asked.

"I mean there's little you can do to stop him now," Henry said. "If his system goes off-line for any reason, the network will continue trading. Everything was programmed in advance so that, if an emergency arose, his chips would automatically carry out his instructions through the Chicago exchanges. It's a crude process, only seventy percent effective. But it's still worth billions to him. Those mainframes can talk to the whole world. He's buying and selling shares around the globe through Chicago without any intervention whatsoever. And guess what? Only I know how to stop it—"

A sharp crack over the receiver made Julie and Agent Love jump. They could hear shouting at the other end, followed by what sounded like another shot before the connection abruptly terminated.

In Henry's private hospital room, the deputy pointed his Magnum at Agent Johnson and squeezed the trigger. The hollow round struck Johnson in the center of his chest with sufficient force to hurl him backward against the dresser, shattering the half-length mirror behind it. A stunned Agent Beck watched helplessly as the deputy thrust the handgun into his face and discharged another round. Beck died instantly.

Jill heard the blasts at the end of the corridor and whirled. She drew her Beretta 9mm and charged up the hallway toward Henry's room. "What's going on?"

The deputy outside the door had his handgun out and pointed at her. "Now, you just stay right there, honey, and put down that weapon."

The deputy stole glances down the hallway to make sure they were alone. No one was coming. No one had heard the shots. He raised his handgun and took aim down the muzzle at her forehead.

The second deputy charged out of the hospital room, carrying his Magnum in both hands muzzle down. "That asshole was spilling everything—"

Jill fired a single round at the deputy holding her at gunpoint. The bullet struck him in the center of his chest, and he toppled with a grunt.

"I don't appreciate guns in my face," Jill said.

The second deputy raised his Magnum. "Bitch—"

Jill fired another round that tore through the upper left side of his chest. The deputy fell back into the hospital room, still holding his handgun.

Jill was on him in an instant. She stomped on his right forearm, effectively pinning the Magnum to the floor. The deputy lay there heaving, blood flowing out of his mouth and chest wound, and spat at her in contempt. "I'll kill you. . . ."

She surveyed the room's corpses—two dead FBI agents and a patient with a massive bullet wound to the side of his head.

"Jesus . . . you're all in on this!"

Jill heard a definitive click behind her right ear. A voice, cold and vicious, ordered, "Turn 'round and face me."

She raised her hands and turned. It was Sheriff Block, holding a .44 Magnum, cocked and ready to fire at her nose.

"Well, well," he said, his eyes stealing a glance at the bodies inside the room, "looks like I caught me a multiple murderer and cop killer."

"You've got it all wrong—"

"*Shut your damn mouth!*" he shouted. He snatched Jill's handgun from her raised hand. "This isn't your gun."

"What?"

He slipped her Beretta into his back pocket, then stooped to grab the deputy's Magnum. "Yep. This here's your gun—"

Jill clenched her teeth and delivered a goal-size kick into the sheriff's face with her boot. It held all the force behind it she could muster. It felt good to hurt him. His head flew back and his large frame dumped heavily onto its side.

He grabbed the bridge of his nose. "You little tramp!"

Jill resisted the urge to go on kicking him. She leapt over his portly body and bolted down the hallway. The sheriff stood awkwardly and, holding his bloody nose, staggered into the hallway. Jill was nearly to the first stairwell exit. Sheriff Block raised his .44 and fired round after round at her, each blast roaring like a cannon through the empty corridor.

The plaster from the walls and ceiling exploded around her as Jill tore open the metal door and flew into the stairwell.

Michigan Avenue
1540 Hours

Julie keyed in "JUDITH-55S" into the password field and pressed Enter. Twin columns of text and numbers began scrolling down the display.

"We're in!" Julie shouted.

"Yes, but what's all that mean?" asked Agent Love.

Julie watched the columns scroll by. The numbers and letters were moving too fast to see anything specific. But she knew well enough what they meant. "It's a list of executable files. Looks like they've already run." She pointed to the left-hand column. "These are the files." She slid her finger across to the right-hand column. "And this shows their status. You see, they all say 'completed.' "

"And what do they do?" Marshall asked.

"Most likely, carry out specific financial transactions," Julie offered.

"Can you delete them?" Love asked.

"There's no point," Julie said. "They've already done their job. Skile's plan, whatever it may be, is under way."

"Can you send another command to counter those?" Agent Love pressed.

"It would take more time than we have to learn the program and reverse-engineer the code," Julie explained. "That sort of work takes weeks."

Suddenly the scrolling columns on the screen froze. "Oh, no." Julie hit several keys, but the system wouldn't respond.

"Are you hung up?" Love asked.

"The system just took itself off-line," Julie said. The file

314

names began to disappear. "This isn't good. The software is deleting program files and wiping the storage disks clean."

"That's evidence!" Love shouted. *"Stop it!"*

Julie tried more keys but was locked out of the system. "Can't. This routine will take only minutes to complete. We'll need that long just to reboot the system—"

"Is there a Colonel Joseph Marshall in here?" a police officer called through the doorway.

The colonel stepped away from the others. "I'm Marshall."

The officer held up a portable radio. "I've got a call transferred to you."

The colonel accepted the radio and said into the unit, "Marshall."

Jill, desperate and distraught, said, "I had to shoot two police officers. *I think I killed one of them!*"

"Slow down," Marshall said. "Where are you?"

"I'm in a laundromat."

"A laundromat?"

"Across from Silver Cross Hospital. You told me to look in on a patient named Henry Princeton. *I didn't kill him!*"

"Tell me what happened."

"I heard shots," she explained. "The deputy inside the room had shot everybody, including the patient. Then he and the one outside the door tried to kill me! I had to shoot them both. Now the sheriff wants to blame me. He took my gun and is looking for me right now. They're all in on it, Colonel. The sheriff and his whole department have been working for Skile from the beginning. For all we know, the son of a bitch owns Colorado."

"Hang on, Jill." Marshall turned and said to Special Agent Love, "The men you sent to Silver Cross Hospital may have been shot. That would explain why you lost contact." He said into his radio, "What about Henry Princeton?"

"He's dead. His head nearly blown off."

"Jill, I want you to stay hidden while I send help."

"Colonel—"

Marshall waved the radio at the police officer. "How do I call into the precinct's interrogation room?"

The officer patched a call back to their station's command center and gave the radio back to Marshall. A voice on the other end said, "Medlock."

"Jill's in trouble. I need you to get some men over to a laundromat across from Silver Cross Hospital in Colorado Springs and escort her out of there—"

"*Colonel*," shouted an HBT officer from the doorway. "Your sergeant found a body in the basement." Marshall, the phone still at his ear, whirled at the news. "He says the guy can't be dead more than a few minutes."

Chapter Fifty
Genie

Michigan Avenue
Thursday, December 30
1600 Hours

Marshall, crouching next to Williams, performed a cursory examination of the worker's body in the building's maintenance shop. He asked no one in particular, "Exactly how long ago was this man shot?"

The police captain, one of four officers present, said, "Fifteen minutes tops."

"His killer rode down in that service car," another officer said, indicating the elevator behind them. "It's the only car that comes down here. It's also his only way out. We would have seen him come back up through the lobby."

"That means he's still in the building," the police captain surmised.

"Maybe not," said Marshall, standing. "Why would Skile come down here and shoot this man?"

"Besides the fact that he's one crazed mother?" Williams spat.

"No, Skile knew another way out of this building." Marshall eyes scanned the crowded maintenance shop. "This worker got in the way of that exit."

The colonel moved to the back of the shop and opened a door to a smaller utility room. The light inside was on and he spotted the open manhole in the back.

"In here!"

The others filed inside and gathered around the hole in the floor. Marshall, kneeling, peered down into it. A slim metal ladder, embedded in the wall, descended into the darkness; without a strong flashlight, he couldn't see how deep it extended.

"Ah, Jesus," said the police captain, squatting next to Marshall. "This leads to the freight tunnels."

"What about them?" Marshall asked.

"They were built at the beginning of the century to ferry coal and whatnot under the city," the police captain explained. "The utility companies use them now for their cabling. There're fifty fucking miles of tunnel down there crisscrossing the entire Loop. He could be anywhere by now."

"Get your terrorism team down here," Marshall ordered, rising. "We're going after him."

Chicago Mercantile Exchange
1605 Hours

"Nancy Shaw," the public address system blared through the Exchange's common areas. *"Will Nancy Shaw please pick up the courtesy phone on any level. Thank you."*

The crowd milling through the Exchange scarcely noticed the announcement.

No one by that name was present to answer the page.

Chicago Water Tunnel
1615 Hours

General Stryker prodded Nancy through the hundred-year-old brick water tunnel under the lake, which looked like the inside of

317

a huge horizontal wishing well. The tunnel was empty, thanks to a thirty-foot section of the ceiling that had been under repair for the past two years.

Nancy and the general sloshed through nearly two miles of stagnant, ankle-deep mud before a solid wall appeared from the darkness beyond their light and towered over them. They had reached the end.

Mold spores and dust motes, disturbed by their arrival, irritated Nancy's throat and nose, choking her. General Stryker pushed her against the wall and directed the beam of his powerful flashlight up the vertical shaft of the water-intake crib. If everything had gone per schedule, Skile's boat would be moored up there by now. The general ran the beam along the rusty handrails that lined the inside of the tower and saw nothing that indicated recent use. Stryker smiled knowingly. It was just a matter of time until he again met up with his business associate.

He removed a pair of handcuffs from his coat pocket and dangled them in front of Nancy. "These should feel familiar to you."

She viewed them warily. "What are you planning in that sick mind of yours?"

"Only this."

General Stryker attached one end of the cuffs to her wrist, threaded its chain through a hand rung, then secured the other end to her free wrist. Nancy pulled on the chain. The general was right—she felt as though she was imprisoned back in Skile's pit.

"I admit your predicament is not much better than the hospitality Mr. Skile showed you earlier this week," he said. The general's eyes took on a sad look. "I saved your life more than once, yet you left that dreary place without thanking me. However crude this place may be, now we can talk."

Nancy glanced up the shaft and could see light radiating in through the top of the tower. That means there must be a way out from up there, she surmised. She looked at Stryker. "Talk about what?"

Stryker folded his arms across his chest and settled against the tunnel's moss-caked bricks. "First I must explain something to you. Our friend Mr. Skile has a vessel moored at the top of that tower waiting to take him away from all this. Don't you agree that he will be surprised when he finds us here?"

"What fun. Then what?"

"Then the three of us will begin a great journey together, but not to where he intended, I'm sure," the general said. "Prepare yourself for a truly beautiful experience, my friend. It will be my honor and pleasure to escort you to Sirius."

Michigan Avenue
1620 Hours

"Tell me everything Henry said to you," Julie insisted. "Even if it doesn't make any sense."

FBI Agent Arlene Love locked her fingers behind her head and leaned back into the office chair in Skile's ruined trading room. "You heard most of it. He said that Skile's system didn't need his people to continue trading. The computers here in Chicago are trading without human intervention, and only Henry knew how to stop the process. Jesus, why did he have to be killed?"

"Obviously, to keep him quiet," Julie said.

"How much damage can Skile's files do to a financial network?" Agent Love reflected. "There are computer firewalls around every institution, and they all have safeguards against this sort of hacking. And if he's manipulating markets, why haven't we seen evidence on the trading boards? Maybe his plan isn't working after all."

Julie's eyes narrowed, and she shook her head. "I have no doubt it will work. But we're not likely to see anything happen today."

Agent Love noted Julie's intense, faraway gaze. "Keep talking."

"He wouldn't want anything unusual popping up during regular trading sessions," Julie said, shaking herself out of her self-induced trance. "Too many eyes, too many questions. Exchange officials would suspend trading if they suspected their systems were in any way out of control. Instead, Skile's commands will execute only while the networks are off-line, away from prying eyes."

"How is that possible?" Agent Love asked.

"His microprocessors will manage everything," Julie said. "After the markets close today, thousands of financial institutions around the world will take their systems off-line to upgrade and test their software for the new millennium. Skile's instructions don't need that software. Why? Because he's encrypted his own routines into the chips of selected trading computers here in Chicago and perhaps elsewhere—just like he did with Eclipse.''

''What the heck is Eclipse?''

Julie raised a hand. ''It's not important. Believe me, Skile now owns these computers. They'll execute whatever commands he feeds them.''

''How does the Millennium Bug figure in?'' Agent Love queried.

''When institutions around the world bring their systems back on-line,'' Julie said, ''they'll discover that the hardware itself can't handle the date change of the new millennium, thanks to Skile's microprocessors. Chaos will reign in every financial market throughout the world as billions in assets are shifted under Skile's smoke screen. Imagine the consequences—monetary systems will shut down. Banks and savings and loans will be drained. Millions of records lost and backups erased. It will take months and countless man-hours before these systems are even moderately operational again. All this will be blamed on the Millennium Bug. When his microprocessors are finally dissected to find out the truth, Skile will have had ample time to sell and resell his newly acquired wealth perhaps hundreds of times, effectively laundering any financial trails leading back to him.''

Agent Love rocked her chair forward. ''That's the wildest scheme I've ever heard.''

Julie shrugged. ''He's a smart man—smart enough to take down the military's strategic satellite defense network. He was just playing with us then. This has been his pet project from the beginning.''

''If what you're saying is true, we're wasting time.'' Agent Love looked at her watch. ''Unless you want to just sit here and try to conjure up a genie who can turn back time.''

Julie looked up suddenly as an idea struck her. ''Arlene, I don't believe it. You're a genius! That's exactly what we can do.''

Agent Love's expression betrayed confusion, and something else: a fleeting terror that Julie had suddenly lost it. ''Call on a genie? You've definitely been sitting in front of the tube too long.''

Julie stood up, the adrenaline coursing through her. "Let's get General Medlock over here immediately." Her face lit up. "We can't turn back time. But we can temporarily stop it."

Chicago Freight Tunnels
1625 hours

Marshall was the first to climb down the vertical access shaft that connected the building's basement with the labyrinth of freight tunnels beneath the city. Williams followed, as did four members of the precinct's HBT team.

They emerged in a six-foot-high tunnel with a breadth of about five feet. The tunnel had once sported rails for mini–electric train cars. Those tracks were mostly gone, covered with a layer of concrete to facilitate maintenance.

The HBT team leader, an ex–Special Forces officer named Lieutenant Walter Heath, began leading the group east. His plan was to take them under the Chicago River, then toward the heart of the Loop area. As they proceeded, he directed his flashlight beam onto a waterproof map of the tunnel system created by Commonwealth Edison.

"We have officers positioned at each of the outlets in case he shows up," the lieutenant said, studying the map. "However, that still leaves hundreds of local accesses that lead up to various buildings for one reason or another. Fortunately, most aren't wide enough for a man to fit through."

The radio clipped to the lieutenant's collar crackled. He responded, "Heath."

"We're watching a boat attempting to moor at the Harrison Crib," a voice crackled from the command center. The signal in the tunnel was weak and full of interference from the electromagnetic fields of the power lines. "Thought you might want to know."

"Is it a utility vessel?" Heath asked.

"Negative," the radio squawked. "It's a civilian craft, about seventy feet. Maybe we'll take a look."

"I don't see any connection," the lieutenant said, "but keep me informed."

"What's the Harrison Crib?" Williams asked, walking behind the lieutenant.

Heath thrust a thumb over his shoulder and explained, "A round, brick building about two miles from shore. It's one of two water intakes for the city."

"Why would a boat dock there?" Marshall asked.

"For one thing, the piers are closed," Heath explained. "The craft's probably in trouble."

Marshall brought them to a halt with a raised hand. "We may be heading the wrong way. I suggest we check this out."

Lieutenant Heath shook his head. "There's no way he could get out to the crib. Our man wouldn't have gone west. The tunnel dead-ends at North Pier. He'd be trapped."

"Unless there's another access we don't know about," Marshall offered.

Heath flipped through his binder of maps until he found the schematic of the water station. He pointed to a pair of dots about two miles from shore. "Here are your cribs."

Marshall ran his finger along two parallel lines leading out onto Lake Michigan and joining at the cribs. "What are these?"

"The water tunnels," the lieutenant said. "One's the original, ninety feet below the lake. The newer one is made of concrete about one hundred ninety feet below the lake."

"Unless he's got a submarine," Williams noted, "he's not likely to use a flooded tunnel to exit the city."

"Actually, only one's in use at the moment," the lieutenant said. "The older tunnel's been drained for repairs."

"Now you're getting interesting," Williams said.

Marshall indicated a point on the map under Illinois Street, not far from Skile's condo building. "Our freight tunnel crosses beneath the old water tunnel just before your dead end, Lieutenant."

"But there's no access from one to the other," Heath noted.

"According to your map, there's no access," Williams said. "Someone with the resources and the right motivation could figure a way to breach these two tunnels."

Heath wasn't convinced. "Too much of a long shot. Breaching the old tunnel would create a very dangerous flooding situation. He has dozens more options this way. I say we stick to our plan and continue west."

"You're welcome to join us," Marshall said. "Otherwise, we'll meet you topside."

He and Williams turned and headed east down the section of tunnel from which they had come.

Chapter Fifty-one
The Impossible

Michigan Avenue
Thursday, December 30
1655 Hours

"Pull the plug!?" gasped James Rubino, group vice president and the top technical manager of the Chicago Mercantile Exchange's vast computing web. He alone was responsible for the exchange's hardware infrastructure around which the universe of currency, commodity, and futures trading revolved. "You're asking me to do the impossible."

Julie sat with Agent Love and General Medlock in the lobby of Skile's condo building, listening to Rubino and his passion to protect the integrity of the Exchange. In the end, they concluded, he wouldn't be much help.

"It's certainly not impossible," Julie countered. "His commands are still in volatile memory. A simple reboot would wipe them out."

"We'd also be erasing a million lines of trading data," Rubino said. "Without making proper backups, the loss would put brokerage houses all over the world out of business. Take me at my word—it's not going to happen."

Julie shifted uncomfortably in the lobby's cushioned chair. "Backing up data might keep his bogus contracts intact. You must flush the memory. Certainly there is redundant data of legitimate contracts in your system and the brokerage houses. Then there's the issue of your mainframes' microprocessors. Just to be sure, you'll want to replace them before you reboot."

Rubino, sporting a thick mustache in need of a trim, glared at Julie in disbelief through his gogglelike glasses. A seasoned systems manager one year from retirement, he wasn't about to jeopardize his fat pension over a witch hunt. "Now I've heard it all. Even if new chips were available now, which they aren't, it would take months to replace every microprocessor in every piece of hardware connected to the Exchange."

Julie shook her head forcibly. "*No!* Just in the computers that control after-hours trading."

"You don't realize what you're up against," he hollered. "Believe me, you're not going to talk anyone into powering down equipment before day's worth of backups are made."

Julie felt her noose tighten with yet another roadblock. How could she make him understand what was at stake?

"Let me make sure I have this right," Agent Love said. "We're aware that the crime of the century is about to be perpetrated, which could cost consumers untold billions of dollars, leave the economy in shambles, and make the nation's most wanted criminal one of the richest and most powerful men in the world. And we're going to let this happen because we don't want to lose any records, mess up files, or delay financial trading while we figure out a workable solution. Have I got that right?"

Rubino's expression turned vicious. "Frankly, I think you're both full of crap. Christ, you can't even show me a single file so I can see what your master criminal might be up to. You're asking me to shut down our entire system and postpone trading indefinitely on your unsubstantiated hunch alone. Have I got *that* right?"

Julie, startled by Rubino's outburst, felt her emotional walls crumbling. Her altruistic, though admittedly tenuous, passion to single-handedly save the nation's economy was rapidly eroding. There were just too many obstacles. Was it madness to persist?

General Medlock, who had been sitting on a leather bench listening to Rubino, raised his hand for a time-out. "We don't have time to argue about this. If this asshole has free rein of your network, it'll make the Year 2000 problem seem like a skirmish. That kind of hit could cost twenty times more than the Millennium Bug—"

"It's bullshit," Rubino spat, letting all his anger and disgust surface. "Not even an order from the President of the United States will shut down these systems. Who's going to put his neck on the block and dump the fortunes of a lot of powerful people? No, sir, it's not going to happen." He looked at his watch. "Excuse me, I've got a network to run." He adjusted his thick glasses and riveted a piercing gaze at Julie. "Have a nice day."

Rubino picked up his overcoat and hat and worked his way through the contingent of police on his way out of the building.

"Well, that got us nowhere," Agent Love said.

Julie sank back in her chair and, totally exhausted, groaned. "If either of you have an ATM card, I suggest you use it to take out as much cash as you can. Come Monday, our banks will be out of business."

General Medlock punched a key on his cellular phone and put it to his ear. "We still have options as long as I can appeal to a higher authority." He said to Julie, "Sit up straight, Dr. Martinelli. I want you to talk with a good friend of mine at the White House."

Chicago Freight Tunnels
1705 Hours

Marshall and Williams reached the end of the freight tunnel, an area as claustrophobic as the inside of a concrete closet. They played their beams along the walls and ceiling searching for a possible access to the water tunnel above.

"I've got it!" Williams hollered.

Marshall swung his beam around.

The sergeant indicated one of several metal rungs in the wall that had been hammered firmly in place. "These are brand-spanking new."

They both directed their lights to the ceiling over the rungs. A manhole-size opening had been bored through, revealing a hollow space above. Its metal-plate cover had been pushed aside.

"Find something interesting?" a voice called to them.

Marshall and Williams turned and directed their beams into the face of Lieutenant Heath.

"Where are your men?" Marshall asked.

"Heading into the city per our original plan," he said. "I decided your theory was too compelling to ignore. If we don't find anything here, we'll retrace our path and join them."

Marshall indicated the rungs in the wall. "Well, we found something."

"Holy Mary . . ." The lieutenant grabbed one of the rungs and tried to wiggle it, then inspected the access hole in the ceiling. "This is a very professional job."

"Call your men back," Marshall said. "We're going to need backup." He flung his Franchi over his shoulder and hoisted himself up onto the first rung. "When you've finished your call, I'll expect you to join us."

The White House
Washington, D.C.
1830 Hours

Kenneth Roberts, the President's national security adviser, walked smartly through the Oval Office to a private sitting room. Its door was closed.

Sandra Tobias, the President's secretary, rushed after him. "Sir, let me announce you."

"Then please hurry." Roberts's features reflected an unusually high level of stress and frustration. He rapped his knuckles sharply on the door.

Sandra stepped in front of him and entered the small, smartly appointed sitting room where the President of the United States and the Canadian Prime Minister had been enjoying a productive policy chat.

"Sorry, sir," she said. "Roberts says it's very urgent."

The President appeared visibly annoyed. "Tell him he'll have to—"

"This can't wait, Mr. President," said Roberts, slipping inside behind the President's secretary.

The Canadian Prime Minister stood. "Perhaps I should wait outside."

The President waved him back into his chair. "This won't take a minute."

The President ushered the two out into the Oval Office and closed the sitting-room door securely behind them.

"What is this, Roberts? What's so damn important?"

"I just spoke with General Medlock in Chicago," Roberts said. "He's taking you at your word to help him."

The President grew very quiet.

"In the interest of national security," Roberts said, "it's imperative that you order the powering down of all computers networked into Chicago's financial exchanges. This must be done immediately."

The President stared vacantly at his adviser, unable to fathom doing what Roberts had just requested. "That is preposterous. And what if I don't?"

Roberts riveted his boss with a deadly glare. "Our economy will be left in shambles, sir. And you will be remembered as the President who did nothing to prevent a financial disaster with implications far more devastating than the Great Depression."

Lake Michigan
1745 Hours

A police launch and a Coast Guard cutter converged on the Harrison Crib and effectively surrounded it. Moored to the brick structure was a handsome seventy-four-foot motor yacht with the name *BRAVO!* painted on her fiberglass hull. With twin 820-horsepower diesels and a four-foot draft, the craft could do twenty-five knots in a heartbeat, waves permitting, giving even a well-tuned cutter a run over the Lake.

The police launch's loudspeaker blared, *"This is the Chicago Police Lake Patrol. We are boarding."*

The officers on deck received no response to the message either visually or over the mariner's radio. Nor could they see any activity on or around the vessel.

The police cutter maneuvered alongside the derelict yacht. The waves were high, the wind bitter. While crewmen secured the two craft together, a team of HBT officers donned bulletproof vests and took up shotguns before boarding. Once on board, they moved quickly belowdecks, methodically searching the spacious living area and cabin bedrooms. The yacht was fully prepped and loaded with supplies, clothing, and personal effects. The liquor cabinet was stocked, including an impressive collection of European wines, and someone had arranged fresh flowers in each cabin. But there was no one aboard to enjoy it. The vessel was deserted.

The officer in charge returned to the yacht's bridge and said into his radio, "Captain, she may be a beautiful vessel, but she's got ghosts for a crew."

Chicago Water Tunnel
1752 Hours

Two Hispanic seamen climbed down the hollow tower that took them ninety feet beneath the lake. As they approached the bottom, they heard a woman's voice call up from the tunnel below. "Hello? Be careful you don't step on me."

The lower of the two climbers withdrew a flashlight and directed its beam down into the black void. It revealed the face of a woman staring up at him, chained to a rung not twenty feet below.

As they finished their descent, Nancy stepped aside as far as her cuffs would allow to let them pass. She was grateful to see them, whoever they were; that meant there definitely was a way out up there. When they reached the bottom, she had to squint through the glare of the flashlights to see their faces. The two weren't much older than teens.

One of them spoke to her in Spanish: *"Quién es usted y qué hace usted aquí?"*

"I'm sorry. I don't understand."

Another flashlight beam snapped on and illuminated the pair. General Stryker, his Mauser out, made his way down the tunnel toward them.

"Señor Stone?" one of them asked.

"No, I am not Stone," Stryker said. "Nor can I allow you to proceed to find him. You must return the way you came."

"What's going on here?" Nancy asked. "Who are these guys?"

"Mr. Skile's crew. He won't need them." Stryker directed the two up the ladder with his handgun. "Start climbing."

One of the crewmen pointed up the tower and said, *"No se puede volverse. La policía está allí!"*

General Stryker discharged a single round that transfixed the crewman's neck. Both hands flew to his throat. Nancy shouted in surprise. He let out a gargled gasp and, blood oozing between his fingers, keeled over into the mud.

The second crewman, his hands extended in a gesture of surrender, stared at Stryker, terrified.

"Go," Stryker ordered, pointing his handgun up the rungs. *"Climb!"*

The crewman grabbed the rung and quickly disappeared into the darkness above.

"You killed this man for no reason," Nancy gasped. "I thought for a moment that you might possess a shred of moral decency. But you're worse scum than I dared imagine."

Stryker returned the Mauser to his pocket. "I am not in a position to be tolerant of Mr. Skile's friends or his employees. After Skile left the chateau yesterday, he had my men massacred in cold blood. I am only too eager to retaliate in kind."

Nancy grew still as the general's eyes took on an unbecoming coldness fueled by rage.

"When he passes this way," Stryker said, "I intend to kill him. And God help you as well if you were in any way part of his hideous crime."

Chapter Fifty-two
Maniac

The Oval Office
1900 Hours

"I feel good about this decision," the President said. "I should have demanded this action the day Senator Lloyd died."

Jeremy Springfield, the President's chief of staff, thrust a finger at the treasury secretary. "Are you certain there won't be permanent damage to the economy?"

Lance Holliday, scribbling notes on a pad of paper, adjusted his thick-rimmed glasses. "None that I can foresee. In fact, the economy could use the breather. Your action could potentially stop huge losses in the market, Mr. President. And you may have just short-circuited a recession."

There were whistles and applause from the other members of his staff. The President, standing behind his desk in his shirt-sleeves, put his hands on his hips and took in a deep breath, feeling invincible. "I'm going to miss this office. There's so much more I could have done."

There came a sharp rap on the open door frame to the President's office. All heads turned. It was National Security Adviser Kenneth Roberts. The President winced when he saw his adviser's familiar anxious look.

"It's too early to start popping champagne corks," Roberts said as he joined the room's party. "We're not out of the woods yet. In fact, the forest just got a little darker."

The Millennium Project

Marshall led Williams and Lieutenant Heath through the tunnel's unvarying darkness. They had made respectable time, considering how the ankle-deep mud felt like a death run in a nightmare.

"What's the latest word from your boys about that boat?" Marshall asked.

"Haven't heard a thing in fifteen minutes," Lieutenant Heath said. "The deeper we go, the worse the radio reception."

"That's terrific," Marshall spat.

Before the echo of their splashing had faded, a figure stepped from a maintenance crevice behind them and watched their collective light recede in the distance. Alexander Skile held a portable cellular telephone in both hands as though it were the most precious artifact in the world. And so it was for those inside this tunnel. He alone held their fates, and the death he could unleash with it would be formidable.

Chicago Precinct Fourteen
1810 Hours

"What's the word from the White House?" asked Special Agent Arlene Love as she, Julie, and General Medlock returned to their command center in the police station.

One of Love's agents, a black man named Jeffery Jones, leaned back in his chair at the head of the interrogation table and stretched his already impossibly long arms. "I've got good news and bad news: The good news is the President ordered the suspension of trading on all exchanges nationwide effective immediately. He also ordered the physical shutdown of all machines connected to the Chicago exchanges."

"That's everything we asked for," Love said. Then she looked at him, suspicious. "Our bad news must be the response to that mandate."

"Bull's-eye," Jones said. "Brokerage houses are screaming. The exchanges are scrambling to confirm. This is going to take time."

"That's unacceptable," Julie said. "They've got to power

down the network immediately. That's all that matters now.''

Agent Jones shook his head. "You can forget it. Shutting down a network and losing data is a system administrator's worst nightmare. Presidential order or not, no one—and I mean *no one*—will deliberately power down a server without making backups. That's going to take all night."

"That's too late!" Julie shouted. "By morning the damage will be irreparable."

"My people have talked with Commonwealth Edison," General Medlock said. "They say they can shut down the power grid to their data center."

"They'll have backup power," Julie said. She appealed to the general. "We're going to need military assistance—and lots of it."

General Medlock admired her persistence. "You got it straight to the White House. Just tell me what you need and I'll get it for you."

Julie retrieved her bag from beneath the table, opened it, and withdrew her Compaq notebook computer. "I need a fast, reliable link from this precinct station to Cheyenne Mountain's network. Tell Cheyenne's network administrators to hook into the Chicago exchanges' central hub. As soon as we're connected, I'll bring Anthony on-line."

The general frowned. "I don't know any Anthony at Cheyenne. Who is he?"

"It's a what," Julie said, plugging her computer into the wall outlet. "Our only chance is to persuade the world's fastest computer to turn off a few light switches."

Chicago Water Tunnel
1820 Hours

Williams spotted it first as a metallic reflection off the brick walls. The sergeant waved Marshall and Heath to a halt and moved cautiously forward to investigate.

"This isn't suppose to be here," he said.

Williams waded closer, his beam focusing on the knee-level reflection. He crouched for a better look. The abnormality was metallic duct tape mostly concealed behind a piece of warped plywood. He directed his beam under the sheet and saw fresh green and blue wires.

"Houston, I think we've got a problem."

The others approached slowly. Williams carefully moved aside the wood to uncover an elaborate package of explosives.

"Houston, I *know* we've got a problem."

"How bad is it?" Marshall asked.

"Real bad." Williams moved his light over a brick-size packet of gray material connected to a radio receiver. "We've got what looks like plastique."

Marshall let out a whistle.

"I may be able to disarm it," Lieutenant Heath said, moving forward.

"Don't count on it." Williams ran his light along a set of exposed copper wires that secured the package to the brick wall. "This is slick. And it may be booby-rigged."

Lieutenant Heath crouched beside Williams. "I did a stint with Chicago's hazardous-materials unit and bomb squad. I won't touch a thing if I'm not absolutely certain."

"Damn right you won't," Williams said.

The lieutenant, directing his own light at the package, scrutinized the circuitry embedded in transparent thermoplastic acrylic. No one could access the electronics without cutting apart the entire unit.

"The bastard who engineered this wants us to see how dangerous it is and back off," the lieutenant said. "We've got about five pounds of Semtex and a very sophisticated remote-controlled detonator, possibly a phone receiver." He pointed to a small tube embedded inside the plastic. "That's a simple mercury switch. We can't move it without setting the whole thing off."

"If this detonates, you'll have one hell of a mess to clean up," Marshall said. "Call your bomb-squad buddies."

The lieutenant shot a severe glance over his shoulder. "No one uses a radio in here until I determine how this receiver works."

"I don't like this," Marshall said. "If Skile can't access this tunnel, he's likely to get pissed off and detonate that thing. And if he's already gone through, he can effectively close this route after him and stop anyone who tries following. Either way, we're standing in a very bad spot."

"We can't be more than a quarter mile from the end," Williams said. "I suggest we get our asses out of here damn fast."

"Let's go," Marshall ordered. "You too, Heath."

"I'm not going," the lieutenant said. Heath took off his lapel radio and handed it to Marshall. "When you're out of the tunnel, make contact with the team and tell them to get a bomb squad down here. We're going to have to freeze this thing. Meanwhile, I'll study the circuitry to figure a way to move this without setting it off."

"Like hell you will," Marshall said. "I'm ordering you out of here."

"Sorry, Colonel," Heath said. "Even if there was martial law, I can't take my orders from the military. My job right now is to keep the lake up there where it belongs."

Marshall attached the radio to his jacket lapel. "I'm through arguing. Good luck, Lieutenant." The colonel pushed past them and continued down the tunnel.

Williams grabbed the lieutenant's shoulder. "Do me a favor and keep that ass of yours in once piece."

Lieutenant Heath placed a hand on Williams's and squeezed it. The sergeant put a cigar stub between his teeth and bolted down the tunnel after Marshall.

Precinct Fourteen
1825 Hours

"I'm on-line," Julie announced. "I've got a solid T1 with Cheyenne."

"Good work, girl," Agent Love said. "You're in the driver's seat. Just tell us what you need."

"I could use Nancy's help," she said. "Anyone heard from her?"

"She didn't answer her page at the Merc," Love said. "She must've gotten lost finding her way back here."

Chicago Water Tunnel
1827 Hours

"Someone's coming," Nancy said.

General Stryker peered down the tunnel and saw a ring of light accompanied by the distant echo of footfalls. "He is a very predictable man."

Nancy pulled on the cuffs that bound her to the wall. "Get these things off me, please."

"Nonsense," Stryker said. "You are my decoy. While he is pondering your presence here with his jaw open, I will have the advantage."

The general extinguished his light and moved back into a maintenance crevice that offered enough depth to conceal him. Stryker held in his laugher as he thought how easy it had been to confront his comrade in this death trap.

A minute passed before two men splashed past the hole in which Stryker hid. The general's triumphant grin vanished. Skile was not alone. Who was this other man?

All Nancy could see were approaching twin headlights. She attempted to raise a hand to shield her eyes, but the short length of chain binding her wrists wouldn't allow it.

"I don't believe it," Marshall said.

Nancy, startled, managed, "Joe?"

The light from the sergeant's beam washed over Marshall's solid features as he stepped up to her.

"*Joe!*" Nancy shouted. "Stryker's behind you!"

Williams reached for his side arm.

"Don't touch it," Stryker warned. He had his Mauser pointed at Williams's chest. "Throw down your lights. I wish to remain in the dark."

Williams did as instructed and dropped his light into the mud.

"You too," Stryker instructed Marshall.

The colonel likewise dropped his flashlight.

"Now your side arms."

The two removed their handguns and dropped them.

Stryker scrutinized the Galil hanging over Williams's shoulder, then Marshall's Franchi. "Remove your shoulder weapons."

As they complied, the general noted, "A sniper's rifle for long range, and a shotgun for close work. Who are you men?"

"For the moment, we're working for the FBI," Marshall said.

"Such unconventional weapons for the FBI," Stryker said. "You are better equipped for a strike team."

"Let's discuss this topside," Marshall said. "There's a large cache of explosives about a quarter mile back just itching to bring down this tunnel. Maybe it belongs to you."

Stryker drove Williams at gunpoint back toward the colonel so he could easily cover both of them. "I am many things some would call monstrous, but I am not a terrorist. A bomb is an act of cowardice." The general looked directly into Marshall's eyes. "When I kill a man, I must see his eyes."

Marshall grabbed the chain linking Nancy's cuffs and pulled them so the general could see. "And women too?"

"As an enemy, a woman can be just as deadly," he said. "I am not certain if Dr. Shaw is my enemy. I suspect she may have struck a deal to flee with Skile before he betrayed me. I will deal with her accordingly when I know the truth."

"Let her go," Marshall said. "She had nothing to do with the deaths of your soldiers."

"How could you possibly know anything?" Stryker asked.

Williams chanced a glance at the colonel. How much should he tell this maniac?

Marshall riveted Stryker with a dark, serious glare. "Because I'm the man you're looking for."

Chapter Fifty-three
Detonation

"We're in!" Julie shouted.

Thanks to the Cheyenne's network administrators, Julie's notebook computer now had a solid computer connection to Chicago's financial nerve center. Weaving through more than one hundred miles of fiber-optic cable and two hundred data-traffic routers, she had isolated a single diesel generator the size of half a railroad car. This generator represented the moat around Skile's fortress—it provided backup power to the exchange's forty-seven refrigerator-size mainframe computers that controlled after-hours trading.

That was her target.

Before she could shut down that generator, Julie needed full administrative privileges to the Exchange's power station, something even a seasoned code cracker didn't come by easily. That meant breaking an encrypted code—a task not unlike finding the combination to a lock with 128 ten-digit tumblers. Julie had prepared a rudimentary computer script that would hold open the "lock" while trying every variation of that combination until it received an "open" ping. If she enlisted the help of IBM's "Deep Blue" supercomputer with its ability to calculate one billion combinations per second, breaking the lock could take weeks.

But Anthony conservatively offered at least a hundredfold boost in computing power. Could she harness that power? Well—that was their only hope.

General Medlock, the phone to his ear, informed Julie, "Com Ed is ready to take down the exchange's power grid."

"Not until I disable the backup," she said. "A loss of power now could lock us out of their network. I can't risk losing this connection."

Julie wheeled her chair up to her keyboard. Everything—theoretically—was ready.

"Wish me luck, folks." She drew in her breath, held it, and pressed the Enter key to load her tiny script. Anthony took her command and, like a father checking the validity of a child's request, began calculating.

The effect was astonishing. Julie let out her breath slowly as a column of 128-digit numbers scrolled down her screen. The characters flew by too fast to see anything beyond a digital blur, and gave her only the vaguest awareness of Anthony's awesome capability.

Chicago Freight Tunnels
1840 Hours

Three HBT tactical officers directed their lights at the open access plate above them. Squad Leader R. L. Garrett, a tall, able commando, ordered his team members, "Follow me."

Garrett scrambled up the rungs and squeezed his large frame through the opening. He played his light beam along the tunnel's corroded walls, its bricks muddy and caked with moss. The tunnel reminded him of the inside of a century-old brick drainpipe. And so it was.

While his team members followed him through the opening, Garrett shouted down the tunnel through cupped hands, *"Lieutenant Heath!"*

His voice echoed eerily back. The officers listened for several seconds and heard nothing in response, only the disturbing sound of water dripping somewhere ahead and behind them.

Something Garrett spotted gave him pause. He extinguished his light and ordered the others to do likewise. They all saw it, a distant ring of light moving toward them.

Stryker thrust his handgun to within a breath of Marshall's face. "What do you know about my men?"

"Enough," the colonel said. "The raid on Skile's chateau was a U.S. military operation to recover a surveillance satellite data module. The unit was equipped with a homing beacon, which one of your men stupidly brought to the chateau. Your troops were at the wrong place at the wrong time, caught with the wrong merchandise."

Stryker cocked his head toward Nancy. "And her?"

"She had nothing to do with any of this. We found Dr. Shaw purely by chance. Let her go. You and I are here for the same reason, and it isn't about killing innocent civilians. I want Skile as badly as you do."

General Stryker pulled back the hammer of his Mauser. "You are a dead man."

Marshall didn't blink. "We're all dead men after tomorrow. You would be doing me a great service by hastening my journey to Sirius. But please, not before I complete my final mission on Earth and find Skile."

"You're not one of us," Stryker hissed. "You would profane the sanctity of our afterlife with your presence."

"To the contrary," Marshall said. He pulled down his sleeve to expose the drawing of Sirius on his wrist. "I've been anointed by God himself to lead your troops in the afterlife. You, my friend, are out of a job."

Officer Garrett snapped on his light to illuminate the approaching figure. "Hold it right there," he ordered.

Skile stopped suddenly and squinted at the harsh light directed into his face.

"He's got something in his hand," one of the officers warned.

"Show it to me!" Garrett ordered.

"It's just my telephone," Skile said in his most disarming manner. He raised his arms and held up the cellular phone in plain view.

"Who the hell are you?" Garrett demanded.

"Jonathan Stone," Skile said. "I woke up this morning a very important man. I am not sure who I am anymore."

"That's him!" exclaimed one of the officers. "That's the bastard we're looking for!"

Garrett approached him. "Consider yourself under arrest."

Skile waved his phone at them. "Then I'm entitled to one phone call."

"Like hell you are." Garrett grabbed his arm, but not before Skile pressed a single button on his phone.

The call completed automatically and began to ring.

Lieutenant Heath heard a click inside the explosives package and saw a series of red pin lights blinking within its clear acrylic casing. He remained in a crouched position, staring stupidly at the circuitry, his mind unable to comprehend the unthinkable.

Suddenly, panic-induced adrenaline shot through his bloodstream, and he scrambled blindly backward against the tunnel wall with enough force to break his collarbone. His flashlight rolled into the mud, plunging the tunnel into darkness. He sat against the wall, his chest heaving, watching the red glow of pin lights stare back at him like the eyes of a demon.

The plastique detonated, producing the equivalent of two thousand pounds of dynamite. Lieutenant Heath and all that he was vaporized in an instant.

Lake Michigan

Police officers on Skile's luxury yacht were handcuffing the Hispanic crewman when a spectacular geyser blew several hundred feet into the air a half mile away. Almost a full minute later, a spray of water swept across the deck, carrying with it chunks of century-old mortar and bricks.

Chicago Water Tunnel

Each second, twenty thousand gallons of Lake Michigan water poured through the gash in the tunnel created by the explosion.

The force of the inrush, driven by the pressure of water above it, rivaled the power of Niagara Falls.

A quarter mile farther east, a deep rumble shook the bottom of the intake crib. Marshall and the others felt the tremor beneath their feet, which carried with it sufficient force to jog bricks loose. The sound came an instant later. A dense roar, amplified by the tunnel, quickly exceeded their pain thresholds.

Stryker whirled to see a great cloud of smoke billowing down the cylindrical corridor. Williams lunged and drove the general against the wall. Stryker pulled the trigger of his Mauser. The round tore through Williams's upper right arm and struck the mossy wall behind him.

"Son of a bitch!" Williams yelled.

The sergeant hurled his weight onto him. Williams drove the general's gun-toting hand against the wall, cracking the bones in three of Stryker's fingers. The Mauser fell from his grip.

Marshall felt his utility belt for the pick to unlock Nancy's cuffs.

"Joe . . ." she said, unable to find the words to describe what she saw rushing toward them.

Marshall glanced over his shoulder. A raging waterfall hurtled down the tunnel at the speed of a freight train.

"*Sergeant!*" Marshall shouted.

Nancy pushed him awkwardly away from her. "Get out of here before you drown!"

The roar became debilitating.

Williams glanced up from his hold on Stryker just as the wall of water crashed over them. He instinctively wrapped his arms around his head as the water swept him off the general like a doll.

The surge slammed Marshall against the tunnel wall with enough force to kill him had the old mortar not yielded and turned into mud on impact. For several stunned moments the onrushing water pinned him against the wall in a death grip. Not until the tunnel filled could Marshall move against the strong current and make his way to Nancy.

Williams had no choice but to ride the swift current up the black tower, where the force nearly lifted him out of the frigid water. He thrashed about trying to gain his bearings, then began feeling his way along the wall for the hand rungs. His right arm was numb with pain. Besides taking a bullet, it had broken in two places when he used it to cushion his crash against the wall.

He coughed up water in his lungs. *"Colonel!"*

Ten feet below, Marshall found the bottom rung. His hands moved from one rusty piece of metal to the next until he felt Nancy still bound to the wall by the handcuffs. She exhibited amazing presence of mind. Her hand squeezed his, not in a desperate panic but in a reassuring touch of trust.

Nancy pulled the short length of chain tight for him. Marshall removed the stiletto from his utility belt and opened the blade. He thrust the blade under the links and, applying pressure upward, moved its serrated edge back and forth like a saw. He worked the blade through the links until it broke free.

Nancy vanished, carried to the surface by the swift current.

Chapter Fifty-four
Swept Away

Chicago Water Tunnel
Thursday, December 30
1843 Hours

Skile heard it first. A deep rumble followed by the cracking of mortar. The roar of the blast came seconds later like a huge, hungry beast. Nothing in their experiences prepared them for the horror the noise invoked.

Stunned, the officers directed their beams into the blackness behind Skile. The specter of the water raging toward them compounded their dread.

"Holy shit!" Garrett gasped.

The officers scrambled toward the access hole. Skile drew his Walther and opened fire on them to clear the opening. They yelled, stumbled, and fell. Skile secured his handgun, rushed to the access, and swung his legs into the hole.

A hand grasped his arm. Garrett, his eyes pleading, said to Skile, "Help me . . ." His words were all but lost in the roar of the approaching water.

"Sorry." Skile shook away his hand and began climbing down the rungs into the freight tunnel below.

The enormous wall of water crashed over the officers and carried their bodies into the black tunnel beyond. A column of water burst through the access opening and blew downward with twice the force of a fire hose.

The column struck Skile like an avalanche of stone and hurled him to the concrete floor below. He landed heavily on his knees and felt the bones in both his legs shatter. The unrelenting column of water mercilessly hammered and pounded him against the walls of the freight tunnel.

He reached for a handhold, something to stop his movement. But it was futile. Skile's fingers slipped ineffectively over the smooth surface of the concrete walls as the water swept him away.

Precinct Fourteen
1850 Hours

The lights in the precinct station dimmed and extinguished, plunging the interrogation room into darkness. Shouting and questions erupted throughout the room. The emergency lights in the hallway snapped on with a thud, and Julie's notebook's computer screen flickered as its batteries took over.

She scrambled for a look at the display. "I told Com Ed to wait!" Mercifully, the connection was still intact—all signs indicated that Anthony's calculations were proceeding at an impossible speed.

"Jonesy, tell me what's going on," said Special Agent Love.

Agent Jones, a phone already to his ear, spoke to his colleagues posted in the operations room of Com Ed's Substation Seven. Seconds later he reported, "Massive shorting in the Loop's power grid." He paused to collect more information. "It's the freight tunnels. They're flooding."

Agent Love threw her hands into the air in frustration. "That's all we need. The phone lines will be next, and it'll take your connection with it."

Julie whirled away from her keyboard. "Joe and J. C. are down in those tunnels!"

The others in the room grew quiet. General Medlock stood and looked at her. Agent Love stepped behind Julie's chair. "We'll find out everything we can. Meanwhile, I need you focused on this. You're the only chance we've got."

Chicago Mercantile Exchange Data Center
1852 Hours

"What the hell happened?" someone shouted from the darkness.

James Rubino ignored the question to which no one had an answer and stormed down the hallway under the glow of emergency lights. Members of his staff were scurrying about, assessing the severity of the situation, while others stood in darkened office doorways watching. On more than one occasion in the past, a power interruption at this data center had proved disastrous. Rubino had dedicated the last year of his career to ensuring that this would never happen again—his pension depended on it.

He stepped briskly to the bank of elevators and slapped the Down button before realizing his error.

One of his assistants stated the obvious: "We'll have to take the stairs, Jim."

Rubino led the way into the cement stairwell and down to the lower level of the center. He and his entourage stormed into a huge, climate-controlled room, which contained the exchange's forty-seven network computers. Emergency overhead lighting was in effect, creating the sanctimonious effect that this was a holy place. Rubino's dark eyes surveyed the tower units and saw nothing indicating that power had been denied to any of his computers.

"Someone give me an update," Rubino demanded.

"The backup generator is fully functional," a deep voice replied from behind a console. "There's been no network interruption, and all systems are on-line."

Rubino's abundant mustache lifted with a grin of satisfaction. *Nothing can take down my machines,* he thought. *Nothing and no one.*

Chicago Water Tunnel
1855 Hours

Inside the Harrison tower, Williams pulled Nancy from the rapidly rising water with his good arm. She was coughing terribly. The sergeant placed her hand securely on a rung and held it there until he was certain she was capable of holding on herself. One of her wrists was bleeding from a deep cut.

"*Go!*" she shouted up to him between fits of coughing. "Just go!"

"Yes, ma'am." Williams reached up and began climbing.

Marshall's head broke the surface of the water, and he drew in great lungfuls of air between fits of coughing. He grabbed a rung.

Nancy looked down to ensure he was behind her. "Joe . . . thank God—"

She saw Stryker's face rise to the surface beneath him. The general lifted an arm stiffly from the water and reached for Marshall as he hoisted himself out of the water.

"*Joe!*"

Stryker grabbed the colonel's ankle in a viselike grip. Marshall looked down into the general's gray, determined eyes that were full of rage. An alarming stream of blood flowed around Stryker's left eye from a forehead gash. Despite his wound, his grip exhibited surprising strength. Marshall could see the general's wrist tattoo on the hand that held him.

"We'll go to Sirius together," Stryker called to him.

Marshall removed his stiletto and swung open the blade. "I've decided to let you have it all for yourself."

The colonel reached down and plunged the blade through Stryker's tattoo, then twisted to sever his artery. Stryker let out a howl; his hand slipped off Marshall. His cry fell abruptly silent when his head vanished beneath the raging surge of water.

Joseph Massucci

Colorado Springs
1800 Hours

Jill knew she was screwed the moment the parade appeared on the street outside. She stood at the laundromat's front window, watching Sheriff Block lead a squad of deputies down this quiet business district like a posse in an old western, complete with side arms and shotguns. All they needed were horses.

As the parade passed each storefront, the two leading deputies would break off to investigate. Once they determined that the establishment was clean, the pair would return to the street and join the rear of the procession.

Jill moved away from the window and scanned the inside of the laundromat with its dozen washers and dryers. The laundromat needed no on-site attendant, just a twice-daily visit to empty the coin caches and replenish the detergent dispensers. There was only one customer, a woman with long gray hair pulling clothes from a basket and folding them on a table.

Jill moved to the rear of the shop and found no other way out. Her first instinct was to climb into a dryer like a child to hide. But even her petite frame wouldn't allow it. She was trapped.

The parade of officers passed before the laundromat.

"Get down!" Jill shouted to woman.

The woman, puzzled by this strange behavior, ignored her and continued to fold clothes.

Jill moved beside the door and collapsed into a sitting position. Her mind was numb with fear. She had no options left, no plan.

The door opened and several pairs of boots entered. Jill looked up at them, dazed by what she saw. These boots didn't belong to deputies carrying shotguns, but to U.S. soldiers with assault rifles.

A soldier in combat fatigues walked briskly to the back to check behind the washing machines. His serious eyes locked with the old woman's look of bewilderment.

"Are you Captain Larson?" he asked her.

The woman frowned.

The other soldier spotted Jill sitting beside the door.

"Captain Larson?" the soldier asked.

Jill nodded.

"I'm Lieutenant Marks," he said. "We're here to escort you to Patterson Air Base."

"What!?"

Adrenaline of a different sort kicked in as Jill scrambled to her feet and peered out the window. More jeeps were pulling up in front and soldiers disembarking. The parade of deputies had come to a halt. Farther down, Jill could see an armored personnel carrier turning the corner.

"Well, I'll be . . ."

Jill burst onto the street and, racing toward Sheriff Block, shouted, "That man's a conspirator and an accomplice to murder!"

The sheriff whirled and pulled out his .44 Magnum.

Jill froze and spread her hands before her.

"Let it go," said Lieutenant Marks, rushing after her. "We're getting you out of here."

Sheriff Block raised his gun to Jill. "She dropped two of my deputies and a couple of FBI agents. I'm not letting her walk outta here."

"He's lying," Jill shouted.

"Put down your weapon," the lieutenant ordered the sheriff. "This is a military matter."

"Like hell it is!" the sheriff shouted. "She's mine."

"I'm *ordering* you to put down that weapon," the lieutenant repeated, raising his rifle.

The sheriff, sporting a grin, pulled back the hammer of his .44 and leveled it at Jill. Her eyes widened—she had never looked down the muzzle of a loaded weapon wielded by someone who full well intended to use it.

"Oh shit!" She dove to the ground as the sheriff fired.

A blast changed a portion of the sidewalk into shattered cement.

"Drop it!" shouted the lieutenant.

Sheriff Block ignored him and, following Jill with his weapon, fired two more desperate rounds. A soldier standing in front of the laundromat howled as the third hollowpoint bullet clipped his leg viciously.

The lieutenant opened fire and hammered the sheriff with a burst from his M-16. Sheriff Block's body dropped onto the snowy street. Soldiers with assault rifles braced for firing surrounded his deputies. Jill sat up on the sidewalk, cradling her bruised leg where she had landed hard on it.

Sheriff Block died glaring at her, his look of surprise hardened into a permanent mask of contempt.

Chapter Fifty-five
Wealth

Precinct Number Fourteen
Thursday, December 30
1915 Hours

Julie nearly missed the *ding* her notebook computer made. When she rolled her chair around to look at the screen, to her astonishment the word OPEN was blinking at the top of the screen above a 128-digit number.

The footnote below read:

SUCCESSFULLY UNLOCKED AFTER 17,901,787,425,874 ATTEMPTS

"We're in!" she screamed, upsetting the room's solemn atmosphere. The interrogation room exploded with questions as the team jumped to their feet.

Agent Arlene Love and General Medlock rushed to her side. Love scrutinized the display. "Now what?"

"Now we find the right switch and throw it." Julie cleared the screen and pulled up the network's interface that controlled the Exchange's backup generator. There weren't many options available. A single readout showed the percent of available electrical power—the system drain, in heavy demand because of the blackout, indicated 45 percent remained. Below the readout were several virtual switches. It seemed straightforward enough.

Julie's heart was racing. She couldn't believe she had penetrated one of the thickest corporate firewalls in the world. She glanced at Agent Love, who watched stonefaced, then over at General Medlock.

Medlock gave her a nod. "Proceed."

With shaking fingers, Julie moved her cursor over an orange icon that said "Emergency Shutdown" and pressed Enter. The words SHUTDOWN IN PROGRESS appeared across the display and began flashing. Less than a minute later, the words were replaced with SHUTDOWN COMPLETE.

Chicago Mercantile Exchange Data Center

"All systems are on-line," reported the network administrator, a young Asian man named Wu. "Generator voltage stable."

Rubino nodded. He rocked back comfortably in the office chair in the dark computer room and asked, "Any word from Com Ed about when our power grid will be back up?"

"Might be another long one," Wu said. "Now they're saying the flooding is worse than '94."

"Good Lord!" Rubino groaned.

Wu scoffed at Rubino's concern. "Relax. Our backup is fully capable of weathering this. That generator can power a community of ten thousand for two weeks."

"I want you to shut down all nonessential CPUs, servers, drives, monitors, the works," Rubino ordered. "Notify me the instant anything varies on that generator—even if it heats up by two degrees—"

Suddenly, an alarm blared on the console. Wu swung his feet off the desk and stared at the words EMERGENCY SHUTDOWN on the display.

"Man, oh man!" Wu said. "Something's grabbed our system."

Rubino appeared instantly at his side. *"Override it!"*

Wu attempted to move the cursor, but was locked out of the system. "It won't let me."

The two could only watch helplessly as the words SHUTDOWN COMPLETE flashed onto the screen. The data center suddenly fell dark, followed by the sinking whine of the climate-control fans coming to a halt. Then silence. There wasn't a single pin light left on any of the units or consoles.

Without power, every one of Skile's commands, every one of his financial contracts in progress, disappeared from the computer's virtual memory. All the wealth he so brazenly presumed to own vanished in an instant, unrecoverable in any form.

At that moment, Jonathan Stone's virtual world, everything he owned and everything he claimed to be, simply ceased to exist.

Lower Wacker Drive
1920 Hours

Alexander Skile pushed aside the steel grating and pulled himself out of a stone shaft that provided ventilation to the freight tunnels. He dragged himself onto the elevated sidewalk that overlooked a row of parked cars, where he propped his back against a stone foundation.

The concrete slab on which he sat reeked of urine. His legs were useless and he could not fully comprehend the unnatural pain coursing through his body. He could go no farther. He touched the sharp splinter of bone jutting from his trouser leg and rubbed his fingers together. He held them before his eyes to inspect the blood. But he couldn't see anything—all lights along the drive were out. The river beyond the pilings reflected nothing from the city, which stood dark and faceless. *Perhaps I'm going blind.*

He heard a voice nearby. A face appeared from the darkness and hovered at his shoulder. It was an old man with an overgrown gray beard, his lean face withered from too many nights with too many bottles. He obviously hadn't bathed in a month.

"You look a sight," he said to Skile. "Do you know you're bleeding?"

Skile ignored his question. "Why is it so dark down here? Am I going blind?"

"The lights are out," the old man responded. "Not a single building's lit anywhere in the Loop. It's the beginning of the end. Soon the people themselves will disappear. I won't miss the people, only the booze." His high, uneven laugh reminded Skile of a bird cackle.

"The world's not ending," Skile growled. "The tunnels are flooded. The electrical lines down there must have shorted."

"I wouldn't know anything about that," the old man said. "I tried living down there once, but they kept chasing me out."

Skile grabbed the front of the man's coat into his fist. "What about the financial exchanges? What about my money?"

The old man just looked at him, baffled.

As the realization settled in, Skile burst into laughter at the irony of it all. No power, no computing, no wealth. They had found his Achilles' heel and wiped out his virtual assets. His hand slipped from the man's coat. "A man can't exist without money."

The old man grinned, showing off the few yellow teeth he had left. "All you really need are a few dollars for beer money." He dangled his fingers tentatively. "You wouldn't have any change, would you?"

Skile reached into his trousers pocket and pulled out a money clip. The wad of soaked bills was fat and impressive. He tossed it at the man. "Have a beer on me. Have several."

The old man examined the money clip with squinting eyes, marveling at the quantity and size of the bills.

"Is this for real?" he asked. "It looks like all the money in the world."

Skile nodded. "It's real, and it's all the money in *my* world."

"I'll split it with you," the old man offered.

"Keep it all," Skile replied. "I won't need it where I'm going."

"Oh? And where's that?" the old man asked.

Skile pulled out his Walther PPK and checked to see that a round .was chambered. "To Sirius. I'm meeting my wife and a few close friends there this weekend. We're celebrating the end of the world together." His eyes grew wide. "Gosh, I hope they take credit."

Skile burst into another round of uncontrolled laughter. He put the gun to his right temple and pulled the trigger.

Instead of a bright star in the midst of the galaxy, he saw only blackness.

The Harrison Crib
1925 Hours

Williams was the first to climb down the stone tower's ladder onto the seventy-foot luxury yacht moored there. It was dusk, and the city's skyline stood dark and mysterious behind them like a deserted metropolis from a lost world. The sergeant showed no signs of being in pain. The police officer who escorted him to the bridge for questioning had no idea that his right arm had been drilled by a bullet and was broken in two places.

Nancy climbed down after him, followed by Marshall.

"We need a first-aid kit," Marshall said to the officers. "This woman has cuts on her wrists. Has anyone checked the sergeant?"

One of the officers radioed over to the police launch for a kit.

Marshall stepped into the bridge, where he inspected Williams's wounds. He frowned and chided him, "That's what happens when you play in sewers."

Williams, cradling his arm in his lap, let out a huff. "Screw the bullet. That water was friggin' cold."

Marshall admired the yacht's spacious bridge and said to the police captain, "Nice boat. Whose is it?"

"Belongs to a man named Stone," the captain said.

"Stone?" Marshall said. "Who's Stone?"

"That's what we'd like to know," the police captain said. "So far, we haven't come up with anything."

An HBT officer said to Marshall, "I thought Lieutenant Heath was with you guys."

Marshall's expression turned hard. "Sorry. I'm afraid he didn't make it."

The officer grew silent and nodded.

A police officer with a radio announced to the group on the bridge, "They've pulled a body from the flooded freight tunnels. His license says 'Jonathan Stone.'"

"Can I hitch a ride back with you for a look?" Marshall asked the police captain.

The captain nodded. "Sure, why not?"

The colonel said to Williams, "Not you, I'm afraid. I'll meet you at the hospital later."

Lower Wacker Drive
1955 Hours

"That's him," Nancy said.

The coroner draped the sheet back over Skile's remains. Nancy turned to Marshall and laid her head on his chest. "He took his own life," she said. "He lost everything and knew it."

Marshall was disappointed. He had expected Skile's features to reflect a brilliance that could command great resources. Instead, he saw the shell of a frail man. This was a mere child who one day decided to play God. And that childishness had killed a lot of good people.

Marshall put his hand around Nancy's shoulder and led her off the elevated sidewalk toward a waiting patrol car that would take them back to the precinct station.

They had kept Julie waiting much too long.

Day Five
Friday, December 31, 1999

"Man is still the most extraordinary computer of all."

John F. Kennedy, May 1963

Epilogue
Bravo

Lake Michigan
Friday, December 31, 1999
2350 Hours

The seventy-four-foot yacht *Bravo* slipped from the Chicago police dock and headed toward Navy Pier. Thanks to its previous owner, the craft was fueled and exquisitely stocked for a journey that could take her from Chicago, across Lake Michigan, and well into Canada.

Belowdecks, Agent Arlene Love emerged from the galley with a tray of prawn and crab-claw hors d'oeuvres and set it on the bar in the ship's spacious living area. She announced to her guests, "Last call before midnight, courtesy of 'Mr. Stone.'"

"My appetite just came back," Olin said, sitting on the couch with her casted leg propped on a leather ottoman.

Jill, seated at the bar draining a Heineken, grabbed the tray of shellfish and presented it to her. Olin selected a particularly healthy prawn from the lot and placed it on a napkin on her lap next to her third glass of very cold Vouvray.

Jill offered the tray to the others. "Who else?"

"They look incredible," Julie said. She and Nancy helped themselves to the feast.

"Where did these come from, anyway?" Nancy asked, dipping the oversized prawn into cocktail sauce. "Three Mile Island?"

"The box says 'Thunder Bay,'" Love said.

"How much time left?" Olin asked, eager.

Julie looked at her watch. "Eight minutes." She moved to the bar and pressed the intercom button to the bridge. "Are you guys coming down or what?"

In the enclosed bridge above them, Marshall leaned over the intercom and replied, "We're almost at Navy Pier. You should see this. The pier's lit up with *candles!*"

"I want you down here with me where it's nice and warm," Julie said. "We're breaking out the champagne. It's Dom Pérignon. And we've got lots of seafood."

"We're on our way," Marshall said. He turned to General Medlock, sitting at the helm in the captain's chair. "It's almost time."

"You throw one hell of a retirement bash," Medlock said, pulling himself from the chair. "I'll remember this night for the rest of my life."

"Let's toast Agent Arlene Love," Marshall said, raising his schooner of beer. "This boat's technically in FBI custody."

Medlock extinguished the engines. "I think I'll just let her drift for a while. I don't think we'll be running into any other traffic out here."

Marshall extended a hand to Williams, who was sitting comfortably in a crewman's chair. "I'll help you downstairs."

"Thanks," Williams said, "but I'd like to stay up here for a while where I can enjoy a little solitude. Nothin' personal. I just like the view."

"Suit yourself," Marshall said.

Williams grasped Marshall's extended hand with his left hand. A cast covered his entire right arm. "Happy New Year, Joe."

Marshall returned a broad grin. "Same to you, my good man."

The colonel and General Medlock went below and joined the small party teeming with anticipation. Agent Love hurled a handful of confetti at the two as they entered. Marshall sidestepped the wad and let it hit the general square in the face, where it exploded in a flurry of colored speckles. There was laughter all around.

Everyone wore a party hat and wielded an exotic musical wind or percussion instrument they had found in storage. Julie gave Marshall a black derby and a cornet, then handed the general a felt jester's cap and an African drum made from a ceramic jar.

"Two minutes," Agent Love announced, holding her wrist-watch like a racing chronometer.

Marshall tipped his derby to Julie before pushing it down onto his head, then blew a note through his cornet that sounded like a VW horn.

"There's something I need to tell you," he said to her.

"Oh?" Julie said.

"This isn't working."

"Your horn? I agree. Give it up."

"Us," he said, setting aside his cornet. "I'm talking about us being apart."

"What are you saying?"

"I'm saying that I don't want to remain a soldier if it means not being with you."

"Is that so?"

"So I've decided to follow the general's lead and retire. I've always wanted to open a little neighborhood tavern."

"Why, Colonel Marshall, I do declare," Julie said in her best Southern drawl. "If I didn't know better, I'd say you were proposing."

Marshall pulled Julie close to him. "I don't know what I'm saying, but I do know I don't want to lose you again."

"I'm not going anywhere," she said, putting her arms around his neck. "And if you are proposing, I accept."

"Ten seconds," Love announced.

"Kiss this millennium good-bye," Jill shouted, adding, "and good riddance!" She began beating her bass drum in time to each passing second.

"You heard the captain," Marshall said. "Let's kiss this millennium good-bye."

He brought his lips to hers.

Love announced: "Five . . . four . . . three . . . two . . . one. *It's HERE!*"

Cheers rose from the party while confetti rained down. They struck up their instruments for a chorus of something passing for "Auld Lang Syne."

Suddenly, all the lights in the vessel blinked out, leaving them in total darkness. Their instruments fell silent.

Finally, Arlene Love's voice broke the awkward silence. "Did anybody bother to check whether this boat is Year 2000 compliant?"

There came twitters of nervous laughter from the darkness.

Up on the bridge, Williams switched the generator back on. The lights returned. The sergeant pressed the intercom and announced to the party below, "Just kidding!"

A roar of disapproval erupted through the deck. Williams leaned back in his captain's chair and laughed uproariously.

A bang in the direction of Navy Pier caused Williams to swivel around in time to see a streak of golden light sail high above the darkened pier and explode in a magnificent shower of stars.

The sky show of colors unfolding above them was truly magnificent.

RED SKIES
KARL LARGENT
"A writer to watch!" —*Publishers Weekly*

The cutting-edge Russian SU-39-Covert stealth bomber, with fighter capabilities years beyond anything the U.S. can produce, has vanished while on a test run over the Gobi Desert. But it is no accident—the super weapon was plucked from the skies by Russian military leaders with their own private agenda—global power.

Half a world away, a dissident faction of the Chinese Red Army engineers the brutal abduction of a top scientist visiting Washington from under the noses of his U.S. guardians. And with him goes the secrets of his most recent triumph—the development of the SU-39.

Commander T.C. Bogner has his orders: Retrieve the fighter and its designer within seventy-two hours, or the die will be cast for a high-tech war, the likes of which the world has never known.

_4117-0 $6.99 US/$7.99 CAN

Dorchester Publishing Co., Inc.
P.O. Box 6640
Wayne, PA 19087-8640

Please add $1.75 for shipping and handling for the first book and $.50 for each book thereafter. NY, NYC, and PA residents, please add appropriate sales tax. No cash, stamps, or C.O.D.s. All orders shipped within 6 weeks via postal service book rate. Canadian orders require $2.00 extra postage and must be paid in U.S. dollars through a U.S. banking facility.

Name_____
Address_____
City_____ State_____ Zip_____
I have enclosed $_____ in payment for the checked book(s).
Payment <u>must</u> accompany all orders. ☐ Please send a free catalog.

LADY OF ICE AND FIRE
COLIN ALEXANDER

Colin Alexander writes "a lean and solid thriller!"
—*Publishers Weekly*

With international detente fast becoming the status quo, a whole new field of spying opens up: industrial espionage. And even though tensions are easing between the East and the West, the same Cold war rules and stakes still apply: world domination at any cost, both in dollars and deaths. Well aware of the new predators, George Jeffers fears that his biotech studies may be sought after by foreign agents. Then his partner disappears with the results of their experiments, and the eminent scientist finds himself the target in a game of deadly intrigue. Jeffers then races against time to prevent the unleashing of a secret that could shake the world to its very foundations.

_4072-7 $5.50 US/$6.50 CAN